DESCENT: LEGENDS *of the* DARK

Terrinoth: an ancient realm of forgotten greatness and faded legacies, of magic and monsters, heroes, and tyrants. Its cities were ruined and their secrets lost as terrifying dragons, undead armies, and demon-possessed hordes ravaged the land. Over centuries, the realm slipped into gloom…

Now, the world is reawakening – the Baronies of Daqan rebuild their domains, wizards master lapsed arts, and champions test their mettle. Banding together to explore the dangerous caves, ancient ruins, dark dungeons, and cursed forests of Terrinoth, they unearth priceless treasures and terrible foes.

Yet time is running out, for in the shadows a malevolent force has grown, preparing to spread evil across the world. Now, when the land needs them most, is the moment for its heroes to rise.

DREAMS
of FIRE

Davide Mana

ACONYTE

First published by Aconyte Books in 2023

ISBN 978 1 83908 243 6

Ebook ISBN 978 1 83908 244 3

Cover art by Adrien Gonzales.

Distributed in North America by Simon & Schuster Inc, New York, USA

Printed in the United States of America

9 8 7 6 5 4 3 2 1

ACONYTE BOOKS

An imprint of Asmodee Entertainment Ltd

Mercury House, Shipstones Business Centre

North Gate, Nottingham NG7 7FN, UK

aconytebooks.com // twitter.com/aconytebooks

PROLOGUE
Memories: The Broken Lands

The sky was clean, untouched by violence or death.

And above everything that they loved, Vaerix loved flying.

Vaerix had been raised for battle, and their skills had been honed by dozens of fights in the service of their brood mother, Levirax.

But still, as exhilarating as it was to cross weapons with a worthy enemy and vanquish them, the pure pleasure of gliding from one thermal to the next, feeling the sudden rush when caught in the updraft, the world dropping away under them, the pale blue line of the horizon stretching in every direction where the land faded into the sky... that was what Vaerix truly cherished.

To a creature like them, who did not know poetry, flying *was* poetry.

Vaerix twisted a wing enough to start gliding to their right, dropping in altitude. Drys, who flew just above them and to the left, mirrored their maneuver.

There was no need for communication between them.

Their shadows grew larger on the blur of the grassland

below. Pinpoint-like arrows in the sky shot toward them. Vaerix signaled with their spear and both they and Drys dropped farther down, swooping over the small band of orc archers below and avoiding the assault.

As usual for a flightless people, the orcs met the incoming dragon hybrids with a volley of arrows, trying to kill as many enemies as possible before the two lines made contact. In the past, Vaerix had seen them use slings instead of arrows and knew many in the Levirax army that had their wing membranes pierced with holes as a result.

But now the orcs' attack was useless. Vaerix and their companions wore armor, and it would take a lucky shot indeed for an archer or a slinger to drop them.

As Vaerix closed in, the smell of the battle replaced the silence and cleanliness of the upper atmosphere, and Vaerix singled out their target. The dragon hybrids flew in for the kill.

An orc archer let loose one final arrow, dropped his bow, and grabbed the axe he had stuck in the ground by his feet. The arrow bounced off Vaerix's pauldrons and they closed the distance and struck with their spear, putting all their weight and speed behind it. The orc was lifted off the ground as the volcanic glass point passed through him. He fell on the ground and was still.

Vaerix braked, opening their wings to decrease their speed. They did a tight turn, the ground a couple of feet under their claws. A second orc warrior charged them. Vaerix pulled another spear from the holder they carried on their shoulder and thrust it at him. The orc parried the attack, but the sheer impetus of the flying dragon hybrid caused the orc to stumble back and fall.

Vaerix did another tight turn, the ground now dangerously

close, and swooped around in time to catch the orc as he was getting back on his feet. The spear caught the warrior between neck and shoulder. The orc fell back as Vaerix landed, their powerful legs flexing.

Two crescent obsidian blades were in their hands and a war cry trumpeted through their throat as four other orcs came for them, brandishing axes and maces.

Before they could reach Vaerix, Drys swept in from above and speared one of them in the back, dispersing the others. Then Drys landed and moved to Vaerix's side.

Together they stood side by side, the excitement of the battlefield replacing the ecstasy of flight, and they ran to meet what was left of the orc forces.

The battle did not take long.

"They fought well," Vaerix said afterward, to their long-time companion.

"They bought time to allow their elders and the hatchlings to run," Drys said as together they walked among the bodies toward the burning orc camp.

"A worthy stance," Vaerix replied.

Orcs, like many of the mortal races, spawned younglings, and were willing to fight and die to protect them. Not all the dragon hybrids shared Vaerix's views, but they respected a warrior's willingness to lay down their life for a higher cause. And they imagined it was so for the orcs too. Preserve the species. Save the little ones and give them a chance to grow and fight on their own.

One of the huts, little more than a husk of blackened poles and charred skins, collapsed in a blizzard of flying sparks.

Many of the other hybrids had already taken flight, regrouping to go back to their camp. There was nothing else to do here. There were no secrets learned from the defeated orcs. No hidden runes. No shards of power. Dragonlord Levirax would be disappointed, just as Vaerix was.

Today, theirs had been a purely tactical victory. A move on the chessboard of the Broken Lands, meaningless in itself, but important in the larger scheme of things. And it had been a good fight. Sometimes that was all that mattered: the warrior's exercise of their weapons.

CHAPTER ONE
Razorcliff

Tall, flat slabs of rock flanked the road that led to the top of the Razorcliff ridge. The members in good standing of the Explorers' Guild had long debated whether those rocks were a natural formation or the remains of some ancient structure. No definitive answer had ever been found to those questions. White as bones and scarred by the elements, the stones trapped the road in a corridor of perpetual shadow, whispering wind and deceptive echoes.

Right in that moment, such deceptive echoes were a broken melody with the garbled words of an old dwarven song, belted out with such enthusiasm and in such a thick Dunwarr accent, even Brockton the Map Maker, a Dunwarr dwarf himself, was unable to understand its verses.

With a grimace, he turned in the saddle of his pony and cast a pained glance at Grisban the Thirsty, who rode behind him. His white-streaked beard flying in the wind, Grisban threw his head back and launched into another howling verse.

A warrior undefeated, Grisban was, and Brockton started to believe the reason was because he had sung his enemies to death.

"Oh, dwarf," Quellen called, his sharp elven voice piercing the din of Grisban's song.

Grisban stopped in the middle of the chorus and turned in his saddle. "What ails you, O wizard?"

"It's mage, if you please," Quellen replied, piqued. He was third in their file and sat atop his stocky ride with a hunched, tired stance, wrapped in his green cloak like an old man in his blanket. Brockton did not know how old he was. It was hard to tell with elves. "But I was wondering," Quellen went on, "how many songs do you know?"

Grisban pulled at his beard. "Ah! Hundreds. Thousands, probably."

"Thousands, indeed." The elven mage arched his eyebrows. "And do you plan to sing them all to us?"

Grisban opened his mouth, and then closed it. He turned to glance at Brockton, and then back at the elf. "What if I do?" he finally asked.

Quellen shrugged. "Then I think we'll need to buy more supplies."

Grisban's frown deepened. "What do you mean?"

"That we'll find no game on the road," Quellen said. "Because you'll scare away anything that lives in a ten miles radius."

Grisban's cheeks burned red against the snow of his beard. "You little–"

"He's right," One Fist called from the back. "You sing like a rotten tooth." The orc's legs were so long his feet brushed the ground as his pony kept plodding on. He lifted the metal hook that replaced his left hand and the sharp end glinted in the shadows. He straightened his back and his leather armor creaked. "And you know what happens to rotten teeth."

"Is that a challenge?" Grisban growled. His hand caressed the war hammer hanging from his pony's harness.

One Fist's grin widened.

"Enough of this," Brockton finally called. "We are not here to fight among ourselves."

"Come on, Master Brockton," Grisban said, smiling grimly. "Just for fun. Without weapons."

"I do not pay you for song or pugilism," Brockton replied. "Save your fight for our enemies, should we meet any. And your songs for when we'll have reasons for celebration."

Grisban looked at him, and his scowl relaxed. "Sorry, boss."

In that moment Quellen lifted his right hand. "Listen."

They all turned their heads around. Apart for the slow clopping of the horses' hooves, all sound had died, and the darkness was growing thicker. The wind too was gone, the air strangely still.

"Maybe what they say is true," One Fist mumbled.

"What do they say?" Quellen asked.

"And who are they?" Grisban added.

"There are stories," One Fist said, "told around campfires, that the Razorcliff is haunted. By ghosts and, maybe, by other things." He made a gesture against ill luck.

"Rubbish," Quellen said. "I'd be much more concerned about cutthroats and ruffians, as Last Haven sits yonder–" he pointed with a hand, "–at less than three days. But to worry about ghosts? Why should they bother us?"

"So you say," One Fist conceded. "But I've been around enough–"

Distant thunder rumbled.

Brockton shivered and looked at the strip of sky above them, where dark clouds had been chasing each other for the best part of the afternoon, and now piled up into a boiling mass the color of a bruise. A single drop of rain hit him right between the eyes.

Just what they needed, he thought. Spring came late in the mountains.

"Haunted it is," he said, turning again to face the road, "by rotten weather." He gently kicked his pony to get it to move faster. "Come," he commanded. "Let's make the top before we're soaked."

As he said so, rain started falling, cold and insistent. Thunder sounded again, this time closer.

"Won't be that lucky," Grisban said, pulling up the collar of his coat.

Behind him, Quellen had pulled up his hood and tucked his head even more into his shoulders. One Fist cursed and tugged his cloak up to cover his head. The ponies marched on, heads low under the rain.

Soon the path curved around the side of the hill and they finally saw their destination, some way up the slope, stark against the tempestuous sky.

The Razorcliff rose like a tall blade of pale rock at the top of the hill, and Brockton's trained eye could see even in the fading light how wind and rain, working patiently for long ages, had sharpened it and dug deep holes in its sides. Man-made walls of dry stone and timber had been added, turning the caves into chambers and stores. A wooden balcony ran along the face of the rock, and a gallows-like post supported a battered sign carrying the words "Razorcliff Inn" in bold if uneven letters.

"The place does look haunted," Quellen said over the sound of the rain.

"Or abandoned," Grisban grumbled.

"Or both," One Fist said.

They drew their ponies to a stop by a stone basin in the front yard of the inn.

"Of the inn!" Brockton called, wishing his voice had the bellows-like power of Grisban's. "You have customers!"

The door opened, pouring out warm golden light, and a man and a boy appeared in the door frame.

"Master Brockton?" the man called. "The map maker?" He was tall and round-shouldered, with a pointy beard and shocks of black hair over his prominent ears.

Brockton dismounted, while Grisban maneuvered his pony into a better defensive position to cover his back.

"I am Brockton the Map Maker," he said, taking one step forward. "I sent word, four weeks ago."

"So you did, master, and we are glad to see you," the innkeeper said. "My name is Zayn, and I welcome you to the Razorcliff Inn." He glanced at the sky, straightened, and smiled. "It's lousy weather to be on the road, but we have a fire and good food for you."

"That's what I like to hear," Grisban said, and dismounted. They had a long road both behind and before them, and fire and good food would be welcome.

One Fist and Quellen dismounted in turn and joined them at the inn's entrance.

"Come inside, gentlemen." Zayn rubbed his hands together and stepped aside. "Your rooms await, and dinner will be served presently. My son will take care of the horses."

He nudged the child forward. The boy ran to take the ponies' reins, watching the travelers with curiosity and awe.

Grisban brought his hand to his belt. He flipped a coin to the boy.

"See that they are well tended and fed," he said. "Then bring our things inside and there will be another like this one for you."

The boy smiled, pocketing the tip. "As you command, master."

"And do not meddle with our stuff," Quellen added, with a sly smile. "Because I am a mage. You know what that means, I am sure."

The kid's eyes widened. His smile vanished.

One Fist entered first, nodding his head at the innkeeper.

Behind him, Brockton stopped on his way in. "We are expecting one more," he said. "They should join us here soon."

Zayn nodded. "Your... friend is here already, Master Brockton," he said in a low voice. His eyes darted toward Brockton's companions and he licked his lips. "Waiting for you."

Brockton arched his eyebrows at the innkeeper's conspiratorial tone. "Here already?"

The man nodded again but would say nothing more.

A sound of thunder, and Grisban's impatient grumble, caused Brockton to move on, pondering the innkeeper's mood.

Quellen was the last in, and then the innkeeper closed the door as he followed them, leaving the rain and the cold night outside.

Grisban pulled off his gloves and tucked them in his belt.

"Is there mulled wine to be had in this place?" he called as he walked to the fireplace.

The room had a low ceiling and a stone floor, bathed in the amber light from the fire. Grisban stretched his hands to the heat with a satisfied groan.

"Mulled wine, straight away, master," the innkeeper replied.

The others started removing their cloaks and unbuckling their sword belts.

"And more light," Grisban went on. "We like to see each other's faces."

"Of course, sir."

Another boy, so similar to the first one they were obviously brothers, appeared out of nowhere, and using a thin stick to catch a flame from the fireplace, went around the room lighting up the oil lamps.

Grisban combed his beard with his fingers and let out a sigh.

Just then, something stirred in the deeper shadows at the dark end of the main room, and a large shape moved forward, obsidian talons clicking on the stone floor.

Grisban cursed, took a step back and his hand ran to his sword. "What in the name of Kellos–?"

The others gasped and cursed, echoing his surprise.

The creature's teeth glinted in the trembling light of the lamps.

Brockton's cold hand gripped Grisban's wrist, stopping him from drawing his weapon.

"It is fine," Brockton said. He underscored his level words with an increased pressure on Grisban's arm.

Grisban glanced at One Fist, who had moved further away to have enough maneuvering room. He was ready but had not yet released his sword from the scabbard. Meanwhile, Quellen was leaning forward, wide-eyed with surprise, one hand fiddling with a polished pebble that he had apparently pulled from his sleeve.

A low sound, like the purring of a giant cat, came from the

creature in front of them. The triangular head rose, the back stretched, and long thin horns almost touched the ceiling. Powerful legs, and a lizard-like body that was too large for the benches and tables, gave the creature an impressive stature. The thing flicked its tail.

Dragon hybrid, Grisban thought. The stuff of legends and scary stories, the long arm of the dragonlords of the Third Darkness. Made and trained to enter the dwarven corridors under the mountains, where dragons could not go. Seldom heard of but in old ballads these days, seldom seen out of the wilderness and the lost cities of the south. He had never crossed swords with one and did not relish the opportunity. He hadn't been aware this was the friend Brockton had said would be waiting for them.

"It is fine," Brockton said again, his voice steady.

A scaly hand stretched toward them, in what Grisban realized was a welcoming gesture.

"They're with us," Brockton said.

Finally, Grisban turned to look him in the eye. "With us?"

The younger dwarf nodded and let go of Grisban's wrist. Then he walked toward the dragon-creature. "It's been a long time, friend Vaerix," he said.

"Verily, it is so," the dragon hybrid said. Their clawed hand touched Brockton's shoulder.

Grisban eyed One Fist, who shrugged. The old dwarf relaxed, trusting Brockton.

"Thanks for accepting my call," Brockton said, and he touched the arm of the hybrid, responding to their greeting.

"You knew I would," Vaerix replied.

"But I am grateful anyway."

Brockton turned as the innkeeper appeared by Grisban's

side, carrying a tray of steaming mugs. "Your mulled wine, master," he said.

That seemed to break the spell, and everybody sighed in relief. Grisban accepted the mug with a grateful nod. Brockton looked back at his companions, the dragon hybrid towering behind him.

"This is my friend Vaerix," the young dwarf explained. "A fine warrior, and wise. We met many years ago–"

"Fifteen years and seven months," Vaerix said.

"–back when I was surveying the Howling Giant Hills, southeast of Frostgate. I asked them to join us on this venture."

One Fist studied the dragon hybrid, wide-eyed. "You are Vaerix?" he asked. "Vaerix the Wanderer? That Vaerix?"

"So I am," Vaerix replied, nodding their head.

One Fist whistled softly.

"They said…" Quellen started, then he shook his head.

"What?" Grisban asked, glancing sideways at the elf. His instincts still commanded him to keep his eyes on the dragon hybrid.

Vaerix tilted their head to the side, like a bird, waiting for the elf to speak.

"Nothing," the mage said. He waved his hand. "Forget it."

Grisban regarded the elf. Since the mage loved the sound of his own voice, his sudden reticence was unexpected. Maybe mere courtesy, maybe something else: elves were a secretive bunch. Grisban would have to keep an eye on Quellen.

Coming closer, the innkeeper clasped his hands together. "If the gentlemen please," he said, "Dinner will be served presently. We have spicy mutton stew with honey-glazed parsnips, and a fine soup of wild herbs and beans."

The mulled wine had helped Grisban find some of his good

humor. "That will do, for starters," he said. "Bring also bread and ale."

"Of course, master."

"Wine for me," Quellen added.

"We do not have much choice, I am afraid–"

Quellen waved a hand dismissively. "Any wine will do, as long as it comes from grapes."

"Let's sit down," Brockton said as the innkeeper disappeared back into his kitchen. "We need to talk."

"And eat." Grisban nodded.

They settled down at the table Vaerix had occupied when they came in. Brockton quickly introduced the others by name to the hybrid.

"Are these all of your companions, friend?" the hybrid asked, while Grisban slid down the bench to make room for Quellen.

Brockton looked at Vaerix, and then at his three companions. "Yes. Why?"

The other's amber glance passed over them. "Nothing," they said. They squatted on their haunches at the head of the table. "I was expecting there would be more of us. A dream of mine, probably."

Grisban caught a fleeting expression on One Fist's face, but when he turned, the orc was hiding behind his mug of hot wine.

Then Zayn and his son emerged, bringing pots and pans and the sweet smell of good food.

CHAPTER TWO
The Widow

Long years on the road had taught Vaerix that being alone, which was a thing composed of numbers, did not mean being lonely, which was a thing of the soul. For this reason, they did not care for long days spent in the wilderness with the sole company of their own thoughts and dreams at first. But that was how things were. And soon, the acceptance of solitude made unexpected company even more welcome and fascinating.

Now Vaerix sat at their end of the table and studied Brockton's three companions as they all attacked their food with good cheer. The dragon hybrid could hardly imagine a more unlikely group.

Stocky and belligerent by his looks, Grisban was full of talk, and he discussed the food, the ale, and the weather, recalled old stories and close acquaintances, jumping from one topic to the next, talking with his mouth full. Every bite and sip of drink seemed to bring him memories of previous adventures, of battlefields and companions long gone, of heroic dinners and long nights spent drinking, and he would start remembering one event to then move on to the next as he brought a spoonful of soup to his lips. And yet, Vaerix could detect something else underneath the boastful attitude of the older dwarf. A trained care, a habit of caution, an attention to his surroundings that spoke of an experienced fighter that matched the calluses on his hands. A respect, too, for his companions, which the jokes and barbs were not enough to hide.

He had discarded his chainmail coat, to be more at ease, but kept his axe by his side, propped to the side of the bench.

Sitting in front of Grisban, One Fist the orc grinned and shook his head at the dwarf's stories. He was tall and wide of shoulder like many of his people, and young. His skin had a gray-greenish hue, and tusks jutted out of his mouth. He kept his hook in his lap, and sometimes massaged the skin where the straps kept the metal tool attached to his left arm. He had slackened the fastenings of his armor, but he had laid his dagger on the table by his bowl. He ate slowly, seeming to savor the taste of the food while scanning the room. A big warrior with a braid of black hair falling over one shoulder, still he tried to disappear in his corner, silent and inconspicuous. He cheered when the serving boy placed a large bowl of roasted chestnuts in the middle of the table and popped one in his mouth. Then he hissed and steam escaped from his lips.

Quellen the mage had barely touched his food, and glanced at Vaerix above the rim of his wine cup. Of the four sitting at the table, the elf was the one Vaerix found hardest to read. There was a hint of briskness underlying his natural elegance. Something elusive about his attitude, too. His ironic smile was a mask through which Vaerix was not able to see. But they had often found the Latari a hard people to read, in the few and far between occasions they had met one of them. Quellen contributed little to the conversation and his brief comments went often unheeded by his companions. And yet, the elf had Brockton's trust, and that would have to be enough for Vaerix.

After a while, Grisban undid his belt buckle and let out a thunderous burp. The sound brought Vaerix back to the present.

"That's better," Grisban said, patting his belly. Quellen arched his eyebrow.

The others commented in soft voices. One of the boys came and took away the bowls and the plates, and at Quellen's request brought him more wine.

"Fine," Brockton finally said. "Let's talk business."

Studying Brockton, Vaerix could see the young dwarf they had met in the Howling Giant Hills, hiding under the fine coat and the measured manners of the Guild Master Surveyor. The youth and curiosity that had brought Brockton to strike a friendship with one who was dragon-kin still animated the gestures of his usual dignified demeanor.

He looked at the others, as if expecting comments or objections, and when nobody spoke, he placed a scroll on the table in front of them. He unrolled it and used mugs and pitchers to anchor its corners.

Brockton tapped the map and made Vaerix's memories fully fade, only to replace them with others. Ink lines and patches of color spread in front of them. Vaerix felt a strange sensation in their chest, like a memory of flight that sometimes came to them in their sleep. They leaned forward.

"What are we looking at?" One Fist asked, munching on a chestnut.

"It's a map," Grisban replied. The orc snorted.

Ignoring them, Brockton ran his fingers over the parchment. "This is the lake south of Thelgrim," he said, pointing at a blue shape. His fingers danced on the map, moving right. "Black Ember Gorge. Last Haven. The ruins of the Karok Doum." He looked up at the others. "These are the mountains we are traveling through."

He put his finger on a small point. "This is where we are now. The Razorcliff."

"And this," added Vaerix, their talon tracing a circle on the blank sector of the map in the top right corner, "is the Molten Heath."

The name had a strange taste in their mouth. In many years of travel, they had never gone back to the Heath, but the region had often been in their thoughts and their dreams. The same dreams which now told Vaerix it was time to return to that place. They still struggled to understand those night visitations, to fully ascertain their meaning. But there was little doubt in their heart that this was the time. Brockton provided them with the reason and the means to travel back to the place they had once called home. Beyond that, the future was still unwritten.

"A big chunk of nothing," Grisban mumbled. "Surrounded by what once was ours."

The Heath had been the domain of the dragons since the world's inception, but in the dim and distant past the dwarves had built cities on the periphery of that area. Dragons and dwarves had lived side by side for centuries, and the dwarves called the place Karok Doum, the Dragons' Gift. But then the War of Fire erupted over a matter of magic and secrets, and the dwarves were exiled from the Heath.

This had been many millennia before Vaerix's time and before the Third Darkness, when the dragons had unleashed their hybrid armies on Terrinoth.

"Where the dragons retreated," Quellen added, "to die after they laid our world to waste during the Third Darkness."

He looked at Vaerix, as if expecting a challenge.

"Dragons do not die," Vaerix finally said, their eyes fixed on the elf. "Retreat, yes. Die? Unlikely, if not by violence."

Quellen frowned, and then nodded a thank you for the explanation.

Clearing his throat, Brockton unrolled a second map, showing a ring of mountains surrounding a featureless area in the middle of which more mountains stood. It was an enlarged detail of the previous map. Scrawled names dotted the parchment.

"This," Brockton said, "is the best map we have of those regions. Our mission is to draw a better one, on behalf of the Explorers' Guild of Dunwarr."

"The gentlemen footing our bills," Quellen added.

"Where does this come from?" Grisban asked, nodding at the new map.

Vaerix was struck by the colors on the parchment and the fine detail. Place names were penned in a neat, precise hand. This was not simply a map, but a small work of art.

"I drew it," Brockton replied. "I spent a few months in the Guild library, working on ancient chronicles and old maps, putting the pieces together–"

"Indeed, you deserve the name of map maker." Grisban pulled his beard.

Brockton cleared his throat. "This is based on second- and third-hand information. Very few documents survive from the time of the War of Fire, and the Guild Librarians won't let a lowly surveyor put their hands on those."

"So how precise is this?" the dwarf warrior pressed, indicating the map.

"As precise as second-hand hearsay," Quellen said, and smiled.

Brockton nodded. "And that's exactly the point. We want an accurate map, and that's what we'll be doing."

"Is Dunwarr going back to the Karok Doum?" Quellen asked. "Now the dragons are no more?"

"I know nothing of such plans," Brockton replied, a little stiff.

"Then why go and map a place that, forgive the term, eats travelers alive, and none of them are ever heard from again?" the elf asked. "The Guilds guard Black Ember Gorge to stop people from going east."

"Well, now they are paying us to go east," Grisban said. "But not through Black Ember Gorge."

Quellen shrugged. "All I'm saying is if we are scouts for the dwarven armies, I am not being paid enough. None of us are."

Vaerix looked closely at the elf, certain, as Quellen's smile curled his lips again, that much of what he had said had been to probe Brockton and the others for information.

"There are no armies and no plans to take back the Karok Doum," Brockton said. Still, Vaerix caught a hint of uncertainty. "We will be working on a new map only, to update the centuries old ones archived in Thelgrim. We are seeking knowledge. That's all."

His tone was final.

There was a moment of silence. Then Brockton cleared his voice.

"The Guilds are looking east again," he said, serious. "Maybe they once again feel the lure of the treasures of the Karok Doum and the riches of the Verdant Ring calling to them. I do not know. Maybe their fear of the dragons and the unknown dangers of the Molten Heath have been dulled by long years of peace and by well-stuffed coffers."

He looked at each one of them in turn. "But our mission is listed as exploration in the official records of the Council. I am not here as a scout for the armies of Dunwarr, I have been watching the world through old dusty maps for too many years. It's time now to see the real world and draw a new map of it."

Brockton's eyes sparkled with a passion Vaerix remembered from their first encounter. "And I will be by your side," they said.

"As will we," One Fist said.

"After all, that's what we are paid for." Grisban grinned.

Quellen looked at the bottom of his wine goblet. "But we are grateful for your sincerity, Master Brockton."

"We are looking forward to five, possibly seven weeks of field work," Brockton went on, again all business-like. He tapped the blank area with his first and second fingers. "We want to look at what the chronicles call the Verdant Ring, a grassland stretching from the Karok Doum to the fire mountains at the core of the Heath, and all around those. And while we are on our way, we'll also take a look at the remains of the dwarven cities at the western edge of the Heath. As Quellen reminded us, our destination is dangerous. We can expect bandits in the mountains, and wild beasts in the plains beyond. That's where your swords will be useful."

Grisban glanced at Vaerix. "What about the dragons?"

"Contrary to what Quellen said," Brockton replied, "no one

in Dunwarr or in the whole of Terrinoth really believes the dragons are truly gone. But they have been quiet for many years now–"

"And the Guilds want us to go and poke their lair," Grisban said, "to see if they are still around."

"Maybe not," Brockton replied, with some embarrassment. "But yes, I too believe the quiet activity of the dragons this past century has caused the Guild Council to approve of our expedition. I will not complain about this. I asked Vaerix along to deal with all that has to do with the dragons and their ilk, if we encounter them."

Grisban arched his bushy eyebrows at Vaerix. "You're familiar with the region?"

"I was hatched there," Vaerix admitted. "But it's been many years since I last visited."

Centuries, in fact.

"I am curious to see how my old homeland has changed," they added.

"And what of the treasures buried in the dwarven ruins?" Quellen asked, with half a smile. "Are the Guilds interested in that? Are we?"

"This is not a treasure hunt," Brockton replied. "We will avoid danger when possible."

Vaerix knew, as they all did, treasure hunters would often brave the mysteries of the land beyond Black Ember Gorge, seeking the fabled riches presumably buried under the remains of the dwarven cities. Few ever returned, and those who did carried little treasure and scars enough, inside and out, to last them a lifetime. Quellen had been correct when he had said the land beyond the mountains, that once Vaerix had called home, ate travelers alive.

"Is that the official policy of the Explorers' Guild," the elf asked Brockton, "or just your personal view on the matter?"

"Your caution again, elf?" Grisban snorted.

But before Brockton could reply, One Fist placed a hand on the map and leaned in closer. "Something's happening," the orc said in a low voice.

He nodded toward the open door, a cold wind blowing in. In front of it, Zayn and his sons spoke among themselves, waving their hands around and casting glances at the darkness outside.

Grisban prodded Quellen with his elbow and the elf stood and let the dwarf pass.

"Let's go and see what's up," Grisban said. His tone was light, but Vaerix saw the hard set of his features. The dwarf rested a hand on his sword as he walked toward the door. Grisban anticipated trouble.

The others followed him.

Outside, the downpour had turned into a fine cold drizzle, like a mist of icy needles in the yellow rectangle of light projected by the open door. All else was darkness. Brockton knew the mountains were home to bands of robbers that preyed on travelers, even besieging inns and trading posts. Nearby, Last Haven was a hive of outlaws. While his companions would surely keep such rabble at bay, the prospect of a violent confrontation, so soon in their mission, made him nervous. Brockton the Map Maker deemed himself a peaceful dwarf and would rather avoid the use of weapons.

But there were no bandits in the darkness outside. No torches raised high in the wind, no blades gleaming in the light. There was only darkness.

Then he spotted, sitting cross-legged by the water basin, a shape wrapped in a leather cloak, the face invisible inside the black shadow of a fur-rimmed hood. A staff, stuck in the soft ground, stood like a flagpole by the figure's side. Feathers and strings of glass beads hung from its top end, shaking in the cold wind.

Brockton and the others crowded into the doorway, while Zayn fussed around them, wringing his hands and casting wary glances at the seated figure.

"I am sorry, dear gentlemen," he said in a conciliatory tone. "I did not mean to interrupt your dinner."

"Dinner's over," Grisban replied. "What's going on here? Who's that?"

"It's a poor welcome you give your customers," Quellen said, with half a smile, "and bad business, if you leave them sitting out in the cold, and your inn half empty."

"I…" Zayn began. Then he coughed. "It's not like you think, good sir. She refused to come in."

"She?" Brockton said.

Again, he studied the shape sitting in the mist-like drizzle. Whoever she was, she was as still as a statue. Her hands were on her knees and she kept her shoulders straight. Pale in the amber light, her hands were large and long-nailed. Only the thin cloud of her breaths confirmed she was alive. He shivered.

"She says the place is haunted," one of the boys said, his voice uncertain, and then stepped back under the hard stare from his father.

"You spoke to this woman?" Brockton asked of the kid.

Not a ghost, then, or a creature of the wild.

"By your leave, sir, yes." He glanced at One Fist. "She is an orc."

Now he looked at his father. The innkeeper shrugged and gestured for him to go on. The boy found his voice again. "She inquired after you, gentlemen."

"Did she, now?" Brockton was surprised.

Their mission was not secret, but certainly it was not widely known. Who was this orc who came out of the dark to seek them out?

"She described your party, and your horses," the boy said. "She is here for you."

Grisban grunted and moved forward, a hard look on his face, but Brockton stopped him. He turned to One Fist.

The orc shook his head and sighed. "Bring me my cloak," he said to the kid. He used his hook to tighten the straps of his armor. "I guess I am the one that will have to go and unravel this mystery."

Brockton patted him on the shoulder. One Fist was a level-headed orc, well suited to parlay with the mysterious orc woman.

"Do you need any help?" Vaerix asked.

One Fist gave them an amused look. "No, friend," he replied, taking the cloak from the boy's hands. "I believe I can handle this alone. But thanks for the offer."

He draped the cloak around his shoulders, pulled the hood up, and walked to where the mysterious woman was sitting.

Standing in the doorway, Brockton and the others watched him spread his hands in what he imagined was a greeting. One Fist then squatted in front of the sitting shape. He heard his armor creak as he did so. He adjusted the cloak around himself.

If they spoke, their words did not carry to where the other adventurers were staying and were just puffs of mist in the cold air.

Once the sitting figure extended a hand, pointing east. One Fist spread his hands again, and his metal hook caught the light from the door, glinting in the dark. The mysterious woman shrugged and moved her hands as they went on speaking. One Fist turned to look at them and then turned back to the sitting woman.

Something in the way the woman moved, so slow and deliberate, oblivious to the cold and the sleet, made her look like a ghost herself.

A few moments more, then One Fist stood, turned, and walked back to the inn. Behind him, the cloaked woman stood, picked up her staff from where she had stuck it, and marched slowly toward the stables.

"She won't come into the inn," One Fist said. "For as the boy told, she claims it's haunted. But she is fine with sheltering with the horses. I mean, we can't keep her out there in the cold, right?"

Before the innkeeper could have his say, Brockton nodded. "You did good."

One Fist placed his left hand on Brockton's shoulder. "We need to talk."

"Her name's Tarha," One Fist said, as they moved far from the innkeeper's ears. "She's from a southern tribe in the Broken Plains. Hard as flint, but in good health, and smart. She's a spirit speaker. You know, a speaker with the dead."

Haughty and dismissive, she had called him a Stone Dweller, the name the tribes gave to those living in cities like the humans. But One Fist did not think it worth mentioning now.

"An orc necromancer?" Quellen asked in a puzzled whisper. Grisban shuddered. "What does she want?"

"She claims her spirits talked to her," One Fist went on. "Told her we would be passing by, and she should join us."

"What for?" Grisban asked.

One Fist shrugged. "To help us. She claims we need her with us if we want to come back from the Molten Heath in one piece. Says we will not make it without her."

"How does she know about our destination?" Brockton asked, his tone both curious and worried.

Another shrug. "Says her spirits told her."

The young dwarf stared into his eyes. "What do you say?"

"She's young. Tough. Stubborn."

"And this spirits thing–?" Quellen asked.

"She is not boasting. I have seen others like her. Not so young, not so..." For a moment One Fist searched for words. "Intense. Doesn't look like one that would take no for an answer."

"Doesn't she, now?" Grisban scoffed.

"She said if we turn her away, she will follow us. I do not doubt her."

"Well, she can suit herself," Grisban said. "We're not here to collect strays."

"This thing with the spirits of the dead," Quellen said, slowly. "I am curious and would like to know more."

Brockton looked at Vaerix. "What do you say?"

"You are the leader of this expedition," Vaerix said. "The decision is yours."

The dwarf grinned. "Humor me."

"I know nothing of the spirit world," Vaerix said, and they glanced at Quellen. "But this is a strange occurrence and not to be dismissed. We should learn more."

"Maybe you should talk with her yourself," One Fist said to Brockton.

Vaerix nodded. "The decision is yours, my friend, but methinks it might be good to have a spirit speaker with us. It cannot be denied the dead far outnumber the living where you are taking us."

Tarha had found a corner in the stables and draped her cloak over a pile of hay to use as bedding. Underneath it, she had been wearing a traveling harness, from which hung pouches and bags, and a belt with a sheathed dagger. She had propped her walking staff against a wooden pillar.

When Brockton entered the horse shelter, she was talking, and running a wide-toothed bone comb through her hair.

Brockton stopped in the doorway, listening to the sound of her voice. Her tones were gentler than he had imagined. Yet he did not recognize the language and imagined it to be some sort of Broken Land dialect. Some kind of prayer or chant, he guessed, but upon listening a moment longer, he did not perceive the rhythm and pattern he expected.

And she was not talking to herself, as he himself did sometimes to put order in his ideas. No, this sounded more like a dialogue, one of which he was hearing only one side.

She was brisk as she spoke, using short, clipped sentences.

Then she stopped suddenly, and he felt more than saw her eyes on him.

"You are the map maker," she said.

"Why won't you come and sleep in the inn?" he asked, coming forward.

"Tell your men to come in," she said in turn. "It will be pouring again soon. Or tell them to go. I won't bite you, you know? You don't need protection. Not from me, at least. And leaving them outside to linger is silly."

Grisban and Quellen had insisted on accompanying Brockton and were waiting outside, within hearing distance, in case of trouble.

"You go back in," Brockton said to them without turning. This was something he needed to face alone, as the leader of this expedition. He heard the dwarf and the elf move away, mumbling among themselves. He looked at the orc expectantly.

"As for your question," Tarha said, "the inn is haunted. But you knew that already. In your bones, if not in your head. Bandits used this place as a retreat. In the end they were captured and executed, out there. It was in the time of the old baroness, but their spirits still cling to this place."

It was a well-known story, often told, and it did not prove the woman's powers. Yet Brockton could believe she was what she claimed to be. One Fist believed her, and Brockton trusted One Fist. And now he looked at her closer, Brockton understood what One Fist indicated when he described her as intense.

"I'd like to ask you a few questions," he said.

She shrugged. "I hope this won't take much time," she said, sitting on her makeshift bed. "We have a long road in front of us, and we need all the rest we can get."

This, Brockton thought, was going to be complicated.

"Also, I'll need a horse," she said matter-of-factly.

Very complicated.

"Yes, about this, too," he began. "One Fist said you want to come with us."

"I am coming with you, yes."

"That's for me to decide," he replied. "I am the leader of this expedition."

"No. It's been decided already. I am here to help. Without me, you will not come back from the Karok Doum."

The dwarven name sounded weird and ominous in her orcish accent. She waited for his response, impassive.

"Who says the Karok Doum is where we are going?"

Her face changed, suddenly young and mobile, and Brockton thought she was about to roll her eyes. Her hand closed on the pendant around her neck. A small figurine carved in bone, maybe one inch long.

"Little can be kept hidden from the spirits," she said.

"So the spirits told you?"

"They did."

"Why do they care?"

She shrugged. "They are spirits. They have their reasons."

The spirits, he wondered, or someone's loose tongue in a Thelgrim tavern?

Brockton was uncertain. And curious, too. As Vaerix had pointed out, her necromantic powers, if authentic, would complement Quellen's spellcasting and give them an edge as they faced the unknown menaces of the Molten Heath.

"I can't promise you payment," he said warily.

The saying went friends should be kept close, and enemies closer. He'd keep Tarha close and ask One Fist to keep an eye on her.

She shrugged again. "I don't need payment. But I will need a horse."

CHAPTER THREE
The Nameless Mountains

They left the Razorcliff, Tarha riding on the most docile of their two packhorses. The inn disappeared quickly behind a bend in the rising valley as they moved east.

"That's the last of civilization we'll see in a long while," Grisban said.

"If you call it civilization," Quellen replied.

Brockton would not risk the ponies' legs on the narrow path they were following, and so they journeyed at a plodding pace, and often had to dismount and lead the beasts on loose gravelly ground, or up some zigzagging track. They climbed higher, their slow mounts keeping their heads down, in what to Brockton looked like a resigned attitude. The sawtooth peaks drew closer, covered in snow. The air grew colder.

Vaerix became aware of the changing colors around them. The blinding white of the snow-capped mountaintops, the dull dark gray of the moraines, the banded greens and hazel of the sheer cliffs. They had learned to pay attention to such details during their travels but had failed to take notice the last time they had crossed the mountains.

Brockton jotted notes in his diary, and scrawled quick maps, and explained he'd draw them again in a cleaner hand that night when they settled down to rest.

The whole mountain range north of Last Haven and south of Black Ember Gorge was a vast labyrinth of hanging valleys and ravines, mountains raising proud against the blue sky, nameless and undefeated.

"A new viable traveling route is an important commercial asset," Brockton explained, "and one the Guilds of Dunwarr will welcome."

Reason enough, maybe, Vaerix thought, to justify the expense and risk of Brockton's expedition. A risk, the hybrid considered grimly, only Brockton and his companions were running, while the Guild Masters rested in their safe homes.

The air grew cooler as they climbed, but the sun was deceptively hot. Brockton commented on how the skin of his cheeks tightened under the sun's glare, his mouth drying out.

They paused for lunch on a table-like slab of black slate jutting above a narrow creek. They filled their canteens at a small waterfall while their horses grazed on bottle-green lichens on the nearby rocks.

"This place is a true maze," Grisban said, drinking a long gulp of cold water. He dipped fingers in the cold spray of the waterfall and splashed his neck. He removed his leather cap and rubbed his temples, and finally washed his face. "We could wander between these valleys for weeks looking for a way through to the east, being baked by this merciless sun and freezing in the night."

Vaerix shuddered, recalling the last time they had been through these passes.

"We will not," said Quellen, sitting on a square stone, his hands hidden inside his ample sleeves.

Grisban combed his beard with his fingers and cast a questioning glance at Brockton.

"What do you know that we do not, mage?" he asked in a harsh voice.

"Quite a lot, I believe," Quellen sighed. "I am a geomancer."

"No kidding," Grisban replied.

Quellen arched an eyebrow. "In case you are not familiar with the word–"

"A rock mage," the warrior said. "We have the likes of you in Dunwarr, too."

"I am impressed," the elf said in a low voice.

"You can throw stones without a sling," Grisban added, crossing his arms.

For the briefest of moments, Vaerix feared Quellen would choke. His throat contracted and his eyes bulged. It looked like the elf mage was about to reply harshly to the warrior, a dangerous light in his eyes.

"You have not shown us your powers, so far," Grisban said.

"And we have heard your endless boasts about your martial prowess," the elf replied.

Grisban's cheeks burned. "Let me show you my boasts!"

"Enough!" Brockton snapped. The elf and the dwarf fell silent.

"I am quite happy," Brockton went on. "Neither of you need give us a demonstration. I am a peaceful individual. But rest assured your skills are not in doubt."

He looked at them expectantly. Elf and dwarf exchanged a nod.

"As for finding our way," Brockton continued, "let's not forget Vaerix knows these mountains, too. Right?"

Vaerix stood. "I will admit I have only a vague recollection of these valleys, from the last time I came through here. Much has changed in the intervening years." They paused and turned their amber eyes on the elf. "And I will appreciate a demonstration of Master Quellen's powers."

Quellen shrugged and stood in turn.

"The reason I was invited to join this expedition," he said with a dramatic flourish, "is my intimacy with the earth itself. While you look upon the cliffs surrounding us and only see rocks, or maybe a nest to raid for fresh eggs, to a geomancer this whole landscape is like a symphony, a sweeping music in which every sound follows the next in a perfectly logical succession. A symphony I am able to read and interpret."

"I am impressed," Grisban mumbled.

Quellen pointed a finger at the rock face on the other side of the valley they were following. The rock strata rose and fell in a mighty fold, bright white marble alternating with thin black layers of slate.

"See how the stone bends and flows like waves?" Quellen said. "Your dwarven craftsmen can read the grain of the stone like a master carpenter can read the grain of a fine piece of wood. But a geomancer takes that further. Just like a sailor can read the waves and thread the waters of the ocean, so the geomancer can read the flow and rhythm of the rocks themselves and plot a course through an uncharted mountain range as surely as a navigator does, following the stars and the sea currents."

He turned his gaze on Brockton.

"It was wise of our master map maker, to have me here with you on this expedition," he said.

Brockton cleared his voice. His cheeks were burning, whether from the sun or the embarrassment, Vaerix could not say.

"It is good to have you here with us," he said.

"Does this mean you will find a quick way to the plains?"

They all turned to Tarha, not yet used to her voice.

Quellen arched his eyebrow. "Indeed. That's what I will do."

The orc woman gave a sharp nod. "This is good, sailor-carpenter."

The following morning, when they lifted their camp and started climbing again, Brockton asked Quellen to take the lead. The elf agreed, somewhat haughtily. "You just follow me," he said over his shoulder. He sat on his saddle and drove his pony up the slope, across a stretch of gravel and into a narrow hanging valley, all green grass and white rocks.

"This way the climb is easier," Grisban said, pointing at the top of the gorge they had been following the whole morning. The pathway climbed easily and disappeared, circling past a rock spur.

"But once you reach the top," Quellen replied without turning, "you will need the wings of an eagle to go on. Yonder lies a sheer cliff, you see, with a two hundred foot drop." He pointed again. "This way is better."

The old dwarf harrumphed but did not say anything more. He kicked his mount into motion and followed Quellen.

"I will pick up the rear," Vaerix said to Brockton as they passed each other. The dragon hybrid's long legs made it easier for them to keep pace with the ponies as they slowly walked along the path.

Vaerix taking the rearguard meant Brockton would be in the middle of their column, together with Tarha, and then One Fist, who was leading the remaining pack horse.

They rode in silence for one hour, the ground rising fast in the shadow of a nameless, ice-covered horn of rock.

It was cold in the shadow, and Brockton shuddered.

"Death is commonplace," Tarha said suddenly.

Brockton saw she was now riding by his side. She held the reins of her horse in her right hand and caressed the cut bone amulet on her neck with her left. Her eyes pierced through Brockton.

"I guess it is, yes," he said.

Tarha was not the talkative sort, and Brockton felt the chill in his bones deepen when she smiled at him.

"In these mountains, I mean," she added. "But the spirits of the dead are quiet and lonely in this place. They do not like the company of the living and do not wish to linger close. That's uncommon."

She looked around, turning her head slowly.

"See there?" she said, pointing a finger. "In that cave?"

Brockton squinted at a darker patch in the shaded rock and was able to make out a narrow crack. "Yes," he said.

"A man died there," she said. "A human, I mean. A lone hunter. He was poorly, due to the cold. In a fever, he slipped and fell on a sheet of ice. Both legs broken, he crawled in there, and died alone as he had lived."

Brockton stared at her, his eyes wide. He suppressed a shiver.

"He knew these mountains like the back of his own hand, could navigate them better than your elf," Tarha went on. "He might be a good guide. But he won't come forward to talk to me."

Brockton kept his eyes on the patch of darkness that was the cave. "Why?"

Tarha shrugged. "It seems he is just not interested, has no reason to. He lacks the will, or the need. I should use some form of violence to bring him here."

"Please don't," Brockton said hastily.

Tarha grinned. "I don't have any good reason to."

He swallowed. "Good."

She turned to stare at the cavern.

"Is it different elsewhere?" he asked. "With the dead, I mean. Down in the plains, say."

Again, she caressed her amulet.

"Often," she finally said. "Many who are no more have unfinished matters they want to see done with. Messages they want delivered. Old friends or, most often, enemies. Cities are particularly busy. And battlefields, of course." She turned to cast a look at Vaerix, and then turned back. "But not here. Here among these peaks, the dead have come to terms with their condition. They are at peace and want to be left alone. I do not know why. I just see it."

"These are lonely places," Brockton ventured. "Loneliness can become a habit. Maybe that's the reason why."

He felt stupid, but Tarha's observations intrigued him.

She tucked her amulet back in her leather tunic and snorted. "Yes, maybe it's that."

Again, they rode side by side for a few moments in silence.

"I just wanted to explain why I am not earning my keep," Tarha said then.

"It is fine," he said. "As I said before, I am a peaceful man. Do not get me wrong, but I'd rather not need your help in the days to come."

"But you will need it," she corrected him. "Peace is a luxury."

And then she laughed, and her laugh echoed in the valley.

Just then, they came out of the distant peak's shadow and Brockton welcomed the warmth of the sun.

They stopped for the night on a high saddle-like notch between two blunt rock humps, overlooking the eastern horizon and the lower peaks they still had to negotiate. A thick layer of fog was laying on the lower valleys, obfuscating the sight. Clouds, actually, Brockton realized. They were above the clouds.

Watching the canyons flooded with mist and darkness, Brockton was happy they had Quellen to help them cross the labyrinth stretching between them and the plains.

As they watched, light chased light through the darkness. A storm was raging on the lower hills. It was the first time Brockton had seen a storm from above. He was fascinated.

"We'll need to look for fuel tomorrow," One Fist said, striking his flint to make fire. He looked around at the barren stone landscape. "Unless we want to use the horses' dung."

Quellen grimaced. "To cook our food?"

Now that the sun was going down, the cold stretched its skeletal fingers to grab them. They would have to keep a fire going and huddle close to it, wrapped in their blankets.

"Exploration is often a miserable business," Brockton said.

"Well, thank you for making us part of it." One Fist grinned. The fire caught and he pocketed his flint.

"You were looking for adventure, you said," Brockton retorted.

They were interrupted by Grisban, who had climbed on top of a low granite spur and was looking east and north. "Look at that!" he exclaimed, awed.

They all followed his stare and watched as the darkening sky acquired a faint red tinge, like a false dawn, that now intensified as the sun sank beyond the mountains at their back. For some reason Brockton could not name, the view drew them closer, in a tight group under Grisban's perch. They looked at the strange spectacle of the scarlet sky.

One Fist whistled slowly.

"The fires of the Heart," Vaerix said, their voice startling the rest of them. The dragon hybrid was larger than any of them, but so silent and aloof, sometimes they seemed to fade away. Now there was a note of veneration in their tone, and maybe, Brockton thought, of longing.

"The Molten Heath?" One Fist asked.

"We are too far to see the fire mountains," Grisban said.

"So we are." Vaerix nodded. "What we see are the fires of the very core of the Molten Heath, reflected in the clouds above them. One of the mountains is breathing its fire to the sky, as sometimes happens. We see its reflection, like the light of a torch mirrored in a pond."

"And the clouds themselves," added Quellen, "are a billow of shards of glass, as fine as hair, and smoke and cinders from the volcanoes, churning into a great gyre above the fire-belching mountains."

"And that's where we are going?" One Fist asked.

"We do not plan to go there," Brockton said.

"Only close," Quellen added.

"Close enough to hear the Heart of the Heath beating," Vaerix said.

CHAPTER FOUR
Memories: The Broken Plains

One of the things Vaerix found hard to understand was the habit of the orcs to take prisoners.

They understood, of course, that sometimes it was necessary to capture and interrogate an enemy, to gather intelligence about their foes' plans. But it was an activity better suited to the commanding officers.

And yet it was disquieting, the way in which the orc warriors would throw down their weapons and raise their hands, stopping the fight as if they expected to survive afterward.

As if they expected mercy.

This was contrary to everything Vaerix knew or understood.

Intrigued, they decided to learn more.

Of the force they had met here on this windswept stretch of nothingness, three orcs had survived, and were currently standing with their arms raised to the sky and shouting as a circle of spear-carriers drew closer around them. Maesix and Drys had been debating whether any one of the prisoners could provide the information Levirax required. It did not look likely, but one of them was higher-ranking by his looks.

Vaerix was fascinated by the way in which their friends' arguments matched their physical demeanor: long-limbed, graceful Drys rebuking with elegant ease Maesix's short argumentative outbursts. Maesix flexed his powerful shoulders and made fists of his hands as he spoke, ready to move from discourse to physical confrontation. Drys stood in a relaxed stance, apparently oblivious of Maesix's brisk menace. A cloud crossed the sun, robbing Drys' gray scales of their sparkle, and made Maesix's brick-red skin look like blood.

"You, there," Vaerix said in a commanding voice to the orcs. They left Drys and Maesix behind. The other hybrids opened a way in their circle for them to reach the orcs. "What is your name?"

"Kurdan," the warrior said, straightening his back. His armor was battered and he had a bad cut in his side. "I am chieftain–"

"That is irrelevant," Vaerix said. "I am Vaerix. I want to talk to you, Kurdan."

"You are talking with me, Vaerix."

Another of the orcs, a young female with a scar on her chin, chuckled.

For the briefest of moments, Vaerix felt like they had had this conversation before. It was just a thought, like an echo. Like a fleeting image after a night's sleep.

With a repressed shudder, they focused on the issue at hand.

"You surrendered," Vaerix said.

The orc looked for a moment at the ground and then up into their eyes again. "We did. It is said your people will show no mercy, but–"

"Why should we show mercy?"

Kurdan looked at them, the honest surprise on his bruised face mirroring the surprise in Vaerix's.

"It is a common practice among my people," he said slowly. "We would rather take prisoners than kill our foes, most of the time."

Vaerix frowned. "Why?"

The orc lifted his shoulders and let them drop in a slow shrug. "It is our way." He placed a hand on his wounded side with a grimace. "It was not always like that. But the old wars bloodied the Broken Plains, and we saw it was madness. We changed our ways. Our elders would rather parley than fight, and even when weapons are drawn, we would rather not waste more lives than needed." He shook his head. "You should talk to one of the elders, they are better with words. I am a warrior–"

"Yet you speak of mercy."

Kurdan was looking closely at Vaerix. He spoke slowly. "I am a warrior, not a madman."

"Don't you want to defeat your enemies?"

"Defeat does not mean kill. Dead enemies are nothing but poison for the land and fuel for feuds. Every child learns that when they receive their first axe. Prisoners, on the other hand, can be traded after the battle as part of the peace talks. Or can be ransomed for treasure or resources. Or put to work, if none would have them back. Some even decide to stay, and it is rare but not unheard of that they become part of the clan."

Vaerix was baffled. This was contrary to all that governed their people. Yet they thought they could see the point of some of the orc's words. "Won't your enemies come at you again if you let them live?" they asked.

Kurdan scoffed. "They should know better. Have we not defeated them once already?"

"The next time it could be different."

"Then we'll see what happens the next time. We are warriors, right? Warriors live to fight another day." A strange smile lingered over Kurdan's face. "So, Vaerix, are we your prisoners? Or is it true your kind does not know mercy?"

Vaerix looked back at their companions.

"What are we waiting for?" Maesix asked them impatiently.

"We are taught that mercy does not belong on the battlefield," Vaerix said, turning back to Kurdan. They wished they could have more time to talk with the orc.

"That's unfortunate," Kurdan replied.

"Are you ready to die?"

The orc sighed. "No, not really. But I guess it makes no difference."

And he stood in front of Vaerix, shoulders squared, arms relaxed along his sides.

Vaerix had never felt like this before. Never before had their deep respect for martial prowess and courage in the face of death clashed so jarringly with the consequences of their actions. In the face of death, very little made a difference, and yet Vaerix felt it should.

Kurdan had renounced his dignity as a warrior the moment he and his companions had thrown down their weapons. For the laws that governed the hybrid armies, they barely deserved a second thought. They were no longer warriors, just an accident, a momentary waste of time. But something in Kurdan's words resonated with Vaerix. It reminded them of the strange images that had been running through their mind over the last few nights. Flashes that had broken the hours of nothingness while their body rested.

Something was happening, and Vaerix did not know what it was. Something fearful and exhilarating at the same time. Something that had to do with… with the *visions* that had been creeping into their sleep ever since this campaign had started. They felt this, here and now, was part of it. Vaerix struggled to make sense of it.

Live to fight another day.

They needed time to think about this.

Vaerix turned on their heels. "Let's go back to camp," they commanded.

"What about these three?" Drys asked, running after them.

"Let them go."

"What?" Maesix called, his voice incredulous.

"You heard me."

With a low growl, Maesix suddenly stood in Vaerix's way, wings splayed in challenge. A puzzled expression warred with fury on Maesix's face. "Why?"

The hybrid was clearly trying to keep his temper at bay.

"We are warriors, not madmen," Vaerix said.

That did not dispel Maesix's puzzlement.

Vaerix opened their wings and caught the wind, rising in the sky.

Drys followed them, and then the others, one by one, leaving the three orcs behind.

Five days later, Dragon Rex Shaarina ordered the dragon

armies to retreat from the Broken Plains and all the other realms they had invaded.

The war was over.

CHAPTER FIVE
Dragon Hills

Quellen led them down a zig-zagging path, past a staircase of black rock, each step ten feet tall, over which small waterfalls dropped with a twinkling sound, white like steam. They looked for a pathway and helped the ponies down.

The expedition had finally started its descent to the lowlands and the Verdant Ring.

The sun kept burning them in the day, and the nights were freezing cold under a star-studded black sky. They used up all their fuel and had to resort to the methods that One Fist had suggested. They sat close to each other in the dark, ate their dwindling provisions, and told stories in turn.

Grisban sang a few old ballads, and One Fist told them of the people and things he had seen in his time as a sell-sword, in places like the Tanglewood or the Starfall Forest. Tarha would sometimes ask him questions or correct some of his observations.

Brockton did not have many stories to tell, and so he spoke of their current mission.

"Already we have done well," he said one night. His

surveyor's book was open in his lap and he had been revising his latest map. Now he placed the carbon stick between the pages and breathed into his cupped hands to warm them. He wore fingerless gloves, but they were barely enough. His fingers felt stiff and frozen.

"We are tracing a new path across the mountains, from the Razorcliff to the plains below," he went on. "A new route, from the Lothan River valley to the Verdant Ring. One that could be faster than the Black Ember Gorge, and certainly safer than going through Last Haven."

He looked at each one of them in turn.

"This alone might make the Guild Masters happy. And we are just starting!"

Grisban groaned. "Will they pay us a bonus? Your Guild Masters, I mean."

Brockton looked at the old dwarf. The cold made him grumpy.

Well, he corrected himself, grumpier. Grisban belonged to the Warriors' Guild, that did things differently from the other, less belligerent Guilds.

"I mean no disrespect, young master," the old dwarf said, "but some of us do not share your passion for discovery. A bonus would make us happy. Will we get one?"

Was he pulling his leg? Brockton wondered. The last thing he needed was for his companions to think more of loot than of the mission at hand.

"They might grant a bonus, yes," he said. In truth, the Council paymasters had deep pockets, but painfully short arms. "Much will depend on the quality of the information we bring back."

"That would be good," said One Fist. He held a steaming

cup of broth in his hand, balancing it against his hook on the other side. "The bonus, I mean."

"And well deserved," added Quellen.

"You will also share the honors–" Brockton began, but Grisban stopped him, raising a hand.

"No disrespect again, but a bonus would be better than a plaque or a parchment."

There was a glint in his eyes.

"You will be paid," Brockton said seriously. Fair pay at least he could promise. "And Tarha, too. We are all equals in this adventure."

"That's nice to know," Grisban said with a quick glance at the orc woman.

The night continued on in silence.

The next day, they entered the cloud layers, and suddenly the warmth of the mountain sun was gone. Grisban cursed and wrapped himself in his cloak as they all dismounted and started leading their horses through the thick fog. He stopped, along with Brockton, at the start of a shelf-like ledge suspended between a tall cliff and the whirling mists.

It looked to Brockton as too narrow for them to walk along, and Grisban clearly thought the same.

"You don't expect us to go there," Grisban said, belligerent. "Not with the horses."

"It is perfectly safe," the elf replied. "The rocks can stand our weight. Only allow about ten steps between each other. It's no more than two hundred yards, then we'll be on the pathway again. I am not particularly happy about this choice, but any other course would take days to negotiate."

"We might need to blindfold the horses," One Fist said.

Grisban looked at him. "You must be kidding."

The orc shook his head. "I'd rather lead a blind horse than a scared one."

"He's right," Brockton said. He unwound his woolen scarf from his neck and tied it around his horse's head. The pony shook its head and neighed, but then he patted its neck and calmed it.

Grisban shook his head just like the pony and grumbled. "Tell me again about how pleased the Guild Masters will be, Master Brockton."

One Fist laughed at that.

But the dwarf, too, blindfolded his pony, and then stood aside as Quellen led the way, followed by One Fist leading his horse. Vaerix was third, unbothered by the fall, walking slowly in long steps, the packhorse's bridle in their left hand.

"Careful where you step," the orc called from up ahead.

Grisban was next, and then Tarha with her packhorse on a leash.

"I'll go last." Brockton nodded at her.

She took a deep breath and stepped on the ledge.

Brockton followed carefully. The rock ledge was about five feet wide, but because of the wall on one side and the drop on the other, it felt much smaller. Brockton brushed the wall with his right shoulder. There was a deceptive wind, blowing from the bottom of the chasm, causing his cloak to fly around, and making the going trickier and the fog thinner as they went on.

"It's easier than it looks," Grisban conceded, his voice lost in the fog.

"Two hundred yards," One Fist called.

Brockton peered forward and could clearly see the tall

silhouette of Vaerix. The dragon hybrid moved slowly but steadily, the docile horse following them.

"About halfway," Brockton said, more to give himself courage than for any other reason. His pony snorted and shook its head.

Right then, One Fist slipped on the wet stone.

"Fortuna!" he croaked.

A faint shadow in the mist, he held on to the reins of his pony for dear life as he tottered on the edge of a sheer drop. His hook scraped on the rock surface, sparks flying, as One Fist tried to find purchase. He managed to keep his balance, and in a quick leap Vaerix was by him, stretching their hand across the orc's ample chest to grab his arm and hold him steady.

The orc thanked them with a nod and started again, walking carefully.

They reached the safety of the mountain path, leading their horses to a shallow creek, gravel sounding under their feet and the horses' hooves.

Brockton accepted a wineskin from Grisban and drank a long gulp, then handed it to One Fist.

"Easy, man," the older dwarf said. "That's the last of it. Next, we'll only be drinking water."

"Soon we'll be out of the mountains," Quellen said.

"Really?" Grisban replied. "Do you know a good wineshop down there?"

"I do not," the elf said, serious. "No one does, I believe." He pointed. "But I can tell you there is a spot, half a mile in that direction, where we can make camp."

"Just what I needed," Grisban snorted. "A night spent in this fog."

●●●

In the end the clouds parted, around midday the following day, the insufferable drizzle stopped, and the expedition slowly descended through valleys and canyons, following a stream that soon turned into a singing creek with trout swimming happily over a bed of pebbles.

There were sudden showers, cold water pouring down their collars and into their clothes, but these were brief, passing over the land as though in a hurry to reach the bottom of the slope. A sentiment Brockton, wet and miserable, could appreciate.

The ponies found better footing, and finally Quellen left the head of the column, handing the lead back to Brockton. They entered a low hill country, gentler and more pleasant after the harsh, sharp edges of the frozen peaks. Shrubs and small gnarly trees appeared, and soon little thickets dotted the hummocky landscape. Tamarisk, mostly, thick clumps of small pink flowers. Tall green grasses replaced the velvet-like mosses, and brightly colored flowers of gentian, so incredibly blue, dotted the landscape. Bees buzzed unexpectedly in the air and birds sang at dawn. After the late winter of the heights, the lowlands were welcoming them with the sights and smells of spring.

As soon as the ground leveled out, Brockton dismounted, took some tentative steps on cramped legs, and patted his coat. Coughing due to the dust, he looked at the rest of them where they sat on their saddles. One Fist peeled off one layer of clothing. Quellen brushed his long hair with his fingers. Tarha was impassive as ever, but looked around, curious.

Vaerix stood by one of the gentian bushes, leaning on their staff, expectant.

"We might need a rest," Grisban said. "And a good bath."

Brockton agreed. He could smell his own clothes, and it was not pleasant. He ordered a three-day stop, for them and their mounts to rest, and also to replenish their supplies and, in Quellen's dry words, "To go back to a semblance of civilization."

They camped close to the water of what was now a proper torrent, one of many that poured down from the sides of the mountains, flowing into a larger river.

One Fist went by the river to catch some fish for dinner, while Grisban mumbled and collected firewood together with Vaerix.

They had left their ponies unattended, to graze by the water. The beasts seemed as happy as their masters to be back on level ground.

While the others worked, Brockton sat down on a rock. He had dropped his saddle and part of his luggage upwind of the fire. From his saddlebags, he had taken his leather-bound notebook and now browsed through the stained pages. The small maps and the scrawled notes looked like breadcrumbs along a path and, in a way, they were. Brockton felt a small spark of pride in his chest and the tiredness that weighed on him suddenly felt accomplished. They were doing a good job, and their fatigue and discomfort were being repaid. They had crossed the mountains and found a new route. His map alone would silence those older members of the Guild Council who had said his dream was a waste of time and money. To the old Guild Masters, a young journeyman's desire for foreign lands and adventure was little more than whimsy. Brockton had suffered through dull long hours in the archives, straining his eyes by candlelight, planning his expedition to the Molten Heath and the Karok Doum. And now here he was.

And there was so much they would see and learn, so much he could tell the world.

He started writing a diary entry, to mark that turning point in their expedition, and then, as he re-read it, the echoing silence struck him. He looked up, carbon stick still in his hand. At first, he thought he was alone in their makeshift camp, everybody else out somewhere doing their part, looking for firewood or provisions, minding the horses or setting up a defense perimeter. But then he spotted Tarha, sitting cross-legged by the fire, perfectly still. He strained his ears. She was whispering something in her language. Some kind of prayer or incantation, he thought. He wished he knew more about her powers, and the reasons she had forced her way onto their team.

Not that she had needed that much force, he smiled to himself.

Grisban had his misgivings, but he was less suspicious. The orc was a grim companion, but he detected a dark strain of humor in her. And a speaker with the dead could be a precious source of information on their next leg of the expedition.

He stared at the page. It would be nice to have colors, to bring the small maps alive. He looked west, at the dark silhouette of the peaks they had crossed. Night came early, in the shadow of the mountains. In the opposite direction, the red sky over the Heart of the Molten Heath was bright, like a hot spot in the dark sky. It cast an eerie light over their camp, almost as bright as the embers in the fire, a red counterpart to the glowing of the moon.

He wondered if they would manage to catch a glimpse of

the fiery mountains at the center of that region. Quellen had spoken of rivers of molten rock, and big clouds of glass shards. Brockton was curious.

He was also curious at the fact that Vaerix had not denied the elf's words, but neither had they added any further comment. There was something there, Brockton could feel it, but he was unable to put his finger on it.

Maybe he should just ask Vaerix. And yet…

A dark shape loomed over him, startling him out of his reflections.

"There is something you need to see."

Brockton looked at Tarha, who nodded in the direction of the river and walked away. Still holding his notes, he followed her.

They walked along the bank of the river. One Fist was knee-deep in the water, catching fish with his hands and his hook, or trying to. He caught sight of Brockton trying to keep pace with Tarha, and splashing loudly, joined them on dry land. The orc had a bunch of fish on a rope, tied to his belt, and his trousers were soaked to the knee.

Tarha led them, Brockton about five paces behind, One Fist running to catch up, down the stream and to a wide bend where the water ran around a large black boulder, like a giant blacksmith's slag heap. The stream had excavated the foot of the rock formation, running around it.

Quellen came in sight.

He stood in the middle of the stream, his long coat tucked in his belt to avoid getting it soaked.

He looked at Brockton, and a displeased expression passed like a shadow over his pale features. But it was just a heartbeat. Then he looked at Tarha.

"I should have guessed you'd find this place," he said.

"Just as you did," she replied.

"But by different means."

She shook her head. "Not so different, sailor-carpenter."

Quellen grimaced, but did not say more.

"What happened?" One Fist asked, finally catching up with Brockton. He was a little breathless.

Brockton shook his head.

"Tarha..." he said.

She turned toward him. "Come and see," she said.

Quellen still did not look pleased.

Brockton walked to the edge of the water and was surprised when Tarha stepped into the stream and walked past the elf to the middle of the current.

She looked at Brockton, arching her thick eyebrows as though in a question.

He sighed, handed his notebook to One Fist, and took his boots off. If there was one thing he could not stand, it was walking with water-filled boots. And he could not allow his notes to get soaked. He shook his head as he slowly waded to where the orc woman was standing.

"What does this mean?" he asked, trying to keep irritation out of his voice. She just pointed.

Brockton looked, and at first, he did not see.

"What?"

Quellen was by his side, pointing in turn. "There," the elf said. "It starts close to the water. Can you see it?"

Following the geomancer's finger, Brockton finally saw.

He gasped.

On the side facing the river, the black rock had the texture of rough compacted sand, tiny iridescent strands sparkling in the rapidly fading light. And encased in the rock, the pale bones of a colossal spine arched like a cat stretching. Brockton took a step back, careful of his footing on the uneven bottom of the stream, and tried to catch a better glimpse of the skeleton.

He spotted a line of flat scales and thinner, longer bones, cracked in foot-long fragments. He thought at first these formed the forepaw of the long dead creature, but on a second look they turned out to be the bones of a large wing, partly folded over the body of the monster. Upstream, the skeleton faded into the rock, its long tail disappearing, but downstream the water had further exposed the bones. A long serpentine neck and a large, massive triangular head. A single horn jutted out of the rock face, pointing at the sky like an accusing finger, and a brace of sharp conic teeth showed from a half-submerged jawline.

"Aris!" One Fist cursed under his breath.

He had tucked Brockton's notebook inside his shirt and had joined him in the middle of the stream. Brockton glanced at him, worried about his notes. Running a hand over the back of his head, the orc whistled softly. "Well," he said, "at least it's dead."

"Long dead," Tarha said.

"That's why she knew it was here," Quellen said.

The spirit speaker ignored him. She climbed on top of the black rock and perched there, like she was riding on the dead dragon. Water dripped from the hem of her cloak and ran down the rock and around a large eye socket, like tears.

"A single tooth," Quellen said in a low voice, "is worth its weight in gold."

But Brockton was not listening to him.

Something which Brockton could not exactly put his finger on, told him no dwarven rune magic had killed this creature. He had heard, like everyone else in Thelgrim, of the great dragon whose skeleton, stabbed by a basalt spike, marked the eastern end of Black Ember Gorge, where Helka the Bold had unleashed her power against the wyrms. But this was something different.

"How did it die?" he asked. "When?"

"Your War of Fire?" One Fist asked.

Brockton smiled at the idea that the War of Fire had been the dwarves' war. It was true the dragons' feud with Helka the Bold had started the war. But when the dragons had come from the heart of the Heath, the dwarves themselves had had little control over the war that had followed. "That was three thousand years ago," he said.

"And this is much older," Quellen added. "Probably as old as the Great Cataclysm. He leaned closer to the rock. "Some mighty explosion," he continued. "Look at how the body is warped. Volcanic ashes buried it after it died. It's been thousands of man-years."

Tarha nodded grimly. "It's been so long," she said in her low, ominous voice, "much of its spirit is but an echo, a misshapen shadow of what it was when in life. Only rage remains. It burns like a weak candle, sounds like a distant horn in the wilderness. It calls, but does not know why anymore."

"That's unsurprising," Quellen said. "The remains were buried so long ago, they turned to stone. Only the teeth and the claws are left of the living creature. Not much for a ghost to cling to."

Tarha gave him a look.

"Or so I presume," he added, with the briefest of bows.

"We need to tell the others," One Fist said.

He looked into the darkness, trying to pinpoint where Grisban and Vaerix had gone. By now, only the opposing glows of the Heart and the moon cast light over them. In the red light from the Heath, the shape of the buried dragon was lost in the blackness of the rock that trapped it.

"I will need to come back here with the light of the day," Brockton said. "Tomorrow morning. To sketch this and make measurements."

"It is not the only one you'll see," Tarha said.

He stared at her as she stood tall on top of the outcrop and made a wide gesture, encircling the horizon. "There are more of them," she said. "Buried in the rock, burning with fading rage and choked with meaningless memories."

"More?" One Fist whispered.

By his side, Quellen looked with new interest at the orc woman.

"So much death."

Vaerix stood at the edge of the water, their eyes glowing faintly in the dusk, like a cat's. Before Brockton could say anything, the hybrid waded into the water, pushing past One Fist. They came to the rock and caressed the surface with their taloned fingers.

"My friend…" Brockton said, moving closer. By Vaerix's drooped shoulders and the tilt of their head, he sensed overwhelming grief. Vaerix leaned on the rock, their hand on the buried bones, their breath a low rattle.

"So much death," Vaerix said again.

"They speak the truth," Tarha said. "Never have I witnessed so much death." Again she gestured at the black landscape around them. "It is like a sea of candles, like a chorus of bullhorns," she continued. She nodded at Quellen. "He feels it, too, in a different way."

Reluctantly, the elf nodded. "These hills are made of petrified dragon bones."

CHAPTER SIX
Memories: The Molten Heath

Just like the storm front against the side of the volcanic mountains, the two armies of dragon hybrids crashed into each other, their war cries and clashing of weapons drowning out the rumble of the thunder. The rain turned the black ash into a slippery sludge that clung to the feet of the fighters on the ground, hindering their movement.

The battlefield was also a stretch of black powdered glass, churned by the trampling feet of hundreds of hybrids. The front line had quickly become ragged. Lost in the chaos, a red sash tied to their right arm, Vaerix faced a large, blue-scaled hybrid armed with a long-handled axe, a green scarf tied to his biceps. Vaerix ducked to avoid a chopping attack and responded with the spike at the end of their staff. The blue one parried and pushed forward. He slipped on the treacherous ground, allowing Vaerix to step away from the hungry blade of the axe.

Above them, two hybrids crossed the sky, screaming, twirling through the air in a tangle of limbs and wings. In a blinding blast, a burning line of white lightning passed through the bodies, connecting the sky and the earth. The air crackled with the fizzy smell of the storm as the two bodies fell, trailing black smoke.

There was wisdom in fighting on the ground, Vaerix thought as the axe hissed by their head.

The blue hybrid groaned, flexing his muscles, and in that moment Vaerix swung their staff and hit him on the side of the head. There was an unpleasant crack. The warrior collapsed and slowly sank in the mud. Vaerix moved on.

At dawn the dragonlord Levirax had arbitrarily divided her army into two forces, the Reds and the Greens, and had pitched one against the other. Let the strong survive, and the weak be forgotten.

Vaerix wanted to survive. For the glory of Levirax, yes, but also for something much more primal and raw. There was little else in their mind but the craving for air and light, and a roaring emptiness that had no name.

Two Greens came for them through the veil of the rain, wielding longswords.

Vaerix parried the closest attacker with their staff. The other one moved to their side to stab them, but Vaerix swept them off their feet with their tail. The foe splashed on his back in the mud. Vaerix disengaged from their first attacker, kicked him back, and speared the one on the ground with their staff.

Vaerix realized their mistake just as the other Green cut at their exposed side. Vaerix tried to dodge and fell on one knee. The blade ran along their ribs, drawing blood.

Suddenly, a gray-scaled hybrid ran out of nowhere, wings flapping, and grappled the Green from behind, breaking their comeback. He leaned into the Green with all his weight, and he lost his balance and roared in fury.

As the Green tried to dislodge this new enemy, ignoring the burning pain in their side, Vaerix caught the neck of the Green in the U-shaped end of their staff. The trapped warrior struggled, but the gray-scaled newcomer held his arms. Vaerix twisted the staff and broke the Green's neck.

The dead hybrid fell, dragging the gray-scaled one to the ground.

Carefully, Vaerix moved closer and offered their new ally a hand. He took it, allowing Vaerix to help him up. He was unarmed and wore a red sash on his arm.

"Thank you for your help," Vaerix said, wary. Something sparked in the vast emptiness inside of them, and every breath of air was charged with energy.

"I am Drys," he said.

"Vaerix."

The rain was now a solid gray wall hiding all sight and sound. It felt like the battle was so far away.

Vaerix picked up the fallen Green's sword and offered it to him.

He accepted it and weighed the blade. "A beautiful weapon." He tilted his head to one side and looked at them. "But these are your spoils of war."

"Have it," Vaerix replied, feeling tongue-tied. "It suits you better."

"Thank you," he said softly. "What do we do now?"

He was not afraid. The spark in Vaerix's spirit grew and crackled with sympathy. The emptiness retreated like night from the rising sun.

The intermittent lightning bolts flashed over the landscape, and it did not make finding their position any easier. Everything was black and gray.

Vaerix picked a direction at random.

"We go that way," they said. "The Reds we find, we take along. The Greens, we fight."

Drys sighed. "How long?"

Vaerix squeezed Drys' shoulder. "As long as we must."

CHAPTER SEVEN
Ruins

Quellen was right.

The dragon bones in the hills peeked like ghosts through the rocks, surfacing where the rain had excavated them. Some were the size of a horse, others were so huge the mind and eye failed to encompass their size.

As they resumed traveling east, Brockton observed Vaerix.

In the week since they had lifted their camp, three days after finding the first skeleton, the dragon hybrid had barely commented on the crowd of dead dragons that littered the landscape, and had offered little by way of answers to Quellen's insistent questions about their past and the dragons' society. Now, as the column of ponies moved through the hills and toward the thin green line of forests in front of them, Vaerix walked slowly by their side, scanning the land around them. Sometimes they would stop, or walk a short distance away, and stand for a few moments by a single skeleton, their hand caressing the thick ridge over an eye socket.

Brockton was worried, and had the following night, as they made camp, shared his preoccupation with Grisban.

"I'm more worried about the elf," Grisban said with a quick look at Quellen, who sat at a certain distance from the fire, his head bent, wrapped in his cloak. "The man is probably planning to mine these hills for dragon teeth, to then sell them wholesale to the Greyhaven wizards." He chuckled. "But I see your point."

He glanced at Vaerix, who stood tall against the dark blue sky, having taken up watch duty.

"Not much of a talker, our friend Vaerix," the old dwarf commented, lighting his pipe. "But they keep going, so that's good."

Brockton looked at him. "How so?"

Grisban sighed a cloud of blue smoke. "Walking is good to cast out a grim mood," he said. "Warriors know that. Ask One Fist. Walking away from the battlefield means leaving dead friends behind, more often than not. And pain and suffering. Even more, uncertainty. Doubt. You are alive, and yet your mind turns to dark thoughts and a black cloud smothers your spirit. Some cry, some are silent and dazed. That is the reason why warriors often seek peace, or at least oblivion, in wine and revelry – but a long walk is often enough to find, if not peace, at least relief. As you walk, feeling the weight of your armor and your weapons, and the fatigue…" He sighed and shook his head, unable to explain. "Walking helps you put your mind at rest."

"And you think that's what Vaerix is doing? Walking to find relief?"

Grisban sucked on his pipe for a long moment, the embers burning brighter. "Stands to reason. Those bones that got both you and the elf so excited, albeit for different reasons, are Vaerix's people, right? It's normal to feel mournful. We should not be surprised, and respect that."

Brockton weighed the other dwarf's words. He had known Vaerix for some time, and he knew the dragon hybrid had always been on the move, walking across Terrinoth in search of something unknown. Relief, maybe – and, Brockton wondered, relief from what?

He wished talking to the hybrid was easier. But Vaerix was as reserved and quiet as Grisban was loud and outspoken. Brockton found himself wary of infringing on the hybrid's privacy.

"You are probably right," he said finally. "But I really wish Vaerix would talk more openly with us."

Or the other way around, he admitted to himself, feeling guilty. He was failing as an expedition leader and, more importantly, as a friend.

"Or at least put to rest the questions of the elf," Grisban grumbled.

"They will talk to us when they are ready," Brockton replied. "I hope."

The two slowly stared at the campfire.

"We fought among ourselves," Vaerix said.

They were following a path along the bank of the creek, that had become wider and deeper as they descended through the hills. Yellow gorse swayed in the breeze, and the world seemed at peace. Vaerix walked by Brockton's pony, their long legs matching the speed of the plodding beast.

Their voice came as a surprise, and Brockton, who had been lost in his reveries, blinked as he grasped the leading strand of that unexpected conversation.

"Fought?" he said.

In front of them, Grisban rode in silence, smoking his pipe.

Brockton and Vaerix followed, and behind them, Quellen seemed to be asleep in his saddle. Tarha came next, riding the first packhorse and leading the second, silent and grim as ever. One Fist completed the line, his tall frame bent over the back of a seemingly too-small ride.

"You have to understand, friend," Vaerix said, "that my people were created for one purpose, and one alone. We were warriors, and fighting was the very air that we breathed, so that, lacking a foe, we would fight among ourselves and thus select the stronger."

Brockton frowned. "Was it training for the dragon armies?"

Vaerix shook their head.

"It was our dragon heritage. Our blood, you might say. And yes, later we did fight the dwarves and the orcs, and sometimes the humans, too. We left the Molten Heath behind and searched for war, at the dragonlords' bidding. But always we battled among ourselves. That was the way we had been taught."

Across the river, in a tall cut in the flank of the hillside, a jumble of pale bones peeked, too deformed and broken to show any shape.

Truth dawned in Brockton's mind.

"And this is what happened to these dragons, too?" he asked. "Is this what you mean? It was their nature to fight each other, and this is what killed the dragons we are seeing?"

Vaerix nodded. "This I believe."

The hybrid turned their gaze around the hills, reminiscing.

"Dragons are lonely creatures," Vaerix said. "They cherish their individuality, and seldom form alliances, or at least, Levirax, my dragonlord, was that way. Each clan of hybrids used to have a chieftain, a dragonlord. You remember them from the Third Darkness." They frowned. "The dragonlords gave my people their laws, according to their inclinations, and the dragonlords follow the Dragon Rex, the strongest among them. In my time, she was Shaarina, a fair ruler. I do not know who is Dragon Rex now, if indeed someone occupies that role. But strength is all-important for dragons. They are forever looking for ways to affirm their strength. Hence their fighting spirit."

"This could be the rage the spirit speaker claims to feel."

They both turned. Quellen had opened one eye and brought his horse closer.

"You were listening," Vaerix said.

"These hills are so silent," he added, opening his other eye, "that voices carry."

Brockton grunted. "There are many stories about the dragons," he said, "and their armies, when they came against my people. Back when Gehennor sent his hybrids against Thelgrim. But I never heard of a war among the dragons themselves, never knew of them fighting each other here." He eyed the bones in the hills. "Not in these numbers. Maybe Grisban–"

"No, please." Quellen lifted a hand and chuckled. "He might want to sing us a ballad."

Brockton snorted.

"Because it was not war," Vaerix said seriously. "This you fail to understand, my friend. Not because of a fault of yours, or out of ignorance, but because of the eyes through which you all see the world. What you call war, was just like breathing for these whose bones mark the land. It was life as they lived it."

Quellen grimaced. "It must have lasted for decades. Centuries."

"It did," Vaerix replied. "Thousands of years before the dwarves and the other young races rose from the mists."

"And those that survived it…?" Brockton asked, fearful to hear an answer.

"They grew stronger," Quellen said. "Smarter, probably."

Once again, Brockton felt a chill as he realized how silent the hills were around them.

"They became the first dragonlords of the Molten Heath," Vaerix said.

Two more days and the hills faded into a green wilderness of conifers and heather grasslands, the river slowing down in ample shallow pools and peat bogs.

As they warily entered the shadows under the trees, One Fist turned in his saddle and unhooked his crossbow.

The clicking of the cocking mechanism caught Grisban's attention.

"Keep an eye out for rabbits," the dwarf called over his shoulder. "I am growing tired of eating smoked trout and biscuits."

But they saw nothing more menacing than a few squirrels and a hedgehog that retreated under a root as they passed along. One Fist deemed them unfit to become dinner.

But he spotted other things.

There was a ghost of a road winding brokenly through the trees, stones too flat and regular not to be flagstones, half sunk in the ground, the trees holding onto them with finger-like roots. And once, in the distance, he saw what looked like an obsidian obelisk, broken and covered in brambles and other crawlers, some pale red flowers dotting its surface.

The broken road became more defined as it went deeper

into the woodland, and ended, after an almost pristine stretch of fifty yards, in front of a pair of tall brass doors, bent and corroded and stuck in a gateway, carved deep into a high black wall as polished as glass. The surface of the wall curved away into the trees on both sides of the gate. The ground had crept up the wall, piled by wind or weather, covered with thorny bushes. A huge crack ran through the dark material from the top of the ramparts to the ground, and a tangle of vines had insinuated itself within it.

Apart from that, only the wrecked doors signaled that the city past the wall had been in any way touched by time. The metal plates were encrusted with grime, bent and warped, leaving room enough to allow the passage of a man mounted on a horse.

"Herd of Kurnos," One Fist breathed, giving voice to everybody's silent awe. "This place is larger than Frostgate."

"Was richer, too," Quellen added.

Brockton dismounted and walked up to the gate. He placed his hand on the ruined metal.

Grisban stood behind him, axe in hand. "Careful," he whispered.

The door was six feet thick. Whatever had slammed into it to bend it must have been as large as a mountain. Brockton looked through the gap, knowing from his studies what he should expect. A tunnel-like passage burrowed under the wall, leading to a wide boulevard scattered with rubble and wild vegetation.

He looked at the sky.

"We have about five hours of light," he said.

Grisban's eyes widened. "You don't mean to go in there?"

"We are here to explore–"

A blast of hot hair engulfed him, cutting his words short. He turned in time to catch a dark shadow rearing behind the broken doors, and then a serpentine form slithered through the gap. Furnace-burning maws opened, trying to grab him.

Grisban yanked him back by the arm. Brockton thought the violence would dislocate his shoulder. He staggered on the stone pavement just as One Fist's crossbow snapped and the quarrel flew past Brockton's head and struck the creature, which responded with an infuriated screech.

Brockton was slammed on the ground and Grisban stood between him and the monster. He brandished his axe and stepped nimbly to avoid a sweep of the monster's tail.

Brockton tried to stand. The horses neighed in panic as the beast hissed and roared. A clawed hand kept Brockton down as Vaerix pulled him further out of the way and pushed the creature's writhing tail away with their staff.

In the open sunlight, the creature's scaly hide shone like iridescent metal. It pulled its triangular head back and hissed at Vaerix, arching its back, bone plates sliding over each other as it adjusted its position to strike.

A single note rang, followed by a sequence of loud pops. Three rocks, as big as Brockton's fists, shot through the air and hit the creature.

The creature rose on its hind legs and screamed its rage at the sky.

Grisban hit it squarely with his axe, burying the blade deep into its exposed gut. The monster gurgled and fell back on all fours. From that position it twisted and again whipped its tail around. The club-shaped end of the tail hit the old dwarf squarely in the side, lifting him off the ground, but Grisban held onto the axe handle. A second crossbow bolt from One

Fist hit the creature in the mouth. Roaring an appalling string of bad words, Grisban struck again with the axe. Black blood gushed through the open wound and the creature tottered, tried to retreat behind the doors, and was struck by Vaerix's staff. Bones cracked and the thing collapsed in a heap of iridescent scales. It shuddered, coughing blood, and was still.

Tarha was calming the horses, talking to them softly as she patted their necks.

Vaerix prodded the carcass with the end of their staff. "Salamander," they said.

"I thought they were bigger," Quellen observed. He came closer, examining the remains.

"It was big enough for my tastes," Grisban replied, massaging his side.

"Its breath," Brockton said, finally standing and dusting the bottom of his pants. "Its breath was like fire."

"A young one," Vaerix said. "Still drowsy after the long winter sleep."

Grisban had recovered the two bolts. He shook them clean and handed them to One Fist, who accepted them back with a nod. "Still want to go in there?" the older dwarf asked Brockton.

"I wonder if its skin could be fireproof," Quellen mused.

Brockton eyed the gap in the smashed gates. "We are here to explore," he said again. "For all we know, we are the first to visit this place in centuries. Hazards are to be expected."

Grisban snorted. "I trust you are keeping track of all those bonuses."

CHAPTER EIGHT
Encounters

Grisban slipped into the passage, holding his axe in his right hand and a torch in the left. He kept the torch high, illuminating the ceiling and the walls of the tunnel. Behind him, Vaerix and One Fist put their shoulders against the left door and pushed it back, widening the gap.

"Not for going in," the orc had explained, "but to make it easier to come out in a hurry."

The groan of the ancient hinges echoed through the corridor.

"This will attract every varmint in the city," Grisban said.

"Or scare them off," One Fist replied.

They walked to the end of the tunnel and back.

"Nobody in here," Grisban said, his voice multiplied by the echo.

He dropped the torch and remounted his pony.

He gave a sideways look at Brockton as the younger dwarf took the lead, and then they followed him. They stopped just outside the gallery. Two other tall metal doors stood open, their bottoms partially buried in the debris. The metal was green with a patina of age. The door on the left was dented and battered. Clumps of grass grew around its base.

Grisban squinted in the sudden light. "Nordros' breath!"

The city was a forest-choked wasteland of rubble and broken buildings, a ceaseless field of destruction that stretched to the other side of the obsidian wall that stood in the distance, a hazy black line against the thundercloud darkness of the sky over the Molten Heath. Past the inner gate where they had stopped, the main avenue of the city was a swamp. Vegetation had conquered the once proud dwarven city. Willow trees stretched their branches, like curtains, over still water pools and clumps of reeds. The putrid smell of the marsh hung in the air. Grisban sneezed and stifled a curse.

Clicking his tongue, Brockton led his pony forward, and the others followed him under the canopy of the willows. They were going slowly, Grisban thought, like a funeral.

When they entered the shadows under the trees, he felt a chill.

Here and there, chunks of wall emerged through the dirt and the greenery, like rock ridges, and an occasional broken column still stood, as white as bone, wrapped in ivy and crawlers. The center of the town had suffered less from the destruction, and as they went, they saw clearer signs of the ancient structures. Brass plates, that had once covered the plain stone walls, laid half-buried in the dirt, the metal bent and made dull by time.

According to the ancient chronicles preserved in Thelgrim, Brockton explained as they journeyed, each dwarven city in the Karok Doum had been planned as a wheel, with avenues as spokes radiating from the central square, and ring-like roads following the curve of the obsidian wall, crossing them. He hid apprehension behind the mask of his knowledge.

No one truly listened, each of them too busy looking around in awe, and finally Brockton fell silent.

They approached the crossroads where the ring avenue was obstructed by piles of smashed masonry and loose stones. The statue of a warrior was half-buried in the mound of wreckage, his features broken, a beard of moss on his chin.

Somewhere, a frog or some other small animal jumped into the water with a plop, and the sound broke the stillness in the air.

The group formed a column as was by now their habit and went on.

After about a hundred yards, they stopped on a strip of dry land as Brockton tried to spot a path through the mire, following the remains of the old pavement. "This is not fire damage," he said.

They all looked at him, confused.

"According to the histories, the cities of the Karok Doum were destroyed by the dragons, enraged by what our ancestors were doing here."

"Their stolen rune magic," Quellen said in a low voice.

"Raging dragons and drakes came from the Heath," Brockton continued, "and burned the cities to the ground. This claims the chronicles I was able to peruse. But what we see here is not fire damage. The dwarves of old built all of this using volcanic glass. Fire would be of little consequence. The buildings were destroyed by impact. Like, by catapults. Look at the defense wall as it still stands. The city was fireproof."

"The population was not as fireproof, I guess," Grisban said.

"And a dragon's fury," Vaerix added, somberly, "can be harsher than a barrage of catapults."

"There were legends among my people," Quellen said, voice low. "About the cities of the Karok Doum. Cities built in obsidian and brass. Whole cities turned into tombs, with dwarven warriors buried there..."

"Waiting to rise again to fight once more for the clans," Grisban said, and seemed surprised at the bitterness in his voice.

"And chambers filled with treasure," Quellen went on. "For the brave to come and take them."

Grisban snorted. "What madness!"

These were not abandoned halls in which carved sarcophagi preserved the ancient defenders. This was a shapeless wilderness, empty of any trace of civilization. Only the wall remained, and the shattered doors.

How many adventurers had been lured to this wasteland by the dream of untold riches?

"This place is a tomb," Tarha said, echoing his thoughts. "No more, no less."

She dismounted and walked up to where Brockton stood. The beads hanging from her staff tinkled. "This place has been a tomb far longer than it has been a city. Thousands are buried beneath us, in the dark."

Her low-pitched voice echoed over the ruins, evoking the ghosts of which she spoke. Grisban shuddered.

"And some, yes, are waiting," Tarha continued. She slowly turned, scanning the mounds of ruins surrounding them. "Some went down in battle, and some did not, and that's their torment. They are ready to defend this place because that is all they know."

Grisban caught One Fist making a hand gesture against ill luck.

"Do you...?" Quellen started, and then stopped, frowning.

"I feel them stirring," Tarha said matter-of-factly. She closed her hand on the pendant around her neck. "Most of them are mere shadows, or even less. But some others…" She stopped, like she was listening. "There is one…" she said slowly. "One of us…" She turned to Vaerix. "One whose presence here is making them angry."

"It makes sense," Grisban said.

Vaerix looked from Tarha to him.

"No offense meant," Grisban added.

"None taken," Vaerix replied. "You are correct. Alas, it was my dragon forebears who did this, if not my people."

They paused. Grisban was unable to read their expression, but Vaerix's eyes narrowed. "Maybe I should go," they said.

"Maybe we should all go," Grisban said, with a meaningful look at Brockton. "Get out of this place while there is still light. There is nothing here for us. No shelter, no supplies."

"Tarha can keep the ghosts at bay," Brockton said. His glance at her betrayed his uncertainty.

"This I can do," she replied without much enthusiasm.

Grisban took a deep breath, but he was interrupted before he could vent his objection.

"I know nothing about the spirits of the dead, or their feuds," One Fist said suddenly. He had dismounted and was down on one knee, looking at the ground and frowning. "But somebody came through here, about one day ago. And they were not ghosts."

"How many?" Brockton asked urgently.

One Fist shrugged. "Five, maybe six. Seven. Man-sized, wearing boots." He pointed east, and north. "They went that way."

"Adventurers looking for treasure?" Quellen asked.

One Fist grinned. "Can't tell you that from their footprints alone."

"Let's get out of here," Grisban said, disturbed.

Vaerix was the first to catch the sound. Their body reacted to the ringing of metal on metal even before their brain processed what the distant echo could mean.

"Fighting," they said, and tilted their head to pinpoint more precisely the sound's origin.

They had been following another rubble-strewn avenue of the ancient city, leading the horses carefully on the uneven ground. Brockton had decided they would try to reach the east gate, having entered the ruins from the south. This meant going along what had once been a ring-road, but was now a jumble of contorted trees and smashed buildings.

Now Brockton turned to Vaerix, his eyebrows arched questioningly. "What?"

Grisban was by their side, his axe glinting in the setting sun. "They're right," the old dwarf said. "There's a fight going on."

"Smoke, too," One Fist added, sniffing the wind.

Brockton looked from one to the next, frowning. He was clearly unable to catch the sound or smell.

"About a quarter of a mile," Vaerix said, pointing north, beyond a tall mound of ruins. "Maybe less. Echoes can be misleading."

"Any good reason why we should care?" asked Quellen behind them.

Astride the lead packhorse, Tarha looked at the elf and grimaced.

"We might not have any choice," Vaerix said.

Just then, coming from a side path between two crumbling walls, a gray horse came galloping at them, hooves thundering madly on the broken flagstones. It neighed wildly, its eyes wide with fear.

Grisban cursed as Vaerix leapt in his way and spread their long arms, at the same time making a soothing noise. The runaway horse stopped and reared, scared anew. It kicked the air less than a foot from Vaerix's face, but they were able to stretch and grab its reins. They brought it closer and then gently caressed its heaving side to calm it. The beast shuddered, but seemed to like being petted.

"Something's happening for sure," Brockton said.

"You stay here," Grisban said with a dangerous grin, thumbing the edge of his weapon. "I'll go and take a look."

"No, friend," Vaerix said, taking a step forward. They handed the reins to the dwarf. "I will go. With One Fist if he is willing. You stay and protect the others."

Grisban bristled. "Why on Yrth–!"

"Our legs are longer." One Fist winked and slapped Grisban's shoulder as he passed him. Vaerix and One Fist ran to the intersection, Grisban's rumbling curses sounding behind them.

About a hundred swift steps along the narrow alley the horse had come from, the ground descended into a small, bowl-like depression, already filled with the shadows of the evening. There was what was left of a wide flight of steps, covered with moss and yellow grasses, leading downward into what might have once been a minor square of the city, maybe a local marketplace. A small pool of water occupied the farthest corner of the clear space at the bottom of the depression, mirroring the sky.

A misshapen chunk of rock rose in the middle of it. What was left of an ancient fountain, Vaerix imagined. The water had pooled at the feet of a tall slab of gray stone, probably a half-collapsed wall of a long-gone building. In ancient times, an unknown hand had carved spirals and other designs over the face of the rock, but time and weather had made the low reliefs as faint as ghosts.

Yet, it was not the ancient carvings that caught Vaerix's eye, but the unfolding scene beneath them.

A small camp had been laid out in a nook on the south side of the carved rock, a smoky fire burning maybe ten steps away from the edge of the water, where a woman stood, two short swords in her hands. She wore a sky-blue tunic over rust-colored trousers. She had hair like a raven's wing and skin the color of terracotta. Her elegant stance was what caught Vaerix's eye, the easy way with which she moved as six other figures, dressed in dusty rags, milled around her, speaking in a rough accent Vaerix did not recognize. They brandished swords and daggers, and those weapons were the only things clean about them. Dust flew when they moved, and their faces were smeared with dirt. They were all human, and at least one of the ragged ones, Vaerix believed, was a female.

"Now this is new," One Fist said in a low voice. He huddled by Vaerix's side behind a pile of broken bricks and dirt with his sword drawn.

Vaerix nodded, tightening their grip on their fighting staff.

As they watched, one of the men ran forward with a mighty curse. He stomped on the shore, spraying water around, and with a vicious lunge he slashed at the woman.

She turned on one foot, crouched, parried with the blade in her right hand. At the same time, the blade in her left hand drew a silver crescent in the air, and then a red brushstroke. The man gurgled and fell back, hitting the water with a loud splash.

"She's good," One Fist said.

As the man thrashed in the water, his companions circled the lone woman, cursing and hissing at her, feinting to test her defense.

The man in the water kicked his feet one last time and was still.

"Good, yes." Vaerix nodded. Then they glanced at their orc companion. "Yet, five against one is not fair, methinks."

One Fist grinned, his eyes ablaze. "Let's go."

They climbed past the crest, and as they ran down the slope, a loud war cry erupted from One Fist's throat, echoing in the small, enclosed space.

Down by the water, the woman had parried an attacker with her crossed blades, and as Vaerix and One Fist ran to her, she turned again and kicked a second adversary in the knee, causing him to collapse. She disengaged and again parried the first man's sword with her right blade as she buried her left blade in the fallen man's chest.

A third attacker was on to her, slashing down at her head with a square-pointed broadsword. They caught his wrist in the fork of their staff, blocking the attack. The ragged man just had time to look at his new foe with panic-wide eyes, and Vaerix twisted the staff, cracking his wrist and disarming him.

One Fist slammed into the next man, pushing him to the ground, and then caught the fifth man's blade on his own, parrying his attack.

Screaming incoherently, the man with the broken wrist pulled a dagger from his belt with his off hand and rushed at Vaerix. They swept at his feet with their tail and he crashed on his back on the ground.

The black-haired woman slashed at the throat of her last adversary, bringing him down, and turned to stare wide-eyed at Vaerix, who held their foe down with a foot placed on his chest. Her nostrils flared as she breathed hard. She straightened up but did not lower her weapons.

"Are you all right?" Vaerix asked her.

One Fist was still trading hits with the last standing fighter, taking his time. The woman was holding her own, retreating slowly.

"Come on!" One Fist said with a laugh. "You can do better!"

A loud twang sounded in the enclosed space of the square, and a crossbow bolt bounced off Vaerix's shoulder armor. They turned to see another ragged man, up high on a mound of ruins that blocked a side street like a dam. The man was busy cranking his crossbow as fast as he could.

A blur of gold and silver arced through the air and an axe buried itself in the crossbowman's chest. He made a croaking sound. The crossbow escaped his grasp, rattled on the rocks below him, and he crumpled to the ground.

Both Vaerix and the swordswoman turned to stare at Grisban, who stood at the head of the buried staircase, his hands on his hips, his white-streaked beard thrown back over his shoulder.

The dwarf smirked. "And you call yourself warriors? Ah!"

One Fist's adversary dropped her sword and raised her hands. "Peace," she said. Her gaze kept going to Vaerix. Her scarred face was wan, her eyes wide. Vaerix now judged her to be young but aged by a harsh existence.

The orc scoffed and kicked the sword out of the way.

The man under Vaerix's foot moaned. The one that One Fist had slammed into was on all fours on the ground, shaking his head.

Slowly, the swordswoman sheathed her twin blades and placed her hands on her hips.

They stood like that, staring at each other, until Grisban spoke again. "A thank you would be nice," he said, walking down to them.

The swordswoman turned to face him, and in that moment the man on all fours sprung forward, roaring, and tried to tackle her. There was a short blade in his hand. She waited for him and then she rolled back, grabbing his wrists. As she fell on her back, she planted a knee in the man's chest and sent him vaulting over her and back on the ground.

By the time they were both back to their feet, the man was disarmed, his blade now in the woman's hand. Then the dagger flew through the air, burying into the man's right eye.

He went down on his knees then to the ground. She dusted off her clothes and finally turned to Grisban. "Thank you," she said with a nod.

She had a low contralto voice, and an accent that Vaerix could not place. Her green eyes sparkled with humor. She kept glancing at them, but did not seem willing yet to acknowledge their presence. Vaerix could not deny they were intrigued, but remained silent, observing her.

"And you," she went on, talking to the woman standing in front of One Fist's sword point, "it has been said that a true sword master does not kill their foes, but gives them life. These fine warriors–" she eyed Grisban, "–have done just that. Take your lives, then, as they were given to you, and begone."

The woman looked at her with wide eyes, like she was struggling to understand. Then she nodded, her hands still in the air. "Yes, my lady," she croaked, with a bob of her head that was intended as a bow. "You are most merciful, my lady."

She made to step aside, but One Fist stopped her.

"Merciful does not mean stupid, my friend," he said. "Drop

all your weapons and everything else you carry. Then take
your friend–" he nodded at the one Vaerix was still holding
down, "–and make sure we don't see your faces again."

"But…" the woman blurted, "in the mountains and with no
weapons… the night is coming."

"One more reason to make haste," One Fist said.

Grisban huffed. "We could just slit their throats and be
done."

His words put a spring in the woman's actions. She undid
her belt, dropped it on the ground, and then hastened to help
her surviving friend up. They limped off without turning and
took the closest alleyway, headed south.

Grisban let out a big guffaw. "Idiots," he said.

"Dangerous idiots," One Fist said, putting back his sword.

"Idiots are always dangerous," the dwarf said with a shrug.
He walked grimly to the body of the man he had killed to
retrieve his axe.

The neighing of a horse announced that Brockton and the
others were here, having followed slowly down the overgrown
alley.

The red sun burning at their backs, the young dwarf and
Quellen were leading the animals, and Tarha was still sitting
astride her packhorse. Vaerix saw they had added the gray
horse to their train. The beast followed them easily, towering
over their smaller mounts.

"I was told you had wings."

Vaerix turned sharply to the woman, who now stood in
front of them. She leaned forward and studied at them with
open, honest curiosity. There were tiny golden specks in her
irises.

She smelled of sweat and lavender.

"You are a dragon-kin, right?" she asked. "A dragon hybrid, like in the Third Darkness."

She struggled with the syllables. Her Rs were strangely grating, but not in an unpleasant way.

Vaerix leaned on their staff. "That I am," they replied. "I am Vaerix."

"I was told your kind had wings," she said again.

Breath escaped through Vaerix's nostrils at her rudeness. "Many of us do, yes."

Something in their voice must have betrayed their emotions, because she frowned and grew sober. She looked down, and then up again. She cleaned her right hand on the front of her tunic, then offered it.

"I am Cyra Kurkuan. Once of Lorim, now..." She shrugged. "A poet of the open road." She turned around, looking at each one of them in turn. "I have not much of a campfire, but you are welcome to share its warmth, gentlemen." A glance at Tarha. "And lady," she added. "Night is coming, and we can all share a bite of good food."

CHAPTER NINE
Memories: The Molten Heath

The city stretched in every direction, as far as the eye could see, a checkerboard of light and shadow under a sky so white it was almost blinding. Angular buildings without windows cast their solid black shadows over the large, deserted avenues.

Empty of people, the city was perfectly silent.

Vaerix had never seen such similar architecture in their travels as of yet.

This was not the black glass and bronze of the dwarven ruins, nor the rough dry walls of the Broken Land villages. No city built by humans they had ever seen was like this. There was no surrounding wall, no towers.

Elves then, Vaerix concluded, must have built these edifices.

Yet no trees lined the boulevards, no birds sang. The architecture had nothing of the fabled liquid curves of elven make.

This was a straight-lines place of stone, of blinding light and deep shadow.

Vaerix walked along the straight streets, looking this way

and that, but no one welcomed them, no one challenged them. They were the only ones here.

And they were weaponless.

The realization caused a momentary spike of panic that instantly changed into aggressive fury. Gone was the sword that had been a gift from Levirax herself, as a sign of her appreciation for the one she had called her champion. Gone was the spear whose head Drys had captured and given to them as a token of affection.

Their senses on edge, Vaerix continued their exploration.

After ten thousand paces, they came to a sunken plaza, a circular space surrounded by descending steps, like rings in the water of a pool.

As they descended the steps, other dragon hybrids appeared, coming from the many streets that converged on this place. Vaerix witnessed a kaleidoscope of scale design and color, a variety of body shapes, a gallery of jewels and ornamentation. Horns were capped with gold filigree, wing claws and fingers sported silver rings. Dress ranged from the strictly utilitarian, with simple loincloths and harness, to the extravagant, silk and brass and polished leather.

Alone or in small groups, none of the newcomers seemed to mind them, and drifted away when Vaerix tried to strike up a conversation, ask them any of the questions that were clogging their mind.

They just gathered in the plaza, and an air of expectancy grew as the place became more crowded.

Vaerix's instincts awakened.

So many hybrids closely packed in one place would lead to violence. The hybrids were trained from their early years to defend their personal space, roughly defined as a circle as wide as their outstretched wings or arms. Anyone within that range was either expected to back off or attack.

Indeed, a commanding officer's first duty was to instill in their troops the capacity to turn on a designated enemy the boiling aggression that being packed in close ranks would cause.

Therefore, now they prepared for the worst.

There would be some pushing and shoving, possibly some harsh words, maybe a challenge. The ensuing fight was generally considered a good thing, a way for the weak to be eliminated, but Vaerix was not sure they wanted a brawl to erupt in this place, surrounded by these strange buildings.

They moved to the edge of the crowd, surveying the gathering hybrids for signs of the coming violence.

But there were no such signs. Vaerix realized not one of the hybrids gathered here carried any weapons, and many wore jewels over their talons and horns that made them useless in a fight.

As Vaerix scanned the crowd, a commotion toward the center of the plaza caught their attention. The hybrids were pulling back, clearing a circular space in which four individuals walked purposefully, each of them carrying some kind of weapon.

So, this *was* to be an arena of sorts.

Vaerix pushed forward to see better. They navigated through the press without difficulty and as they reached the first line, the four hybrids lifted their tools. Notes tumbled over each other as the first strains of a soft melody spread across the crowd which cheered and then settled down to listen.

As the sinuous music rose in volume, Vaerix started to awaken, amazed at what they had seen.

They were in the barracks of Levirax's army, and their world had changed forever.

"I do not understand," Drys said.

Vaerix shook their head, frustrated. "It is like flying," they said. "No one can explain it, one must experience it for themselves. And just like flying, once you've experienced it, you will never forget it."

"But we can't do it," Maesix said. Vaerix's brood brother and a fine warrior, gifted with an inquiring mind and a quick temper. "That's the whole point, right? Flying is something we do not need to understand because it is part of us from the moment we hatch. But seeing visions in the night?"

Vaerix sighed and took a look around.

There were about a dozen dragon hybrids, sitting together in the temporary barracks they had set up in an old ruin in the land that had belonged to the orcs. Everybody was listening to Vaerix as they relayed their latest night visions.

But it was not their number that Vaerix noticed.

It was how bleak and bare their quarters were.

Vaerix had never been bothered by that in the past. But now, after what they had seen in their dreams, the barracks were little more than a plain wooden box in which they were kept between one battle and the next. A roof over their head. A place where they could hunker down and rest. Room for their weapons and armor.

It was not so in their dreams.

Vaerix still struggled with their experiences. Dreams were common to many other creatures of Mennara, but unheard of in dragons and their kin.

In their sleep, Vaerix visited strange, wonderful cities, where the hybrids lived in peace, surrounded by beauty. Brightly colored flowers, shadowy tree-lined boulevards, sun-bathed plazas bustling with activity.

Its strangeness should have been horrifying, yet Vaerix found it intoxicating.

They did not know where these dreams came from, or why they were experiencing them. Did it mean there was something wrong with them? Or maybe something right?

Vaerix only knew they had to share them with their companions.

"It is like a memory," they said now, striving to explain. "Like when you recall things you have seen or done. Only it is nothing you've ever done that comes to you. No place you have ever been is what you see."

"So what's the use?" a voice asked among the small crowd. "Is it actually real, these things you see? Or is it make believe?"

They also knew both men and orcs, and dwarves, too, had these nightly visions, the same as Vaerix was experiencing. It was even said these lesser peoples had among them individuals trained, or gifted enough, to read future auspices into these dreams from which those people suffered.

"Methinks it is just imagination," Maesix said.

And that alone was an accusation. Imagination was not considered a good trait for a warrior.

But Vaerix knew their dreams were not just imagination. They had seen some of these visions, these dreams, come true.

They had experienced snippets of conversation between them and Drys come true, snippets they first heard while they had been asleep. Places Vaerix had visited first in their dreams, and then encountered as the Levirax army advanced across the Broken Plains.

This was, in fact, the crux of the whole thing. Because if those dreams could be a premonition of things to come, then what about the world in which Vaerix spent most of their sleeping hours? What of the peaceful, fulfilling life those dreams promised?

What of the white city of light, peopled with dragon hybrids that did not know war?

"Why you?" one of the others asked.

Vaerix shook their head. "I don't know."

"I have never heard of anyone else doing these dream things, among our people," Maesix said.

"Or if they did, they did not tell," Drys said.

And there was a true sadness in his voice.

CHAPTER TEN
Cyra

"Thanks for retrieving my horse, by the way," Cyra said, taking the reins from Brockton. "I call him Cloud, because he's gray and wanders around." She patted the side of the beast and then dropped the reins on the ground. "He's not very smart, and he's stubborn like an old bock. Not a very good horse, but he's all I have. I traded a poem for him, in a place west, called Red Bridge."

"A poem?" Brockton asked, intrigued. "For a horse?"

"It was a long poem," she replied with a lopsided grin. She looked affectionately at the horse and caressed its neck. "But I guess it was not a very good poem after all, huh?"

She laughed and went back to the campfire, where she had placed an iron teapot close to the flame. A plume of steam escaped the spout.

"I did not expect this place to be so crowded," she said, sitting on a square block of masonry and gesturing for them to do the same. "Busier than the Orc Market in Dawnsmoor, it turned out to be. But I must say I am happy you are here."

Introductions had been made, and Brockton's companions

were setting up camp in the shadow of the stone wall, where the night wind would not find them.

Cyra pulled her hand back from the hot handle of the pot and shook it, clicking her tongue. Then she used a rag to handle it and pour the tea.

"You were doing all right before we came," One Fist said, squatting down in front of her, the fire between them.

Cyra smiled. "I'm not so proud I can't appreciate help on the battlefield."

"You are a long way from home," Brockton said, coming close to the fire. Quellen followed him.

She answered his observation with a shrug. "I guess so."

Grisban was standing aside, minding their ponies.

Tarha was slowly circling the plaza. Brockton thought he saw her lips move. She sometimes stopped and used a tool like a long iron spike to carve signs on the rocks. Then she walked to the pool and washed her hands.

Brockton thought about the ghosts she had mentioned before. He had said she could keep them at bay, and he believed that was what she was doing.

He shook as if waking from a dream and realized Quellen and Cyra had been talking this whole time. Now the woman was looking at him. He smiled.

"You knew those who were attacking you?" Brockton asked.

"One does not need to know someone to kill them," One Fist observed. Cyra handed him a tin cup filled with tea and he nodded as he took it.

"But I did," she said. "We came here together."

"Here?" Brockton asked, looking around. She had this way of speaking that left more questions open than she answered. "In this city?"

"Treasure hunters," Quellen said, a hint of contempt in his voice.

The woman Cyra grinned. "Explorers," she corrected him. Then she looked sideways at Brockton. "I meant here in this valley."

"Grave robbers," Quellen said.

She ignored him.

"Are you really from the Lorimor Empire?" Brockton asked.

"By way of Last Haven, and a lot of places before that," she replied in good cheer. "But Last Haven is where we set up our little venture. There was a young mage that hired us. A Greyhaven apprentice. A guy called Carthos."

"You're a sell-sword?" One Fist asked.

"She's a sword poet," Quellen said, with a smirk.

She looked at him with a brief frown and then nodded at him. "That I am."

"Sword poet?" Grisban rumbled. "A bard, you mean?"

"Afraid she's a better singer than you?" One Fist grinned.

The old dwarf huffed. "Bards and minstrels," he said, "they are strange. I met one, once, that could sing people to sleep."

"You ever tried that?" the orc asked.

Grisban replied with a rude word.

"Not a bard," Quellen said. He was keeping his eyes on the woman. "A sword poet. A very special kind of warrior from the Lorimor Empire."

Grisban moved closer, one hand on the handle of his axe. "How special?" he asked, suspicious.

"The people in my land," Cyra said, "have found out that the same discipline is required to wield words and blades. Both poet and warrior, we say, require eye–" she counted on her fingers, "–hand and heart. Perception, technique and instinct. Some of us devote our lives to perfecting the twin arts of poetry and swordplay. We train in both, and both we practice, striving for perfection."

"You call yourself a sword poet," Grisban said. "Yet you fight with two knives."

The woman arched her eyebrows. "These are short swords," she said, humor draining from her voice. She lifted one of the blades. It was about two feet long, narrow at the waist and thicker at the point. A groove ran along all its length. It looked heavy, for its short length. "They are the weapon of choice, in my land, of the higher classes, and mentioned in the ancient imperial laws. Commoners are forbidden from carrying them."

"They look like knives to me." The old dwarf shrugged.

"Maybe you would like to taste their bite?"

Brockton looked from her to Grisban and back. Were they really starting a quarrel? Could fighters really only think of fighting?

Grisban grinned. "Is that a challenge?"

"It might help you appreciate the difference."

They were. Brockton tried to think fast of a way to pour water on that unrequited fire.

"They are fine blades," Vaerix interjected. "Beautifully made and, by their looks, ancient."

Their quiet voice seemed to soothe the two warriors, and Brockton silently thanked their quick wits. Cyra sheathed the sword and then caressed its hilt, a faraway look in her eyes. "They belonged to an old friend of mine."

Grisban was about to say something else, but Tarha chose that moment to stick her staff in the ground by the fireplace and sit by the dwarf's side. He started, and stared at her, and closed his mouth. He moved aside a little. Ignoring them all, the orc served herself some tea.

Brockton was eager to resume the conversation and steer it as far as possible from anything involving swords. Cyra had so far dodged Brockton's questions, and this felt to him the right moment to further change the subject from her choice of weapons and to get some answers.

"What brought you to the land of Terrinoth?" he asked.

"And to these ruins," Quellen added.

She looked into the fire and took a deep breath.

"I was west of the mountains. Our mountains, that is. The ones you call Lorim's Gate, where Bueldan's Tears Lake feeds both the River of Sighs and Riya's Run. There was no real reason for me to be there. Rambling, you know. Anyway, I was in this village on the shores of Bueldan's Tears. And as I watched the snowy peaks to the east, I found myself wondering what might lay beyond them. We hear stories, you know, about fabled Terrinoth, where the dragons roam…"

She stopped and glanced at Vaerix. Then she shrugged.

"So I put my things in a bag–" she pointed at a satchel laying on the ground by her saddle, "–and started walking. That's another thing poetry and swordsmanship have in common. Much of the work is done on your feet. I crossed the mountains to a place called Summersong, and from there I went north, skirting the Tanglewood, to Dawnsmoor. An interesting place I was quite happy to leave behind." She chuckled and sipped her tea. "That was seven months ago. I went south to Riverwatch and spent some time there. Then north again. I wintered in Cradle Fort, and then skirted the place they call the Tangle, which is rather confusing, considering there's a Tanglewood in the west, too, and headed north into the mountains to Last Haven." She grinned and massaged her jaw. "Now that's a town that works hard to deserve its name."

She stretched suddenly and retrieved her bag. From it, she pulled out a square, thick leather-bound book, not different from the one in which Brockton kept his notes.

"Here," she said. "I took notes along the way."

She showed the pages to Brockton, who squinted at the small writing and nodded at the finely drawn sketch map.

"I've been to Tamalir, too," he said, recognizing the name.

Cyra smiled. "That's the sort of place where one could happily spend the rest of their days, isn't it?" She turned a couple of pages. "I wrote some good poems there."

"I see." He nodded.

Then she sighed. "Anyway, in Last Haven this young mage, this Carthos, who looks like a stray cat, but he's pretty quick, was setting up an expedition to this place he called the Molten Heath. Spoke of dwarven ruins and dragon hoards. Ancient wonders and strange perils. He needed blades, and I had never met a dragon. So, I got myself hired. We came north through the low passes and did a bit of exploring, a bit of adventuring. But our companions got cold feet and Carthos was not, let's say, the most sympathetic of masters."

"What happened to him?" One Fist asked.

"Snuck away two nights ago," she said. "Taking all our findings with him."

"What findings?" Quellen asked. He sounded casual, but Brockton perceived his interest.

"Just stuff." Cyra waved a hand and went on. "That was when my companions turned sour. I was the odd one out, and I thought it better to part company. I guess Carthos had the same idea, only a lot earlier. As I said, he's quick. Anyway, I thought I had given them the slip, but apparently, they were able to follow me here."

"Looking for the stuff," Quellen said. "The stuff you did not have with you in the first place. Because the mage stole it. Right?"

Cyra stared at him for a moment. "Exactly," she said. She turned her empty teacup upside down, ending the conversation. "Then you came."

They shared some food and then settled down for the night.

"I'll take first watch," One Fist said.

"You think those two fools will come back?" Grisban asked him.

"Not tonight, no," the orc said. "But they likely will, because they are fools. And there might be other dangers roaming these streets. Salamanders and such."

He looked questioningly at Tarha, but she shook her head, and One Fist gave her a grim smile.

Brockton left the orc and Vaerix to set up the watches and walked by the small lake. The day had been cloudy, but now the night sky was clean, framed by the snowy caps of the mountains which reflected the light of the moon, that the fires of the Molten Heath tinged a bloody hue.

He caught himself naming the constellations. He took a deep breath, pulling his cloak closer.

"Do you remember what I told you in Razorcliff?"

He turned sharply and saw Grisban standing there, his features lit by the red glow of his pipe. "About picking up strays?"

"She's a map maker and a fellow explorer," he replied defensively.

"She's a sell-sword from a foreign land and a rambler," Grisban countered. "And already we have the orc woman tagging along."

"Cyra is different."

"Sure."

That was disrespectful to Tarha, Brockton realized. The orc had been a good, if somewhat grim, companion so far. "I don't mean—" he started, but Grisban cut him short.

"I'll concede Cyra's not as sinister as the spirit speaker. But she was here to loot these ruins. She admitted it herself." Grisban caressed his beard. His pipe burned bright. "And we have only her word about her fallout with this mage. This Charos—"

"Carthos."

"Whatever. For all we know, he may be lying dead in some underground chamber hereabouts. If he ever existed."

Brockton fell silent. He valued Grisban's pragmatism but felt the old dwarf's disapproval of his decisions was undeserved. Already Tarha had proved herself a valuable addition to the expedition, and Brockton was sure Cyra might prove useful too.

And the last thing he wanted was to antagonize Grisban.

"I am the leader of this expedition," he said in a level voice. But this, too, was the wrong way to handle it.

"And this is what you always wanted," Grisban said quietly. "The opportunity to go beyond the mountains, beyond the borders of the map, and see what's here. Basically, what our friend there by the fire has been doing, if we are to believe her. An adventure."

"If we are to believe her." Brockton looked at the campfire and then back at him. "You think she's lying?"

"Her story is dodgy."

"She has maps and sketches of her travels."

"You are the first to know that maps can be drawn in the safety of one's home. Maps in a book don't prove anything."

Brockton felt a sting of pain. He had spent most of his life at home, drawing maps based on other people's stories. He had a bad taste in his mouth. "And you don't trust her," he said.

"I trust no one." Grisban smirked.

"That's harsh."

"That's kept me alive for more years than I care to count. And I'd like to stay this way, if you don't mind. You know, alive. It's a strange and dangerous place we are in. There will be dangers, and it is likely things will try to kill us. Things far worse than a lone salamander, or a bunch of fools with rusty blades. So I will be harsh and distrustful any day of the week. I understand you cherish the excitement of discovery. But you are paying me to make this expedition as uneventful as possible."

Brockton shook his head. "I do not believe she'll be a problem."

"She's a stranger we met in a ruined city. That's a good beginning for a ballad, but this is not a ballad. We should be careful. Already the orc woman–"

"I trust Tarha," Brockton said. "I think in this very moment she is protecting us from the ghosts that haunt this place."

"Ghosts only she can see," Grisban replied. Then he smirked. "That's fine. But as I said, I am the one who will trust no one. That's what you are paying me for."

Brockton felt a spark of irritation.

"Are you really afraid I might put us all in danger because I fell for a beautiful stranger's green eyes?"

Grisban chuckled and shook his head. "It's not the green eyes, my friend, but what those eyes have seen that you fell for." He laughed out loud and slapped Brockton on the shoulder. "But I am glad you noticed our new companion has green eyes. There is still hope for you, expedition master!"

Still laughing, he turned and walked toward the campfire.

"Goodnight, Master Brockton," he said over his shoulder.

CHAPTER ELEVEN
Levirax

Deep in the caldera of the volcano she called her fortress, Levirax planned her future conquests. She felt a mounting excitement, like none she had felt for many centuries.

Curled under an overhanging spur of volcanic rock, the dragon inhaled the inebriating sulfur exhalations from the boiling magma below. Her ennui was fading, replaced by a cruel bloodlust.

One from the ragtag tribes that constituted the lower ranks of her army had confirmed the presence of a band of dwarves, delving into the ruins of their lost cities in the forests at the edge of the south-western mountains.

Dwarves in the Karok Doum, Levirax thought, was the best new thing in long decades of planning and preparation, a sign from whatever power cast the dice of Mennara's history.

She had no doubt this small band of "explorers" currently making their way at the margin of the Verdant Ring was just the vanguard of an invading force. The greedy Dunwarr guilds had finally summoned up the courage and the resources to cross Black Ember Gorge and come to reclaim their lost kingdom after four millennia of cowardice.

Their wounds healed, their memories faded, the dwarves wanted to steal again what their ancestors had stolen from the dragonkind before. Shaarina's policies of isolation and caution were to be blamed if the righteous fear of dragonkind had eroded in the dwarves' hearts, making them bolder than they had been for one hundred generations.

They would come with their axes and pikes, their war songs and their trumpets, believing they would meet no opposition. For this reason, now, they had sent an advance party to learn the lay of a land from which they had been expelled four millennia before.

The earth rumbled, like the volcano itself shared Levirax's mounting fervor. A war was coming, and war was to Levirax as welcome and comforting as the fires that burned in her fortress.

Levirax had no doubt her armies would be more than enough to shatter the dwarven forces and forever bury their power and arrogance. She had been working ever since her return from the Broken Plains eight centuries before. She had gathered around her hybrids and had sought and nurtured those that had been left behind by the dead dragonlords. Forged them into a rough but effective weapon against Shaarina's conservative, over-cautious policies. And now in this new war, her dragons and her hybrids would push back the dwarves in their warren in the eastern mountain, to cower in fear. She anticipated the pleasure of the fight, the triumph of her will.

But it was not just that.

An invading army would force Shaarina to make a stand.

Levirax was quite certain the Dragon Rex was too tired and weak to counter the dwarves. She still remembered how Shaarina had balked during the invasion of Terrinoth, turning her own forces against the other dragons. She remembered the dragonlords that had been slaughtered on Shaarina's orders. Punished for being bold. For being victorious.

Shaarina was too cautious.

She had always been, and in her old age she was even more so.

Caution, Levirax knew, could be crippling. A cautious warrior would not charge their enemies, crushing them under their feet. They would sneak and hide, like the orcs did, or the cursed Latari.

Every dragonlord shared that conviction.

And Shaarina's predictable hesitation in the face of the dwarven army would signal that the time had come for a new Dragon Rex. A younger, bolder one. One that knew no fear.

The dwarves were bringing more than war to the Molten Heath.

They were bringing revolution.

Levirax could see the future events unfold. Her defeat of the dwarven army would draw to her the younger dragons, who chafed under Shaarina's lethargic rule but were not yet committed. Proud, if simple-minded, individuals like Archerax, that would welcome the opportunity for battle and for conquest.

Because once Shaarina had been taken out of the picture, either killed or faded into languor, and the dwarves' army had been shattered, then Dragon Rex Levirax would turn her gaze back to Terrinoth. She had unfinished business there that was long overdue. She would unleash her armies and bring the baronies of humans and the chiefdoms of the orcs to their knees. Then, she smiled grimly, she would take care of the Latari.

Everything was clear now, in Levirax's mind.

She could hear already, in the low thrumming of the volcanic chamber boiling under her, the drone of the voices of her followers, invoking her name.

Levirax, Dragon Rex.

It was time to make her next move against Shaarina.

With a roar that echoed in the hollow mountain, she summoned Archerax.

The night was perfectly still. The moon had disappeared behind the top of the obsidian city wall. The wind had fallen and nothing stirred in the darkness.

The travelers were in a circle around the dying embers of the campfire.

Grisban was snoring. One Fist turned in his sleep, pulling his tan blanket over his head. Brockton had fallen asleep sitting against the carved wall. Vaerix was somewhere out there, silently pacing the edge of the pool, watching over them.

Tarha sat with her legs crossed, her eyes on the orange glow of the coals slowly fading to dull black. She took a deep breath and closed her hand around the bone amulet hanging from her neck.

It felt like fire in the palm of her hand.

She breathed out slowly, through clenched teeth.

She could feel the ghosts of the city circling outside of her wards, probing, sniffing the air. Ragged remains of the area's old citizens, they were scared and confused. But there were others, too. Dwarven warriors as tight bundles of fearlessness and anger. Anger at them. At all intruders.

Long burning anger at the dragons. At Vaerix.

But they would keep away, at least for this night.

In her mind's eye, her wards burned like beacons, casting the darkness away. The raging ghosts would not dare come closer. But they paced the perimeter, following Vaerix as they did their rounds.

She had told the dragon-kin to remain inside the wards.

And then there was another. One that would not stop at her carved wards.

With a loud crack, one of the last remaining logs in the campfire snapped in half and fell in the embers, causing a column of bright specks and smoke to rise in the air.

As the sparks faded, the smoke started spiraling as it rose, forming a cone that widened and changed shape. The beads, mirror shards and bones hanging from the top of Tarha's staff jangled. Still no wind reached so deep into the ruined city.

The pain in her hand grew, like a hot iron being pushed into her palm.

She looked at the shape hovering above the embers and that pain was forgotten, replaced by a cold stab of anguish that went through her heart.

Tarha forced her eyes not to linger on the broad shoulders, the thick neck, the fierce face of her visitor. She knew every swirl of his tattoos, every scar marking his ghostly skin. She pushed her own self to the back of her mind. This was no time for longing.

Dead is dead, she reminded herself.

Even to those like her.

"What wisdom do you bring me tonight, spirit?" she asked.

A part of her rebelled. Not spirit, it screamed. Husband. Mate. Companion. Friend.

Ughat the Mace. Her Ughat.

But no more. She ignored the ache in her chest, and in her soul.

The spirit spoke to her. Words like from a great distance, forcing their way through the thin but resilient barrier between the worlds.

She turned to look at the sleeping form of the stranger Cyra Kurkuan, who slept curled up in a bundle under a checkered blanket, her hands crossed over her chest.

"No," she said softly. "I do not trust her either."

CHAPTER TWELVE
Woodland

Vaerix walked into the shadow of the eastern gate, their staff clicking as it hit the ground.

There were thick, deep grooves on the surface of the inner doors. Beyond them, the passage in the obsidian wall was half choked with wreckage, like flotsam carried by a flood. Patches of moss, faintly glowing, hung on the walls of the corridor, and the other end was a pale strip of light, tall and narrow.

Vaerix took a step into the shadows, their eyes adapting to the dusk, painting the scene in shades of gray. The ground was scattered with the rusty remains of shattered armors and broken weapons, and pale bones peeked through the felt of sickly molds and fungi.

"Now this is the spot where I'd try it," Grisban had said, "if I were those two jokers."

Brockton had been unconvinced. "You really think they might want to ambush us? Two against seven?"

"We sent them on after taking all they had." The dwarf had cast a glance at Cyra. "There's a downside to being merciful."

"And street ruffians are not the only danger here," Quellen added.

So Vaerix had offered to go in first, beating One Fist to it.

The weight of their staff felt good in Vaerix's hand as they took two more steps forward. The plan was for them to clear the passage before the others came through with the horses.

Behind them, they heard One Fist cranking the crossbow, ready to cover their back. Then, unexpectedly, Tarha was by their side. "I am coming with you," she said.

Vaerix did not debate the issue. They had learned through observation that the orc spirit speaker would not be swayed by argument when she was set on her course.

They walked on, side by side and maybe two yards apart, the gentle jingling of Tarha's staff accompanying their steps, a counterpoint to Vaerix's staff tapping.

Something moved in front of them, crossing the blade of light at the far end. It slithered, it ran, it surged. A scaly creature, red eyes blazing.

Vaerix stepped in front of Tarha as a cloud of flames erupted before them. Tarha drew back and crouched in Vaerix's shadow. The fire caressed Vaerix's skin, burning the edges of their garments, but leaving them otherwise untouched. Their dragon heritage did count for something still.

With a furious roar, the salamander pushed through the fiery cloud of its own breath and snapped at Vaerix with its jaws. It was larger than the first one they had encountered, and its bulk filled the tunnel. Its long triangular head featured a mouth riddled with sharp teeth, and its eyes burned in the darkness. It also appeared to be completely awake and not drowsy like the one they had defeated. Vaerix responded to its attack by clocking its head with the heavy end of their staff. The creature retreated and screeched in fury.

Behind it, a second shape moved.

"There's two of them!" One Fist's shout echoed farther back in the corridor.

Steps approached, running.

The second salamander climbed over the back of the first, trying frantically to get to Vaerix and Tarha. This one was older, Vaerix saw, its left eye bisected by an old scar. Steam escaped its nostrils as it opened its mouth, showing rows of dagger-like teeth.

Vaerix smacked it with their staff and the salamander ducked to avoid the hit. Its tail swept the floor.

One Fist's crossbow twanged. The salamander shrieked, a dart stuck in its mouth. But the wound only made the beast angry.

Its younger companion shifted underneath it and moved to the side, flanking Vaerix.

Vaerix changed position, now facing two enemies from two different directions.

Tarha, still crouching where she had found shelter behind them, was chanting a repetitive string of words Vaerix did not understand.

They caught the older salamander as it opened its mouth, filling its lungs with air as it prepared to belch fire upon them.

The smaller one tried to claw at them. Vaerix parried with their staff and pushed the menacing paw back. They could feel the heat growing in the older salamander's maws.

Tarha stood, her humming now a sharp-edged litany, rising and falling in volume, amplified into a chorus of voices by the echo in the tunnel. She gripped her staff in both hands and the crooked end glowed with a faint, ghostly light.

Vaerix hit the smaller salamander squarely on the head. They heard the running steps draw closer, just as the older creature snapped forward and belched a colossal ball of fiery gas at them.

Tarha was suddenly silent as she hit the ground with her staff, and the light at the top of it blazed like a bright star, and then vanished.

Vaerix felt the tickling of the flames. Ignoring the burning gas surrounding them, again they hit the younger salamander. The fire dissipated, and Grisban was by their side. The dwarf swung his axe with both hands, a war cry escaping his lips. The salamander tried to catch the blade in its jaws and was too successful.

The blade cut deep into its snout and the creature shuddered and rolled on its side, gasping breaths escaping it.

Such was its weight that Grisban stumbled and let go of his axe. Instinctively, Vaerix helped him keep his balance.

He looked up, squinting. "Fortuna's tears!"

Vaerix followed his stare.

The floor of the corridor was shifting, like bubbles rising to in a bog.

With creaking and metallic clangs, armored shapes began to stand. Old chainmail failed and rusted rings dropped to the ground. A neck snapped, the skull falling and the helm crashing with it. A bent blade was dragged along the stone pavement with a nerve-wracking screech.

Two, then three dwarven warriors rose from their death slumber. Dragging their feet, they crawled to where the larger salamander was retreating, hissing in panic.

Vaerix felt a chill in their bones. They had met magic before, but there was something so profoundly unnatural, so utterly wrong, in the way the three crooked shapes advanced on their prey, that for the first time in more years than they cared to count, Vaerix felt the impulse to run.

But they stayed, and Grisban with them, and watched as two more skeletons rose and moved against the surviving salamander. One of them dragged it's leg and the other carried half a broken shield and a grime-encrusted mace. They followed the others and slowly surrounded the creature. Once again, the salamander disgorged a cloud of smoldering fire. The skeletons ignored it, even when they burst into flame, the dried-up remains of their bodies flaring. But they kept pushing on, illuminating the corridor with the fire that consumed them. And by now they were close enough to attack.

Tarha was still standing, still humming her incantations, her staff high above her head.

The reanimated dwarven skeletons moved in fits and jerks, like marionettes, their arms rising and falling, their ancient blades biting in the scaly skin and flesh of the salamander. Vaerix watched in horror as the flame-shrouded bodies snapped and fell to pieces, and still continued to hack and slash. An arm hit the floor, its armor rattling. A body crumbled into a pile of crackling remains. Still the remaining skeletons kept hitting with their time-blunted blades.

The salamander roared and screeched and finally crashed to the ground, a lifeless body surrounded by five sinister funeral pyres.

Tarha let out a choked gasp and went down on to her knees, coughing.

Vaerix was the first by her side.

She leaned on her staff and looked up at them as they placed their hands on her shoulders.

"You hurt?" Vaerix said.

"I'll be fine," she replied, her voice but a whisper. "In a moment."

Vaerix helped her up. The woman's taut muscles trembled under their hand.

Grisban was checking the remains of the large fire lizard, prodding it with his axe. As he passed by the smoking remains of one of the skeletons, the pile of fire-burnished armor and burned bones collapsed.

The dwarf cursed.

Nothing else bothered them as they continued on their journey.

Vaerix waited in the center of the tunnel, their vestments still smoking. The others went through leading their horses, Grisban at the front, carrying a torch. They went slowly, careful on the uneven ground, and they skirted the dead salamanders and the smoking remains of the skeleton warriors.

Vaerix was still thinking about Tarha's display of power, about the darkness they had perceived in there. The orc was leaning against the wall of the passage, obviously weak and in pain.

There was a hard price to pay for her magic.

One Fist handed Tarha his waterskin, and she drank a long gulp and nodded a thank you. Then, walking side by side, they both rejoined the file.

"These are your buried halls of the dwarven heroes," Grisban said to Quellen as they went. He pointed at the scattered armor and dried up bones of the ancient defenders. "These are your lost treasures."

Vaerix let One Fist and Tarha pass through the metal door at the end of the tunnel and then followed them, squinting briefly in the sudden light as their eyes adjusted.

The metal doors were bent, the brass pockmarked and

cracked. The ground had risen, cementing them in their half-open position.

Just past the deformed doors, the ground dipped into a circular depression about fifty yards wide and six feet deep. It was surrounded by what looked like a rough embankment, covered in thorny bushes, and it was filled with what sounded like broken glass under the horses' hooves. Pools of dirty water occupied the bottom.

Quellen stopped and picked up a shard of the material. He turned it in his fingers and lifted it to examine it in a better light. It refracted the rays of the sun, bluish and translucent.

"It is glass," the elf said.

Brockton had his book out, taking notes.

Beyond the crater, the forest's trees were young and grew close to each other, pines and firs, and clumps of ferns. An animal of some kind scuttled away as they came into the sun. Birds flew off in panic.

"When the dragons attacked the city," Cyra said, "this must have been their first line of defense."

"And their last," Vaerix replied.

"Horns of Kurnos," Grisban whispered.

Vaerix stopped and pointed toward the north, where black ash and fire painted the sky. They could see plainly what had happened here and believed their companion might want to know, too. Brockton was here to learn, after all, and what he might discover was important.

"They flew in from that direction," Vaerix said, pointing north. They turned around slowly, until they faced east. "Over the forest, they banked on the updraft currents, aligning with the gates."

What a mighty sight they must have been, Vaerix thought.

Powerful wings beating, stretched in the wind, only the blue of the sky above them forever. Their scales glistening in the sun, defying the arrows of the defenders.

Vaerix pushed those feelings back, relegated those images to the place where dreams happened.

"They approached and dropped their altitude, gliding close to the ground. They came in fast, brushing the top of the trees."

The others were looking at them and then in the direction they were pointing at, expectant.

"Then they breathed their fire," Vaerix said.

Vaerix could hear, inside of their mind, the war chants of the dwarven warriors turning into screams, and then falling silent. The roar of the earth turning into smoke, the moan of the metal deformed by the heat. The triumphant screeches of the dragons.

For the time of a heartbeat, the gruesome smell of the battle replaced the sweeter, rich smell of the nearby woods.

"Dragons," One Fist whispered, almost echoing their thoughts. "Not salamanders."

"Dragons indeed," Vaerix said, and the word had a strange taste in their mouth. "And after they blasted the doors and the defenses, they vaulted over the wall and laid the city to waste."

"Were you here?" Cyra asked, her tone awed.

Vaerix turned to look at her. "No, the War of Fire was long before my time."

"The way you spoke of it," she said slowly. "It was like you saw it happen."

"I did," Vaerix replied. "But not here."

They entered the shadows of the trees and traveled in silence until they met a stream. Whether it was the one she and her wayward companions had followed out of the mountains, or just another one running parallel to it, Cyra could not tell. The stream widened and faded into an ample swampland in which the trees grew wide apart, leaving room for reeds and tall grasses. The ponies found their way following sand bars and soon Brockton and his companions looked over a green plain dotted with clumps of red and blue flowers. The forbidding peaks of the western mountains were at their back, and in front of them the Molten Heart clawed at the sky with angular peaks, bathed in a crimson light under a black cloud of cinders.

"The Verdant Ring," Brockton announced, making an annotation in his book. He was somehow able to ride and write at the same time.

A useful skill, Cyra conceded. Yet there were other questions in her mind.

She had expected more resistance from the dwarf about her joining the expedition. She had ample faith in her powers of persuasion, but had prepared a specific ditty anyway. There was power in words, and while she was no mage, she knew a short poem, like a song without music, designed to ease acceptance. Yet there had been no need for her meager magic or for her well-trained gift of gab. Brockton had simply said they could not leave her alone in the wild and had offered her the chance to go along. Cyra had been genuinely surprised.

This was not what she had expected from the dwarves, not the way a secret mission from the Dunwarr Guilds was supposed to be conducted. Brockton was as serious and committed as a schoolteacher, and his companions behaved like the crew of a pirate ship. And then there was the dragon hybrid, who was a walking enigma.

But later in the day Brockton called for a stop, and while the others set up camp, Vaerix walked to the side, and removed their singed garments and examined the damage they had suffered.

Cyra had wondered so far about the warrior's wings, imagining Vaerix was an individual belonging to a family of wingless hybrids or maybe someone born without, simply because she could not fathom a dragon hybrid without wings.

But now, as the dragon warrior turned the garment in their clawed fingers, Cyra was for the first time able to see their arms and sides. Scar tissue marked both the bottom of Vaerix's arms and the sides along their ribcage. The marks were irregular and ragged, like the flesh had been brutally torn away without the help of a blade. Cyra shuddered. Those were not battle wounds. As the hybrid dropped their garment on the ground and retrieved a new one from their satchel, Cyra watched while Vaerix shook their spare clothes and shrugged into them.

Cyra felt a chill. More questions flourished in her mind.

Who, mostly, and why?

She imagined cutting such a creature's wings was akin to chopping off a man's hands or feet. Punishment for a crime.

"Don't throw that away," she said to Vaerix. The hybrid turned to look at the burned raiment they had just discarded.

"I can darn that," she said. "If you want."

"I'd be grateful," Vaerix replied.

She shrugged. "You're welcome."

As the sun went down, they sat around the fire and Brockton updated them on his plans.

"We will turn north," he said, showing them his map.

"Toward the Molten Heath?" Grisban asked. He frowned

and sucked on his pipe, making it clear that he was not happy with the idea.

"Toward the grasslands," Brockton corrected him. "We will travel for a few days in the plains of the Verdant Ring. I do not expect to find any interesting feature, but who can say? Then we will turn back west again, toward the lost ruins of the Karok Doum and the mouth of Black Ember Gorge. And through there, back to Thelgrim. Nice and smooth."

"Hopefully," Quellen added with a cynical smile.

Cyra nodded.

She had been in Highmont when news had reached her of an expedition moving out of Thelgrim, on the Guild Council coin, and headed for the Molten Heath. As soon as her informants had confirmed the story, she had dropped what she had been doing there. Her masters in the Lorimor exchequer would be much more interested in the dwarves' plans than in the local rumors she had been collecting for weeks. She had hastened to cross the Lothan river, trying to dream up a way to track or follow the dwarven explorers. The little magic she was able to wield brought her to the bandit town of Last Haven. There, the offer from the mage Carthos had seemed to her a blessing. And now, after some unexpected ups and downs, she knew she had made all the right choices.

Now she kept her counsel while the others debated the logistics of the coming weeks. Brockton's planned course seemed to confirm her suspicion that this expedition's purpose was to investigate the lost dwarven runes of the Karok Doum, a magic that had always had piqued the interest of the Imperial Court of Lorimor.

"Will we be visiting any more ruins?" Quellen asked.

And the interest of the elven court of Lithelin in the

Aymhelin, too, Cyra said to herself, glancing sideways at the mage.

"You have a lot of interest in those ruins, mage," Grisban said casually.

"Just as our Master Brockton," Quellen said, "I have an undying thirst for knowledge."

Sure, Cyra thought. Her line of work was making her cynical, she reflected.

Vaerix remained silent.

Cyra wondered what was going through their mind.

CHAPTER THIRTEEN
Memories: The Chamber of Levirax

The Heart of the Molten Heath thrummed like a colossal drum. The ominous rumble reverberated through the black obsidian floor of Levirax's grand chamber and along Vaerix's bones. Over their head, a great swoop of rope-like stone filaments intertwined into a rough cupola, black and silver in the red light of the fires. Sulfurous smoke seeped through the cracks in the floor, like breath counterpointing the heartbeat, so that the hall was veiled by a thin, acrid mist.

Two lines of twelve dragon hybrids, their wings folded in a sign of respect, formed a corridor along which Vaerix followed Wing Captain Xenith, Drys, and Maesix walking behind them in turn. All four wore their battle armor. They also had the privilege of keeping their weapons in the presence of the dragonlord, as a sign of the trust they enjoyed.

On the elevated dais at the far end of the chamber, Levirax stirred and uncurled her spines. Her serrated crest rose, her wings stretched, and finally eyes like suns focused on the approaching warriors.

Vaerix felt like the flames in those eyes were searing through their very soul. The thought surprised them. Rarely if ever had they thought of themselves as possessing a soul. Such things were of no consequence to a warrior.

Or so they had been taught.

But things, they imagined, had changed.

About fifteen yards from the ledge on which Levirax lounged, Xenith stopped and saluted, his moves sharp and precise. He bent his leg, and his right wing extended and fanned in front of him, brushing the glass floor.

"Vaerix is here," he said. "As you commanded."

Levirax flicked her tongue, tasting the sulfur-rich air. She changed position, her head rising higher.

"Vaerix," she said. Her voice resounded in the cavern-like chamber, resounding with an accusatory tone.

Vaerix took a step forward and saluted in turn. "Levirax."

In general the dragon hierarchy had little time for the titles and ceremonies the Terrinoth royalty was said to cherish. Pageantry was a waste of time and a distraction on the battlefield. Status and power were innate to the dragons, part of their very nature, and individual class was projected by the brood parents into their hybrids. However, under Levirax, everybody knew their place by these titles, like Wing Captain Xenith, and recently Vaerix had come to believe those titles were to Levirax but a tool to better control her warriors.

This was how Vaerix and all their brothers and sisters had been raised, this was their way.

Levirax's eyes burrowed into Vaerix.

Then she turned slightly, focusing on her guards. A sharp-clawed paw flicked. "Leave us!"

A ripple of hesitation ran through the two lines of guards, but it lasted less than a quarter of a heartbeat. Then the dragon hybrid warriors turned on their heels and marched toward one of the arches that lined the northern wall of the chamber. Their armors clanging, their talons clicking on the black floor, they were soon gone.

Levirax's gaze shifted again. "And these two?"

Both Xenith and Vaerix were standing again and they turned to look at the two that had followed them.

"These are Drys," Xenith said, "who according to our rules shall speak for Vaerix. And Maesix, that will speak against them."

With an effort, Vaerix resisted the urge to look at their old companion. Maesix would speak against them? It was not unexpected, yet for a brief moment Vaerix wondered if Maesix's role in this was more than met the eye. It was customary for these kinds of trials to have two speaking for and against the one standing judgment. But for the last three days Vaerix had been asking themselves who had betrayed their trust and denounced them to Xenith. They felt a pang of sudden hostility for Maesix, their dragon-spirit ready to catch fire. But reason prevailed over fighting instinct. It was unlikely Xenith would have exposed his informer, and Vaerix accepted the fact that flaring into a fury here and now would be useless. Maesix was a brood-brother and a friend. More than that, a companion, a comrade at arms. He would never betray Vaerix's trust. And it was quite the consolation to learn that Drys would be speaking for them, and not against. Vaerix focused on the warmth of gratitude and pushed back their doubts.

Levirax sat up, her spine curled in a rising spiral. Again, she gestured with her claw. "They may go. Their testimony will not be needed."

Xenith seemed taken aback. Drys and Maesix looked at each other.

Vaerix squinted at the brood mother. What did her words bode for their plight?

Levirax's temper flared. "Begone!"

The command exploded like thunder through the dragon's throat.

With a last glance at Vaerix, Drys turned, and together with Maesix walked back to the gates through which they had entered. The gong sound of the bronze doors closing brought them back to the here and now. All that remained in the Great Hall was the rhythmic booming of the Molten Heart, Xenith's ramrod stillness, and Levirax's purr-like breathing.

She kept her lantern eyes fixed on Vaerix for a long moment.

They stood straight, wings folded, head held high. This, they knew, was not a moment to show uncertainty, no matter how uncertain they were feeling.

"I am disappointed," Levirax said.

Vaerix held her gaze and said nothing. What was there to say, after all?

"Of all my soldiers," Levirax said, "you were one of the strongest, Vaerix. Braver than many, loyal and faithful. More importantly, intelligent. A smart warrior is worth fifteen dumb ones. But it seems to me your smarts have turned against you. Against me."

"I would never–"

"Silence!"

Levirax's voice shook the very walls of the chamber.

"Your brood siblings are talking," the dragon continued. "Stories are circulating about you, Vaerix. And not, I am disappointed to learn, about your battle prowess and your loyalty. Not about the qualities that have made you a paragon for our troops, and your wings my most valuable tool on the battlefield. That would've been good because the duty of a warrior is also to inspire their companions. That would've been good, but it is not what the rumors are about. No, what I hear is some nonsense about visions in the night and other such strangeness."

She changed position again and stretched her long neck, bringing her head and her cruel maws closer to Vaerix.

"This is bad for the morale of the troops. In the battlefield of the mind, uncertainty and doubt are enemies as dangerous as axe-wielding orc berserkers can be in the Broken Plains."

She paused, her eyes darting toward Xenith.

Then she spoke again, her tones mellifluous. "But our troops are no longer in the Broken Plains, Vaerix, are they?"

Something akin to relief blossomed in Vaerix.

So, this was it. The real crux of the matter. Not their dreams, and what they might mean for the future of dragonkind, but something done and finished.

"Why have my armies retreated from the Broken Plains, Vaerix?"

An edge of anger glinted underneath the mellow tones of the dragon's voice.

"A command was issued," Vaerix said. Their voice was steady, trained by long years of battle discipline. "To cease hostilities and immediately retreat to the Molten Heath."

"A command? Who issued such a command?"

Vaerix nodded. "Dragon Rex Shaarina herself."

Silence rang like a bell under the black and silver dome. Levirax expanded her chest like bellows, her eyes flaring. "Shaarina?!"

Her voice caused the yellow mist to billow and a dusting of debris to fall from the ceiling of the chamber. "*Shaarina*?!"

New cracks opened in the obsidian floor and the whole mountain shuddered, as though in fear. Xenith tucked his head in his shoulders and Vaerix had to call on their battle-hardened spirit to stand still.

"Shaarina," Levirax said, her voice suddenly thick with poison honey, "may be the Dragon Rex, but you answer to your dragonlord first. And I am your dragonlord!"

Levirax lashed the air with her forked tongue and turned sharply to Xenith. "What do you say, commander?"

The wing commander tarried.

"Did you," Levirax asked, slowly speaking each syllable, "receive such an order from Shaarina?"

Xenith's nostrils flared. "The point is moot, Levirax," he said. He took a deep breath. "I am one of yours, and I take my orders from you." He eyed Vaerix. "And you alone."

"Even if the commands come from the Dragon Rex herself?" Levirax's voice dripped venom.

"If the Dragon Rex wishes to impart me and mine any command, she will go through you, Levirax. You are our dragonlord, the only one that can impart any order."

Levirax turned to Vaerix. "And what do you say to that, Vaerix?"

Vaerix considered Xenith's stern look. Then they spoke. "The order came as we were on the battlefield," they said.

Levirax made a show of being surprised. "Does that make any difference?" She looked at Xenith. "Does that change the chain of command?"

"It does not," the wing commander replied.

"Time was critical. By disengaging and retreating, right then and there," Vaerix said, "we avoided a useless loss of life."

Levirax straightened her neck. "Loss of life?"

"The orcs were not giving us quarter," Vaerix explained. "Many orcs and dragon hybrids would have died had we waited to relay the order at the end of the fight–"

"Loss of life?"

Again, the chamber shook and creaked under the onslaught of the dragon's fury.

Vaerix could see that Xenith was shivering. The wing commander's life was on the line, as was theirs.

The echoes of Levirax's voice faded. "What is the alternative to life, for a warrior?" she asked.

"Death," Vaerix and Xenith answered as one. It was one of the tenets of their army, and their army was their whole people. Levirax had carefully imprinted on them her rules, her worldview.

Fighters fight and fighters die.

"That is so," she conceded. "Then why should I care for the death of my warriors on the battlefield if I see fit to spend their lives so?"

Vaerix felt a tingling at the back of their mind. This was wrong. Levirax was wrong. The sudden awareness made their head spin. Just entertaining such a thought was treason.

"A life spent without achievement is a life wasted," they said. "To die on the battlefield without purpose is a waste."

Levirax was silent again. She changed her position and stretched languorously on her rock ledge.

"Maybe I was wrong," she said. "I should have raised you to the rank of Wing Commander instead of Xenith."

The wing commander's eyes widened.

"You seem to know everything there is to know. You know how my warriors' lives should be spent. You know what commands should be followed. You do not hesitate to take matters in your own hands. So maybe you should lead my army."

Her eyes turned into two burning slits.

"Or maybe not. Maybe you are just a traitor to your brood and your people." She turned to Xenith. "Remove this creature from my presence," she said. "Permanently."

Xenith froze for a moment.

Vaerix observed him as though from a great distance. A sudden emptiness made them numb and indifferent. As unprecedented as this was, it was also something they could have seen coming had they not been blinded by... what?

Hope?

"You mean, executing them...?" Xenith began, uncertain.

Levirax flicked her tail and snapped her tongue. "Do so according to your ways of the battlefield," she said. A tone of boredom crept into her voice. "I have wasted enough time with this creature."

But still Xenith did not seem willing to let go.

"Maybe... considering the traitorous way they undermined the troops' morale..." He tilted his head to one side and then straightened it back. "There are rules. And traditions. For dealing with traitors."

Levirax frowned. Then a cruel smile curled the lips of Levirax and her sharp teeth glinted. "I approve of the way you think, Wing Commander."

She made a dismissive gesture with her forepaw. "Take the wings of this heretic creature, just as I now take their name from them. And cast them out forever."

Vaerix felt their heart stop, squashed by an ice-cold hand.

CHAPTER FOURTEEN
Dragon Dreams

Shaarina was tired. Tired with an ages-long fatigue that weighed down her limbs, cramped her wings, caused her bones to feel like stone. Movements that had been natural and nimble now required an effort, a strength of will that sometimes she thought was the only thing in her that time had left untouched. It was her will, not her muscles, that kept her going.

Her heart beat slowly, heavy with fatigue and memories.

She stretched her limbs, perceiving the closeness of one of her people.

A young one.

That was in itself unusual, and one reason among many to become vigilant. Shaarina's ilk were not keen on companionship, and a young dragon entering the personal space of an older one was normally perceived as defiance. A provocation, the prelude to a challenge.

But what young dragon would dare to challenge her?

She was still Dragon Rex and had clung to her power for two millennia.

She was the strongest fighter, the most ruthless schemer.

Yet the young one still approached. A male.

Shaarina's curiosity was piqued. Such a novelty injected her with new energy. She lifted her head over the surface of the fire lake in which she spent most of her time and turned a fierce stare at the youngling slithering toward her in an attitude of submission. Her skin cracked and split as she moved, covered in lumps of rock-like barnacles, her scales grown thick with age. She noted the proud way in which the newcomer held his black wings. Not in open challenge to her authority, but an attitude that spoke of arrogance. The young one was too sure of himself.

She searched her mind for a name and found it. She made a point of knowing by name all the dragons and drakes on the Heath.

"Archerax," she said.

Strident for the long years of silence, her voice rumbled under the volcanic glass ceiling of her chamber, causing the molten rock in which she sat to ripple.

"Hail, Dragon Rex," Archerax said, bowing his head even closer to the cracked surface of the obsidian floor.

"Do not hail me," she replied. Old age had taught her patience but shortened her temper. Dragons had no such need for honorifics. "Why do you disturb my meditations?"

She caught a cruel flash in Archerax's eyes.

By showing her irritation, she was implicitly admitting Archerax had the power to touch her. And he liked power, this one.

Her memory served her well. Her visitor was one of the young would-be conquerors that had sided with Levirax at the end of the war, when he was but a hatchling. Not very smart. Ambitious, with a taste for violence and destruction, and a lack of restraint that was excessive even by the standards of dragonkind.

Her people had forgotten the age of the ancient Yrthwrights when the dragons had been stewards of this world and not brutal conquerors. Shaarina longed for those ancient times.

Archerax had been marked down for execution at the end of the invasion of Terrinoth. Yet she had spared Levirax and her underlings, and Archerax with them.

Often had she wondered, in recent years, about the wisdom of that choice.

"I bring news," Archerax said. "Things are happening in our domain of which you should be informed."

She took exception at his reference to their domains. He was lord of nothing, this conceited upstart. A rumble of laughter shook the hall and a small cloud of burning gas escaped Shaarina's lips. "Things of which you presume I have no knowledge already?"

She appreciated the hesitation in Archerax's response. The young one was not smart enough to avoid his blunder, but smart enough to be afraid of the consequences.

"I just thought—"

"Yes," Shaarina purred, her voice like an earthquake, "that's a practice to be encouraged in the young, thinking."

She perceived a change of stance in Archerax, a sudden tension rippling under the black and blue scales. She could smell his emotions. Anger.

Thin skinned, this Archerax.

How touching. Yet, she should tread lightly with this one. If he was here, either he was being an instrument of his dragonlord, or he was willing to betray Levirax. Both hypotheses were interesting. Learning which of the two was true would be useful and would condition her reactions.

"What of the news, then?" she snapped.

Keep the pup unbalanced, let him speak more than he should. Bubbles rippled on the surface of the molten rock around her. Steam erupted.

"Vaerix is back," Archerax said.

"Vaerix?"

She searched her memory, long centuries of events and experiences. Had there ever been a dragon called Vaerix?

"The dreamer," Archerax said. He stepped forward, coming closer to the edge of the fire lake. "The one that was cast out."

"A soldier," Shaarina said, recollections coming back to her. "One of Levirax's. After Margath's fall."

The sole utterance of the old dragon's name seemed to brighten the light out of the great hall. The fall of Margath at the hands of a human warrior had been a happy day for Shaarina.

But she now remembered the other incident, too. A minor quibble, a welcome hiccup in Levirax's plans, back in the hectic days at the tail end of dragonkind's misguided Terrinoth adventure. She should have done away with Levirax back then, she thought.

But regrets were meaningless.

A flick of Archerax's tail brought her back to the present.

"Why do you think the return of this wingless exile should be of concern to the Dragon Rex?"

Archerax's eyes narrowed. Shaarina could almost feel his thoughts crawling in his skull as he tried to devise a response. The Dragon Rex was not responding to his news as he had hoped.

He had been sent to her, now she was certain. Levirax was trying to play her.

"Vaerix comes to the Molten Heath with a force of dwarves," he said finally.

Shaarina stretched her neck and snorted fire. This was interesting, if true. Shaarina was old enough to know that interesting and dangerous were often the same.

"As it was to be expected, and known," she said. Let the youngling and his dragonlord wonder how she knew. "Is there anything else you want to waste my time with?"

"Our defenses..."

"What of those?"

"We cannot appear weak."

The sheer impudence was such that Shaarina knew this stupid male had been sent to try and play her for a fool. Not even Archerax was so foolish to think by himself with such an attitude. Those words had been spoken to him. She allowed a burst of welcome wrath. Her roar shook the walls of the chamber.

Archerax retreated, keeping his head low, his tail curled between his legs. But still there was that dangerous fire in his eyes.

"Go now," she hissed.

Then, as he was about to disappear in the shadows at the edge of the hall. "You are a good ally, Archerax," she said.

Archerax distended his wings, grateful.

Shaarina watched him go. Kindness after contempt, to sink a hook in the stupid young one's soul. Build loyalty. Something was on the move, and she might need every tool she could find.

The dwarves' coming, if it was actually a fact, might put

ideas in Levirax's mind and force Shaarina's claw. But Shaarina could still turn all that in her favor. Time could have robbed her of her strength, but her ruthlessness remained untouched, as hard as diamond.

Vaerix woke up in the misty light of the early dawn, their mind still in turmoil for the dreams the night had brought.

It had started with them walking along a road. A long, straight road, built like the dwarven roads of the Karok Doum. Large slabs of black stone, aligned on the plain and unmarked by time. It was a desert road that went from horizon to horizon, and Vaerix had been alone on it. Then, the scene had changed, as it so often did in their dreams. There had been fire and great billows of black and purple smoke, and the earth shook.

In the shadow of a tall black tower, hybrid fought hybrid, heeding the call of strange war cries. Some of the warriors wore full suits of armor, while others were garbed like the orcs of the Broken Plains in rough leather and furs. It was like in the old days, when they did not have another foe, when they had fought among themselves to cull the weak ones.

Wing Captain Xenith had been there, holding his scythe that was the token of their rank, and the weapon he had used to cut Vaerix's wings. His armor was silver-bright and there was a ferocious expression on his face. In their dream, Vaerix moved through the crowd of fighters, untouched by their struggle, and heard voices calling their name, at first in surprise, and then as a chant, dozens of voices joining in.

"Vaerix!" they called. "Vaerix!"

The name that had been taken from them so many years ago, with their rank and their wings.

Drys looked at them, infinite sadness in his eyes.

"This is not what you wanted," he said.

Then the thunderous roar of a dragon's rage tore through the sky and the black tower toppled, as Vaerix had startled awake.

"Bad dreams, huh?"

Wrapped in her cloak, Cyra tended to the fire. She poked at the embers with a stick and leaned forward, blowing gently. As the fire burst back to life, she dropped the stick and stretched her hands to the flames.

"You were making noises," she said by way of explanation. "In your sleep."

"I see," Vaerix replied.

They came closer to the fire.

The others were still asleep. Grisban paced the edge of their camp, axe in hand. The dwarf caught Vaerix's eye. He nodded.

"It's not like you were talking in your sleep or anything," she added. "But you sounded... distressed."

Vaerix sensed her curiosity.

"It was a bad dream," they admitted. They knew humans sometimes told each other of their dreams, but they did not believe this would be proper.

"Those happen," she said with a shrug.

She had placed her iron teapot by the fire. A thin wisp of steam rose from it.

"You shouldn't be worried," she continued with a lopsided smile. "They don't have to be an omen for the future, right? I mean, sometimes dreams are just dreams."

She poured the tea.

"I believe dreams are like riddles," Vaerix said, accepting a cup of tea. "For us to solve."

Cyra sipped her tea. "Like I said, dreams about the future?

Sent by the gods to set us on our rightful path?" She shook her head. "That's something I always found sketchy. I mean, if Fortuna wants me to buy a new pair of boots, why does she have to send me a dream of dancing foxes in silk slippers?"

She laughed suddenly and drank some more tea.

One Fist groaned and sat up. The camp was waking up.

"That's not what I meant," Vaerix said.

"Yeah, I know. I was just being silly. I meant no disrespect."

"Of course."

"So," Cyra asked conspiratorially, "what was your dream's riddle about?"

Vaerix considered that for one minute, the tea getting cold in their hand. "I don't know," they said finally. "That is part of the riddle."

The voices chanting their name still echoed in their memory. What did it mean?

One Fist yawned, staggered to the fire, and burned his fingers on the iron teapot. "And good morning to you," he said grumpily.

After two days, they were back in the saddle and heading north, riding in the tall grass in a double column, Brockton and Grisban leading.

"This looks like a big chunk of nothing," the warrior said, scanning the horizon.

"There used to be villages," Brockton said, "and fields, providing food for the big cities to the south and west. Roads connecting them, too, and signal towers. But all that's long gone, of course."

"So where are we going, exactly?"

Brockton reached into his saddlebag and pulled out his

notebook. On the first page inside the cover was a simplified sketch of the map he had shown his companions back at Razorcliff. "There used to be a city," he said, showing the map to Grisban, "about two days to the north. One of the first settlements in the Ring, walled with an earthen rampart. Ninaedur, it was called in the ancient maps. We'll try to get there."

"Ninaedur," Grisban repeated. "The city of the plain. Sounds like a nice place to visit. But I guess we're late for that. You think we can really find it?"

Brockton turned in his saddle to put the book away.

"I don't expect a proper ruin. But on land this flat, the remains of the rampart should stick out."

Vaerix chose that moment to run up to their side. "Look," they said, pointing at the sky.

Brockton squinted against the glare. Three birds hovered on the horizon, gliding gently in the sky, black specks against the intense blue sky.

"Any idea what birds those are?" he asked.

Surely, they were no ducks. Raptors of some kind, probably. And yet, did hawks fly in formation?

Vaerix laid a hand on his arm. "Those are not birds," they said.

Brockton frowned at Vaerix for a moment, then turned swiftly, searching the sky for the creatures. "Are you sure?" he breathed.

Vaerix's lips curled in a smile, revealing their sharp teeth. "I am."

"Back to the trees!" Brockton commanded in a low voice. "Now!"

"And scatter!" Grisban added. He pulled the reins, forcing his pony to turn sharply.

The others did not ask for explanations. Kicking their

mounts into motion, they ran the five hundred yards that separated them from the sparse treeline. Once under cover of the vegetation, Grisban and One Fist dismounted, weapons at the ready. Cyra joined them, slapping her horse to push it out of her way.

"Were those dragons?" she asked in a breath.

"Dragon hybrids," One Fist replied. He leaned against a tree, crossbow ready, and scanned the sky through the overhanging branches.

Brockton was both excited and scared. The presence of dragon hybrids in the area had always been a given and that was the reason he had wanted Vaerix with them. A hybrid themselves, Vaerix could be a useful negotiator and help Brockton find some common ground with the locals. Or so Brockton had imagined. On the other hand, he had not expected to meet any of the hybrids so far from the volcanic domain of the Molten Heath.

"Can't see them," One Fist said.

"They probably landed," Grisban mumbled. He was looking at the open field. "Can't fly at us through the treetops."

Holding the reins of his pony, Brockton automatically turned to Vaerix.

"They are gone," they said.

Brockton was not sure he should feel relieved yet. He eyed Tarha, who was standing by a tree, one hand on her bone amulet. She was looking at the plains. Then he looked back to Vaerix. "Did they see us, do you think?"

"Yes."

"Fortuna's Eyes!" One Fist cursed under his breath.

"We should move," Grisban said without turning. "Fast. Go back into the foothills, go to ground for a couple of days."

Brockton raised his hands, trying to placate him.

"They will be back in force," the old dwarf said. "And we are not equipped to take them on. Those are dragon hybrids."

"We mean them no harm," Brockton replied.

Grisban snorted. "Do they know it?" He turned to Vaerix. "What say you?"

"They will be back," Vaerix replied after a moment. "I can't say more."

"Can't or won't?" Quellen asked, holding a pebble in his hand, playing with it.

Vaerix held the elf's gaze. "Much will depend on their commander," they said finally.

Grisban huffed. "I say we don't wait to find out."

Brockton took a deep breath. They were wasting time in useless chatter. It was time to be the leader of this expedition. "We retreat into the woods," he said. His map-making would have to wait for the time being. Their safety came first. His tone did not leave any room for discussion.

Grisban and One Fist nodded.

"We go about two miles," he continued. "Then we turn west and keep going. We'll try as long as we can to keep the trees and the marshlands between us and anyone who would try to follow us. Vaerix, you will take point."

The dragon hybrid nodded and in three long strides was gone, invisible in the shadows of the undergrowth.

"Quellen, you keep an eye on the sky," Brockton went on. It was time to see if what was said of elven eyesight was true.

"And One Fist," he said, remounting his pony, "you stay behind and follow us, keeping closer to the edge of the woods."

"I'll go with him," Cyra said.

Brockton hesitated. That would leave him, Grisban and the

two mages as the main party. "Fine," he said. "You want to see us, but we don't want to see you."

"Understood." One Fist shouldered his crossbow and nudged Cyra. "Let's go hunting."

She moved to get her mount, but he stopped her, his hook catching her wrist. "Leave the horse."

She stared at him and freed her arm from his hold. "Really?"

Brockton raised his hand in salute.

Cyra turned her cloak inside out, midnight blue replacing the red. Riding on, Grisban picked up Cyra's horse's reins and tied them to his saddle.

Brockton turned to look at them one last time, but just like Vaerix, One Fist and Cyra were now invisible, shadows in the woodland.

The sword in the sheath hanging from his saddle seemed to burn against Brockton's leg. He had brought it along out of custom and hoped he would not have to draw it.

CHAPTER FIFTEEN
Arwyia

They were moving as fast as the terrain allowed, and both One Fist and Cyra were already covered in mud up to their knees. The air was hot and humid under the trees, and they were both sweating, only to feel a chill when a gust of breeze dried the sweat on their skin.

They stopped to catch a breath.

"What about the wings?" Cyra asked.

One Fist gave her a look and started running again. It was not the best moment to make conversation, and her questions made him uncomfortable.

"Vaerix," she said, trying to keep pace. "What happened to their wings?"

"You should ask them," he replied.

"Well, but–"

"Not now."

"Vaerix's been talking in their sleep," she said, her voice a low hiss. "And it has to do with their wings. You have to admit that's a nasty wound they suffered. But I asked and they became cold and distant. So, what is it?"

One Fist stopped and she bumped into him.

"There are stories," he told her. It was out of place to gossip about comrades at arms.

"What stories?"

"I am a warrior, not a storyteller. You should ask them."

He had heard stories about the flightless dragon hybrid that roamed Terrinoth. Heard them ever since he had been on the road himself, selling his services as a warrior. A powerful if reluctant fighter, the hybrid was said to have been exiled from their people for some crime committed during the Third Darkness. They had lost their wings, chopped off as punishment, and now traveled the world to atone for their offenses.

Which was a nice story, and One Fist believed it or not, in part or whole, depending on his mood. But if it truly was Vaerix's story, the orc still believed it was for Vaerix to tell. Brockton had vouched for Vaerix when they first met at the inn and that was all One Fist needed to know.

Cyra snorted as he leapt from root to root to avoid a wet patch. She did not seem to feel the fatigue. In fact, One Fist was impressed by Cyra's ability to follow him without making any noise. As quiet as an elf, as the saying went.

If she only would stop talking. The woman could give Grisban a run for his money as far as talking went. She had, admittedly, a better voice.

They followed their course due west, keeping inside the treeline, the shadows hiding them, the spongy ground helping them remain stealthy while hindering their progress at the same time.

One Fist could still spot the rear end of the packhorse in front of them, where the others were riding. He stopped for a moment by a clump of reeds, in the shadow of a forked tree.

Cyra moved close to his side, and for a moment he thought she would speak again. Like many humans, she seemed to have a hard time keeping silent.

But she just touched his arm and offered him her canteen.

He shook his head.

Cyra drank and then made to move on, but he stopped her, hooking her wrist. She freed herself and gave him a hard look.

He touched his ear, and then made a show of looking around.

The birds in the branches had fallen silent. An ominous stillness had fallen on the marshy grassland.

Cyra nodded, catching on.

They waited, scanning the terrain around them.

It could be the birds had just been scared by them, One Fist reflected, and the longer they tarried in this place, the farther behind they would be to Brockton's band. And yet, better safe than sorry.

Cyra brushed her fingers against his arm.

Stifling a sneeze in the musty air, he turned. She pointed. One Fist froze.

A dragon hybrid squatted in the tall grass about thirty yards away. Only the horns and the hooked tips of their wings were visible, especially when the breeze caused the grass to ripple and bend.

Had the dragon hybrid seen them? Why were they not attacking?

One Fist cast off those questions. The only thing that mattered now was the danger at hand.

Thirty yards was well within range of his crossbow. But he had seen a crossbow bolt deflected by Vaerix's shoulder padding. He doubted his would be more effective against this adversary.

Around the fire, a few nights before, Quellen had said the salamanders were better at seeing in the darkness, and in full daylight they could spot a foe only if it moved.

One Fist now wondered whether that was true for dragon hybrids, too. It was said salamanders shared some sort of kinship with dragons, just as the hybrids did. And Vaerix's soft-glowing eyes seemed to have no problem with the darkness. They had keen eyes in broad daylight too.

Minutes dragged on and the shadow of the forked tree shifted. It had to be hot under the sun out there in the tall grass, One Fist thought. And yet again, Vaerix never seemed bothered by heat. They had shrugged off the salamanders' fire breath, after all.

With a sudden chirping cry, a large pheasant sprang from its hideout in the shrubs and took flight, flapping its wings.

Cyra started in surprise, but One Fist held her down with his good hand.

The bird flew away and after maybe thirty heartbeats, the hybrid stood.

One Fist heard Cyra's sharp intake of breath.

Having known Vaerix, One Fist was not surprised by the hybrid's stature, but the wings, even folded, made them look much larger than Vaerix. Standing tall on double-jointed legs, they turned their long horse-like head, yellow eyes running along the treeline. A set of bony ridges ran between their horns, and their upper chest and shoulders were covered in rough skin. In one of their clawed hands, the creature held a spear, the head a rough piece of metal, somehow hammered into shape, and kept in place by a strap of leather wound around the wooden shaft. Not an elegant weapon, but certainly effective when backed by the muscular arms of the hybrid.

The creature opened their wings.

By One Fist's side, Cyra's eyes widened.

The sun filtered through the wing membrane, the skin punctured in a few points, the lower edge ragged. As they watched, the hybrid took three running steps and jumped into the air, flexing their powerful legs. They flapped their wings, much as the bird had done a few minutes before, and slowly rose in the sky. Then their wings were still and the wind filled their taut skin, lifting the creature in a sharp climb.

Soon a black silhouette against the sky, the hybrid drew two ample circles and then flew north, soon too small to see against the sun's glare.

Only then did they dare to move.

"Are they going to call others against us?" Cyra asked.

"Likely," One Fist said. He felt like their problems had just begun.

Vaerix felt the presence of the dragon hybrid before they saw them.

They slowed down in their tracks, their tail swinging slowly as they sniffed the air. They sifted through the kaleidoscope of smells that colored the air of the undergrowth.

A young one, female, no more than ten yards away.

Muscle memory kicked in faster than their instincts as a shadow fell over them. Vaerix lifted their staff and parried a slash from a strangely shaped blade.

The other hybrid flapped her wings and disengaged. She fell to the ground, and as she did, she tried a lunging stab. Vaerix deflected that easily.

Then they lifted their right hand in a fist, hiding their talons in a sign of non-aggression, a request to stop, as it was used on the battlefield. "I am not an enemy."

"Intruder!" the young one hissed, cracking her tail like a whip.

Her accent was uncouth, as was her appearance. She wore no armor or garments of any sort. Simple leather straps crossed her chest, like an impromptu harness, from which hung a series of pouches and a simple loop holding a triangular glass shard, about a foot and a half long, the blunt end wrapped in leather to use it as a knife. Her sword was just as ugly, a strip of metal hammered into shape and probably sharpened against a rock.

"Not an enemy," Vaerix repeated, slowly circling their foe. They stretched up to their full height. "I am Vaerix, that some call the dreamer."

Offering her their name could be interpreted as both an act of good faith and a possible challenge. But it was worth trying.

The other looked at them, giving no sign of having recognized the name.

Vaerix felt a small pang of disappointment, followed by a bitter splash of self-deprecating mirth. Thus were they repaid for their vanity, they thought. With oblivion or indifference. Levirax has ensured it.

But if she had not recognized their name, the other dragon hybrid at least had a rudimentary knowledge of common courtesy. She straightened her back, tucked her wings in a respectful position and lifted her makeshift sword in an awkward salute.

"I am Arwyia, of the Burning Lake."

Her name was a corruption of an old word meaning "Unconquered." Her scales were a burnished bronze color with iridescent hues, witnessing an ancient lineage. Beautiful, but scarred and dirty, just like her talons. Her left horn was broken, and when she extended her wings, Vaerix saw a number of cuts and holes in the flight membrane. A larger wound had been roughly stitched together, leaving behind an ugly scar.

Arwyia's life had been hard for one so young, a witness to her dragon heritage. Several questions arose in Vaerix's mind, all of them boiling down to who or what could be the enemy this young one had fought. No possible answer pleased Vaerix.

Her next lunge was so swift, Vaerix was surprised, and they managed to avoid her blade only by ducking and sliding back. It helped that Arwyia's left wing was caught in a low branch and her jump was cut short. She landed in a clump of ferns, crushing it under her feet. Bad idea, fighting in a forest, Vaerix thought grimly, if your wings are that important to your fighting style. They parried the three successive slashes with their staff, holding their ground.

They could see the fury mounting in Arwyia, her movements becoming broader, less effective. Not properly trained, Vaerix thought.

"I am not here to fight," they said. They held the staff in one hand, parallel to the ground, like they were offering it to her, in a non-aggressive stance.

"You are fighting!" she hissed in reply. Two more downward slashes tried in vain to penetrate their defenses.

Vaerix did not follow up their parries, giving her room to spend her energies and grow tired. They wondered passingly how long it would take for Brockton and the others to get here. A crowded battlefield could actually be an advantage for such a sloppy fighter.

They'd have to put a stop to this.

Once again, she tried to rush them, spreading her wings to lift herself from the ground in a mighty jump, loading her full body weight into the slash. Once again, the trees hindered her movement. The cut was unbalanced. Vaerix intercepted the blade with the forked end of their staff and twisted it out of her hand. The sword flew in the air and landed with a thump to the ground.

With a roar, Arwyia tucked her wings in and charged them headfirst, the glass knife flashing in her hand.

Vaerix sidestepped her and she swept at their legs with her tail.

Vaerix laughed as they fell. They had forgotten the excitement of battle.

As they fell, they in turn tripped Arwyia with their staff.

Both hit the ground at the same time. Growling, the female tried to slither to where her sword had fallen, but Vaerix was standing over her now, and they pinned her neck to the ground with the forked end of their staff.

"Enough!" they said.

She half-turned, looking at them with a golden eye.

"Kill me, then," she hissed.

"I am not here to kill," they replied.

A flash of anger lit Arwyia's eyes. "I was a fair opponent," she said. "You owe me my death!"

"No one owes death to another," Vaerix said. But there was a tingling of recollection at the back of their mind that forced them to instinctively change their stance. Like they wanted to instinctively pull back from their fallen foe. Memories swept over them in a tide of deja vu. They had dreamed this.

"The defeated do not deserve to live," she spat at them.

"That is madness," Vaerix replied.

Her tongue lashed the humid hair. "Why shame me?"

Vaerix stared at her.

The shame of defeat, a stain worse than death for a warrior. One of Levirax's most cherished precepts. Death as the only alternative to life for those who fight. How many battles had Vaerix themselves fought under that rule? How much had Vaerix paid to try and counter that credo?

They shuddered.

"Who do you serve?" they asked in a low voice. "Who is your dragonlord?"

But they knew in their heart that it could only be Levirax. Dragonlord Levirax, still alive after all these centuries. Just like in their dreams.

Arwyia hissed again and twisted to free herself. Vaerix avoided her tail but was caught on the side by the hook in her wing. They pulled back, freeing her. Arwyia scampered away, pausing for but a moment to retrieve her blade.

"Is it Levirax you serve?" Vaerix asked urgently. But she only laughed at them and kept running.

Vaerix chased her, but as soon as she came to a clearing, she jumped in the air, extended her wings and took flight.

"I will see you on the battlefield, Vaerix the Dreamer!"

Vaerix caught a glint of flashing metal before she disappeared beyond the green canopy. They heard the ponies making their way through the ferns and the shrubs.

Off to meet her tribe, Vaerix imagined. They wondered briefly if any of the tribe's members would remember Vaerix, and what that could bring to the expedition. Maybe oblivion and indifference were not such a bad thing.

But Levirax would certainly remember Vaerix. That did not bode well.

"On the battlefield," they whispered.

"We always knew there were dragon hybrids at large," Brockton said. "So it should really come as no surprise that we found them here, so close to the Molten Heath."

And yet he had been surprised, and scared. Not that admitting the obvious would be of any use. They had retreated further into the hills, where the trees were thicker, and were passing the night without fire.

"Well, that's certainly a consolation," Grisban said.

"They inhabit the southern wastes," Brockton went on, ignoring the warrior. "All over Terrinoth, many make a living as sell-swords or enforcers in the service of petty lords and dark wizards."

"Those were no sell-swords, the ones we met today," One Fist said. "Too badly equipped. Looked more like brigands to me."

"Brigands require someone to rob," Quellen said.

Grisban grunted. "Well, I guess that was us, right, mage?"

Quellen closed his eyes for a moment.

"He means brigands require a trafficked road," Brockton said. "And a steady supply of travelers to rob. But here in the wilds?"

"It would make for very lean pickings," Quellen said.

"And they are clearly no marauders," Brockton went on, trying to sound reasonable, "as there is very little to maraud around here."

"They looked more like scavengers," Cyra offered. "Going from one ruined city to the next looking for loot."

"Dragon hybrids have a thing for ruins," Grisban admitted. Then he glanced at Vaerix. "No offense meant."

Vaerix just waved the words away with their hand.

"Or a band of hunters," Cyra said. "Maybe they were looking for rabbits and waterfowl, just like us."

"They've got to be big rabbits," One Fist replied, "considering the sort of weapons they carried."

"Hunters want bows," Grisban nodded. "Or slings."

"The one we saw had a spear," Cyra said, but she sounded uncertain herself.

"A spear that looked like a shovel," One Fist corrected her. "If they were hunting, they were hunting larger game. And we saw none of that."

"Or maybe they were hunting for us," Grisban said.

"Why don't you let Vaerix speak?" Tarha said, her voice startling them.

Brockton gave a grateful nod in her direction, then turned to Vaerix. "What can you tell us, old friend?"

"Much has changed since last I spoke with mine," Vaerix said gravely. "The one I met today was undisciplined and badly trained, if trained at all. She had power but no restraint. Yet she spoke the old language, and she seemed to follow the old rules."

"What rules?" Cyra asked.

"Before we were a people," Vaerix replied, "we were an army. Like a weapon, not made or born, but forged. Rules were part of such forging. They were designed and imparted to make us more efficient in battle. A set of beliefs my people lived by. And died by, too."

"And killed by too," Grisban said.

Vaerix's reply sounded like a sigh. "Yes."

"You mean like a religion?" Cyra asked.

"Religion means gods," Vaerix replied. "My people have no gods."

But Brockton had a more urgent question. "And you say this hybrid you met today, they…" He searched for the right word. "…they shared these beliefs?"

"You had time to discuss philosophy?" Quellen asked with a chuckle.

It was Cyra who answered him. "To a true master swordsman," she said, her rolling Rs suddenly stronger, "there is no difference between the discipline of the sword and their life path, what you'd call philosophy. No separation, no difference. Because how could I drive my blade in one direction if my heart is going another? This is a truth we sword poets acknowledge." She looked at the dark shape of Vaerix. "And something akin, I believe, to what your people called their rules. A thought that gives shape to our life."

"It is so," Vaerix replied.

"So, what you are saying is, this is–" One Fist frowned, "–an army? A dragon army, like in the Third Darkness?"

"A tribe. She mentioned belonging to the Burning Lake."

"You sure had a long time to spend in conversation," Quellen said.

It was Grisban who answered this time. "You want to know who you are fighting, mage," he said. Then he turned to Vaerix. "A tribe under a dragonlord?"

"They seem to live by the same credo as my old dragonlord imprinted on us," Vaerix said.

"But it's been centuries," One Fist protested.

"Dragons are long-lived," Quellen said.

They remained silent for a minute.

"This dragonlord…" Brockton began.

"Levirax," Vaerix replied with finality.

Silence weighed heavily on them following Vaerix's words.

"This is bad," Grisban then said.

Brockton took a deep breath. He looked up at the sky, at the slice of moon hanging in the vast blackness. He felt his responsibility weighing down on him, like a giant hand trying to squash him. A dragon out of the Third Darkness, lording over a nation of warlike hybrids was not what had been on his mind when he had dreamed of exploring the world. His expedition could trigger a new war, a new invasion of Dunwarr. A new Darkness. This was not the sort of discovery he had imagined would put him in the annals of the Guilds.

"We stick to our course," he said finally. "We will move west under cover of the woodlands. We will keep our eyes open but will not seek out these dragon hybrids. We will move faster than planned…"

"Difficult, in this woodland," Grisban interjected.

"We will try." Brockton gave him a hard look. "But other than that, we will not change our plans because of them."

The old dwarf grunted. "I hope they don't change our plans for us."

CHAPTER SIXTEEN
Swamp

Three days later, they came to more ruins, half-sunken in a swamp.

They had not sighted the dragon hybrids anymore and had followed the course planned by Brockton, riding west under cover of the canopy of the trees. By night they shielded their fire as best they could but, as One Fist observed, the risk of attracting possible enemies was nothing compared with Grisban's fury at the idea of eating cold food.

Then, on the morning of the third day, the ground became spongy with water and the distance between the trees increased, allowing more light to penetrate to the forest floor. Quellen pointed out a red stone statue sticking out of a murky pool, a bearded face framed by an abstract frieze. A dwarven warrior, part of his twin-bladed axe hidden by a clump of reeds.

By noon, they were surrounded by the remains of what Brockton identified as a trading outpost along the old Karok Doum merchant road they had been following.

"I did not realize we were following more than your whims

and the sun," said Grisban. But One Fist, as everyone else, had seen that the trees were strangely aligned and now could spot the moss-grown remains of the ancient city. He could also see his own wonderment in the faces of the others. The glass wall of the ruined city had been impressive, but the sheer extension of what surrounded them caused the legends of the lost dwarven domain to take shape in front of his eyes.

A poor shape, admittedly, but still awe-inspiring in its magnitude.

By the sight of it, Brockton declared that this outpost had been larger than Twelve Oaks.

"Who knows how much of this town is buried under our feet?" Brockton said, giving voice to One Fist's thoughts when they stopped for rest.

Grisban dismounted and the ground squelched under his feet. "Or rather drowned," he said.

They found a clearing and welcomed the rays of the midday sun. Bugs buzzed in the air, chased by birds that snapped them up in mid-flight. A wall ran parallel to the animal tracks they had been following so far and disappeared into a swampy stretch of green, still water. Beyond that, three broken columns marked the gateway to a half-crumbled building, the polished brass tiles on its face mostly gone.

Another structure, low and boxlike, sat at the other edge of the clearing, wrapped in vines and crawlers. It almost looked, One Fist thought, as if it had pushed up from under the ground, like a fungus of some kind. Its low, wide entrance was like a gaping mouth, six feet tall and fifteen steps wide, curtained by a screen of hanging vines. When Quellen tried to enter, Cyra following him up the broken steps, a burst of scared birds flew out, screeching.

Cyra started, and there was a sword in her hand. Then she laughed.

"Careful," One Fist called out. "The whole thing could collapse on you."

"Or worse," Tarha added.

One Fist would have asked her what lay in wait inside the ruin, but the whole woodland was becoming animated around them. Chirping wildly, more birds took flight from the bushes at the edge of the water and unseen animals rushed through the undergrowth, too excited, or scared, to keep quiet as they went.

"Something's coming," Grisban announced, unhooking his axe from his saddle.

One Fist turned to Tarha, but she frowned and shook her head.

"Look!" Cyra called, pointing. The water in the nearby bog was boiling.

Fish started jumping out of the water, many of them landing on the grass on the edge of the pond.

"What in the name of Kurnos...?" Grisban started, looking around.

One Fist had his blade in his hand, but he could not spot any enemy.

Suddenly Quellen gasped. "Brace yourself!" he shouted. "And stay clear of the ruins."

The elf ran down the steps and moved to the center of the small clearing, grabbing Cyra by the wrist, bringing her along.

Now the ponies were panicking, too, and Brockton was trying to keep them at bay. The scared ponies dragged him along, his heels digging two parallel grooves in the soft ground.

Then One Fist's ears caught a distant sound, like the rumble of thunder, but one that did not seem to fade. Like the long deep wail of the Mag Ukluk war horns.

Leaves started raining on them as the trees groaned and shuddered.

"Earthquake!" Brockton shouted.

He let go of the ponies and hunkered down on the ground while Cyra pulled free of Quellen's hold and turned around, her eyes huge and wild with anger.

One Fist could now feel the earth shuddering through the soles of his boots. With a loud crash, a tree fell into the nearby pond, spraying them with water and mud, sinking slowly.

Chunks of rock and debris fell from the abandoned buildings.

The rumble was now an all-encompassing sound that reverberated in his chest.

One Fist swayed and went down to one knee. The others were all on the ground now. Only Tarha and Vaerix stood, each one leaning on their staff. The dragon hybrid had tucked their head between their shoulders, as one expecting to be hit, and was pressing on the ground with their tail to keep their balance. Tarha clutched her pendant in her fist.

Then the world was silent and still so suddenly that One Fist felt like his very breath had been taken away from him.

"It passed," Brockton said.

"There might come another," Cyra replied, standing up and brushing her knees with her hand.

"It was to be expected," Quellen said. "So close to the volcanoes of the Molten Heath."

"That's really a consolation," Grisban said. He used his axe to help himself to his feet and then helped Brockton stand. "So much for your powers of geomancy."

"Vast as my powers are–" the elf squared his shoulders haughtily, "–I cannot command the earth to stop shaking. But I'll try to keep the largest chunks of debris from hitting your head, if you want."

Grisban grumbled.

"Such events are common in the south of Lorimor," Cyra began, but a look from the dwarven warrior silenced her.

"Everyone all right?" Brockton asked.

"No," Tarha said, her voice sounding like a bell.

Screams suddenly rent the air as a cloud of faintly glowing mist erupted through the low vine-covered entrance Quellen had tried before the earthquake. One Fist caught an impression of panicked faces, of gaping mouths and empty eyes, as the radiant mass rushed toward him, rolling on the ground like water spilling from a tub. The grass blackened at their passage, frost covering the withering blades. Cries and curses came from his companions.

"Run, you blockhead!" Grisban shouted, but the orc stood his ground.

No sense in trying to outrun something so fast and large. Breath escaped from One Fist's mouth in thick clouds of steam and his hair stood on end as a chill burned his skin.

This was it, he thought.

What a stupid way to go.

Then Tarha stepped in front of him, holding her staff out. Her tresses flew as if in a strong wind. The ghostly torrent surged toward her, the sound of its lamentations increasing to deafening, and then split into two streams rushing past on either side. It further separated into a swarm of cackling luminescent tendrils that wound through the trees and the ferns and disappeared.

"Now they are gone," Tarha said. She leaned on a nearby chunk of wall, breathing hard in the still cold air.

"Can I help?" One Fist asked.

She shook her head. The steam from her breath waned as her chest stopped heaving.

"By the Chaos Serpent, what was that?" Grisban said.

"The earth shaking," Tarha said. "The ghosts were as disturbed as we were."

Grisban cursed again.

"We need to get the horses back," Brockton said.

"I'll go," One Fist offered. He needed to move and do something normal, to push back the memory of the ghostly flood. He glanced at Tarha, and she nodded, as grim as ever.

"I am coming with you," Cyra said.

Brockton was still scanning the empty spaces between the trees. "Make it quick."

"Yeah," Grisban called after them. "This place gives me the chills."

After retrieving the horses, the expedition went further west. The road they had been following became more defined, and the shattered buildings emerging from the ground became more common and larger. Brockton ordered One Fist to take point on foot, one hundred yards ahead, and Vaerix picked up the rearguard.

"We want to avoid bad encounters," he explained as Vaerix fell back.

After the earth shaking, the forest had returned to being a peaceful wilderness. The ground was slowly rising as they went and it was no longer water-soaked like before. Birds chirped in the trees, eyeing the travelers warily from the branches.

Small animals moved in the undergrowth, and One Fist had managed to capture a couple of rabbits.

"For Grisban's dinner," he joked.

Yet the old dwarf was not in the mood for laughter, and Brockton was not shy in admitting the billowing outpouring of spectral mist had scared him much more than the prospect of facing dragon hybrids or even their masters. Those were scary enough, granted, but solid, material creatures that could be reasoned with, or fought.

Ghosts were beyond his comprehension, and where his reason was unable to go, fear bloomed. And despite the fear, or because of it, he decided to interrogate Tarha.

"There are ghosts here," Tarha answered to Brockton's questions. "Clinging to the stones like men drowning, trying to resist the current that might carry them away. Not as many as you fear, but some."

"Same as in the old city," Grisban said dismissively.

"No two ghosts are the same," Tarha replied. "I believe that ancient magic was practiced here, by your people or by Vaerix's. A power that twisted and warped the spirits and made them… different."

She turned in the saddle, scanning the landscape. She pointed at a lone archway, all that remained of a lost building whose shape Brockton could not imagine. Two crooked trees grew on either side of it.

"In that doorway," Tarha said. "A lone warrior, defending something she does not even remember, her ferocity and her duty all that remains of her. That, and the memory of her chainmail and her sword, shape what's left of her. She is telling me to stay away. I am quite willing to. And over there, by that column–"

"Are they a threat?" Grisban asked, interrupting her.

Tarha turned her grim look on him.

Grisban cleared his voice. "An immediate threat, I mean."

"None you can hold back with your axe," Tarha replied.

"What's that supposed to mean?"

"These ghosts are ancient and have grown strange," Tarha replied, "twisted by time and loneliness and by some ancient power. Do they wish us ill? No. Would they harm us? Probably. We are the intruders here and they wish us gone."

Brockton stared at the broken column Tarha had indicated. He thought he saw green dots of light, as large as a coin, dancing around the eroded marble. He shuddered. There were things, he admitted to himself, he had not considered when he had planned this expedition.

Grisban cast a glance at the sky, scoffed, and turned to him. "A nice choice we have. But I'd rather risk being spotted by the dragon hybrids on the plain than risk spending the next night in this forest graveyard."

Brockton could see Cyra shared the dwarf's misgivings, while Tarha was impossible to read. As for Quellen, the elf was riding with his hood up, his shoulders curved, like he was sleeping in the saddle.

"We will look for a place clear of ruins. Tarha can protect us. And we will not enter the buildings anyway," he said.

"And yet–" Quellen said.

Brockton cut him short. "We are not treasure hunters," he said with a quick glance at Cyra. "We'll stay out of the buildings."

"I was just saying," Quellen replied in a conciliatory tone, "that spending the night with a roof over our head might not be unpleasant."

"Until it falls on our heads," Grisban said.

"And that's the least of our worries," Brockton agreed.

"The necromancer can protect us as easily inside a building as out in the open." Quellen's tone was reasonable.

Tarha glared at him.

"One does not go and poke an anthill," Cyra said.

"We will avoid the ruins," Brockton repeated, "as much as we can."

Up ahead the land rose some more, a large complex of buildings buried under a mountain of rubble that the vegetation had colonized and turned into a hill. The ancient road cut through it like a straight, narrow canyon. On either side, old gateways were still exposed, some curtained by hanging vegetation, some clean and open like eye sockets in a buried skull.

One Fist was waiting for them, crouching behind a slab of black obsidian that jutted out of the ground like a shard of a colossal broken bottle left behind by a passing giant. The ancient material was supposed to be perennial, but the fury of the dragons that had shattered the city had also broken down its volcanic glass walls.

"There's smoke in the air," he said when Brockton went to him.

"A campfire?"

The orc shrugged. "Horses went this way," he said. "Say, two days ago. Maybe more."

"Cyra's old friends? Waiting for us?"

"Likely. This place screams ambush. It would be nice to find a way around."

"We'll need to back up and–"

"We might have no time," a low voice said. Brockton turned,

his hand on the hilt of his sword. One Fist spun around, his blade ready.

Vaerix appeared and squatted by their side, placing a placating hand on Brockton's shoulder. One Fist snorted and lowered his sword.

"Some of my people are following us," Vaerix said.

"Kurnos's teeth," One Fist hissed. "How many?"

"How much time do we have?" Brockton asked in turn.

"Five warriors. Three minutes behind. I ran."

Nothing in Vaerix's demeanor betrayed any fatigue or distress.

Brockton nodded. There was a tight knot of fear in his belly. Five dragon hybrids was probably more than they could take.

"We'll run, too," he said. "There is no time to find a way around this pass."

He looked at One Fist, who again shrugged. "We have little choice."

They ran back to the horses. The hybrids were too close for comfort.

"What happened?" Cyra asked, looking at Vaerix.

Grisban had unhooked his axe from the saddle. "Trouble."

"Both ahead and behind," Brockton said. "So we are running. Through that passage."

"Running away from trouble?" Quellen asked with a smirk. "Or toward it?"

"Running where we are expected to walk," Brockton retorted, thinking of the highwaymen more than likely waiting for them. "Hoping the snare will close behind us."

One Fist had made certain their things were securely tied on the packhorses. Then, with a nod, he jumped in his saddle and drew his sword.

Grisban and Cyra had their weapons ready, too.

Brockton unsheathed his sword. The blade glinted, as if happy to be finally be free.

So much for his hopes of never having to draw the weapon. The sword was heavy in his hand and his heart was heavy with anticipation.

"Let's go."

They spurred their mounts on, galloping through the narrow canyon as fast as they could. Brockton led the charge, followed by Grisban and by Cyra, whose horse's long legs helped her overtake the head of the column.

Quellen and Tarha followed, with Vaerix and One Fist at the rear, running side by side, the orc on his minuscule pony, and Vaerix taking long strides with their powerful legs.

They were about one hundred yards in when a chorus of twittering sounds echoed between the narrow walls of the passage. Brockton's heart sank.

These were not highwaymen laying in ambush as One Fist had predicted.

This was another unknown horror of this land.

He leaned on the pony's neck, kicking its haunches to make him go faster.

The white blur of Cyra's horse led the way, the woman's red and blue cloak flying behind her like a banner, a sword blazing in her left hand.

Then the horse reared and Brockton's pony reacted by slowing down, scared. Brockton cursed.

There were shapes holding the far end of the canyon. But not the foes One Fist thought would ambush them. Tall and powerful, their hooked wings spread menacingly.

More dragon hybrids poured through the black holes of the

buried building's windows and gateways. They were making that continuous sound, like high-pitched trumpets, like colossal birds.

Cyra turned her horse around. Brockton stopped fully.

Another band of hybrids, probably the one Vaerix had spotted, came up through the gap behind them.

Hybrids flew above them, bounding across the canyon.

Soon, they were all huddled together, their mounts neighing in fear, as dozens of dragon hybrids closed in on them.

Like the ones they had seen a few days before, they did not wear armor and carried an assortment of rough weapons, spears and axes made with bent rusty metal and shards of colored glass. Brockton could not tell their age or their gender. All were scarred and fierce looking.

The twittering war cry subsided and silence hung over them like an executioner's axe.

"Here is your anthill," Quellen said to Cyra.

They were trapped.

CHAPTER SEVENTEEN
Memories: Upper Lothan River Valley

"Let's kill it."

"Shut up, kid."

"Breath of Aris, it's been badly mangled, ain't it?"

"Wonder what did it."

"I wouldn't want to meet them."

Vaerix willed their eyes open. Their eyelids were caked in grime and glued together. It took them a moment to focus on those surrounding them. Vaerix smelled horses and dust. And the bad sick smell that had accompanied them these last few days.

"Look out, men. It's moving."

Vaerix tried to get on their hands and knees and failed.

Breath came ragged out of their throat, with an unpleasant rattle.

"What if it's plague?"

"I told you to shut up."

A man entered Vaerix's field of vision.

Tall boots, a pair of blue trousers. He crouched down and his gaunt face came into view. Vaerix squinted, trying to focus.

Bearded chin, metal breastplate, a bowl-like helmet over long brown hair.

The man leaned on a sheathed sword like it was a walking stick.

"Can you speak?" the man asked. Then he looked to the side. "Bring me some water."

Someone handed him a waterskin, and he drew closer and poured some water into Vaerix's mouth.

Vaerix coughed and again tried to stand.

"Easy," the man said.

"Why are we wasting time with this thing?"

The man turned sharply. "Kid, I won't tell you again…"

"But–"

"Oh, shut up!" somebody else said. Other voices agreed.

Finally, Vaerix managed to sit up on the ground. The movement caused them searing pain, and their arms felt as if they were on fire. Barely healed wounds, opened again. In the glare of the low sun, they tried to focus on their surroundings.

They were out of the mountains. That was the first surprise. Vaerix had no memories of leaving the high gorges behind. The last few days had been a haze of pain and confusion, a fever dream that had left no tracks in their mind. Their muscles had done the walking, while their mind was far away and dazzled.

Now they were on a gentle knoll, green grasses and yellow flowers around them. It was mid-morning, and there were people there.

Humans.

Five men surrounded them. A faraway corner of Vaerix's mind found time and energy enough to marvel at the variety of the humans, in terms of size and color. One of the men was staying behind, taking care of the horses Vaerix had smelled a moment before. Another was crouching in front of them, and by his clothes and demeanor was the leader. Of the remaining three, one was very young, with flaxen hair and a ruddy face, and one was short and had a great belly over which was stretched a rusty chainmail. The third man, tall and lanky, was the one that had handed his chieftain the water and now took his skin back.

"What sort of beast it is, Aedan?" he asked.

They were armed with a mishmash of weapons, swords and pikes mostly. Militiamen, Vaerix thought, a patrol from some human settlement in the Lothan valley. Men who reluctantly made a life of fighting but would pick up arms in case of necessity. Those who had met them claimed they were weak foes and messy fighters.

The bearded one was still looking at them.

"Not a beast," he said now. "At least I think not."

"It's a hybrid, I tell you," the kid said in a wailing voice. "One of the dragons' foot soldiers."

"That ain't no dragon-kin."

"Is too."

"Where are its wings then?" another objected.

Resignation crept into Vaerix's heart. This was what Xenith had planned for them when he had cast them out. There was no love lost between humans and hybrids. They just wished the militiamen would make it fast and not too painful.

The one called Aedan leaned forward. "Do you understand what I say?"

Vaerix nodded slowly. Two of the militiamen gasped.

"Good," the man said. He placed an open hand over his breastplate. "My name is Aedan Couch."

Again, Vaerix nodded. They placed their hand on their chest in the same way. Their arms were in agony. "Vaerix."

They were not going to renounce the name that had been taken from them.

"Vieritz," the man repeated, stumbling on the syllables and mangling their name. "Is it true? Are you a dragon hybrid? One of Margath's?"

Vaerix took a deep breath. If they were to die here, under the pikes of these half-warriors, they'd die standing. "Not Margath's," they said, a hint of their old pride in their broken voice.

Vaerix's arms failed as they tried to push themselves up to standing. Pain flared and their head spun. The man Aedan jumped up and caught them, pushing a shoulder under their arm, and kept them up.

The other militiamen reacted by taking a step forward, their weapons ready. "Careful," one of the men said, but Aedan ignored him.

He helped Vaerix sit on a rock. "It's some bad cuts you have there, Vieritz," he said. "Your arms."

Vaerix looked at the ground, shamed.

"Was it some kind of beast? An enemy of yours?"

Vaerix looked at the man. "Yes," they said. "An enemy."

Aedan nodded. "Is this enemy of yours still hereabouts?"

Vaerix shook their head. "Beyond the mountains," they said.

The man frowned. "Is that where you came from, Vieritz? From the mountains?"

Vaerix nodded.

The man that had offered some water walked around them and stood by Vaerix's side. They made an ugly sound, but they did not touch Vaerix's skin. "The wounds are rotten," they said. Then he invoked a deity Vaerix was not familiar with. "Whoever did this, they burned them cuts to cauterize 'em. Did a bad job of it. Smells like gangrene."

Aedan nodded. "We need to clean those wounds, Vieritz. You understand this, yes?"

"Are you really going to help this beast?" the youngling cried.

Aedan snorted and turned. "This is the last time I warn you," he hissed angrily.

"They are our enemies. They attacked our land..."

"Put a lid on it," the short man said.

"The war is over," the one by the horses added in a weary tone.

"Had it not been for good lord Roland..." the young one tried.

The short one by his side laughed and gently pushed the young one aside. "The lords are all good after they die, right?"

The others laughed, but not Aedan.

Vaerix's head was spinning. They had heard of Lord Roland, who had slain Margath. All the rest was gibberish. They placed their hands on their knees and leaned forward, trying to breathe without pain. It was useless.

"Look at this wretch," Aedan said in a low voice. He leaned down, so close to the kid that their noses almost touched.

"We might end up dead," the kid said.

From where they were sitting, pain and confusion making their sight swim, Vaerix was not able to see the face of Aedan. But they heard Aedan sigh and then straighten back up to full height.

"So we might," he said. "In which case, we'll be dead because of our kindness. There are worse ways, right men?"

His men mumbled something Vaerix was unable to catch. For the first time, a faint realization dawned in their pain-addled mind.

Aedan turned to Vaerix as Vaerix looked up.

"We'll take care of those wounds," he said. "You understand this, yes? You come with us, to Berlam Bridge. It's our village. We clean your wounds. We have food too. Then you tell us your story."

Vaerix nodded, too tired and confused to do anything else.

They had been cast away by their people, and now were being welcomed by their enemies. As they followed Aedan's party, Vaerix's fevered mind tried to struggle with the madness that was their new life. And the unexpected kindnesses they had encountered.

For too long Vaerix had watched the world through Levirax's eyes.

But not anymore.

CHAPTER EIGHTEEN
Guests

"Why are they not attacking us?" Brockton hissed.

"Don't give them any ideas," Grisban replied. He evaluated their odds and did not like the results. There were too many of the brutes and they had the advantage of the terrain.

"See that opening on the hillside?" he said, keeping his voice steady. "The one with the cracked lintel?"

Brockton looked at him, panicking.

Grisban took a deep breath. "One Fist," he called.

The orc kept his gaze on the hybrids. "I hear you."

"The cracked lintel gate," Grisban repeated. "Narrow one. Halfway upslope."

One Fist's pony was turning on its legs, like it was looking for a way out that was not there. "I see it."

"I'll open you a gap," Grisban said. He essayed the edge of his axe with his thumb. "You and Vaerix will take Brockton, the elf and the woman in there—"

"The woman?" Cyra snorted.

Grisban took a deep breath. "It's not the time—"

"I can fight, old man—"

Grisban chuckled. "But not here, it would be stupid. Up there they'll have to come through the door to get you. Three of you'll only face one of them at a time. And Quellen can open a way out somewhere."

"Suddenly you have great faith in my powers, dwarf," Quellen commented with a smirk.

"You'll never hold them long enough for us to get there," Cyra objected.

Grisban closed his eyes. "Fortuna, give me smart enemies but not stupid friends."

Vaerix took a step forward.

The dragon hybrids suddenly stood very still.

Vaerix lifted their staff in front of themselves, holding it parallel to the ground. "They do not want to fight," they said.

"How do you know?" Grisban asked.

"Because if they wanted to fight," Brockton said in a rough voice, "if they wanted us dead, they'd have killed us already." He coughed and cleared his throat.

"It is so," Vaerix said.

One of the dragon hybrids came forward. He was not as tall as Vaerix, but broader of shoulder, wearing what looked like a scrap of some ancient flag as a baldric and a necklace of old coins. His scales had a milky hue with a faint yellow edge. Grisban had seen snakes that pale. A long scar crossed the right side of his face and continued down the neck. The creature walked with a slight limp, as if its right leg was a little stiff, and carried a proper sword, some two-hander Grisban thought would look better in a museum than on a battlefield.

He kept his wings tucked behind his back, the claws on top of them folded into small fists.

Cyra was humming a song.

Grisban stared at her. He felt suddenly dizzy, his limbs heavy. The pale dragon hybrid's head snapped in her direction. "Silence!" the creature shouted.

Cyra hesitated and then stopped.

Grisban's head cleared.

The hybrid stared at Cyra for one long minute, then slowly started walking around Vaerix.

Grisban noticed Vaerix scratching at the scars on their arms, their eyes never leaving their foes.

As the hybrid walked by, Cyra's horse snorted and whinnied.

"Hold your nag steady," Grisban hissed at her.

The creature ignored the horse and completed his circuit of Vaerix, who stood as still as a statue. Then the hybrid's eyes brushed over the rest of the party, his tail slowly swinging from side to side.

Grisban made sure to make eye contact, hefting his axe.

"Do you speak for these?" the hybrid asked Vaerix.

Vaerix turned to look at Brockton, then gave a single nod. "Now, I do."

That seemed to be enough for the other. "I am Brazzax," he said in a low rumbling voice, his eyes on Vaerix. He held his ancient sword in both hands, also parallel to the ground. "Some call me the Pale. I speak for my people, the tribe of the Stone Houses."

Vaerix stood perfectly still. "Greetings."

Brazzax straightened his back and his wings moved, the claws clicking open. "Do you have a name? Or should I call you… the Wingless?"

Vaerix shifted their position. They pulled their staff up and stuck the end in the ground. "I am Vaerix," they replied, their voice cold. "Called the dreamer."

A ripple of voices ran through the surrounding hybrids. Some bodies changed positions. Weapons clicked and scraped.

Grisban caught One Fist's eye and nodded at the gate with the broken lintel. The orc nodded back. Should things get violent, they'd stick to his original plan.

"A name out of old legends," Brazzax said, a hint of mockery in his voice but also, Grisban thought, a quaver of uncertainty. He held his breath. If something was to go down, it would happen now.

Brazzax gave a sideways glance at Brockton, then looked back at Vaerix. "Why are you in the land of the Stone Houses?" Brazzax asked.

"We travel west," Vaerix said.

"We know that. But why?"

Grisban and Brockton traded a look.

"We are explorers," Vaerix said.

"There are no treasures here," Brazzax said, a note of contempt creeping into his voice. "None you can take with yourselves."

"We do not seek treasure. We seek knowledge."

The pale dragon hybrid snorted. "So you say."

"Because it is the truth."

"Then the dragon hybrids of the Stone Houses will share our fire," Brazzax said.

Again, a murmur rose from the gathered hybrids, but Brazzax turned a fiery eye on his companions and the talk died out. "The shadows draw longer, and the ghosts are crawling out of their nests. We will sit by the fire and tell stories through the night, sharing this knowledge."

"So be it," Vaerix said.

Brazzax lifted his sword, still held in both hands like a

staff, and barked an order. Slowly, the dragon hybrid cohorts dispersed in small groups who walked up the hillside to the darkened doorways through which they had come.

Only Brazzax and six of his companions remained.

"We are invited to be Brazzax's guests," Vaerix said to Brockton, in a voice that sounded formal even for the already uptight hybrid.

"We will accept, gladly," Brockton said, finding his voice.

"Not like we had so much choice," Grisban mumbled.

"A warrior cherishes the opportunity to avoid a fight," Cyra said.

He gave her a look.

"It sounds better in Lorimorian." The woman grinned.

They dismounted and led their horses up the hill, escorted by the dragon hybrids.

"This is something I have never seen," Vaerix said to Brockton as they sat around the fire in one of the surviving rooms of the buried complex. The walls were dark with many years of wood burning and the air was stale.

They had left their horses in the hall beyond the gateway and Brazzax had accompanied them through an arch and into this room.

"What if it's a trap?" Quellen had asked.

"Why should they bother?" One Fist had replied.

The orc was right, Vaerix thought. If the warriors had wanted them dead, they could have killed them outside, easily. But they had refused the fight – and this was strange, just as everything about these members of their own people seemed strange in Vaerix's eyes. Arwyia's single-minded aggression had not surprised Vaerix, nor had her adherence to what still sounded like dragonlord Levirax's principles. But what was happening here, this was unprecedented.

They had learned, during their travels before this quest, about the small bands of dragon hybrids haunting the ruined cities of the south and serving mages and wizards as hired muscle. Vaerix had had a few scrapes with some of these that had seen in them an easy prey, and an object of spite and derision. Scattered remains of vanquished armies whose dragonlords had not heeded Shaarina's call for retreat. Left behind and lacking a real purpose, they lived by the sword as they had been brought up.

Like Vaerix themselves, they were remnants of something that was no more.

Brockton's questions, when they had come, had been an echo to their own thoughts.

"What if they want to hold us here, to hand us over to their dragonlord?" Quellen asked. He was toying with one of his pebbles. A sign of preoccupation that Vaerix had learned to recognize.

"Much has changed from the wars," they went on, replying to Brockton but also, obliquely, to the elf. "It seems these that greeted us do not serve a dragonlord, nor do they share the ancient discipline, but still hold a distant memory of it."

Steps came closer, shadows looming and growing larger on the walls.

Brazzax walked in, followed by two warriors carrying torches.

Behind them came a dragon hybrid so old, crooked and stiff, Vaerix for a moment doubted their own eyes.

The old one dragged his left leg, and his right wing was twisted, the bones broken and badly healed. He wore a red garment, carefully darned, over blue scales that turned green in the yellow light of the flames, and he walked leaning on a staff, dragging his tail on the ground behind him.

Another one that would not fly anymore, Vaerix thought, and went through their memories to recall one that must have been old when they had still been but hatchlings. But nothing was there.

The two warriors stopped by the archway, and Brazzax and the other hybrid entered the room, side by side. When he was close enough, they saw the newcomer's eyes were perfectly white, and he moved his head like a bird, trying to catch the faintest sound reverberating in the enclosed space.

"Blind like a bat," Quellen whispered behind them.

"But not deaf," the old hybrid snapped. His voice was a high-pitched croak, but still perfectly clear and full of humor. Then he grinned, showing a long maw in which a few teeth were missing, but those that remained were as sharp as knives. "Where is the one that calls themselves Vaerix?"

Vaerix stepped forward.

Up close, the newcomer was not so old, as rather worn out, consumed by the events of a life that had been long, yes, but maybe not longer than Vaerix's.

"I am Vaerix," they said.

The old hybrid tilted his head to listen. "You truly are," he said, surprise and amusement playing in his voice. Then his grin widened. "Have you had any more of those dreams of yours?"

Brazzax and his warriors escorted them further inside the ruins where the dragon hybrids camped. Time and neglect had damaged the ancient mosaics almost beyond recognition.

"Such fallen greatness," Grisban murmured with awe and regret.

A stretch of glass tiles on the walls still showed a blue sky, an emerald-green hill, or a limb of some noble personage whose name and features had long been forgotten. The obsidian floors were still as polished as the day they had been laid, but covered in dust and debris, marked by black circles where campfires had been set. There was a fine layer of dust in the air that made Vaerix's nose twitch. The once proud building crumbled with age.

"This place is a death trap," Grisban said.

"I agree," Quellen replied in a low voice. "Normally I would assume these ruins strong, especially to have withstood the passage of time. However, given the recent quake, we should be advised to be careful where we step. Places might be weaker than they appear."

"Not much else we can do," Grisban said.

Vaerix appreciated the dwarf's pragmatism. They looked around, taking mental notes about the place. Time had turned what had once been a great building into a hill, terraces and balconies covered in a thick layer of dirt and vegetation. Inside, the air smelled musty and humid, the walls encrusted with fungi and crawling vines. The hybrids had adopted the place as their own, occupying the chambers that, according to Brockton, had once hosted some kind of school or library. More of the structure extended underground.

"Just imagine what treasures must be buried beneath our feet," Quellen murmured.

They marched on. The hybrids, armed with spears, led them through the first two chambers and then stopped to take up defensive positions. Vaerix kept their wits about them. Grisban, they were sure, did the same. No matter the courtesy they were being shown, these dragon hybrids were still enemies. Any detail could become critical in a fight.

"We will take care of your animals," said Brazzax, motioning them on. The Blind One had lagged behind, his pace but a crawl.

A wide staircase, now leaning on one side, led to an empty circular hall so large its edges faded in the shadow. A mountain of wreckage occupied the center of the floor, and over their head, the collapsed dome had been replaced by trees hugging the edges of the hole with gnarled roots. Light from the sky penetrated the tangle of branches in a web of pale shafts, casting irregular pools of brightness on the dirty floor.

More guards were stationed here, and Vaerix spotted a cradle of ropes and rusty chains hanging from the tree trunks some twenty feet above their head. Defenses to delay an intruder trying to enter from above, or an intruder capable of flight.

Like other hybrids. This, too, was important information. Why would they need to ensnare other dragon hybrids, however?

The settlement was arranged in a tight defensive manner, within the occupants' limits. They clearly expected trouble and had rendered any access to the buried palace difficult to breach. Archways opened in the walls and their small procession followed a wide, low corridor past a stairwell and into a square room with a low ceiling. A depression in the center of the floor had been piled with wood and a fire crackled happily, casting light on the stained walls. The smoke was sucked into a vertical shaft above and the air was reasonably clean.

"You can stay here," Brazzax said. "As our guests."

Vaerix thanked him.

"There will be food," the hybrid went on, "and drink. And talk. But now you rest. Also, you are free. But know that there are guards in our encampment."

And with that, he turned and walked away.

Grisban watched Brazzax go, then turned to Brockton. "We've walked into something I don't like," he said in a low voice.

"They seem friendly," Cyra said.

"They seem at war," One Fist replied.

Grisban nodded, but it was Vaerix who spoke the obvious. "My people are fighting among themselves."

"Well, from what you told us in the mountains," Quellen said, sitting by the fire and stretching out his hands to warm them, "that should be the normal state of affairs. A perennial state of war."

It was hard for Vaerix to understand when Quellen was being sarcastic, and when he was being obtuse. They decided to humor him. "Not like this," they said. "Not in scattered bands without a leader."

"The blind one…" Grisban began.

Vaerix sighed. "Is not their leader."

Grisban frowned.

"It is so." The blind hybrid's voice sounded clear, and they all turned as one to see him limping into the room with a younger dragon hybrid behind him who held food and drink. "I am not a dragonlord, but I do have good ears." He grinned at the joke as his companion led him to the fire and he squatted down, his joints creaking. "Who was asking?"

Grisban took a step forward, but Vaerix spoke on his behalf. "He is Grisban the Thirsty," they said. They recalled Brockton's words back at the Razorcliff. "He is a fine warrior, and wise."

"It's rare for a warrior to live long enough to find wisdom," the Blind One said. "Know, then, Grisban the Thirsty, that we are a people of warriors and we fought for our dragonlords, bringing fire to the lands of Terrinoth. Zir the Black was the one I served."

All but Cyra gasped or cursed at that name. She frowned questioningly.

"A dragonlord in the Third Darkness," Brockton said dryly, taking a bit of food. "Second only to Margath in cruelty."

The Blind One nodded. "In Zir's service I had a rank, which I will not remember. In her service I fought, and in her service I suffered these injuries. And with my wings and my sight gone, I also lost my usefulness. Thus, it was in the old times. I should have been killed."

"That is harsh," Grisban said.

"Why did Zir let you live?" Vaerix asked.

"For the same reason Levirax let you," the old hybrid replied. "To be an example. To show why warriors are meant to fight and die and not to live long."

Gently, Vaerix placed their hand on the Blind One's shoulder. "Those days are gone," they said. "And different ways are possible for our people."

A rattling laugh escaped the throat of the old hybrid. "Again with those dreams of yours." He shook his head. "Do not be mistaken, dreamer. I heard about your fables."

"Not fables. I saw what can be."

"That may be so, dreamer. Truly, I can tell you a lot has changed since the time we made war on Terrinoth. But you are wrong. Where it matters, things are still the same."

Frost swept over Vaerix's heart. They knew what the blind one was about to say.

The Blind One nodded, correctly reading their silence. "Because truly, Zir the Black was killed by order of the Dragon Rex, but Levirax still lives, and grows in power."

Brockton believed he would need a new book soon.

But the blind hybrid kept talking, and Brockton scrawled notes as fast as he could while the others listened and ate.

Brockton did little more than taste the food the hybrids brought – well-cooked boar meat and onions baked in the embers. He was too busy writing down everything.

But Grisban and One Fist made sure nothing would be left over.

Meanwhile, Brazzax spoke of how after the Third Darkness, the dragons had returned to the Molten Heath, and those that had not yet faced it, stood in judgment before Shaarina the Dragon Rex. And Shaarina was lenient with those dragonlords who had followed her order to retreat, among them Levirax, whose forces had left the Broken Plains as soon as the order had been received.

For the dragon hybrids, confused times came thereafter.

"Shaarina did not care for us," the Blind One said. "She barely cared for her own brood. She retreated to her mountain of fire and did not turn a second glance on us. Many died in the Third Darkness, and many had been left behind when their dragonlords had been executed, when the dragon armies were ordered to return to the Heath. It was a time of fear and anger."

Brockton looked up from the page, waiting for the old hybrid to continue. Around him, the others were silent.

"Intelligent creatures need purpose," the Blind One finally said, "and with our purpose gone, we fell on each other, because war was all we knew. We had been created for war. Burdened with peace, our people fractured and scattered. Bands of survivors turned into clans and tribes. Villages were built. Others settled in the ruins. Some even tried to make their own way, leaving behind what they had been. Trying to follow the ramblings of mad prophets, who had denied everything they had stood for. Everything they were."

The old hybrid stopped and turned to where Vaerix sat by his side. His blind eyes rested on Vaerix for a long moment and then he quickly tilted his head.

"What, Vaerix the Dreamer? No words from you now?"

Vaerix shook their head.

"I see," the Blind One said. "You have learned at last to keep your counsel. That's wisdom, I guess. Pity it came too late."

That rattling laugh of his sounded once again.

"We were not created for peace," the Blind One continued. "And peace is not for us. Do not expect sympathy from me, Vaerix. The dream of a peaceful life was a poison you poured down the throats of the young ones. Those who sought it found strife and death. As the armies broke up into tribes, the tribes fought among themselves. Not just for pride and glory, but for food, for land. For survival. The peace you had dreamed of, the peace you had promised to the people, turned into desperation. And when again they were offered a purpose, a discipline–"

"Levirax," Vaerix said, and Brockton was surprised at the coldness in the hybrid's voice.

"She is a strong leader and has a purpose, a plan. Shaarina grows tired with age. She sleeps in her mountain and is seldom seen. Soon there will rise a new Dragon Rex, and Levirax is ready. She has gathered many of the tribes to form an army again, and she has a vision. We have yet to decide if we will join her ranks."

"A vision of death," Vaerix said.

"A vision of strength. Of pride."

"A blind one talking about visions to a dreamer," Cyra said suddenly, spite in her tone. "Hilarious."

They all turned to her. Brockton signaled her to keep her counsel, but she paid him no heed. She leaned forward, hands on her knees, and spoke with a bitter voice.

"It seems to me, old one," she said, "you and your people have forgotten that true warriors cherish peace with all their heart. That is the reason why we train and seek perfection in our art, so that our demeanor alone will tell our adversaries all they have to know, and they will lay down their arms, knowing that any other choice would mean their defeat. Much as we love the exhilaration of the fight, it is for peace that we do what we do."

"Nice words from a weak people," the Blind One retorted. "You are not warriors, but performers. Warriors die. That is the ultimate truth: that death is the only alternative to life for those who fight, and we will only know peace in the cold embrace of the tomb. All else is philosophy and empty posturing."

He stood suddenly, and the young one that had accompanied him came to guide him out. The Blind One pushed his helping hand away angrily and walked out alone.

"Well, that was sudden," Quellen said.

Vaerix stood in turn and in silence walked out of the room.

"What have we got ourselves into?" Brockton asked in a whisper, his eyes on the lines of notes he had written. A new Dragon Rex?

This was not what he had planned.

•••

Rain fell over the ruins. A spring shower blown in from the plains. Water poured down through the branches in the circular hall and dripped from the cables and chains that hung from the trees. Rivulets of water ran on the floor of the outer rooms.

Vaerix checked the horses, who rested in a nearby room, to see they were safe and dry. The ponies welcomed their coming, neighing softly. Cyra's horse, Cloud, shook his head and snorted. Vaerix caressed his side.

They spent a few minutes with the animals enjoying their tranquility, their warmth.

Then they walked out again. Trying to quieten their thoughts from the Blind One's story and how Vaerix's dreams had harmed the dragon hybrids, Vaerix reached the gateway through which they had entered the buried palace, stopping under the skewed arch, listening to the rain, smelling its earthy smell. It was like a gray veil had been stretched over the landscape. Low dark clouds ran through the sky, and to the north the red reflection of the Molten Heath's fires had paled to the pink of a false dawn. The narrow stretch of old road at the base of the hill had turned into a stream.

"I fought a troll, once."

Vaerix turned sharply. Grisban approached them slowly, sat down on the doorstep and sucked on his pipe.

"There was this peel tower, in the hills overlooking Blind Muir. A ruin, more than a tower. A burned-out husk abandoned in the time of the First Darkness, so old nobody even remembered its name, if it ever had one. Big piles of rocks and old ghosts. Our friend Tarha would have loved it, I'm sure." He chuckled. "Anyway, there was this troll hiding in there. A big brute of a creature that knew only violence and robbery. I mean, a troll, right?"

He turned to look at Vaerix. Vaerix nodded. Yes, they knew what a troll was.

"I was green back then. Barely had a beard, if you know what I mean. Saw myself as the greatest warrior out of Dunwarr, traveling the world to fight duels and slay dragons. No offense meant. Anyway, I walked into that cursed ruin like I owned the place." Grisban blew a cloud of smoke. "And this mountain of muscles and fury comes at me down this spiral staircase, roaring like a thunderstorm, and wielding a whole tree for a club. And I had an old axe I bought secondhand and a shield made of wood. By the Whispering One, I was scared!"

He laughed loudly. "Are you afraid of trolls, Vaerix?"

Vaerix wondered where all of this was leading. They shook their head. "No," they said. "Wary, but not scared."

"They are not really smart," Grisban said matter-of-factly. "You simply need to keep moving and you're set. Their rage makes them forget to defend themselves. No reason to be scared of trolls, really. No, you know what scares me? Old age."

He sighed, and smoke escaped his lips.

"Old age is a vicious foe. Old age makes you stiff. Not just your limbs, and that's bad enough, but your mind. Old stupid ideas you'd have laughed at in your youth become set-in-stone rules that can't be broken. Rules that govern your life. And you find yourself looking at the past, remembering how good it was. You forget how scared you were of that troll's club and just remember you triumphed. How great it all was. Old age makes you scared because things are changing, and you are no longer nimble enough up here." He tapped his temple. "And still you think you are right all the time. That's a recipe for disaster. Like being so full of yourself you walk into a troll's lair whistling a song."

Grisban looked up at Vaerix. "That blind old coot in there's wrong."

Vaerix felt warmth for the old dwarf. Grisban was not good at this sort of thing, but he was trying.

"Thank you, friend," Vaerix said.

"Respecting the aged is a great thing," Grisban mumbled. "But we should respect them enough to tell them they are talking out of their..." He clicked his tongue. "Out of line, I mean."

CHAPTER NINETEEN
Ghosts

At the edge of the light cast by the hybrids' torches, a tall and narrow door led to a narrower ledge and then to a staircase descending in the dark.

Down this staircase went Archmage Quellen and behind him, stepping carefully not to cause any noise, Cyra followed.

She had come to the conclusion that either Brockton the Map Maker was a better liar than anyone she had ever known, or he really had no interest in the dwarven treasures of lore supposedly buried under the lost cities of the Verdant Ring.

Quellen, on the other hand, clearly had such an interest.

So, when the elf had silently walked out of their quarters, she had thought it might be interesting to follow him. She had watched him use one of his flying pebbles to make a sound in a side corridors, distracting one of the sentinels long enough for him to sneak past, but she had kept him in sight. There was a faint luminescence about him, a clear sign the old story claiming elves could see in the dark was not completely true.

His long tunic brushed the floor as he circled a corner of the staircase. Cyra listened for a moment, just making out the sound of the mage's steps. Then she followed, one hand brushing against the wall, the other on her sword hilt. Soon, a cold light reached her and she passed a crystal as large as her fist set into the wall, which cast an eerie light on the steps.

She reached out to touch it. It was cold.

She went on. More crystals lit her descent and dark tracts alternated with bright ones as she continued deeper. At this point she could no longer hear Quellen's footsteps, and she figured she must now be at least fifty feet beneath the level the hybrids occupied. The deeper she went, the warmer and more humid the air became. And the more she thought this had been a bad idea.

The hybrids would catch her, and that would mean trouble. Trouble, she believed, from which neither Brockton nor Vaerix would be able to pull her out. But she wanted to know what the elf was doing and what he might discover.

Suddenly she was on level ground, debris crunching under her feet. A corridor going left and right was before her. No lights to the right, a faint glow to the left.

Cyra cursed and chose left.

There was a sharp turn after five steps, and one of the light rocks emitted a soft brightness that briefly blinded her after her time in utter darkness. The corridor did not go farther than fifteen steps, a solid wall of rubble marking its end. Cyra frowned and turned.

Quellen was there, holding one of his small stones. "Found something interesting?" he asked in a low voice.

"You should not go out alone like this," she snapped, thinking quickly.

He arched his eyebrows. "And you are here to protect me?"

"To bring you back, actually."

"You took your time. You have been following me for quite a while. Why not stop me as soon as you saw me leave?"

"I was curious," she confessed in her most sincere voice.

"That I can believe."

"What are you looking for?"

The elf smirked. "What I am looking for is irrelevant," he said. "I'd rather talk about what you are here to find. You have never told us the whole story."

"There is no story…"

Cyra stopped. She saw Quellen's eyes widen. The mage started backing up slowly.

She turned on her heels and stumbled back two steps in horror.

A faint blue-green substance was filtering through the wall of debris that blocked the passage. It oozed out, pooling on the floor and hanging in the air, at the same time both liquid and mist. It extended an arm, a hand with spread out fingers, and then it pushed a shoulder through the wall. There were rings on the translucent fingers, a band on the wrist, half-hidden under the cuff of a coat that had once been rich.

The head followed the shoulder, and then the rest of the upper body. An embroidered coat, a thick chain of office around the neck. Nice, braided beard, hair in a sort of topknot. A dwarf by his looks and proportions, and yet not like any dwarf she had ever seen.

The lower half of the evanescent body, that cleared the bottom of the obstruction, had no ghostly legs, but rather tapered to a lump of twirling miasma, which dragged on the ground. Where it passed, it abraded a path in the dust and debris on the floor. And yet it appeared to have the substance of smoke.

Its other arm swept through the wall, holding a ghostly staff, and it was fully free. The thing advanced faster than should have been possible with its grotesque shape. It rolled like a cloud rather than slithered like a creature made of mundane substance.

But it was the face that caused Cyra to gasp and retreat further, finally slamming into Quellen. The features of the apparition shifted, like a face reflected in a pool of water. The eyes floated in the face, moving up and down at the sides of a nose that was, at times, just a gnarled hole. And the mouth hung open, a black pit gaping in a protracted, silent scream.

"Out of the way!" Quellen said, recovering his wits and pushing Cyra to the side.

The stone in his hand shot out with a faint pop. It splashed into the advancing apparition, passed right through it, and hit the wall of debris behind with a solid thunk, rising a small cloud of dust.

The thing kept advancing.

"Run!" Quellen snapped and, pulling his robe up, he retreated.

Cyra followed him, but a ghostly hand closed on her arm. She cried out in pain, a burning sensation searing through her sleeve and into her skin.

In front of her, Quellen cursed and stumbled on the staircase, landing at the foot of the steps with a groan. "You cursed–"

Cyra was having difficulties focusing, the pain spreading from her arm up through her shoulder. It split her head and pressed down on her heart.

Tarha stepped down the staircase suddenly and walked past Quellen, ignoring his protests. She was chanting one of her litanies. Her staff burned in the dusk of the corridor. Cyra was relieved to see her.

The pale blue thing let go of Cyra and retreated.

Free of the ghostly grasp, Cyra staggered forward, her arm hurting and shaking. She caught a glimpse of a second shape in the corridor by Tarha's side. A tall orc wearing a chainmail coat, a fierce look on his ghostly face.

Then Tarha belched out a single, uncouth sound that had to be some orcish word, angular syllables running into each other. Holding her staff in her right hand, with the left she grabbed the front of Cyra's tunic and pulled her to her side, and then pushed her back. Staggering in pain, Cyra helped Quellen stand.

The semi-transparent shape of green and blue light was crawling back, covering his face with his crossed arms. He retreated behind the corner and once again Cyra was sure she saw the ghostly orc warrior pursuing them, pushing the other apparition back.

Then it was over.

Tarha grasped her staff with both hands, her shoulders hunched. She was breathing hard, a wheezing sound coming from her throat. She turned to Cyra and Quellen. "Begone," she said.

"Are you all right...?" Cyra began.

"Go, you fools!" the orc hissed.

Quellen ran up the stairs. Cyra still felt dizzy, and her legs were like stone. She staggered, leaned against the wall and then decided she would wait for Tarha, who seemed to be struggling after the fight with the ghost. The orc gave her a hard frown and then accepted Cyra's help. The two women walked slowly up the staircase, side by side, their shoulders brushing the ancient walls.

Cyra felt a sudden pressure at the base of her throat and

stopped. "I can't breathe," she coughed. Something was wrong with her. She didn't know what.

Tarha stopped and helped her sit on one of the steps.

Just then, the faint echo of metal on metal reached them. There was a thunderous crash and the walls shuddered.

"Earthquake..." Cyra said in a broken voice. Was the staircase growing darker?

"No," Tarha said. "Not an earthquake."

The walls shuddered and a landslide of broken masonry, crushed stones and other debris poured down the staircase, shrouded in a thick cloud of dust.

The dwarven fire jewels in the walls twinkled and died, plunging the steps into complete darkness.

A metallic tinkling came from above and then two of the defense chains fell, hitting the pile of rubble at the center of the circular hall and crashing on the obsidian floor. A cloud of dust rose through the air as dark-winged shapes dropped through the green canopy and folded their wings as they landed.

Cries of alarm rang through the air. Weapons clashed as dragon hybrid fought dragon hybrid.

"Alert the others," Vaerix cried to Grisban.

The dwarf was already running.

Vaerix had left their staff with the rest of the luggage. Courtesy demanded for them to go unarmed among their hosts. Now, as one of the attackers approached, they picked a chunk of rock from the floor and tossed it at them. The dragon hybrid parried the projectile, awkwardly raising their pike-like weapon, just as Vaerix closed their distance in two long strides and swept their enemy's feet with their tail. The intruder fell and Vaerix knocked them out with a kick. Then they took the intruder's weapon, crude as it was, and used it to parry a slash from the sword of a second enemy.

Vaerix recognized the brutish sword and the aggressive deportment of this new adversary before she spoke. "On the battlefield, Vaerix," Arwyia said as a greeting.

Vaerix did not reply. If they survived this battle, they would investigate the enmity between the Burning Lake and the Stone Houses' hybrids.

The sound of battle rose around them. Spinning the pike around to keep Arwyia at a distance, Vaerix assessed the attacking forces. The Stone House guards were rushing to counter the invaders.

There were half a dozen hybrids currently engaged with the Stone Houses defenders. The echoes of the great hall made it hard for them to pinpoint other noises, but there seemed to be a major clash of arms at the entrance of the complex.

Arwyia feinted and closed the distance, trying to catch them with a backhanded slash. Vaerix parried with the shaft of their pike and pushed against her, forcing her back against the wall to hinder her movements.

A second attacker cut through one of the defenders and rode the momentum of his charge to close in on Vaerix's left side. Vaerix tripped him with the butt of the pike while using the head of the weapon to deflect Arwyia's blade.

At the edge of their field of view, Vaerix caught two warriors grappling with each other. They spun in the air and slammed into a column. The stone crumbled and a section of the ceiling fell in a landslide of wreckage, burying them.

More invaders came from above, and there was an acrid

smell in the air. In the distance, there was a hollow crash and the whole building shuddered. One of the trees on the edge of the hole in the ceiling was dislodged and crashed onto a group of fighters.

The building, Vaerix realized, was a lot worse for wear than it seemed.

Taking advantage of that brief interruption, Arwyia tried to move to the side, and as soon as she was able, she opened her wings and flexed them over her head so that her next slash was followed by her wing tips, trying to claw Vaerix's eyes out of their sockets.

Vaerix parried, retreated, and felt the fiery bite of the blade as the very tip caught them in the arm. Gritting their teeth, they changed their grip on the pike and slammed the shaft in Arwyia's side. She gasped, ribs creaking, and in that instant of hesitation, Vaerix slammed the flat of the pike's blade on her wrist and disarmed her. Then they swept her off her feet with their tail and turned to push away the next attacker.

"Stop!"

The sound of the battle was dying down.

The commander of the invading forces stepped forward. While their troops wore mismatched furs and leather, and carried old weapons, the commander wore a fine breastplate over glinting blue-gray scales. He had not even drawn his sword.

"Put down your weapon, Vaerix," he said.

Vaerix clutched at the pike's shaft like the earth had opened beneath their feet, and that length of polished wood was all that kept them from falling forever into the earth's core.

"Drys."

Memories flooded Vaerix. The battles fought, the

camaraderie, the intimacy. The hours spent talking, the secrets shared. The centuries since they had last been together dissolved as if they never were.

"Put that down," Drys repeated, and a note of concern crept into his voice.

The air thickened with black smoke. The bitter smell brought Vaerix back to reality. Back to a world where they were an outcast and the dreamer and no longer a companion with Drys.

A fire had been started by the gates.

"We are not here to kill," Drys said.

He was still nimble and fit as a whip. There were new scars on his wings, and his gray scales had earned a darker bluish tinge with age. There was a hard set to his jaw that had not been there in his youth, and Vaerix wondered what else had hardened in Drys, and why.

Behind them, Vaerix heard Arwyia scramble to her feet. They were still holding the pike in a defensive stance.

"Dragonlord Levirax is eager to see you," Drys said to Vaerix. "And your friends."

"They are mine!" Arwyia spat. "By right of combat!"

Drys turned a steady gaze toward her. "They belong to Levirax," Drys replied coldly. "You will have to discuss your rights with her."

Arwyia folded her wings in a sign of submission.

"Let's go," Drys said, turning again to Vaerix. "We don't want this place to collapse on our heads."

With a sigh, Vaerix dropped their pike.

Arwyia followed behind them with her sword poised to strike. Drys led Vaerix down the corridor and to the room where the expedition camped.

One of the Levirax hybrids ran to meet Drys and spoke briefly, in hushed tones, with the commander.

"We want them alive," Vaerix heard Drys say.

Vaerix forced down their turmoil about seeing Drys again and the memories that raged in their mind. The fight was not over, it had just moved to a different battlefield. They should keep their wits about them like Drys was doing. Clearly, seeing them hadn't had the same impact as it had on Vaerix.

They reached the stairwell and the archway to the camp. Three hybrids crowded the space in front of the passage, and three more were on the ground, bleeding. One, a dart sticking out of an eye, was certainly dead, as was the second, the body showing numerous cuts from Grisban's axe. The third was coughing, their wings twitching, the body and the wing membranes riddled with holes.

Past the archway, standing in front of the fire, were Grisban and One Fist, side by side. The dwarf was bleeding from half a dozen small cuts where his chainmail had not stopped the weapons of the hybrids. One Fist was breathing heavily, his breastplate dented, a bloodied sword in his good hand. Behind them, Quellen appeared pale and fatigued, one sleeve of his long tunic torn at the shoulder, and Brockton was helping him remain standing. The younger dwarf was unarmed and very pale.

Neither Tarha nor Cyra were in sight.

Brockton caught Vaerix's searching gaze and shook his head imperceptibly.

Vaerix glanced sideways at Drys, to see whether he had seen the dwarf's signal, but Drys bent to look at the dying hybrid warrior. When he straightened his back and gave the sign to put the wounded out of their misery, he turned to the defenders.

Grisban took a step forward, defiant. "Who's next?" he rumbled.

"We are not here to kill you," Drys said. His voice was level and reasonable, like it had always been. How many times had Vaerix dreamed of him, they wondered.

"For a moment you got me thinking otherwise," Grisban said.

"You have fought well," Drys conceded.

"You haven't seen nothing yet." One Fist grinned.

There was a distant rumble and debris rained from the ceiling.

"Do not waste your lives," Drys said.

"I thought we had this conversation," Vaerix said. "Many years ago."

The shadow of a smile curled Drys' lips, as he leaned closer to Vaerix. "You have not changed," he said in a low voice.

But he had, in ways Vaerix could not yet define.

Grisban eyed Vaerix. "Friend of yours?"

Vaerix looked at Drys. "Oh yes," they said.

CHAPTER TWENTY
In the Dark

Tarha struck a flint and lit a short candle. The bags and pouches on her belt seemed to hold all sorts of items. She used a few drops of wax to fix the candle on the edge of one of the steps and then looked into Cyra's eyes.

"I'm cold," Cyra said through chattering teeth.

She could not move her arm, and she did not feel it anymore. She was scared, but in a faraway, lightheaded way.

Tarha took Cyra's right hand and helped place it on Cyra's heart.

They had moved down the steps, the top of the staircase buried in rubble. Cyra's head was swimming. There had been a sound of battle from above, but Cyra still could not focus on anything but the cold in her chest and the dead weight of her arm.

Tarha took a small flask from her belt and placed it in Cyra's left hand. "Drink this."

Cyra was shuddering as though with fever. She sniffed the strong aroma of raw alcohol. "What's this?"

Fighting, fighting, fighting... her mind ran in circles. Who was fighting?

Things had now fallen eerily silent, except from the occasional creak and groan of the walls, as if the whole building was stretching like a man in his sleep.

"Drink."

The liquor tasted like armor lubricant on her tongue, but soon turned into a burning punch in her gut, like a ball of fire. She coughed and felt a pleasant warmth spread through her body, and her mind's crazy dance slowly wound down and stopped.

"It will keep the cold from reaching your heart," Tarha said.

"What's happening up there?" Cyra asked.

The sound of blades clashing, that was what she had heard. Whose? There was no sound now, not that she could hear, but there had been.

She felt so tired.

The orc did not reply. She peeled Cyra's sleeve off and exposed her arm. Cyra gritted her teeth as the fabric chafed her skin. Now she could feel the pain.

"You'll live," the orc said in a low voice.

From one of her pouches she pulled out a small wooden box and unscrewed the top. A strong herbal smell reached Cyra's nostrils. Under her own hand, her heart was beating steadily, and the shivers that had racked her body were fading. She was herself again.

"It will hurt," Tarha said, scooping up a dollop of the cream in the box with her fingertip.

Cyra bit her tongue not to gasp out loud when the substance first touched her exposed wound. "It does," she said, tears filling her eyes.

"It will be a good reminder," Tarha said, "about acting stupidly."

Wrapped in the lonely sphere of candlelight, it was like they were floating in a sea of darkness.

"What was that thing? What did it do to me?"

So many questions, so much happening at the same time. Her mind was beginning to spiral out of control again.

"It won't come back," Tarha said, and Cyra knew she meant the ghostly apparition.

"Yes, but what was it?"

Speaking helped keep her mind off the searing pain that stabbed through her flesh.

"The opposite of life," Tarha said. "I don't have a name for it. Not one you'd understand." She stopped spreading the ointment. She cleaned her finger on the front of her tunic. "The spreading darkness won't grow anymore," she said, "but it will leave a scar."

"I can live with that."

"You will have to."

Cyra looked down at her arm and grimaced.

"We need to bandage it," Tarha said.

She pulled out the hem of Cyra's undershirt and proceeded to rip it into narrow strips. She wrapped Cyra's arm, tightened the bandages and fixed them with a knot.

"Now we'll have to get out of here."

Having finished her wound-dressing work, Tarha pulled back and sat less stiffly. She ran her fingers over the bandages, smoothing them, and Cyra was surprised at her lightness of touch.

"Thank you," she said.

The walls shuddered again. Tarha picked up her candle and snuffed it out. Cyra felt like she was drowning in the dark, but it was only a moment. Then Tarha's staff came to life, spreading a weak glow.

"Let's go," the orc said, taking her by the hand.

They descended the steps to the junction below and took the other corridor, the one Quellen had explored.

Cyra was suddenly reminded of all that had gone on before.

"What happened upstairs?" she asked.

"I don't know," Tarha replied. "Yet."

They kept going, passing black gaping doorways into black rooms full of wreckage. They walked slowly, until they reached a circular chamber, the walls lined with shelves covered in cobwebs and loaded with books and scrolls. The air was thick with the smell of mold and decay.

"This is what Quellen was looking for," Cyra said. The cobwebs had been torn away from a couple of bookshelves, the books recently disturbed. She took a volume from the shelf. It crumbled into a pile of dust on the floor. The scrolls did not fare better.

"If he was, he was to have been disappointed," Tarha said.

But there were a few gaps in the shelves from missing books, Cyra noticed.

"He has been talking about the buried treasures in the cities since we left Razorcliff," Tarha said.

"Brockton trusts him," Cyra said.

Tarha chuckled. "He also trusts you," she said. "And me. Should he?"

"What do you mean?"

But Tarha did not reply. She had found a chair, the upholstery cracked and as dry as paper. She rapidly dismantled it and piled the pieces in the center of the room. Then she struck her flint and started a fire.

Only then did Cyra realize how cold she still felt.

She sat down and stretched her hands to the flames. "This might attract some unwanted attention," she said.

Tarha shrugged. "Nothing's alive down here. And I need the fire."

She sat on the other side of the fire from Cyra and closed her hand around the talisman hanging from her neck. The light from the fire painted red brushstrokes over her cheeks, turning her eyes into black pits.

"What about what's not alive?" asked Cyra.

"They will not bother us."

"We should go back up."

The idea of being buried under the old building made Cyra's breath short. The darkness of the rooms and the corridors pressed down on her. What if they could not find their way out?

A hissing sigh escaped her lips. Would she be just another haunting shadow in these ruins?

Tarha gave her a look and Cyra thought she'd roll her eyes. But the orc just took a deep breath. "We need to find a way out, yes. This is why I need the fire."

Cyra forced herself to take deeper breaths, trying to stay in control. "How?"

"We need to wait."

Cyra worked her wounded arm and grimaced at the pain. She welcomed it. It turned her thoughts away from the nightmare of being buried alive.

"What creature was that?" Cyra asked. She was not sure whether she had asked already. "The one that hurt me?"

"Some kind of ghost," Tarha replied. "I have never seen the like."

Cyra exhaled slowly. "It looked... different."

The orc looked her in the eye. "Have you seen many?"

Cyra shook her head. "There was an ancient mansion they said was haunted. A senator's ancestral home. Five miles west of Yalefen."

"Never heard of it."

"I spent two nights there. I heard voices. Had some..."

Tarha arched an eyebrow questioningly.

"Bad dreams. That's all I ever saw of ghosts in my life. Before the one that hurt me, at least."

That, and the ghostly orc warrior by Tarha's side. But she did not think mentioning it would do her any good.

The fire was going down, and darkness was slowly reclaiming the room.

"Magic was done here," Tarha said. "In this building. The rune magic of the dwarves. The magic that angered the dragons four thousand years ago."

Cyra nodded. What Quellen had been looking for, probably.

"That magic left a residue." She nodded at the fire. "Like ashes after a fire. It always does. That residue tainted the ghosts of those who died here, like when the ashes stain your fingers. The thing that attacked you spent a lot of time here."

"A lot of time in a room full of ashes," Cyra said slowly. "Your hands will never become clean again."

"Yes."

The last flames sputtered and died. The blackened remains of a chair leg cracked and fell, and a small storm of smoke and ashes rose in the red light of the embers.

"Now we'll know," Tarha said.

Any question Cyra was about to ask was silenced when the smoke from the dying fire started to rise, whirling in a widening spiral, growing with a rhythm of its own. In the still air, the smoke continued to turn and expand until a tall figure appeared, shrouded in smoke and ash, standing in the embers.

An orc.

The same orc Cyra had seen before. Tall and broad shouldered, wearing a chainmail coat and a leather loincloth, his hair falling over his shoulders in thin braids. He stood with his back to Cyra and she could not see his face. But his hands were large and powerful and he had the relaxed stance of one used to battle.

The shape was perfectly still, and so faint Cyra could still see Tarha where she sat across from her.

"What wisdom do you bring me tonight, spirit?" Tarha asked.

She sat still, listening, and Cyra was amazed by the change in Tarha's features. Her grim expression melted into one of warmth and affection. A ghostly smile lingered over her lips, only for her face to shift into a mask of pain. Tears filled Tarha's eyes but did not run down her cheeks, and when she spoke again, her voice was broken.

"What of the others?" she asked.

Again, she was silent, and somehow brought her emotions back under control. She gave a brief nod. "How do we get out of here?"

A few moments, and the last of the light from the fire was gone, and with it, the shadow of the orc warrior.

"Are you all right?" Cyra asked softly.

Tarha looked up at her, her eyes glinting, like she was surprised to discover her sitting there in the dark.

"We are in trouble," she admitted.

•••

"There has been battle up above," Tarha said as they hastened along the next corridor.

"The hybrids had pledged us their hospitality," Cyra objected. Had they caught the thieving Quellen, and that had sparked a fight? Or maybe the onus fell on Grisban, with his penchant for rubbing others the wrong way.

"Not our hybrids of the Stone Houses," Tarha replied. "The ones we met three days ago. The ones we ran away from. They came in force from outside. They captured our companions."

Cyra needed not ask her how she knew this. "What do we do now?"

"We get out. Then we see."

It was a long trek in the dark, the way barely visible in the glow-worm light of Tarha's staff.

Cyra did not know whether the chambers they moved through had been buried by time or had originally been built underground. They followed crumbling corridors and passed over a shuddering bridge crossing a buried chasm. They waded through flooded rooms and helped each other climb up piles of rubble that had once been staircases.

Cyra sometimes wondered what marvels lurked just beyond the edge of the light – many colored dwarven mosaics and wise inscriptions, bas-reliefs and paintings could be seen. Age-old books eaten by mold, ancient weapons rusting, jewels buried in grime and debris.

Twice they heard movement in the darkness and they stopped, holding their breath. But whatever caused those noises never came close.

Cyra had no idea how long they had been wandering, or where they were. Yet Tarha moved with purpose, like she knew the way.

After an unfathomable amount of time, they sat down on a fallen column for a brief rest in the light of Tarha's staff. Cyra's boots had filled with water and she pulled them off, upturned them and wiggled her toes in the stuffy, humid air.

"My husband," Tarha said suddenly, in response to a question Cyra had never asked, but which grew heavy between them throughout their trek. "Ughat the Mace." She hooked the string of her pendant with a finger and lifted it. "This is from his right hand. His thumb."

Cyra shuddered.

"I could not let him go," Tarha said in a faraway voice, and Cyra suddenly realized how vulnerable Tarha really was.

"How did he die?"

"Fighting," Tarha replied with a hint of pride. "Baronial soldiers. They attacked our villages, burned our settlements. Called us invaders. They came in winter, with the snow. A dozen of them he fed to the hounds of Nordros, but even he could not take them all. He had a warrior's death."

She fell silent and tucked the macabre token of her dead husband into her tunic. "And now I see him in the light of the dying fire. That's all that's allowed."

"I saw him," Cyra said. "I think. Before, when you saved me from the pale blue ghost. He was standing by your side."

Tarha frowned. "It figures," she said slowly. "You were being dragged to the realm of the dead yourself. You were able to see beyond the veil."

"So even if you don't see him," Cyra went on, "he is always by your side."

She felt the need to offer some consolation to her companion. She almost took Tarha by the hand, but when she stretched her arm, the stab of pain in her bicep stopped her.

Tarha closed her eyes and took a deep breath. "And a lot of good he does to me, having him by my side," she mumbled in a tone that reminded Cyra of Grisban's grumpy mutterings.

Then she stood and flashed her tusks in a brief smile. Her staff's head burned brighter as she tightened her grip on it and held out her hand to Cyra. "Let's move," she said. "The others might need us."

The echo of their steps told Cyra they had entered a larger space, stretching beyond the pale bubble of ghost light that radiated from Tarha's staff. The orc's hand tightened in hers and they moved on slowly. It took Cyra a moment to realize there were bones scattered on the floor, some still wearing scraps of their clothing, odd pieces of armor. Their going slowed further as they picked their way across the vast boneyard.

"The dwarves came down here to find refuge," Tarha mused, looking around. "While their warriors defended the city above."

"A last redoubt."

"But not a good idea," the orc said. She stopped, looked around and changed her course, pulling Cyra along. "The dragons attacked with their fire," she went on. "Like Vaerix told us, remember? They flew over the walls and breathed their flames on the buildings. It was not a battle, not really. The defendaners never had a chance."

Cyra frowned. "But these here..."

A sitting skeleton stared at her with their empty sockets. From the few patches of bleached cloth hanging from their frame, Cyra could not tell whether they had been a man or a woman, young or old.

"Certainly, the fire could not reach down here," she said.

They had found books and documents, crumbling with age and eaten by fungi, but not burned. They had seen tapestries bleached by time still hanging in abandoned corridors.

"The flame did not," Tarha said. "But the fires above sucked up all the air from below, the staircases functioning like chimneys."

The skeleton Cyra had been staring at suddenly collapsed in a cloud of dust, the skull hitting the floor and rolling into the darkness.

"It was a quiet death," Tarha said.

Cyra turned her gaze away.

They walked on past columns and statues, the silence so heavy Cyra could not take it any longer. "Are they still here?" she asked in a faint voice.

"Some of them."

"Shouldn't we do something?"

Tarha stopped and turned to look at Cyra. The ghost light of the staff painted deep shadows under her eyes and her cheekbones. "What should we do?"

"Can't you help them move on?"

Tarha chuckled, and Cyra shuddered.

"It doesn't work like that. And we don't have time anyway."

Cyra looked around, seeing only darkness. "It's wrong," she said.

"They don't mind we are here," she said. She squeezed Cyra's hand. "But let's not overstay our welcome."

As they continued, Cyra whispered an old song from Lorimor, a song about autumn leaves and quiet herds roaming the grasslands, and men going home from the fields after a long day.

It was not much, she thought, but she felt she had to do something.

The ghosts listened in silence, or so she imagined.

They came to an archway and with a last look back, Cyra followed Tarha through it.

How long they spent in the buried chambers of the ancient dwarven ruin, Cyra was unable to say. She placed one foot after the other and followed Tarha, stumbling on the rubble, her hand brushing the wall by her side.

Time became an abstraction. Her mind wandered, thinking of Brockton and the others. Little sparks of memory mixed with wild speculation. She imagined Grisban would fight to buy time for One Fist to take Brockton to safety. As for Vaerix, they were a formidable adversary, but they'd be facing their own people.

She had come to feel sympathy for that mixed band, and this was not good. Her true purpose of spying on Brockton to ascertain his true purpose required a core of cynicism that Cyra lacked, and she feared the decisions to come. Maybe coming to terms with the fact that her friends were more than likely dead would make it easier for her to leave them behind and save her life.

But it hurt.

Finally, a gust of cold air and a spark of distant light signaled they had come to the surface. They moved cautiously to the end of the corridor they had been following, and Tarha pulled aside a curtain of hanging ivy.

Cyra drew a few deep breaths and stretched her arms above her head. The air was clean and smelled of greenery and rain and cleansed her lungs from the lingering smells of the darkness below. They were out of the underground.

It was late morning, and the sun cast shadows of the clouds on the green stretch of the forest's canopy. No sound of violence reached them, and the birds in the trees seemed to chirpily comment on the quiet of the day.

They had emerged on the side of the hill and had to walk about a mile, following the curve of the slope, to reach once again the narrow passage where they had been ambushed just the day before.

"Harridan's fingers," Cyra whispered.

The top of the hill had collapsed, crushing the top rooms of the buried complex. Tongues of dirt and loose debris stretched down the sides of the mound, partially blocking the canyon below.

Three lines of spears were stuck in the cracks between the flagstones of the old road. On top of every spear was the head of a dragon hybrid.

Walking through that gruesome display, Cyra recognized the pale scales of Brazzax, the Blind One, and many other dragon hybrids of the Stone Houses. Had they been killed in battle? she wondered with a deep shudder. Or had they been captured and then executed?

She stood in front of the grisly trophies until Tarha pushed her gently aside.

The orc approached Brazzax's head and placed her right hand over the crested forehead, her fingers splayed through the bony ridges. She started chanting a strange song, her breathing rhythm picking up speed as the words became more frantic.

A cold chill came out of nothing, and Cyra shuddered and took a few steps back.

Tarha kept repeating her words, her hands pressed on the

dragon hybrid's head, until at the base of the spear a mist rose through the cracks in the pavement. It rose, spiraling up the shaft, and was sucked into the severed neck.

Brazzax opened their eyes.

"Where are the map maker and his companions?" Tarha asked in an imperious tone.

The hybrid's mouth closed and opened two times as their eyes rolled wildly.

"What happened to them?" Tarha asked.

"Gone..." Brazzax said, his voice crushed by weariness.

"Where?"

"The Heath..."

"They were taken to the Molten Heath?"

The eyes stopped in their wild motion and fixed on Tarha. "Levirax," the severed head said. "It was Levirax."

"Levirax!" another voice shouted at the farther end of the line of heads.

"Levirax!" a second voice joined in, and then another.

"Levirax!" they chanted. "Levirax!"

"Where is Levirax?" Tarha asked, her voice rough for the exertion.

"The Tower," Brazzax replied while the other voices died down. "The Broken Tower. On the edge of the fire mountains. She'll come there for the prisoners."

The dead eyes narrowed. "Kill Levirax," dead Brazzax said.

"Kill Levirax!" the Blind One commanded.

"Kill Levirax! Kill Levirax!" the other dead hybrids screeched.

Tarha pulled her hand back again and staggered where Cyra caught her and supported her. The jaw of Brazzax slackened. All the voices died out suddenly, like blowing out a candle.

•••

They found Cloud grazing on the tender grasses at the edge of the marshland. The horse snorted at their approach. He took two tentative steps, like he wanted to signal he was ready to bolt had they tried anything to harm him.

But Cyra cooed and whispered endearments, and called him "you stupid nag", and finally came close enough to run her fingers through his mane and caress his neck.

"We are lucky," Tarha said. "I wonder what happened to the other mounts."

"If the ponies made it," Cyra said, "by now they are halfway to Dunwarr. But not my horse, oh, no. He had to stop and eat along the way."

But they still had lost most of their luggage, and their equipment was buried under a pile of broken stones and wreckage.

"At least we have a horse," Cyra said. "We can ride together."

She waited for her companion to say something, but Tarha suddenly sat on a fallen log, perfectly still.

For a moment, Cyra thought she was conferring with the spirit world.

But then the orc opened her eyes and spoke.

"I am going north," she said.

Cyra snorted and walked nearer. Cloud followed her. "You want to look for this Broken Tower?"

"The men need our help."

Cyra turned her eyes to the north. The fires of the Heath were painting the clouds red. "It does not seem such a great idea," she said. "It seems that we are walking to our deaths."

"We can't abandon them."

Cyra paced up and down in front of Tarha. "What can we do?"

The orc just stared at her.

"There's two of us. You want to take on a whole dragon army? We don't even know if our friends are still alive."

She had hoped they were alive as she'd roamed in the dark and had talked herself into accepting them as dead because it was more expedient. But now in the sunlight she was seeing things differently. The chance they were alive was slim.

"Had they wanted them dead, we'd have found their heads back there with the others."

It made sense. Cyra *wanted* it to make sense.

She sighed, crossed her arms, and shook her head. "Listen, the way I see it, we landed in the middle of a war that is not our own. This is the dwarves' business. The wise way is to turn west and head for Black Ember Gorge. Riding Cloud, we could be there in three to five days. Three days more, maybe four, and we'll be in Dunwarr. Nice and smooth."

"You mean we should run," Tarha said. "And leave our men behind."

"I mean we should save ourselves. And they are not 'our' men."

There was no sense in risking their lives again, Cyra repeated to herself. If they were still alive, Brockton and the others were beyond their reach, on their way to some dragon fortress full of hybrids bristling with weapons. She had the information the empire might be interested in knowing. Cyra and Tarha had no supplies. No weapons. Reaching the border between the grasslands and the volcanic peaks with Cloud alone would be a challenge in itself.

It all made perfect sense. But left her dissatisfied. Tarha's cold determination had pulled some long dormant strings in her heart. There was such a thing as loyalty, after all. There was honor.

"We must be smart," Cyra said, and her words sounded craven to her own ears.

"Fine," Tarha said, standing. "I will go then."

And she started north in long, energetic strides, leaning on her staff as she moved through the grass.

"Wait!"

Tarha stopped and turned.

"It will be dark soon," Cyra said.

She was experiencing the sort of unease that came from unresolved issues. And maybe from the idea of being left behind, alone in a swamp, ten days from safety. She had never been troubled by going alone, but somehow now it was different.

Tarha looked at the sky. "It's at least three hours to sunfall," she said. "We can both make a good head start before dark. In our respective directions."

"You have no provisions."

"I will hunt. It's not like I can't take care of myself."

"And once you find this Broken Tower, wherever that may be? What will you do when you get there, if you do?"

There was a rock-solid stubbornness in Tarha's impassive face. "I will free the men."

"How?"

The orc grinned. "I am not without some powers."

Cyra huffed in exasperation. "You need a plan, a strategy."

"No. I need help."

That stopped Cyra in her tracks. Maybe too much time playing the cloak and dagger game had made her dry and calculating.

That was not the way of the sword poets.

"We can ride Cloud together," she said. "Neither of us is too heavy."

Being a sword poet, after all, was not about weighing gains and losses like a shopkeeper. It was about thought turning into action.

"We'll need to fashion a bridle," Tarha replied and started undoing the straps of her harness.

Hand, eye, and heart, Cyra thought, were the keys to being a sword poet. And now that her heart was set, she'd make sure her hand and her eye followed. And that seemed to answer all her questions but one.

"How do we find this Broken Tower?" Cyra asked, undoing one of her belts.

"We ride north to the fire mountains," Tarha replied. "Once there, I will ask for directions."

CHAPTER TWENTY-ONE
Prisoners

In the fading light of the sunset, Drys was browsing Brockton's notebook when Vaerix went to see him. Arwyia walked behind them, weapon at hand. She was not going to let her earlier promise go to meet them on the battlefield and let both their blades speak.

"You should not have come back," Drys said now, without turning.

It was the first time they were talking properly after the fight in the ruins and Vaerix's capture. Now the open fields of the Verdant Ring were in front of them and a large part of Drys' warriors had gone forward, rising in the sky on their wings, flying further north to the fires of the Molten Heath.

Vaerix and the other prisoners would follow on the ground with an armed escort.

Drys closed the book with a bang. "This time Levirax will take more than your wings, old friend," he said.

Vaerix detected a note of true regret in their old lover's voice. "Warriors die," they said with a shrug.

Drys smiled at that show of bravado. "It is so, isn't it?" He turned to Arwyia. "You may go."

Arwyia made to protest, her wing tips rising, but Drys cut her short. "Do I need to repeat my orders?"

Arwyia lowered her head and pulled her wings together. "Vaerix is dangerous," she said.

"So am I," Drys replied coldly. "You may go."

They watched her retreat.

"Once we were just as full of fire and fight," Drys said.

"But we grew older," Vaerix replied, and it suddenly felt like all those centuries before, their last talk about how things were and how things could have been.

"You were not forgotten," he said. "That's why you should have stayed away."

"I remembered you, too," Vaerix said quietly.

It was like flying against a strong wind, the way Drys seemed to push back against Vaerix anytime they brought up the past and how it made them feel now.

"Levirax remembers you," he said.

"I did not believe she had survived."

"Truly?" Drys asked. "Did you ever consider how your actions saved Levirax's life?"

"How so?"

"Had you not disobeyed her orders and commanded the retreat of our forces from the Broken Lands–"

"The Dragon Rex's orders were clear."

"So they were. And by promptly and loyally obeying them, Levirax escaped the fate of Zir the Black and many others." Drys paused, letting that sink in.

"I did not act to damage Levirax," Vaerix said.

"But by acting the way you did, you actually helped her."

Drys sighed. "And they repaid you by cutting your wings."

"It's a done thing," Vaerix replied.

The pain of their loss had faded and so had their resentment. They still missed the sky, but lingering thoughts about what had been were pointless. It had taken many years for Vaerix to reach that conclusion, but now they were at peace with what had been done to them.

"There were things I found on the ground that I would have missed by flying."

Drys looked at them and sighed. "Why did you come back? Tell me truthfully."

Vaerix shrugged again. "The road I was following led to this place."

"This," Drys said, lifting Brockton's notes. "Are the dwarves preparing an attack?"

"I don't know. I do not believe so."

"Because this is the rumor that's circulating among the tribes and the troops. That Dunwarr is coming to the Karok Doum in force and there will be battle. A war the like nobody ever saw. Is it so?"

"I don't know. But I doubt it. Brockton is a man of peace."

"Already the warriors are fighting among themselves, for the stronger to step up and be ready for the clash to come."

"You know there is another way," Vaerix said.

"No. You claim to know there is another way." Bitterness crept into Drys' voice. "I only know what you told me all those years ago. About peace and dignity and everything else. I still remember. Do you still dream?"

"Yes."

There was a hard light in Drys' eyes. "And what do your dreams tell you?"

"They tell me of a great darkness," Vaerix replied. "And hope, too."

"Nothing I could not have told you myself, and without invoking more than common sense."

"Yet you do not act upon such common sense."

They stared at each other for a long moment.

"It is good to see you again," Vaerix said.

Drys weighed the book in his hand. "The scouts spotted seven of you," he said, ignoring Vaerix's statement. "What of the two that are missing?"

Vaerix took a deep breath. So it was to be like this. They could only respect Drys' choice to ignore Vaerix's opening. Respect had always been part of what had brought them together.

"Two females, a human and an orc," they replied. "Cyra and Tarha. They fought when the Stone Houses tribe surrounded us. Neither survived their wounds."

Vaerix was amazed at how easily they lied to their old companion. So much for respect, they said to themselves. But there was still hope the sword poet and the spirit speaker had somehow escaped the ruins and Vaerix would do all they could to cover their tracks, offer them a chance to escape.

Drys looked at them, frowning. "Unfortunate," he said.

"They made a choice."

"Certainly, they did."

They stood one in front of the other for a little more without talking.

"You may go," Drys said in the end.

"Can I join my friends for the night?"

Drys waved a hand. "Please yourself."

Was there a note of ruefulness in his voice? Vaerix could not say but was grateful for Drys' small kindness. Drys could not be sure they would not betray his trust but was willing to act on their ancient friendship. Vaerix turned and walked to the campfire. They'd have to tell the others about their lie, so they would not contradict their story if interrogated.

They felt a sudden painful regret, but events had forced them to take sides and the choice had come naturally this time.

"I know about you," Arwyia said, appearing at their side. "You were once a mighty warrior. One that struck fear in the hearts of their enemies."

Vaerix shrugged. "That was long ago."

"I see that." She grinned. "Still, it will be a pleasure killing one that was once the champion of Levirax."

Vaerix suddenly felt very old and very lonely.

Riding Cloud from early sunrise to sunset, Cyra and Tarha closed the distance with the party of dragon hybrids that had captured Brockton and the others. They kept out of sight, waiting for the right moment to try and rescue their companions. When the hybrids stopped, so did the two women, allowing their horse to rest for a while. At these times, while Cyra looked for berries and other food, Tarha would send forth one of her spirits to scout the enemy camp and learn how their friends were faring. The land was scattered with ghosts, she claimed, the remains of centuries of strife, and she could cajole or control them.

But what really surprised Cyra was the realizations she, just as Tarha, had started thinking of Brockton and the others as friends and not just as companions on the road.

At night, the two women huddled together, sharing their

body heat and their meager provisions. They did not dare light a fire, for fear of giving away their presence, and talked in hushed tones, because voices carried. They were by now so close to the Molten Heath that the black clouds of ash overhanging it made the stars invisible in the night sky. Yet, when the sun went down, the hot wind from the fire mountains was not enough to keep the travelers warm.

In the absence of a fire, Tarha was unable to contact the spirit of her dead husband, and this both limited her powers and placed her in a melancholy mood. She caressed the bone pendant on her neck with a faraway look in her eyes.

The darkness and the silence felt oppressive to Cyra. She tried to start a conversation, if only to break the quiet, but nothing seemed to drag her companion out of her foul mood.

She decided to go dig at the crux of Tarha's problems. "It must be strange," she said bluntly, "to have your man still with you after his death."

Cyra felt the orc's eyes on her. Silence became as heavy as a mountain. Then Tarha pulled her legs closer to her chest and wrapped her arms around her knees.

"Sorry," Cyra whispered.

She wondered if the orc even heard her. Tarha sat like that for what felt like forever.

"I did not want to let him go," Tarha said in a soft whisper that Cyra strained to catch. "And because I did not want to lose him, now either way I will." A bitter chuckle escaped Tarha's lips, like a nightbird cry. "Foolish, I was."

"There was an old woman," she went on. "Her name was Nargol. Mad Nargol, scary Nargol. She lived in the wild, in a cave, because she wasn't allowed in our village. I went to her. She threw stones at me. Screamed at me to go away. To leave her alone. Five days and five nights I sat outside her cave, but in the end, she accepted me as an apprentice."

Cloud snorted in the darkness and for a moment they were silent, scanning the shadows for some incoming foe. But none came.

"I was a fast learner," Tarha whispered. Cyra was not sure if the orc was talking to her, or to herself. "Even Nargol was impressed. And, I believe, a little scared of me. But I learned everything she could teach me. And then I made this."

Cyra imagined more than saw her holding the sculpted piece of bone in the palm of her hand.

"Nargol was so mad at me. You never, she said, never call and bind the spirit of someone you love. Never. Nothing good can come out of such choice." Again, that birdlike chuckle. "She was right, of course. But I was young and in love, and so I called him to me, and I bound him through this shard of his bone. And thus, I lost him forever."

She shook her head and laughed bitterly. "What a fool."

At this point, Cyra's curiosity burned like a bonfire. "I do not understand," she murmured.

Tarha turned to her, startled, like she was waking from a dream. Like she had just realized she was not alone. "We are the same, you and I," Tarha said. "And likely Quellen, too. But who can say with elves?"

"The same?" Cyra asked warily. This was not going in the direction she had expected, and she was not sure she liked it.

"We serve a master. We spy for them."

Cyra's stance stiffened. "I don't know what you mean."

"Please."

The tone of Tarha's voice was so abrupt, Cyra felt her cheeks burn with shame. "I serve my empress," she admitted.

There was no sense in lying. "As all the citizens of Lorimor do."

"They may as well, but you are the only one that came here to spy on the dwarves' expedition."

"It's not…" Cyra stopped. "You, too? And Quellen?"

Tarha cleared her voice. "Cannot be sure about the elf, but he clearly has some motives of his own."

Cyra shrugged. "I think he's just being an elf." She hesitated. "And you?"

Tarha bowed her head. "There is one," she said. "One that, like me, is intimate with death. A deeper intimacy that stretches long into the past. He commands ghosts and specters and many other unsavory things. And he likes to know everything that happens in Terrinoth."

Cyra felt a chill. "I believe I have heard of the one you mention."

Everybody had. A master necromancer. The night suddenly felt a lot colder.

"And we won't say his name," Tarha admonished.

"We won't, no." Cyra shuddered. She was trying to push the name out of her head. Not even think about it. "And you are in… his service?"

She couldn't keep the horror from cracking her voice. How could someone willingly choose to serve that one?

"Not I." Tarha lifted her pendant. "Him. He is bound to me but serves another master."

She was silent for a long spell while Cyra tried to wrap her head around that new revelation.

"It was my fault," Tarha said finally. "I brought him back where someone stronger could snatch him away from me. Nargol knew. And it happened. And now his dark master wants to know what the dwarves are plotting. He likes to know everything that happens in the realm of the living. Somehow, he got wind of this expedition. And I had to come here, to serve as anchor for my man's spirit, so that he can spy for his true master and report back to him."

She touched the pendant through the leather of her tunic.

"I am just here to carry this." She chuckled again. "Nargol was right. I was a fool."

The warm wind from the Heath couldn't dispel the cold Cyra felt deep in her bones.

After the battle in the ruins, the dragon hybrids' leader, Drys, had dismissed most of his warriors. Only eight remained, the one called Arwyia among them. These would escort Brockton and the other prisoners, that the hybrid kept calling guests, on foot to their destination.

Metal manacles had been locked on the wrists of Brockton, Grisban, and One Fist. Quellen's hands had been tied behind his back and his mouth closed with a strip of silk with a big knot in the middle.

Only Vaerix had been left free of any restraint. They walked behind Drys, who sometimes spoke to them in the strange language of the dragonkind, showing an almost friendly attitude. Arwyia never left Vaerix's side, and never sheathed her sword.

Past the trees and the marshlands, the Verdant Ring spread in an endless stretch of prairie, over which low clouds ran on the wind like flocks of wild sheep. The land was flat and uninterrupted, and they marched north, to the bruised sky that marked the Molten Heath.

The hybrids' pace was exhausting, a breathless canter that

crushed the prisoners. Brockton lacked One Fist's innate vitality, and Grisban's relentless stubbornness, and every mile felt like a stab in his right side. But then he looked at the elf, pale and soaked in sweat, and a cold fury replaced his pain and fatigue.

Still, the prisoners were treated with cold courtesy and allowed frequent pauses during the march. Twice a day they received water, and every evening the guards shared their food with them – mostly the roasted meat of small animals the hybrids had caught during the day. Only Quellen, constantly bound and gagged, did not receive any food or water.

Both Brockton and Vaerix protested against this, but Drys ignored their requests.

Three days into the grasslands, Quellen collapsed and would not move when one of the warriors kicked him. Drys gave the other hybrid a scathing dressing down and then ordered them to settle for the night, despite there still being two hours of light remaining. Brockton pleaded with the dragon hybrid commander for water and permission to remove the elf's gag.

Drys barked an order and one of his warriors pulled out a water gourd and gestured Brockton toward the fallen elf.

"We are not monsters," Drys said, before he turned and walked away.

"And still they would call us guests," One Fist mumbled, as with the others he hastened to Quellen's side.

"Nobody likes the Latari," Grisban commented.

He held the elf's head and shoulders up while Brockton poured some water between the mage's chafed lips. The hybrid guard kept a sword drawn, ready to strike should the mage try any spell.

"It's not that," Brockton said.

"Keep the mage gagged," One Fist commented.

"Exactly," Brockton nodded. He eyed the guard.

Most of Quellen's spells required him to speak words of power and wave his hands in mystical gestures. Brockton had no idea of how such things worked, but it made perfect sense for their captors to keep the elf bound and muzzled. And it could have been a lot worse than that: according to the chronicles, cutting out the captive spellcasters' tongues had been a practice of the dragon-kin armies during the Third Darkness.

Quellen coughed. Grisban pushed him into a sitting position.

"Easy," Brockton said and poured some more water.

Quellen worked his mouth and opened his eyes.

The hybrid standing behind Brockton took the water gourd from his hands. Then he put the gag back on Quellen.

"He needs food," One Fist said. "No one can go this long without food."

But the hybrid just turned and rejoined his companions.

"We are not beasts," the orc mumbled.

Later, the hybrids lit a small fire and food was brought to the prisoners. Brockton was allowed to bring Quellen some food, with two warriors standing over them. Brockton had a wooden bowl of cooked meat and used his fingers to feed the elf.

"They are afraid of your powers," Brockton said in a low voice, stating the obvious.

"Which is bad," the mage replied.

"You, silent!" one of the guards growled. They took a step forward menacingly. Quellen shrugged and allowed Brockton to put one more bite of badly burned marmot meat in his mouth. He chewed slowly.

Then Quellen was gagged once again and Brockton walked back to where Grisban and One Fist were sitting.

"He's surviving," he said.

The others nodded.

A hybrid paced behind them, occasionally stretching his wings.

Grisban gave him a look. "What are you afraid of?" he asked. "That we'll ask for seconds?"

The hybrid looked at him, uncomprehending.

"They think they're pretty smart, these lizards," Grisban mumbled.

"But they are not." One Fist grinned.

Brockton looked at the orc. "What do you mean?"

One Fist was the one that had suffered the least from the forced march. He was younger than both Brockton and Grisban, and he had the natural resilience of his people.

But there was something else.

Catching Brockton's eye, now the orc lifted his hands, holding his wooden bowl, and rattled his chains. His grin broadened.

Brockton frowned.

All three of them had their wrists locked in three-inch-wide iron bands, connected by a span of thick chain. They had not been manacled together, but each of them marched with their hands tied.

The iron manacle on One Fist's left wrist had been latched over the armband holding his metal hook in place. The orc only had to undo the strap holding his hook and it would come off, and with it the manacle.

Brockton looked up from One Fist's hands into his eyes.

"Not so smart," One Fist said.

And then he went back to his food.

"Any marmot left over?" Grisban called.

The hybrids talked among themselves. Then one of them came over, carrying the smoking remains of the dinner.

Brockton started silently sifting through a list of possibilities, a plan slowly taking shape in his fatigued mind.

Archerax did not realize another dragon was drawing near until the shadow of his unexpected guest fell over him.

His instinctive violent reaction turned to submission when he realized who had entered his domain.

His defensive growl died in his throat. "Dragon Rex," he hissed, folding his wings and curling his tail around his hind legs.

Shaarina moved ponderously closer.

"I am pleased to see you, too, Archerax."

Archerax had established his residence in the secondary crater of an old volcano, to the east of the Molten Heath. Lava poured from above, spilling from the higher main crater and filling Archerax's nook. An island of volcanic glass sat in the middle of that incandescent lake, and Archerax was in the habit of idling there, enjoying the heat and entertaining thoughts of future power and conquest.

Now Shaarina settled at the edge of the lake.

"How can I serve you?" Archerax asked.

Shaarina had not left her lair in five centuries. This was clearly not a courtesy visit.

"I have been thinking about our last meeting," she said slowly. She pensively dipped a talon in the magma, stirring it.

"I see," he replied, to dissemble the fact that he did not see at all. The instinct of his species made him quite suspicious of Shaarina's motives and poured the cold water of caution on his fiery attitude.

"You wish for greatness," Shaarina said.

Archerax shuddered. The conversation was veering into a territory fraught with danger. Ambition was a double-edged sword among the dragons, and twice so when the Dragon Rex was concerned.

"Under your enlightened guidance," he said.

"Obviously," Shaarina replied. She looked around. "Are there no hybrids in your service?"

Archerax shifted on his glass pedestal. The magma boiled, as if in response to his nervousness.

"Only a few," he said.

And he had sent them off with Wing Captain Xenith, to supplement Levirax's force against the dwarves.

"Of course," Shaarina said.

Again, she played with her claws in the molten rock.

Archerax exhaled. The silence was grinding on his nerves.

"It won't happen," she said suddenly. Now her eyes were set on him, piercing. "This war with Dunwarr that Levirax fantasizes about."

"Is it so?" Archerax asked.

Levirax was gathering her armies as they were speaking, and Archerax was expecting her command to join her. But Shaarina seemed to have other information, and for all her old age and reclusive nature, Shaarina was Dragon Rex. Her words carried the weight of authority.

"I feel your disappointment," she said, an ironic note creeping into her voice. "Greatness wants for opportunity, and what better opportunity than a war against our ancient enemies?"

"What else, indeed?"

Shaarina drew herself up, towering over Archerax.

"But this war will not happen. Wishing for it is not enough."

Archerax bowed his head, striving to become even smaller in the Dragon Rex's shadow.

"You should look elsewhere," she said, her voice now a low purr, "for an opportunity."

Archerax waited, holding his breath. Was Shaarina suggesting he break his alliance with Levirax?

"Say," she went on, almost casually, "to the south and the east, past the dwarven foundries."

Archerax frowned. "The Ru Steppes?" he breathed.

The madness of all this suddenly faded in excitement. Was Shaarina truly suggesting him to strike an alliance with the Locust Horde?

"The truly great do not wait for others to give them a war," Shaarina said. She stood and slowly crawled to the edge of Archerax's nook.

"Choose your allies wisely, young Archerax," she said by way of goodbye.

Archerax watched her take to the sky on great black wings, his mind already playing with the pieces of a new game.

CHAPTER TWENTY-TWO
Drys

"And this is the plan," Brockton said.

"I think it's plain stupid," One Fist replied.

Another long day had gone by, the prisoners walking across the sea of grass. Brockton noticed how the tall blades were turning yellow as the air grew warmer and drier. The ground, too, was different, the earth darker and sandier, the grains irregular. There were black mountains now in front of them, and the hazy crimson glow of the fires that burned in them made the dark ash clouds look close enough to touch. As they drew closer to the Molten Heath, tremors became more frequent, and twice that day they had felt the earth move under their feet.

When they had finally stopped, they had fallen to the ground, their legs and shoulders aching. Quellen just lay on the greass, still like a corpse. One Fist checked on him and walked back shaking his head.

"He's not going to last much longer."

The silence that followed those words crystallized Brockton's resolve. Not even Grisban found words to comment.

Waiting for their guards to bring them water and, hopefully, some food, Brockton had briefly sketched out his plan.

Once again, the orc was unconvinced. Grisban kept his counsel.

"Why?" asked One Fist.

"Priorities," Brockton said now.

One Fist gave him a hard stare, frowning. "My priority is to see you safe out of here. That's what I am paid for."

"We are in too deep," Brockton said. "We are in the open and our captors can fly. In no way can we hope to make a run for it. But one of us alone could."

"I will not leave you alone."

"You forget who's paying you," Grisban said. "You take his coin, he calls the tune."

One Fist turned to him, but before he could speak, one of the hybrids came to them and tossed him a water gourd. "Drink," she said.

One Fist pulled the cork with his teeth and lifted the gourd in a silent toast before he drank. Then he handed the bottle to Brockton.

"What good would I do?" he asked.

Brockton had anticipated that objection.

"You could go back to Dunwarr," he said, talking fast, in a low voice. "And inform the Council that there are dragons at large in the Heath, and they are planning something. The dragon hybrids and their dragonlords could be a menace for the whole of Dunwarr, Terrinoth, and Aymhelin."

"At least one—" Grisban nodded, "—according to Vaerix."

Brockton kept talking. "I mean, we always knew there were some dragons left behind, but this is different. It's a dragonlord from the time of the Third Darkness we are going to meet. A horror from the past of the world. We must warn the Guilds and the Baronies–"

One Fist shook his head. "I can't leave you behind. I'm paid to keep you safe."

"I'd be with him," Grisban said, but the orc ignored him.

He looked at Brockton. "I can carry you for a while. Then you'll get rid of your chains and we can–"

"No. For some reason, I am the one they want–"

That was what Drys had said when they had been taken. Dragonlord Levirax wanted to see Brockton.

"They are not treating you differently," One Fist objected. "Not like they are treating Vaerix."

"Brockton's our leader," Grisban said. "He'll be the first to be interrogated. Him and Quellen, because he's a mage. The dragons have this obsession with magic, or so they say, and consider it their own. The two of us, we do not matter."

"Whatever their purpose," Brockton whispered, "it means they'd pursue me mercilessly should I try to run."

"While they'd let one thick-skulled orc warrior go," Grisban added. "Especially if he managed to disappear."

"That's the reason why you should strike north," Brockton added. "As soon as we reach the hills. They'll look for you south and west. In the hills you can find a place to hide."

"Without provisions or water?" the orc protested.

"If anyone can make it, it's you," Brockton replied.

"Aye, if…"

"Are you scared, man?" Grisban spat.

"Of course I am." One Fist stared at the ground. "I am not stupid." Then he took a deep breath and shook his head. "I don't–"

"You, orc!"

One of the hybrids was coming closer, pointing a finger at One Fist.

Brockton felt panic rise, like a hand choking him.

"What?" One Fist replied.

"You give water to the elf," the hybrid said.

With a groan, One Fist stood and walked on stiff legs to where Quellen lay on his back. Passing by Grisban, he took the water gourd.

"Can you remove his gag?" he asked the hybrid.

But the hybrid only gestured for him to go on and stood by the side, holding his spear.

With more protests, One Fist knelt by Quellen and helped him sit up.

"He'll do it," Grisban said.

Brockton nodded. "It's all we can do. Now all we need is an opportunity."

The opportunity came early the following morning while most of the hybrids in the camp were asleep. One Fist quickly unbuckled his hook and slipped the manacle off his wrist. He massaged his stump for a moment and then put the hook in place again. Unless he was able to steal a blade on his way, the metal hook on his hand and the chain still attached to his right wrist would be his only weapons.

Brockton and Grisban were awake. Quellen was a motionless shape by the fire the hybrids had built to keep the cold of the night away. One Fist looked at him for a moment to make sure the elf was still breathing. The slow expanding and contracting of his chest reassured him.

He wondered how long the elf could go on.

Pushing such worries out of his mind, One Fist squeezed

Brockton's shoulder in a silent goodbye and then moved away in a crouch. The flames were low, and the little light from the fire competed with the first hints of pink on the eastern horizon. This, he had decided, was the best time – with most of the hybrids still asleep, and the sentry tired at the end of their shift and more likely to be distracted or slower on the uptake.

Moving as silently as a shadow, he reached the edge of the camp. There was only one sentry, a female warrior slowly walking a circuit around the camp. Now she was the farthest away, and One Fist sprang into action.

In three long leaps he cleared the area, aiming for a clump of bushes. Just as he reached the flimsy cover provided by the vegetation, a low rumble cut through the still air and the ground started shaking. The fire collapsed, spitting embers, and the hybrids woke up, startled by the earthquake.

And there was One Fist, standing out like a sore thumb at the edge of the camp.

"By the Whispering God!" he hissed, starting to run just as the first cries of alarm sounded behind him.

He did not turn to look. He ran with all the strength he could muster. He knew it would be useless. The gods had spoken their decision, sounding the alarm themselves. But at least he'd go down like a warrior.

Cold air rushed in and out of his chest and his back tensed, waiting for a spear to catch him between the shoulders. He kept his head down, arms and legs pumping, and he cursed in his heart the dragons of the Heath and their blasted fire mountains, the spirits of the shaking hearth and the dragon hybrids, but most of all he cursed Grisban, who had convinced him to try this foolish ploy.

He surprised himself by laughing.

He only hoped the old owl and Brockton were taking advantage of his diversion to sneak out of the camp.

Great wings were beating above him.

One Fist did not look. Here it would come, he knew, the spear that Kurnos had marked with his name.

But what happened instead was that Drys landed in front of him, holding a spear in his hands.

"Stop!" he shouted.

"Make me," One Fist gasped, without slowing, and slammed into him with his shoulder. Drys held his ground and pushed him back. He stabbed at the orc with his spear, but it was a half-hearted move, and One Fist caught the shaft on his hook and pushed it away. He swung his chain around and struck at Drys' head with the loose manacle. The metal connected with the scaly flesh of the cheek, and Drys took a step back and turned on his feet. One Fist saw the sweeping tail and ducked. A second swing and the chain wrapped itself around the spear shaft. He pulled, trying to disarm his adversary.

Why was no other hybrid coming for him?

Drys held onto the spear and with his free hand punched One Fist in the face. It was like being kicked by a mule. Colored bubbles danced in One Fist's eyes and his ears rang. But Drys had not used his talons, which could have pulled out One Fist's eyes.

"Don't waste your life," the hybrid said.

One Fist stared at him. "Warriors die, right?"

"Not like this," Drys said. "Not for nothing."

Other hybrids were now landing around them.

Drys pushed against One Fist, but instead of stabbing

at him with his spear or using his talons and wing-claws, he spread his wings, buffeting him.

One Fist was pushed to the side. He actually grabbed Drys' spear to keep his balance.

"Live," Drys told him in a soft voice.

There were more spearpoints turned against him now. One Fist stood straight, his breath slowing down.

Drys nodded at him.

One Fist raised his hands and let them take him back to the camp, where Brockton and Grisban were waiting for him surrounded by spear-carrying hybrids.

Vaerix was standing by the side, Arwyia as usual close by with her sword ready.

"Take away his hook," Drys ordered as he massaged his cheek. "And chain him above the elbows. He won't be able to slip out of his chains again."

Then he turned to One Fist. "From now on, you'll carry the elf," he said. "That will make you think twice before you go for another run."

"Why did you come back?"

The question had lingered between them for days now. Drys repeated it, seeming to desire a different answer than Vaerix had provided.

Vaerix sighed. "It felt like the right time."

Drys moved a little closer. "We thought you dead. But I somehow did know–"

The other hybrids were sitting around a small campfire. The days were warm under the spring sun, but the nights still had wintry fingers to caress and grasp the travelers. The prisoners, exhausted, had been lulled to sleep by the heat radiating from the fire. Vaerix and Drys had moved away, stopping where the light and warmth were but a ghost.

"Maybe I should have come back earlier," Vaerix said.

He caught the shadow of Arwyia, following them at a respectful distance.

"She says you shamed her," Drys said, following their glance. "She wants one death to cleanse the insult. She won't let you go. You shouldn't have spared her."

"It would have been a waste," Vaerix replied.

"That's not our way."

"That's why I should have come back earlier."

Drys sighed and shook his head.

"I came here through the southern passes," Vaerix said. "And I came through a place where the mountains themselves are made of ancient dragon bones."

Awe sounded in Drys' voice. "The fighting ranges."

"Yes. The ancient killing fields, where dragon fought dragon for centuries. We have often flown over that area in our days, but it needs walking to see what those years brought to our race. This is the truth of many things, that soaring high above them we miss the truth."

"The truth is that the weak were culled from dragonkind and only the stronger survived."

"The truth is that lives were wasted."

"This is heresy."

There were things Vaerix wished Drys would ask them. The places they had seen, the people they had met. The things Vaerix had learned during their travels. The things they still did not know.

But Drys did not seem to be interested. "You still believe our ways are wrong," Drys said.

"I have seen how it could be different," Vaerix replied.

Drys laughed and then looked at them, a flash of guilt in his eyes. "In your dreams."

"Yes, also in my dreams."

"Where else?"

Vaerix took a deep breath. "Out there, along the roads of Terrinoth. I have seen strange peoples living together, working together for a common goal. We should have learned that, at the end of our campaign…"

"Work together? The baronies are at each other's throats," Drys replied. "Civil war is commonplace. Brother kills brother, as it happened after the passing of Deiterhelm. I will not dispute what you saw, my friend, but peace doesn't seem to be the way of humans. Nor of any other people of Terrinoth. Our way looks to me more honest and more natural. Life is strife. Fighters fight, and fighters die. This is how the world works."

"This is how Levirax says the world works," Vaerix objected.

And Levirax had poisoned them all with her worldview, they thought.

"Levirax knows," Drys replied dryly.

"Truly, Levirax knows a lot about the ways of Terrinoth," Vaerix replied, "for someone who has spent eight hundred years under a rock."

In the back of their mind, Vaerix heard Grisban's distinctive chuckle. That was the way the old dwarf would have put it.

Drys stared at them, momentarily speechless.

All this echoed their old discussions so many centuries before. It pained Vaerix to see how much their old partner was in thrall of the dragonlord, to the point of being shocked by a simple, rational objection.

And in fact, how did Levirax know of the current affairs in Terrinoth?

"Some believed you," Drys said suddenly.

Those words brought Vaerix back to the present moment. "Some?"

"After…" Drys shut his mouth and sighed. It was like he was chewing on a bitter mouthful. "After you were taken to Levirax," he said finally. "When news came of what had been done. They rose in arms. They wanted revenge. They invoked your name."

"I was not aware of this."

"Of course not."

Vaerix felt a cold hand grip their heart. Their dreams about their kin living in peace had caused a riot. What a cruel joke. "What happened?"

"What do you think? They went down fighting."

Vaerix opened and closed their hands. "How many?"

"About two hundred," Drys said in a dead voice. "Levirax had us kill those she had not killed herself."

"Us?"

Drys turned sharply. "What was I to do?"

Vaerix shook their head. "Nothing," they said. "I was the one that should have done something."

"Done what? It is not so easy to turn against a dragonlord," he said. "Against all that we are."

"I should have come back earlier," Vaerix repeated, a stone-cold certainty in their voice.

The yellow, dry grass of the prairie broke against the slopes of the volcanic ash hills. Clumps of broom and lupine dotted the dusty gradient, but otherwise nothing grew on the black dust.

Here and there, rough ridges of glassy rock emerged through the ground and yellowish vapors escaped through deep cracks.

As the party moved north, the plain transformed into a black sand desert, and Brockton imagined it as a black circle, traced on the map with a large soft brush, to surround the Molten Heath.

Or maybe this was the Heath already. He could see how the volcanic landscape was encroaching on the plain. The swamps of the south had been replaced by puddles of boiling mud, and cracks in the ground released foul-smelling vapors and glowed red in the night. The hybrids were used to flying over these faults, but now were forced to slowly walk around them.

In all directions the land undulated in a series of low hills, hanging close to rock formations that rose through the ground and defied the sky. Low blocky mesas of banded rock beds and spurs of sharp volcanic glass, black and white and in strange hues of green. Twisted, stunted bushes clung to the sides of craters of long extinct volcanoes, their conic shapes abraded by the wind. These, too, the hybrids skirted warily, and once Brockton spotted what he thought were the recent remains of a burned-out village, but their captors pushed them on.

The Molten Heath, the pulsating heart of the region, was slowly expanding. Ancient lava flows stretched like cobbled roads, or like colossal braids of petrified ropes, tongues and ridges extending like the arms of a starfish around the seat of an old caldera, obliterated by its own explosive history. Smoldering rock crawled along the ridges, torpid rivers of molten rock slowly pouring onto the plain. The air was furnace-hot and a warm wind blew from the north, making Brockton's mouth even more parched.

On one of the ridges, that in the distance looked like a tangle of rugged roots from some colossal tree, rose like a broken tower of black glassy stone. Trembling due to the heated air in the red-hot light of a nearby lava flow, it was a tall cone surrounded by a lower wall, its massive brass doors facing south. One of the line of towers Brockton had read about in the ancient chronicles, erected by the Karok Doum dwarves to guard the Heath and mark the border that separated their domain from the dragons'. Most had been shattered and burned in the War of Fire, their garrisons slaughtered by the advancing tide of enraged dragons.

From where they stood, about one mile away, the building looked abandoned. No banners flew on its top, and part of the outer wall had crumbled. Twisted, skeletal trees had made roots in some of the arrow slits and now grew toward the ash-black sky like dead arms begging for some sunlight. Fingers of windblown black sand clawed at the remaining stones of the enclosure. All that was left of the once proud defensive system was a ruin sitting by a slowly flowing river of fire.

As they approached the structure, a large campsite appeared on the windward side of the tower, past the river of molten rock. Ordered rows of shelters as far as the eye could see. A small city of huts and tents smeared with the black of the wind-blown ash, crawling with busy winged creatures. A city of dragon hybrids, a whole army of them.

A distant rumble announced a bright red light on the horizon, followed by a brief tremor.

"The fire mountains are awakening," Drys said to no one in particular.

"It is a sign," Arwyia said.

She was as usual by Vaerix's side, her sword glinting in the late afternoon light.

"But a sign of what, I wonder?" Drys replied. Then he sighed. "Let us go. Our guests are tired and certainly eager to be seen to their quarters."

They started again, trudging through the ashes. Then one of the warriors let out a warning cry.

Three winged shapes had appeared in the sky above the tower, jumping from the top of the building, their wings beating with a steady rhythm.

As they came closer, it became evident that, like Drys, they were wearing armor, the hues of the metal matching the colors of their scales.

They drew closer and circled above them, and finally glided down and dropped about one hundred yards from them.

Two of them were holding spears, and the one that appeared to be their leader carried a long sword slung between his wings. He had a long jaw and short stubby horns.

As he approached, his eyes were glued to Vaerix.

When he was close enough, he first ignored Drys and sighed as he nodded at the wingless hybrid. Then he glanced sideways at Drys. "It is true, then."

"As you can see."

"Vaerix," the newcomer said, turning his gaze once again on the prisoner. He said the name in a low voice and looked away.

"Maesix," the other responded, with a hint of a bow.

"I believed you dead," Maesix said.

"But I live," Vaerix replied.

"So you do. Captain Xenith is in for a surprise."

All the broken pieces of Vaerix's past were still here to haunt them. It was like nothing had changed. All that had happened had been for nothing.

"Is Xenith here?" Drys asked.

"In the tower. We are here to oversee the camp and to interrogate the dwarves. Dragonlord's orders." A brace of sharp teeth flashed as Maesix grinned. "But I guess now he'll have other things to occupy him."

He looked at Vaerix, leaning forward.

"You should never have come back."

The road to the tower led them through the dragon hybrid camp.

Maesix talked briefly with Drys, and then together they led the war-band and the prisoners on a circuitous path to the tower. They followed the lava flow for a while, the burning wind carrying a smell like a blacksmith's workshop, and then they circled a long and narrow pool of molten rock. Bubbles broke the red-hot surface, releasing yellow steam, and the fluid curdled at the edges where it touched the colder rock of the shore, frozen waves climbing on each other.

From there, they finally reached the encampment and followed the main avenue across it, in the direction of the derelict tower.

"Why the detour, I wonder?" Grisban said.

"To parade us, apparently," One Fist replied. He was carrying Quellen on his shoulders and was short of breath.

Grisban turned a defiant eye on the hybrids gathering on either side of the avenue.

"Looks like they never saw a dwarf," he said.

And for all they knew, he told himself, they never had. About one in five hybrids they saw was wearing a suit of armor and the colors of their commander. All of them were winged. The others were in more simplistic attire – leather and furs –

and shook their weapons at their passage. Some of them, in the back, had no wings. They screamed insults and challenges, and some of them were pointing their finger at Vaerix. Some of them called them by name. Grisban heard both spite and awe in their voices.

The armored hybrids were shouting orders, trying to keep their less-disciplined companions in line, and were doing a poor job of it.

Which, to Grisban's experienced eye, was unsurprising. Someone was unsuccessfully trying to shape a wild rabble of marauders into a semblance of an army. Good soldiers had been given command, each of them saddled with a score of battle-happy boneheads that had a hard time telling their left foot from their right. This just had the effect of overtaxing the more disciplined troops, who found themselves doing a job for which they were not trained. At the same time, the warriors from the local tribes, unused to the hard-edged discipline, chafed and grew restless and viewed their inexperienced commanding officers with hostility.

It was the worst possible mix.

Maybe that was the reason they were being paraded through the camp, Grisban thought. To give the troops something else to think about.

"There must be two thousand of them," One Fist said.

Grisban nodded and grunted. It was a fair assessment.

"Ain't seen any stores," the orc went on.

Grisban grunted again.

Two thousand warriors needed food and supplies.

"Either they are ready to move..." he said.

Somebody threw a rock at them. It bounced over Grisban's shoulder, unheeded. A hybrid in plate armor moved through the throng and started barking in the face of the one that had thrown the stone.

"...or things will get ugly."

"The volcanoes to the north," One Fist said, glancing sideways at Quellen's head resting on their shoulder, "are not the only thing that's about to blow up."

Grisban grinned. "Maybe we can help."

CHAPTER TWENTY-THREE
Xenith

Wing Captain Xenith was surprised.

As with many fighters, he did not like it. Surprises did not bode well in battle, and battle was all that Captain Xenith knew.

And yet here was the traitor whose wings Xenith had torn off more centuries before than he cared to remember. A turncoat that had lost their place, their status, and their name. A wingless creature that should have had the good grace to disappear and die.

Xenith paced the grand hall of the Broken Tower, his fury boiling in his chest, causing his wings to twitch with every step. His tail snapped left and right as he distilled his surprise into bitter anger.

Drys and Maesix were there. Drys was the one who had captured the dwarves and the wingless creature.

Both them and Maesix were old companions of the wingless one.

Xenith would have to watch them closely.

The wingless one had been a strong warrior before they

turned mystic and traitorous. Driven insane – of this Xenith was certain – by some poisonous elven weapon, some mind-killing magic deployed by the hateful Latari at the tail end of the invasion of Terrinoth. The wingless one's peace-mongering ramblings had damaged the morale of the troops and, again, Xenith was certain that this had contributed to the defeat of the dragon armies.

Few of their companions had paid heed to the creature's folly, and many more had denounced their betrayal to Xenith, but not before Vaerix turned their back on Levirax's orders. The mad traitor had managed to undermine Levirax's triumphant campaign in the Broken Lands by relaying Shaarina's retreat orders to the troops.

The law of war had been clear, and when ordered to remove the traitor's wings and cast them off as an exile, Xenith had been happy to comply. He had even dared to contradict his dragonlord, she who wanted the rebel's life. Xenith had seen no reason to go against the rules that Levirax had imparted on them, with the added risk of creating a martyr. The wingless one would die among strangers as they deserved. Later, he had taken pride in cleaning up the aftermath of the traitor's actions, culling from the army those that had fallen for the disgraced one's mystical visions.

That should have taken care of the problem, as ordered.

Some remained, to Xenith's chagrin, who remembered the wingless one's promises, and sometimes they made their voices heard. It was one of Xenith's duties to silence those voices permanently.

And through the years, Xenith had come to see his worst fears come true. The creature whose name he would not pronounce had slowly turned into a legend. And now, the wingless one was back, leading the vanguard of a mighty dwarven army, coming to reclaim the Karok Doum.

Xenith roared in frustration.

How had they survived all these years out there among the people of Terrinoth? By allying themselves with Dunwarr, obviously, bowing to their avaricious authority. By promising them to guide their armies back to the Karok Doum, deep into the heart of the Molten Heath.

Xenith heard the ominous creaking of the great brass doors of the tower.

The prisoners were flightless weaklings and the gates had to be opened for them.

Xenith would have simply eliminated the intruders straight away, but he had orders. Levirax wanted to know more about the coming invasion. So Xenith had opted to place the prisoners in the abandoned tower. A mixed army, composed of both loyal hybrids from Levirax's force and members of the wilderness tribes loyal to the dragonlord, had been gathered, and Xenith did not want the wingless one too close to his troops. Once already they had caused confusion and disarray, and Xenith would not give them the opportunity to do it again.

Voices sounded in the courtyard, but Xenith paid them no heed.

Not now, his anger freezing as the thought of Levirax caused him a sudden pang of fear.

Levirax had ordered him to rip the wings off the creature and exile them.

Levirax, who had been the foremost victim of the wingless one's betrayal.

She was coming here, any day now, to meet the prisoners,

to interrogate them, and to inspect the army. She would not take the return of the traitorous creature lightly. Heads would roll, and Xenith would have to work hard to make sure his was not one of those.

Then in walked a slow procession.

Xenith stepped on the perch at the head of the hall and watched them as they approached.

There was Drys, obviously tired, their silver and blue armor dusty. Maesix walked by his side, a grim set to his jaw.

Behind them, the prisoners.

Two dwarves, dirty and ragged, one with brown hair and the other with dark graying hair and a white-streaked beard. Behind them came an orc helping an elf stand. The orc had a metal hook where his left hand should be. The elf was gagged and bound. A mage, then. He looked more dead than alive.

And then there was the wingless creature.

They stood proud and defiant, ignoring the warrior by their side, her sword level with their chest. Their eyes found Xenith's and held his gaze for a long minute.

At the sight of the wingless creature standing there, disgust choked Xenith. Fury once again replaced any other feeling.

"Welcome, Drys," he said, because he still remembered protocol.

"Captain, I did not expect to meet you here."

"You did not?"

Xenith narrowed his eyes as he studied Drys' reaction. Could he trust him? He had been the wingless one's companion on the battlefield and off it, and there could still be loyalty there. Or more.

"So, these are the dwarves," Xenith said, changing the subject.

Drys did not reply, but walked up to Xenith and offered him a book.

"This is the journal of their leader," he said and pointed at the younger dwarf. "His name is Brockton the Map Maker. He belongs to Dunwarr."

Xenith flipped through the pages. There were sketches, maps, and line upon line of tiny, neat script.

"A Dunwarr Guildsman making maps of our land," Xenith said slowly.

This fact alone confirmed Levirax's suspicions. The Karok Doum had changed dramatically since the War of Fire, and even more so in the last thousand years. An invading dwarven army would need precise maps. Hence the reason why they had sent a scouting party in the dragons' domains.

"Your forces will have to do without this," Xenith said as he leafed through the book. "A pity that so much work will have to go to waste."

The dragon hybrid called Xenith turned a few pages of Brockton's notebook.

"You have been precise and exhaustive in your spying, Master Guildsman."

Brockton's mouth was as dry as paper. He licked his lips and cleared his voice. The ruined hall that Xenith used as headquarters was hot and stuffy, their voices echoing under the tall ceiling.

"I am not a spy," he said. "Ours is a geographical expedition."

"You drew maps of our territories. Took notes about the land and its inhabitants." Xenith held the book up, showing a page covered in sketches. "Drew the likeness of our warriors."

"Yes, that's what a map maker does."

"That's also what a spy does, Master Brockton." He hefted the book. "On notes like these does an army march and generals make their plans. Traveling routes, foraging, where to make camp. What sort of resistance to expect from the inhabitants–"

"This is absurd," Brockton blurted out.

"Absurd? When you ride into the Karok Doum with a dwarf warrior, an orc fighter and an elven mage at your side? With one of the most infamous traitors of our race as a guide?"

Before Brockton could object, Xenith turned to Drys. "The wingless creature broke our laws. Again," he said. "Throw them in a cage, awaiting execution."

Drys looked up sharply. "Execution?" He looked from Xenith to Vaerix and back.

"Have you any trouble remembering the law, Drys?"

"I believe dragonlord Levirax might want a word with the prisoner," Drys said stiffly.

"Which is the reason why," Xenith said, waving a hand, "we let the wingless creature live, for the time being. You, there–"

"My name is Arwyia, captain, of the Burning Lake," she said, bowing her head.

"Arwyia. You will take the creature to their cage." A cruel smile curled the lips of Xenith. "You want to be careful. I remember they can be quite resourceful."

Arwyia bowed again. "As you command, captain." She hesitated, raising her head. "In fact..."

"What?"

"Vae – this creature, captain, owes me a fight."

"A fight?" Xenith's tone was contemptuous. "You? With this flightless creature?"

"They insulted me."

Xenith snorted. "They insulted our whole race. That is why they are as they are."

"If they must die," Arwyia said, growing bolder, "I swore it will be by my own hand."

Xenith looked at her, and Brockton wondered what was going on in his mind, what Vaerix had done to him to deserve so much hatred. No one, not even the Blind One, had shown such absolute contempt toward Vaerix.

"We will see. Now, to the cages with them."

"Yes, captain."

Arwyia prodded Vaerix with the tip of her sword. The hybrid cast one last glance at Brockton, gave a brief nod at the others, and went through an archway followed by Drys and Arwyia.

"Now that the creature has been taken care of," Xenith said, "we can talk."

Brockton caught a movement in the corner of his eye. He turned as two of the remaining guards stepped back and stopped by the sides of the main door. The hybrid Maesix and two more remained close by.

"I am sure," Xenith went on, "that you will not force me to use torture."

Brockton felt his legs go weak, a weakness that had nothing to do with fatigue. By his side, Grisban cursed.

"Torture is wasteful," Xenith went on, "and unreliable. A lot of the subjects will lie through their teeth and say anything just to make the pain stop. So... Let us just have a peaceful conversation, Master Brockton."

Brockton waited in silence. This was not what he had imagined.

"I see you followed a new route into the Verdant Ring,"

Xenith said, once again checking Brockton's notes. His eyes on the pages, he started pacing the room, his long legs carrying him across the hall in five long strides before he turned. "Through the southern ranges. Is that the route your armies will follow? Is that the direction from which the invasion will begin?"

"You do not understand," Brockton said wearily. "There is no invasion. No armies."

"Oh, no, Master Brockton," Wing Captain Xenith replied. "You are the one who does not understand. There are always armies, you see, following those that draw maps. It can be a large force of warriors marching on to conquest, ready to lay the newly mapped land to waste. Or it can be but a handful of raggedy sell-swords, escorting a column of merchants eager to exchange goods with the people of the land. And then patrols of armed men protecting the trade routes those self-same merchants traced, following your maps, connecting trade posts. And next a small garrison to defend each village that grew out of the trade posts and horse-changing stations. More traders and crafters, their families, their children will be next. To work the fields, to mine the hills. And for each one of them, for each peaceful merchant and quietly living artisan, no less than five warriors, at least two of them ahorse, for mobility. Following that, a line of watch towers like the one in which we are right now, to spot danger from afar and to mark a border, stake out a claim. And an army, a proper army, to defend that border, to man those towers, to fight those dangers. And walls around your cities, where your troops will be quartered. Thousands of men, thousands of spears glinting under the sun."

Xenith stopped pacing the floor and turned an ice-cold eye on Brockton.

"So do not pretend, Master Brockton, that there is not an

army following you. Do not delude yourself that your presence here will not have consequences… and consequences of the kind that's resolved by blades. Do not act as if you are anything but the early scout for an invading army. No matter how naive you are, or claim to be, you and yours are the vanguard of an invasion, and one my people will stop." He dropped the book on the floor with a thump and a small cloud of dust. "There will be blood, Master Brockton. And it will be on you."

Brockton looked down at his notes, some of the pages escaping the binding, and then looked up at Xenith. A painful feeling of betrayal choked him. The hybrid's reasoning made so much sense. Brockton wondered if that was what would really happen and had been planned from the start by the Guild Masters in Dunwarr. He had to convince himself all Xenith said was speculation and madness.

"Maybe you'll need time to think about what your responsibilities are," the dragon hybrid continued. He turned to the hybrid standing to his side in a clean jet and copper armor. "Find a suitable place for him and his companions."

"Yes, sir," the one called Maesix said.

"But not the elven mage," Xenith went on. He pointed at one of the hybrid warriors. "Take the elf out in the courtyard and cut off his tongue."

Brockton gasped. "You can't do that!" he cried.

Grisban took a step forward. "By the Nightlord–"

For a brief moment, Brockton was sure Grisban would try attack Xenith with his bare hands. But one of the hybrid's guards stopped him by pressing the tip of his spear at his sternum.

Maesix hesitated, uncertain. "Dragonlord Levirax might want to interrogate the mage, sir."

"I ordered his tongue cut, not his throat."

Maesix stepped down.

Xenith looked at Brockton and then waved a hand. "Off with the elf's tongue."

Two hybrid warriors approached One Fist, who was still holding Quellen up. The orc tried to stop them, but one of them lashed at him with their tail and One Fist landed on his back, Quellen a bundle of limbs in a ripped cloak by his side. The hybrids grabbed the elf by the arms, lifted him up and dragged him out. He moaned in his gag and thrashed weakly with his feet but in a moment, he was out of the doors and gone.

"We will talk later," Xenith said to Brockton. He grinned. "We that still can."

Maesix placed a clawed hand on his shoulder and led Brockton through a passageway. Behind them, two more guards pushed on One Fist and Grisban.

Barking the names of half a dozen gods, Grisban resisted the hybrids and managed to push one of them back. He waited in a pugilist's defensive stance, but the second hybrid hit him across the back with the shaft of their spear. Grisban coughed and went down on his knees, where the one he had pushed and challenged slapped him in the face, leaving the parallel trails of her talons on his cheek. Then she picked him up forcibly by his belt and dragged him out of the hall.

They descended into the lower levels of the building, past rooms filled with collapsed masonry and barred doors. An iron door was opened and the three of them were pushed in. They did not take the time to remove their chains. The door creaked and slammed shut. A latch slid noisily into place.

They stared at each other in the red light that filtered

through a tall arrow slit in the wall. The air smelled of rust and sulfur and was so hot it made breathing painful.

"They can't cut his tongue, right?" One Fist asked.

Brockton just shook his head, too anguished to speak.

Quellen stumbled on the slate flagstones of the courtyard, staggered and fell on his face. His hands were still tied behind his back, his mouth gagged. He was unable to break his fall or to vent his pain with a cry.

The impact numbed his cheek, his temple, one more strand in the braid of pain that coursed through him, from his feet, worked raw by the long miles he had walked, to his aching empty belly, to the sores in his paper-dry mouth.

He tried to right himself. He was on his knees, swaying uneasily. His cloak, pinned under his right knee, tugged at him and then ripped with a loud sound. He straightened his back and his bones crackled. The abject fear of what was to come momentarily dissolved his fatigue. His hands were icy cold, his nostrils choked with the smell of the exhalations from the nearby lava flow.

One brief glance revealed a dirty space, a half-collapsed wall and a pile of debris. The sun was going down, or it was the glow from the nearby lava he could feel flowing on the other side of the collapsed wall. He still had his powers. He still felt one with the earth, intimate with the rocks, aware of each and every pebble. Not that it made all that much difference now. The river of molten rock just one hundred paces away called to Quellen with its raw power, mocking him with all the energy he could perceive and yet not tap.

The two dragon hybrids were talking among themselves in their uncouth language. Two huge brutes, muscles rippling under their scaled skin, they were probably trying to decide which one of them would pull his tongue out and which one would cut it. Quellen had noticed two kinds of warriors, the armored ones and the ones in raw leathers, and these two belonged to the more unsophisticated lot. Which only made them scarier.

His thoughts in turmoil, Quellen took a long breath through his nose and tried to work his tongue around the gag to wet his mouth.

His head still rang from the fall, and his brains were sluggish because of the pain, the fatigue and the hunger. The fear. He could almost feel his blood running slowly through his veins, made thick by the lack of drinking water, his heart beating like a drum out of time trying to pump it wearily through his veins.

This was no time for being weary, he said to himself.

To cut out his tongue, they'd have to remove his gag. That would give him some time. One, maybe two heartbeats to speak, if he'd be able to gather enough breath, and push some sounds through the parched desert that was his throat. Two heartbeats to cast a spell.

He ran through his mind the list of enchantments he'd be able to cast with his hands tied and maybe five seconds to speak the formula.

There was not much. For all the raw resources at hand in this place, geomancy was still an art that required time. And right now, time was the last thing Quellen had. He could call on small spells that mages learned in their first year as apprentices, or even earlier, as children at their mage parent's knee. Cantrips to light a candle or sharpen a pen or pop a cork from a bottle. A simple spell to make two stones stick together, another to blow sand around in dust devils in the absence of wind.

He racked his memories desperately. There had to be something.

The two guards finally reached an agreement.

One of them pulled out an obsidian dagger, little more than a shard of volcanic glass with a rag for a hilt. The other groaned and snorted, obviously not pleased. He laid his spear to the side, leaning against the black wall of the courtyard, and stood in front of Quellen where he was kneeling on the ground.

The hybrid grabbed Quellen's jaw and held him still. His companion used his blade to cut at the gag, and in doing so he nicked Quellen's cheek.

He did not care.

The one holding his jaw pressed with his fingers, hurting his cheeks, forcing his mouth open. This was it, Quellen thought.

Rough, big fingers pinched his tongue and pulled it out. Quellen gagged and coughed. He tried to shake his head free. His mind blanked.

No spells, no hopes, no solutions.

The black glass blade flashed in front of his eyes.

On sheer instinct, with an energy he did not know he had, Quellen pulled away. The sudden movement hurt his neck. The hybrid did not let go, but pinched his tongue harder, drawing blood. The blade twisted and cut the back of the hybrid's hand.

The creature hissed, let go of Quellen's tongue, and turned to his companion, barking a protest.

A guttural sound escaped its maws just as a sharp metal point erupted through the other hybrid's chest. The warrior's eyes widened and a rattle burst through his throat. His dagger slipped through his dead fingers and rang on the hard ground.

In a flash, two blades crossed under the other hybrid's chin and bit hard into the soft skin of their neck. The hybrid made a short sound like a cough and fell forward, pushing down Quellen and pinning him to the ground with his dead weight.

The impact with the inert body pushed the last of Quellen's breath out of his chest. Crushed on the ground, gasping like a drowning man, he tried to get free. Tarha, by his side, helped him move the body and sit up.

"Hold on," she hissed.

His head spun, his ears ringing.

Cyra was shaking her short swords clean. She sheathed them.

"You take him," she whispered at Tarha. "I'll hide the bodies."

The orc nodded. Standing, she took hold of Quellen's arm and with a grunt, she picked him up on her shoulder and ran.

He wanted to say something, but his mouth would not work.

Then he slipped into darkness.

CHAPTER TWENTY-FOUR
Escape

When Tarha and Cyra had come in sight of the ancient tower, they did not have a plan. Skirting the hybrid camp, made inconspicuous by one of Cyra's songs, they found an access to the tower just in time to see the two hybrids manhandling a ragged prisoner they had almost failed to recognize as Quellen.

Urgency had made planning superfluous.

Now Tarha skipped to the base of the tower and found a passage that led to what had been a guard room. There was the broken remains of a narrow staircase leading up from the bowels of the building, but anything that had not been built in stone had long decayed and vanished. She laid the elf down with a grunt. Cyra joined her and they propped the elf up against the stone wall, to help him breathe. Cyra felt for his heartbeat.

"At least it's steady," she commented after a while, speaking in a low voice. She cast a quick glance at the entryway. Being found here would undo all they had done.

Under the palm of her hand, the pumping was slow and sluggish. Cyra wondered what the norm for elves was, if their heart beat as fast as a human, but had a bad feeling about the mage's health.

Tarha pushed a strand of dirty hair out of his face. "He's had a rough time."

Quellen's soft boots were broken and stained, his feet swelled and bloodied. His bright clothes were stained and ripped, black dust dulling their bright colors. A large bruise was spreading over the side of his face and there was a cut on his cheekbone. His breath was ragged, coming in short gasps, his chest barely moving, and he smelled of rancid sweat and fear.

"But this might help," the orc added with one of her grim smiles.

She had her small bottle again. Cyra remembered the warmth and the vile taste. It had done her good.

Tarha poured the liquor between Quellen's chapped lips.

The elf's eyes opened, and he shook with a coughing fit, sneezing at the same time. Tarha placed her hand over his mouth, hissing for him to make less noise. He bent forward and Cyra supported him.

"Ethana's tears, woman," Quellen croaked, "you poisoned me."

Cyra and Tarha traded a glance.

"Latari gratitude," Tarha spat.

Quellen took a deep breath and licked his lips. His face had regained color, his eyes were feverish. "I thought you dead," he said in a low voice. "Or on your way to Black Ember Pass."

"We followed you," she said simply.

The elf looked at her. He tucked a strand of hair behind his ear. "That was stupid," he said.

"See?" Tarha said.

Quellen gave her a sideways glance. "Make no mistake, I am

grateful," he said slowly. "But still I question the wisdom of your choice."

He took the small flask from the orc's hand and as she watched, as he drank another gulp of the liquor. He coughed and cursed. "I might get used to this," he said, handing her back the empty bottle.

"Now you'll have to help us get the others out, too," Cyra said.

Quellen stared at her like she was foolhardy, but was too spent to further speak his thoughts.

Brockton started, Grisban's hand shaking him awake.

"What?" he mumbled. How long had he slept? His body felt like he had been trampled by an ox. He checked the light in the arrow slit. It must have been no more than ten minutes. His head felt heavy and the warm air made it hard for him to breathe.

"Something's up," Grisban said in a low voice.

One Fist was standing sideways by the iron door, looking through the square spyhole.

Brockton sat up and his ears caught the sounds coming from the tower. Voices calling, feet running, the ringing of a bell.

He looked at Grisban, a question unspoken.

"I think the elf escaped," the old dwarf said.

Quellen? Escaped?

His wrists still manacled together, Brockton rubbed the sleep out of his eyes with the heels of his hands. "How?"

Grisban shrugged. "He's a mage."

"He was more dead than alive–"

A ferocious grin split Grisban's face. "I guess he's really attached to his tongue."

"Someone's coming," One Fist hissed, stepping away from the door.

"Let me do the talking," Grisban whispered, winking at Brockton.

The door swung open and Maesix came in followed by two guards, their leather garb contrasting their officer's metal plate. The room felt suddenly crowded and stuffier. Brockton and the others retreated against the far wall.

"Let me guess," Grisban said with a chuckle. "You lost an elf."

The hybrid looked at him, cold anger in his large eyes. "Where is the mage?"

"How can we know?" Brockton asked back. The chains on his wrists jangled. Grisban gave him a sideways look.

Maesix took a step forward. "Speak!"

"What did you expect?" Grisban laughed cruelly. "You said it yourself, he's a mage. More than that, he's an archmage. No more than a handful in all of Terrinoth can claim such a majestic title. He's a master elementalist, a summoner of great accomplishment, celebrated in the great halls of Greyhaven. He's got the power of the five elements at his fingertips. He can ride the wind and squeeze water out of the rocks. He can shatter one of your warriors by raising an eyebrow. No wonder he slipped away right under your nose."

Brockton had to make an effort not to turn and stare at Grisban. The old warrior had gone mad. None of that was true.

"He will be apprehended," Maesix said coldly. "It is only a matter of time."

"I honestly doubt it."

"He killed two of mine."

"I am not surprised." The old dwarf nodded.

"He will not go far–"

Grisban's laugh echoed in the cell.

"Far?" One Fist said. "Knowing him, by now Archmage Quellen's in Frostgate enjoying a cold beer."

"I told you," Grisban added, "he's an archmage. Distance is meaningless to the likes of him."

Maesix's wings quivered. "He is still here. He won't leave you behind."

"It's an elf we're talking about," Grisban snorted. "He won't risk his skin to save two dwarves and an orc. You've got to face the facts, he's gone."

Maesix looked at each one of them in turn, and then turned on his heels and strode out of the cell, his two warriors following him.

Grisban's laugh followed them out and when the door slammed closed, stopped, the sudden silence like a thunderclap.

"The power of the five elements?" Brockton asked, amusement in his voice.

"Well, maybe that was a little too much," Grisban admitted with a shrug and a chuckle. "But one does not just fight with sword and axe, master map maker. A good lie is both shield and dagger to a smart man. It's just another way to feint, to keep your foe out of balance, waiting for an opening to strike them down."

"But such outrageous falsehood…" Brockton caught himself thinking elven magic only recognized four elements and he felt suddenly very silly. His cheeks burned.

"Quellen won't hate us for making him look better," One Fist said.

"And if he really killed two warriors," Grisban added, clicking his tongue, "maybe it was not all falsehood, what I fed them."

Brockton just shook his head.

"Grisban lit a nice fire under them," One Fist said. "Now they'll be scared and wary. They will overestimate the danger and will have little time to pay us attention. Not to mention–" he smirked, "–I'd love to see what happens when our friend Maesix there goes to report to his captain."

"What do you think happened?" Brockton asked. "With Quellen, I mean. Really."

"I guess they had to take his gag off to cut his tongue," One Fist said.

"And he had one last spell ready," said Grisban. He shook his head. "Never trust an elf, that's what I say. Knock them out before you remove the gag, that's the way to do it."

Brockton shuddered. Grisban's casual truculence never ceased to surprise him. "Maybe he just teleported away," he suggested.

"Two dead," Grisban corrected him. "If he teleported, he took a chunk of them along."

"Fortuna," Brockton whispered, shivering.

"Well, good for him, I say," the old dwarf warrior said. "The only bit I did not need to make up is about this being the last we've seen of Archmage Quellen."

Brockton had to agree. "You don't think he'd come to our rescue?" he asked.

Grisban laughed a bitter laugh. "Not in a thousand years."

"Now that," said Quellen, peeking through the small spyhole in the door, "was just plain rude."

The latch was pulled, and the door swung open. The elf was riding piggyback on Tarha's shoulders and she did not seem to be particularly pleased.

A big grin spread over One Fist's features.

"What are doing here, you fools?" Grisban blurted out.

Cyra peeked over Tarha's shoulder. "Now a thank you would be nice, old man. We're here to save you. Let's move it!"

Then her eyes widened. "Where's Vaerix?"

Vaerix measured their cage in long steps, their mind torn between practicalities and wild fancies. The door had closed behind them with a clang, the latch clicked with a rusty sound.

Vaerix turned. Arwyia studied them, standing three feet away from the iron bars.

The lock on the door to the cage was not overly complicated and only Arwyia was here to guard them. They could crack the lock easily and then fight their way out.

But then what? All the dragon hybrids would swarm them.

"They told me who you are," Arwyia said, looking through the bars. "Who you used to be when you still had a name."

"I do have a name," they replied.

A slip. Silence was all that their guard deserved.

But their mind was spinning, too many things moving at the same time.

She laughed. "Not for centuries, creature. Xenith took your wings and Levirax took your name."

Vaerix looked down at their hands. They took one long breath in, trying to focus. This was not what they had dreamed, so long ago. Not what they had hoped for their people. But regrets were useless when one was locked in a cage.

Arwyia was still talking, but they were not listening to her words any longer.

Vaerix examined their thoughts, dismissing them one by one, uncluttering their mind. This was not the time for confusion.

For disappointment.

It was like everything they had done had turned out for the worst. Every action, every choice, had led to the opposite of what they had hoped for.

The hybrids kept fighting. They kept dying.

Levirax, who had them punished for heeding Shaarina's orders, had actually benefited from Vaerix's decision and actions.

And in the intervening decades nothing had changed for their people. Or, if possible, things had become worse. Levirax had kept poisoning the hybrids with her ruthless world views and her brutality.

Vaerix wondered what their people would look like if not for their dragonlord's dark influence. Maybe, it would be more like what they saw in their dreams.

They had not asked for all of this. They had not asked for the dreams and for the knowledge that came with them. They had not asked for exile and solitude. They had not asked for their long, fruitless quest.

Once, they had been a good soldier in the service of a cruel master, but having known only cruelty, they thought fighting against it would make their future better.

But now the memory of the look in Drys' eyes was enough to confound them.

Can one be wrong if they do not have an idea of what is right?

"Maybe you should never have come back," Maesix had once said.

Maybe I should never have left, Vaerix thought now. But what could they have done staying here? They had no choice. They had been exiled.

"But you know," Arwyia's voice reached them through the noise of their thoughts, "maybe you will get your name back when I kill you."

Vaerix looked at her. All this creature understood was fighting, she only thought about survival or death. The noise of Vaerix's thoughts started to subside.

Arwyia laughed. "I will see you on the battlefield," she said.

Vaerix watched her shift behind a pillar and out of their view. She was poorly trained, but her lack of discipline would work to Vaerix's advantage. A vast quiet suddenly came over them as a plan started taking shape. They'd have to help Brockton and the others escape. But then they would do what was needed for their people.

If all the dragon hybrids understood was the battlefield, Vaerix would use the battlefield to make them see.

"You didn't think about bringing weapons, did you?" Grisban mumbled.

Cyra was picking the locks on their shackles. One Fist asked her to leave the chain hanging from his wrist. The chains and a lone recovered spear were the only other weapons, apart from Cyra's swords and poniard, and Tarha's dagger. But both Tarha and Quellen had other ways to defend themselves in case of need.

"Will a short sword do?" Cyra asked Grisban, offering him one of hers.

The dwarf accepted the blade. "Until I find something better."

One Fist weighed the hybrid short spear, the head a crudely hammered piece of metal. He snapped the shaft, shortening it some more, and then twirled it around like it was some sort of strange axe. He nodded.

"We don't have much time," Cyra said. She led them to a short archway. "This way."

Low steps led up and down.

"Vaerix is upstairs," Tarha said.

"How do you know?" Grisban asked.

"The wingless hybrid is making the local ghosts nervous," she replied, unsmiling.

"Xenith talked about cages," Brockton said.

"We'll see when we get there," Cyra said. "Now move."

"Who appointed you as leader?" Grisban asked in a belligerent whisper.

Below, on the ground floor of the tower, the hybrids were in turmoil, but the upper levels of the ruin were quiet and undisturbed.

"She's good at sneaking," Tarha said, gently pushing him on.

Cyra ignored that barb. "The passages," she said as they walked in the dark, "were probably built in case of siege."

They climbed up, following a very low spiraling staircase that ran inside the outer wall of the tower. Massive stone slabs formed the walls and the ceiling, so heavy and stable, it was no surprise they were clear of debris and secure. Cyra took the lead, with Brockton at her side. Light filtered through cracks in the walls, supplementing the faint glow of Tarha's staff.

"The dwarves built well," Grisban rumbled.

"Tarha was able to discover this corridor thanks to…" Cyra shrugged. "You know."

"They know I speak with ghosts," Tarha said behind them. "Let's not waste time."

"And then Quellen helped us open the way and get to you," Cyra went on. She was inordinately proud of how things had worked out so far.

"It was a nice example of cooperation," Quellen said. He rode on the back of One Fist, who greeted that comment with a groan.

"But not much of a rescue," Grisban grunted. "We're short of weapons, with no horses, and surrounded by enemies with wings. What now?"

"We are improvising," Cyra admitted.

Another low archway led to the next floor.

Cyra stopped them by raising a hand, and then she moved forward to peep around the opening.

She crouched as low as possible and then waved a hand.

Grisban was by her side. She nodded and placed a hand on his shoulder for balance.

The room beyond the archway was partially filled with rubble, as the upper stories had collapsed centuries before, leaving the structure partially open to the sky. The debris and broken rafters had partially buried a large metal cage that sat in the center of the room.

Vaerix was sitting in a corner of the cage, and they looked their way as they moved. Five steps, and Grisban and Cyra were at the cage's door.

Vaerix stood.

Cyra got to work on the padlock while Grisban scanned the shadows in the corners of the room.

"Let's go," the woman hissed, opening the cage.

Vaerix moved toward her and through the door. "Arwyia…"

She looked at them. What were they talking about?

A shadow dropped on them from above. The newcomer pummeled Cyra with the tip of her wing and slapped Cyra away. She kicked Grisban, the clawed foot connecting with the dwarf's chest, and sent him rolling on the floor. Then she lunged at Vaerix with her spear, trying to skewer them. But Vaerix grabbed the shaft in both hands, evading the assault. For a moment it was a test of strength, both hybrids pushing on the spear from the two opposite sides.

"I was expecting this," the hybrid shrieked. "Now you must fight me, creature!"

Cyra cursed and tried to stand, her head ringing from the hit.

The hybrid was screeching at the top of her lungs. Soon more guards would come.

Then Vaerix looked up, and still holding on to the shared weapon, quickly stepped to the side. The other hybrid stumbled, unbalanced, but still roared in triumph. Just then, One Fist came running at her from behind, still carrying Quellen on his back. Vaerix let go of the spear as the orc and the elf slammed into the stumbling hybrid's back. Their joined momentum pushed the hybrid into the cage. They crashed on the cage's floor as Cyra slammed the door shut and snapped the padlock closed.

"You chose the wrong battlefield," Vaerix said. The trapped hybrid roared and grabbed the bars but was powerless.

Cyra helped Grisban up. "Not bad for an improvised plan," she told him.

"Out, before this place crawls with guards," Brockton called.

They ran back to the inner staircase.

Tarha led the way, her eyes on the ghostly shape only she could see. The pathetic remains of a long dead servant, one that had fallen with the defenders over a millennium before, when the dragons had rained fire on the tower. She had called the spirit up from the pocket of nothingness in which it had lingered and ordered it to show her a secure way out.

The enraged shape led her and the others through side passages and narrow stairs, down into the bowels of the tower and away from the noises of the hybrids. Only once did they come out in the open and face one of the guards. Grisban and Cyra pinned the hybrid in a corner and did away with it before he was able to raise the alarm. Then they had gone back into a dirty crawlspace and down steep steps to an underground tunnel with rough stone walls.

The spirit would not go further and slowly faded.

They stopped, and One Fist put down Quellen and stretched his back with a grunt.

"This gallery leads outside," Tarha explained. She had picked that up from the spirit before it waned. "One mile from the tower."

"We could lay low here," Brockton said, "and wait for things to quieten down. Then we can just sneak out and run as fast as we can."

"Have you got our horses?" Grisban asked.

"Only Cloud," Cyra replied.

The dwarf snorted. "Great rescue plan."

Tarha left them to their discussions and walked back to the place where the steps met the rough floor of the gallery. She stretched her senses until she felt the distinctive tingling of another wayward ghost. One of the old defenders, a ragged mind filled with rage and pain due to a fiery death.

Quickly, she dealt with him, placing him at the top of the stairs.

The spirit was too weak to affect the material world in any way, but might act as a sentry. He would also pour all its dread and angst on anyone trying to come down the steps, discouraging them from going further.

The effort of taming the ghost and ordering it around left her weak and drenched in sweat.

She slowly walked back to where the others were still talking.

"This is madness," Brockton was saying, his voice carrying all his weariness.

"It is not," Vaerix replied.

Tarha stopped and looked at them. They were not planning their escape. She perceived the tension in the air. She caught Cyra's attention and gave her a questioning look.

The sword poet frowned and shook her head.

"There is nothing you can do," Brockton said in a low, reasonable tone.

"Yet I must try," Vaerix replied. "My people deserve better than what Levirax has given them."

"And you really believe you can change that?" Quellen asked, his tired voice finding its ironic edge again.

"I do," Vaerix said.

"Rubbish," Grisban said. "You want revenge. You want to close your hands around that Xenith's neck and squeeze until his eyes pop out of his head. I can respect that. That's why I am staying back with you."

"What?" Brockton snapped. He looked around in disbelief. His gaze focused on Vaerix. "After all we went through, you can't just leave us. Not now. Grisban–"

"You can go on without me," the old dwarf said. "Vaerix needs help."

"That is…" Brockton said. He closed his eyes. "That is just wasting your lives. We will need the help of you both."

"We'll keep the hybrids busy while you get as far as you can," Grisban said. "It's worth trying."

"No, friend," Vaerix said. "This is something I must do alone."

Grisban drew himself up to his full height. "I'd like to see you try and stop me."

"I could."

"Enough!"

Brockton's voice did not rise, but it seemed to shake the very walls of the corridor. Tarha saw fury simmering in the dwarf's eyes as he took a step forward. His intensity gave her pause. She had never seen him like that.

"We have half the Molten Heath dragon population out for our blood," Brockton said, "and you two fools want to fight among yourselves? This is not a time for such."

"Show some respect, young one," Grisban replied.

"Or what? Will you fight me, too?"

Grisban growled, but Vaerix placed their hand on his shoulder. "Remember what you told me," they said. "About respecting the elders."

Grisban looked up at them. "Then come with us," he said.

"I can't." Vaerix looked at each one of them in turn and then focused on Grisban. "I must build a road," they said.

Grisban arched his eyebrows. "You're out of your mind."

"No." Vaerix shook their head. "A road to bring my people where I am right now."

"In a tunnel?"

"They want to show them a new way," Tarha said. How could the dwarf be so thick?

"It is so," Vaerix said. "It was easy for Levirax to bring my people to where she is. To war and death. Fear and need are powerful tools and fight is part of our very essence. But there are other places to be. I have been there. And if I want to build a road to lead the people there, I will need to use the tools available. I will need to fight to show them there is more than fighting. Use violence to teach them to be at peace."

They looked at Grisban. "You understand, friend. In a war, any tool is a good tool."

Grisban nodded. "Yet you don't want any help."

"You must protect Master Brockton," Vaerix said.

Grisban snorted. "One Fist can do it."

Vaerix shook their head. "Thank you, friend." They looked again at each one of them in turn as they spoke. "You go forth," they said. "This is something I must do alone."

"I still…" Brockton said. Then he hesitated. "I still think it is foolish."

"I know, friend. But it must be done."

Tarha felt her ghost sentinel pull at her. There were guards sniffing around the head of the staircase. She doubted they'd find the courage to come down right now, but time was running out.

"They are coming," she said.

CHAPTER TWENTY-FIVE
Memories: The Howling Giant Hills

The wind that gave the Howling Giant Hills their name blew an odd storm of scattered papers and parchments, like autumn leaves strewn all over the grass, into Vaerix's path.

Two mules, looking stolidly on the scene unfolding before them.

Two dwarves, one of them prone on the ground, still, bleeding.

The other was young, wearing sturdy traveling clothes.

A man was holding him pressed against the rock with one hand and slapping his face with the other. He kept a steady rhythm, slow but constant. Almost bored in his stance, he did not appear to really enjoy what he was doing.

Three more men, two humans and an orc, stood at his back, laughing and trading jokes. They clearly enjoyed the show for what it was.

Vaerix stepped out of the shadows of the trees and into the clearing. They casually caught a page the wind blew in their direction and looked briefly at the neat lines of writing.

"Let him go," they said, their voice strong enough to force the men to turn.

The mules pricked up their ears and backed away, scared at Vaerix's sudden appearance.

"What is this thing?" one of the men belched. He was wearing a dirty coat and metal plate armor over his right arm. He carried a rusty mace, like something stolen from a battlefield.

"Some kind of freak," the orc said with a grin. He carried a bludgeon made with a thick tree branch, some green leaves still attached.

Common ruffians, bandits of the wild.

"Let the dwarf go," Vaerix said again.

The one holding the dwarf grinned. He was the only one wearing clean clothes and carried a longsword across his back.

"And who are you?" he asked.

He let go of the dwarf, who fell to his knees, coughing.

Vaerix did not waste time answering, their mind focused on what would happen in the next two minutes. Already the other three were spreading out, trying to surround them. A peaceful resolution would not be an option.

The orc was the first one to come at them, screaming, his club held high over his head with both hands. Vaerix stepped aside and cracked their staff against the orc's knee. As the orc cried out in pain and stumbled, Vaerix parried a sweep of the second man's mace and closed their distance with the leader of this sorry pack of would-be wolves.

The leader unsheathed his sword.

Vaerix twirled their staff over their head and broke the wrist of the one with the mace. The man cursed and let go of his weapon.

The third one had a large knife, almost as long as his forearm. He tried to stab Vaerix with an upward movement.

Vaerix caught his arm in one hand. Turning, they used their tail to sweep the man with the broken wrist off his feet.

As the man hit the ground with a grunt, Vaerix used their staff to bludgeon the knife man on the head, hard enough to put him out of action.

They stepped over their last foe and faced the man with the two-handed sword.

"Aren't you a clever one?" the man said with a grin.

Vaerix ignored his words.

The man brandished his sword and took a step forward.

Vaerix held their ground. They guessed this man was used to scaring his foes with his big weapon and his abrupt movements. He was after all the sort of man that ambushes travelers, not a warrior.

Vaerix parried the man's first slash, and then the second.

They stood on their feet and moved the staff to intercept the blade, gently pushing it aside, letting the edge slide along the shaft of their weapon.

"Aren't you a clever one?" the man repeated and spat, moving to the right, trying to get in a better position to strike. "You think you can fight us, huh?"

But his companions were out of the picture already.

Vaerix saw the young dwarf run on his hands and knees to the side of his wounded fellow.

Then the man moved, faster than before, and what started as a slash from above suddenly changed to a horizontal cut plainly aimed at Vaerix's midriff. Vaerix appreciated the ploy, dodged, twisted. They struck their staff in the ground and used it to pivot out of the way of the blade, and then Vaerix leapt and slammed both feet on the man's chest. He stumbled back, hitting the same rock he had pushed the dwarf against a few minutes before.

The impact seemed to have knocked the air out of his lungs.

Vaerix closed the distance, used the staff to further unbalance their adversary. When the man was down on one knee, the sword stuck in the dirt, Vaerix hit them squarely in the face with the palm of their right hand.

The man gurgled and fell flat on his face.

The young dwarf was using a piece of cloth to stop the bleeding of their friend. He stopped a moment to look up at Vaerix.

"You should go," Vaerix said.

The dwarf glanced at the men rolling on the ground.

"They will rise," Vaerix added.

The young dwarf nodded and tried to pick his friend up.

Vaerix helped him and together they placed the wounded one on the back of a mule. The two animals were wary of Vaerix, but the dwarf calmed them.

"Yonder is Frostgate," Vaerix said, pointing.

"I know," the dwarf said. He gave a brief look at the scattered papers. Then he offered his hand. "Brockton," he said. "Junior Journeyman. From the Dunwarr's Guild of Explorers."

"Greetings," Vaerix replied.

After a moment of hesitation, they accepted the offered hand.

The dwarf was looking at them, expecting.

"My name is Vaerix," they said, conforming to the customs of Terrinoth.

Brockton smiled. "Well, Vaerix, it sure was a happy accident meeting you."

CHAPTER TWENTY-SIX
Confrontation

Vaerix watched the others go.

Cyra had to pull Grisban by the arm to make him run. Tarha lingered back, at the side of One Fist, who carried Quellen on his back. Brockton, leading the group, was already out of sight.

With a sigh, Vaerix turned and slowly walked to the steps. They climbed up and found their way to the outside. No one challenged them.

In the shadow of the ruined tower, they walked to the edge of the river of lava. The molten rock flowed in a shallow trench about one hundred yards wide. A black and red lizard skin of hardened slag drifted over the liquid fire underneath that glowed bright red through the cracks. Vapors escaped hissing from the fractures.

The whole of Levirax's army had gathered on the other side of the chasm, or so it seemed. While the whole dragon army would not pursue Brockton's party, Vaerix knew if they had joined the retreat, the dragon hybrids would've hunted them all down.

Hundreds of hybrids were looking at Vaerix in silence as they walked calmly toward them. Hundreds of warriors, some in the polished armor of the regular forces, many more in furs and leathers, members of the tribes that had accepted Levirax as their dragonlord.

Vaerix squinted through the fog, the air rippling from the heath. They looked for Drys in the press of hybrids that were at this point toeing the very ledge overlooking the river of fire.

They could not find Drys, but they easily spotted Xenith, wings unfolded as a sign of authority, with ample free space around him.

The time had come.

With a roaring war cry, Vaerix lifted their spear in the air and the metal tip caught the ruddy light from below.

Silence from across the flow was absolute.

Then they pointed the weapon at Xenith and again pushed all the air in their lungs through their throat, issuing their challenge.

This was the plan, and it was not a great plan – to use the battlefield to teach a lesson to the hybrids, to show them that another way was possible. That warriors died, yes, but not always, and not without purpose.

Vaerix felt a sudden calm spread through them. They were about to use violence against violence. Never a good choice, despite what he had told Grisban.

Or maybe this was just revenge and they were deceiving themselves.

But it was done now.

Once again, Vaerix issued the challenge.

Excitement rippled through the army. A chorus of war cries

responded to Vaerix's, louder and louder, until every dragon hybrid along the banks of the lava river was shouting their welcome for the challenge.

"Vaerix!" somebody shouted.

Others picked up that name and soon a part of the army was chanting it like a battle hymn. The name that should have been forgotten. The name that was supposed to no longer exist.

A sudden gust of air alerted Vaerix to an attack.

They tried to move aside, but claws clamped into their back as a body slammed into them, sending them sprawling on the hot ground. The pain in their back brought back memories of a time long past, and their spear escaped their grip. The weapon plummeted into the magma, bursting into flames before it hit the cracked crust.

With a roar, Vaerix used their tail to dislodge their foe and then rolled to the side, the move causing a second stab of pain in their wounded back muscles.

Arwyia, now free, was standing over them brandishing her spear, a ferocious light in her eyes.

Behind her, more hybrids were running at them from the tower.

"Let us do what is needed," she said.

Before she could stab them, Vaerix kicked her away and then twisted themselves back to their feet.

She did not speak again. She rushed forward, brandishing her spear with a single hand, cutting through the air. Vaerix dodged these cuts easily, but had to bend to avoid a slap from her left wing. They made an effort to ignore the searing pain in their back as Arwyia took to the air, flying over them and landing behind them.

Pain was not important.

If they could feel pain, they were still alive.

Living was important.

Vaerix turned in time to block Arwyia as she came at them, spear pointed, using her wings to gain momentum.

With a quick move of their right hand, Vaerix caught Arwyia's spear just below the sharp head. She whipped at them with her tail and they blocked the hit with their left forearm. Arwyia's right wing claw bit into their shoulder.

Roaring with pain and still holding the spear, Vaerix turned on their left foot and at the same time brought their right arm up, capturing their foe's wing in a lock, the shaft of the spear pressing painfully on the long bone. Arwyia tried to free herself, but her movements just increased the pressure.

With a loud snap, the long bone supporting Arwyia's left wing broke. She cried in pain and stepped back, her wing dragging.

Now Vaerix had a spear again.

The guards from the tower had formed a wide circle around the two combatants and were watching, unwilling to interfere with the feud.

Vaerix did not waste time using it. A lunge drew a red cut along Arwyia's side, then a quick twist and a hit in the knee with the butt of the weapon. She limped back, cursing them. She had a dagger in hand now.

On the other side of the lava flow, the hybrids were screaming, shouting, chanting Vaerix's name, a sound like distant waves breaking on some distant shore. Not "creature". Not "wingless one".

"Vaerix!" they chanted. Vaerix felt a surge of sudden pride. They had given them their name back.

But with recognition came something much darker. The hybrids were mad for the kill. It was like in the old times. Two dragon hybrids fighting, the loser to be killed to make the people stronger.

Vaerix felt nauseous.

"This has no meaning," they said.

This was not part of their plan. Vaerix did not want this young one's life.

Arwyia tried to stab them again, hissing in fury. She attacked with a storm of punches, cuts and tail sweeps, but Vaerix just pushed her back.

The crowd roared as the two adversaries traded blows.

Vaerix pulled back, feeling empty. The heat of the lava tickled their back.

"You owe me one death," she said. She was frothing at the mouth with rage.

Her wing was clearly causing her pain and distraction. Vaerix played every possible variation, adding in their greater experience, and their longer weapon, and her blind fury. Every outcome turned out the same.

"Do not waste your life," they said.

Wasn't this the whole point? Wasn't this what they had tried to tell their people all those years ago? What they had been searching for, and trying to understand through all their travels?

There had to be an alternative to violence.

"Fight me!" she roared.

"You have lost already."

Surely, she could see it, too. She would never be able to beat them, not in the state she was now.

"Then kill me!" she screeched, and she rushed them, head low.

Vaerix took a step back and felt the heat of the vapors escaping the burning river.

No retreat in that direction.

They took a step to the side and lifted the spear to push Arwyia back once again.

But she executed a strange dodge, stumbling, her wing flapping limp at her side, and then there was a wet impact and the shaft in Vaerix's hand shuddered.

"No," they said.

They took a step back, anguish and a sense of futility overwhelming them. But Arwyia's eyes blazed as she pushed herself forward. She dropped her dagger and grabbed the spear with both hands, pulling the spearhead deeper into her ribs.

"I die like a warrior," she grinned. "And you lose, Vaerix."

Cloud was grazing the yellow flowers of a lone brush that grew on the side of the hillock where Cyra and Tarha had left him. He snorted and looked at them as they approached, a reproachful look in his big eyes. He had not enjoyed being alone.

Cyra patted him on the neck, but he reacted haughtily, still offended for having been left alone and with precious little fodder.

"Put the elf ahorse," she said to One Fist.

"The elf would appreciate it, thanks," Quellen said in turn.

With a groan and a heave, One Fist lifted the elf bodily and sat him astride Cloud. The animal did not seem to care for the added weight.

One Fist stretched his back with a moan and then rolled his head, his neck cracking. "What now?" he said.

Brockton pointed west. "Black Ember Gorge."

"We've got no time to waste," Grisban added, gruff. "We want to make the most of any time Vaerix is buying us."

Cloud raised his head, as if listening.

"Move away from the slope," Quellen said.

Cyra had the horse by the bridles. "What–?"

A low hum rose from the ground itself, and with it a slow vibration. The earth shook under their feet.

"Earthquake!" Grisban said.

Remembering what had happened the last time, Cyra sat down and pulled her legs close to her chest. The others were either laying down or trying to keep their balance. Cloud's eyes rolled in panic and he neighed. Afraid, he reared and kicked the air, Quellen holding on to his mane.

A column of red fire rose on the northern horizon, followed by another, and then the distant rumble of two twin thunders rolled through the air.

Chunks of rock fell down the slope. A whole slab of gray stone, a small tree still clinging to its top with skeletal roots, slid down the incline and finally stopped about ten yards from where Cloud was looking at it.

Then everything was still again.

Dark flakes of ash started falling like black snow.

Another peal of thunder echoed in the distance, and then another.

Green and blue lights were mirrored in the black clouds overhead.

"Looks like the fireworks of Riverwatch Festival," One Fist said.

"Old volcanoes are waking up again," Quellen said. "Looks like the Molten Heath is giving Vaerix a big welcome."

Grisban gave a hard look at Brockton. "And we are missing the party."

Drys witnessed Vaerix's duel and Arwyia's death through the haze of the river of molten rock, the hot air trembling and making the scene in some way less real. He wondered whether that was how Vaerix's dreams felt, at the same time heart-wrenching and unreal.

Drys stood with Maesix by Wing Captain Xenith, as they watched the dance of weapons unfolding on the other side of the chasm. Excitement roared around them, the hybrid army enthralled by the clash. Many knew the myth of Vaerix, many more were learning about them now. Some knew and respected Arwyia. And they all knew about the incoming dwarven army, about the war to come.

They had been gathered here by Levirax's command. But they had not expected this. The two fighting in the mist rising from the lava flow was like a prologue, a promise of things to come.

Then it was over, and the shouts and the calls died out as Arwyia sank to her knees and then lay prone on the ground.

In the sudden dead silence, Xenith uttered a curse. He spread his wings and took to the air, crossing the chasm, wielding the scythe-like weapon that was the symbol of his authority.

His personal guard followed him, as did Drys and Maesix.

Together, they flew through the thick, syrupy hot air, breathing iron and sulfur, and landed where the warriors from the tower had surrounded Vaerix, forming a wide ring, keeping at least ten yards away.

Vaerix was standing still over the dead body of their fallen foe.

Wings vibrating in the wind, Wing Captain Xenith landed in the circle and both Drys and Maesix dropped at his back. Behind them, the crowd tottering on the edge of the molten rock river erupted in another cheer.

"Xenith!" they called. "Xenith!"

Vaerix looked up. Their eyes lingered for a moment on Drys', and then they looked at Wing Captain Xenith.

"I heard your call, creature," Xenith said. "I heard your challenge."

Vaerix shook their head. "This was wrong," they said. "Violence cannot teach anything but violence. I was wrong."

Drys was suddenly sure Vaerix was talking to him, not to Xenith. He nodded, signaling he had heard and, in a way, he understood.

Vaerix had never intended to kill Arwyia, never wanted to start a fight with Xenith. Not like this.

"She showed us a good death," Xenith said. "Nothing wrong with that."

He hefted his weapon. Xenith's scythe, a six foot staff with a curved three foot blade, was ideal to attack targets on the ground while flying, but was hardly efficient as a one-on-one dueling weapon.

"We should have done this all those years ago," Xenith said.

"Captain…" Drys began.

What could he say to him?

Remind the captain that Levirax might want to interrogate Vaerix?

Remind him that the dwarves had fled, and were on their way to rejoin with their army, wherever that could be?

Or just ask him to show mercy. To stop wasting lives.

Drys' voice shriveled and died.

"Back down," Xenith said, glancing at them. Then he paused. "But first–"

He handed his scythe to Drys. "Give me your sword."

Drys stared at him.

"Now," Xenith said.

With a glance at Vaerix, Drys unbuckled his sword belt and handed the sheathed weapon to the wing commander. Xenith pulled the blade free and let the scabbard fall on the ground. "Now retreat."

Maesix pulled Drys by an arm and they joined the line of warriors surrounding Vaerix and Xenith.

The wing captain weighed the sword in his hand. "This is better," he said grimly.

A thousand voices cheered as he held the sword high, and then quieted down, expectant. Drys watched in silence, heart in his throat.

Xenith walked up to Vaerix, stopping about five steps from them.

"Any last words?" he asked. "This is how legends go, right? A big rousing speech before you die. You could tell the warriors about your dreams. Many of them have never heard your fables. They might understand what a pathetic creature you are."

Vaerix did not reply.

The silence around them was uncanny, only the low boiling of the nearby lava flow providing a background.

"I don't want this," Vaerix said.

"But you issued a challenge," Xenith replied. "Warriors fight and warriors die, creature. Are you a warrior?"

Vaerix scratched at their scarred arm. "True warriors do not take the lives of their enemies, but give them life."

Xenith laughed. "What does that mean?"

"That you can have your life and walk away with it. Right now."

Again, Xenith laughed. "You are out of your mind."

Drys watched as Vaerix's stance changed. Their shoulders relaxed and they drew a long, deep breath. Preparing for battle, like in the old days.

Vaerix placed the head of Arwyia's spear on the ground, and with a swift kick broke the shaft close to where it joined the metal head. They pushed the metal blade away. This left them with a staff about five feet long.

They held it in the middle with their right hand and stretched their arm in front of them, so that the wooden staff was parallel to the ground.

And they waited.

Xenith grinned.

He stretched his wings, preparing to strike, and he looked so much larger than Vaerix, who stood still, holding their staff. The claws at the tip of the wings clicked viciously.

Vaerix breathed softly, waiting.

In two steps, Xenith closed the distance and slashed at the exposed arm of Vaerix with a powerful downward cut.

Vaerix took half a step to the right. The sword hit the left end of the staff, pushing it down. Vaerix twisted their wrist, used the force of the blow to twirl the staff and reverse it, and used their left hand to push the end in the face of Xenith. The blunt end of the staff stopped just shy of the captain's eye. Startled, Xenith took two stumbling steps back, wings flapping for balance, and only by using his tail avoided falling on his back.

He managed to keep his hold on the sword and when he

looked up, Vaerix was standing there in front of him, their staff again held parallel to the ground at arm's length.

"Are you mocking me?" Xenith asked, simmering with rage.

Drys felt Maesix move by his side, shifting his weight from one foot to the other.

Xenith approached Vaerix again, more cautious this time. He assumed a supple stance, flexing his legs, and then shot forward, feinting to the left before slashing again with his sword.

And again, Vaerix moved about one foot to the right and used the energy of the strike to twirl their staff, deflect the blade and at the same time carry an attack at Xenith's face. They placed their left hand on the bottom of the staff and pushed it forward. The far end of the weapon hit Xenith on the cheekbone and Xenith staggered back, cursing.

A single drop of blood marked his cheek.

A murmur spread through the troops. This was like a warrior playing with a youngling.

Vaerix fell back into their relaxed stance, holding the staff in both hands, parallel to the ground.

"You think this is a game?" Xenith barked.

Drys had never seen Vaerix fight like this.

They had not ceded an inch and remained unfazed, as if it was a breeze and not the captain of the dragon army that they were facing. Their power and their fury, which had allowed them to dominate on the battlefield, had been replaced by control and restraint.

Yet their skill was still unequaled.

Xenith cleaned his cheek with his thumb.

He half-turned, like he was going to walk away from Vaerix.

Then he turned back and lunged, stabbing at Vaerix's chest. A triumphant roar escaped his lips and was reprised and amplified by the crowd.

Vaerix sidestepped him and struck the blade with their staff, about one inch in front of the hilt. The blade slipped from Xenith's fingers and dropped on the ground.

A collective gasp from the army echoed Drys'.

With supreme indifference, Vaerix stepped back, leaving his adversary room to recover his weapon.

"Careful," they said as Xenith stretched a hand to grab the hilt. "It's very sharp."

Grimly, Xenith picked up the sword and, rising up, segued with a sudden attack. He slid forward, putting his weight on his right foot, his wings opening with a loud sound that could have surprised a less experienced adversary. Again, the tip of Drys' borrowed blade sought Vaerix's heart, and again Vaerix dodged and struck the blade out of Xenith's hand. They then followed through with a new hit at the face of the commander, followed by a swing at his head that Xenith barely avoided by jumping back.

They faced each other, Drys' sword on the ground between them. Xenith's breathing was labored, while Vaerix was perfectly unfazed.

"Why is Vaerix doing this?" Maesix asked in a low voice. "Why are they not fighting?"

"But they are," replied Drys, awed.

Maesix was not listening. "Coward!" he shouted.

Others picked up his call among the crowd on the other side of the molten river. But the majority watched in silence, wondering what would come next. Just like Drys and Maesix, they were seeing their captain being humiliated, his martial skills ineffective in the face of the wingless hybrid's detached ease.

"Do you hear them?" Xenith asked. "They know what you are. A wingless creature and a coward."

But if he had hoped to cause an angry reaction, Xenith was once again disappointed. Slowly, his eyes on Vaerix, he retrieved the sword for the second time.

"Do you hope to shame me?" he asked. "Like you shamed Arwyia?"

Vaerix did not reply. They stood, holding their staff, and with their free hand they gestured for Xenith to come near.

Ignoring the invitation, Xenith started slowly circling them, the sword point low, close to the ground. Vaerix turned, keeping their eyes on him.

Xenith's tail cracked like a whip. He feinted with his wingtips, scratching at Vaerix's face. Vaerix just dodged the attacks, their feet planted on the ground, their back and neck twisting.

"Fight me!" Xenith screeched.

Another roar, another slash. The blade cut through the air from left to right. Vaerix's staff hit Xenith's forearm with a loud crack. His wrist broken, Xenith let go of the sword just as Vaerix pushed their staff into the ground and used it as a springboard for a jump. They wrapped their legs around Xenith's long neck and twisted in midair, using their whole weight to sweep Xenith off his feet. The captain tried to use his wings to break the tumble, but landed on the ground on his back. The impact knocked the air out of his lungs. Vaerix rolled on the ground and was back on their feet in a heartbeat.

Maesix took half a step forward, but Drys stopped him.

Vaerix stood over Xenith, the end of their staff pressing against his throat. "You lose."

"Kill me then," Xenith hissed.

"I don't need to."

"Kill him!" somebody shouted in the crowd. More voices joined the chorus. Even some of the guards in the circle around them called for a kill.

But Vaerix would not give them that, Drys thought. They would show the dragon hybrids there was a choice, even on the battlefield. Vaerix would give him life.

Drys looked around. Maesix was shivering with fury.

"Are you scared of killing?" Xenith asked mockingly.

"Are you scared of living?" Vaerix replied.

Someone in the crowd started chanting Vaerix's name.

This caused a commotion. More voices joined in, while many others rose against them. Blades leapt out of their scabbards. Angry warnings were issued.

With an angry growl, Xenith slashed at Vaerix, using the claws at the tip end of his wings. The hooked talons painted two bright red lines across Vaerix's chest. Vaerix took a step back, releasing Xenith, who leapt to his feet and stretched to grab Drys' sword. Vaerix tapped his hand with their staff and Xenith pulled it back.

The disturbance in the crowd was spreading. More and more voices called Vaerix's name, as warnings and menace were giving way to violence.

The clang of weapons rose as hybrid fought against hybrid.

Huffing with fury, Xenith charged Vaerix, wings outstretched, trying to tackle and grapple them to the ground. Vaerix hit him hard in the head with their staff and danced away from him.

Xenith stopped, shaking his head to clear it. He caught sight of the staff as Vaerix swung it a second time at his head and blocked it with his left arm. Vaerix ducked under his guard and caught him in a grapple hold, blocking the left arm. They leveraged their staff and pressed down hard.

Xenith cried out in pain as his shoulder cracked and popped.

Both arms now out of commission, the wing captain staggered back.

Maesix pushed past Drys and ran to the captain's side.

He had his sword out.

"Stand back, coward!" Maesix cried.

The guards in the circle looked at each other, uncertain about their next move.

Across the river of magma, a brawl was spreading through the army as supporters of Xenith and Vaerix fought out their differences.

Xenith leaned against Maesix's side.

"Arrest the creature!" he shouted. His voice rose above the din. "Arrest and put down this wingless aberration!"

"You heard the captain!" Maesix shouted in turn.

But still the guards hesitated.

In an elegant flowing movement, Vaerix picked up Drys' sword and stood holding both sword and staff in a simple defensive stance.

CHAPTER TWENTY-SEVEN
Revolt

Heeding Xenith's call, hybrids took to the sky in one and twos, forming a cloud of wings over the chasm. They had their weapons ready as they flew the brief distance from the edge of their camp to where Vaerix was holding Maesix and the guards at bay.

But there were others now that opposed them. They chanted Vaerix's name and crossed their weapons with the warriors that had been their companions but a few minutes before. War cries and the sound of battle rose above the thrumming of the river of molten rock.

Vaerix parried Maesix's sword with the one they were holding and at the same time tripped one of the hybrid guards using their broken spear staff. They moved with the easy rhythm of the fight, a dance they had been practicing all their life.

This was what they had dreamed about, what felt like a thousand years before, when they camped in the marshlands with Brockton and the others. Fire and madness, and hybrids chanting their name.

If this was the solution to the riddle, it was not a solution they liked.

Rarely if ever was peace achieved with weapons.

Maesix swung at them again, and Vaerix again parried, but did not follow up with a slash of their own.

They were not here to kill. And yet, hybrids were dying all around them.

They died chanting Vaerix's name.

It was a nightmare.

"You do not understand, do you?" Maesix asked.

Vaerix parried another attack, stepping back. They did not have the heart to fight their old comrade, and their preoccupation with Drys was a further distraction. The blue-gray hybrid was being swallowed by the crowd.

"I always knew it would come to this," Maesix said. He parried Vaerix's staff with his wing and tried to slip his blade under their guard.

"Everybody knew you were destined for great things," Maesix went on. "We could see it. But then this curse came upon you." He smirked. "You called it that, do you remember? When you started seeing things in your dreams. Your curse, you called it."

Another slash, and then Maesix's shoulder connected with Vaerix's sternum, pushing them back.

"I was wrong," Vaerix said.

"Oh, no, you were absolutely right. Maybe for the last time in your miserable life, you were right. You had been cursed and you brought the curse upon our people."

Their blades locked. Maesix tried to slap Vaerix aside with his tail, and Vaerix parried.

"I saw how your words inflamed the younger ones. How they were willing to follow you. A new world without rules—"

"Just different rules."

"Anarchy."

"Not so."

Maesix was no longer listening. He brought on more attacks. "Even the older ones were swayed," he said. "Even Drys wavered."

Vaerix's eye caught a movement, saw Drys push through the brawling fighters. Maesix used the moment to scratch at their eyes with his wing talons. Vaerix turned their head sharply, but two parallel lines of blood marked their cheek.

"You must see what I did was necessary," Maesix said, his voice cracking.

"What did you do?" Vaerix asked, but the answer was clear in their mind.

"You had to be stopped," Maesix said. "To stop the anarchy. I stood against you in that trial, but I also was the one who informed our dragonlord of your traitorous dreams."

Drys now pushed between the two of them, his eyes wide in amazement and alight in fury. "You?"

"It was the only way."

Vaerix did not have a name for what was boiling in their chest, but they saw it amplified tenfold in Drys' eyes. He now knew what Vaerix had known for centuries.

"You had Vaerix tortured and cast out," he screeched. "You informed on the ones that kept their memory alive, afterward–"

Maesix laughed, a sound like the rattling of a broken toy. The chaos and madness of the fighting around them was forgotten.

"And it was useless," he said. "Your wings torn off, your name erased, you became a ghost." His eyes widened in a sudden understanding. "To some, you became a dream."

"You betrayed them!" Drys shouted. "You betrayed us!"

"I am loyal to our dragonlord, Levirax."

With a roar of rage, Vaerix rushed at Maesix, their sword poised to kill.

The blades sang, biting into each other. For a moment fury prevailed and Vaerix did not hold back anymore. Then, as their blades clashed, Vaerix relented. It was not Maesix's betrayal so long ago that was moving them, but Drys' recent pain at the revelation.

Fighting hybrids crossed the path of the duelists and were swiftly cut down. It was a death dance with swords and talons, tails and kicks. Maesix's wings gave him a slight advantage, but Vaerix's experience was not dulled by blind fury.

They would impart Maesix a lesson, but would not take his life. Their old duplicitous companion would live.

Then suddenly Drys was between them.

Vaerix missed a step in the dance. A body slammed into their back and they staggered forward, suddenly unbalanced. They used the staff to break their fall, but in this way they left themselves open to Maesix's blade. Vaerix saw what was about to happen in their mind's eye.

A clean cut at the neck, and then oblivion. They knew with the perfect understanding of the accomplished fighter. This was the end.

Maesix saw an opportunity and shifted his grip on his sword. The blade drew a pale streak through the air, seeking Vaerix's throat. With a loud clang, it stopped about half a foot in front of Vaerix's face, scraping sparks along a short, thick blade.

The long-limbed shape of Cyra slipped between Vaerix and Maesix, pushing back the latter with a well-placed kick in the abdomen. Then she turned and parried a slash from Drys.

"Friends of yours?" she asked over her shoulder.

New voices joined the chanting, over the noise of the battle. Vaerix dodged an attack from a stray hybrid and turned. Grisban and One Fist were busy keeping five foes at bay.

One Fist was wielding a rough sword, the blade thick and blunt ended, stabbing left and right, while Grisban pushed through, swinging a stone hammer little more than a big rock tied at the end of a stick. He cracked the knees of a hybrid that tried to stop him and ran over him as he fell without pause, the mad strains of a dwarven war song escaping his throat.

Parrying a slash from a stray sword, Vaerix wondered briefly where the dwarf found the energy to fight and sing with the same wild abandon.

By their side Cyra disengaged and dodged a second attack from Maesix. She parried another slash directed at Vaerix's head using her crossed swords and stepped in front of them.

"Time to go," she said.

Vaerix had lost sight of Drys, carried away into the battle. They caught a sparkle of gray, but it was gone. Vaerix disarmed an attacker with a swing of their staff and then stood behind her, back to back, as more hybrids circled them, wings outstretched.

"Why are you here?" Vaerix asked.

"You know how Grisban is," she replied.

Cyra kicked her adversary in a knee and turned to face a second attacker.

The hybrid fell face first on the ground, Grisban behind him, wielding his hammer.

"Less talk," the dwarf said. "We need to go."

Just as he said so, Maesix came at them from behind and cut downward in a mighty sweep. Grisban caught his movement in the corner of his eye and started to turn. The hybrid's blade cut in his shoulder.

Only then, Vaerix realized the earth was shaking.

More hybrids crossed over the flow of magma, the beat of their wings churning the sour vapors that lingered over the black crust of the molten rock. Others followed and attacked them in flight, chanting Vaerix's name like a rallying cry.

Two hybrids, locked in combat, fell and caught fire as they touched the burning surface of the lava flow in a crash of armor, broken wings and violence.

Where they impacted the surface, the thin black crust cracked.

Molten rock burned bright red underneath.

More steam escaped as bubbles started boiling in the lava and a swell formed in the flow. A wave that surged and rose, brightly burning rock coalescing in a shape. A large smoldering hand, covered in a thin skin of cooling magma. Fingers stretched, the palm crossed with thin cracks, the colossal hand waved in the air and swatted the flying hybrids.

Some were knocked out of the sky and plummeted in flames into the burning river below. Others were grasped and crushed when the smoldering fingers closed over them.

The sight of the molten rock hand put a stop to the brawl among the supporters of Xenith and the hybrids that rooted for Vaerix. They all stared in awe and horror at the portent unfolding before them.

Trailing sulfurous gases, the giant hand swept through the

308   *Descent: Legends of the Dark*

sky and then slammed on the edge of the chasm, like a drunkard slapping the top of a table. The impact scattered the remains of the army as the hybrids flew through the heat and the spray of liquid glass. The closest tents in the nearby camp caught fire, as the hand dissolved in streams of lava that ran in every direction.

"Now that was impressive," Brockton said, looking over the scene from the top of the ruined tower.

"Thanks," Quellen said, his voice little more than a breath.

He leaned on the parapet, pressing down with his hands to relieve some of the pain from his scarred feet, and tried to catch his breath.

They had split, and the fighters had joined the battle. Tarha had disappeared down a dark staircase, and Brockton had been forced to help the elf up the stairs and to the very top of the tower. There, the mage had called on all that was left of his powers.

The tower shuddered.

The show was not yet over, apparently. Brockton gasped, surprised, and tried to keep his balance. The tremor increased and to the north, a sound of thunder announced two tall columns of red liquid fire, that cast their incandescent glow over the landscape as they rose into the black sky.

"Satall's mercy," Quellen whispered.

Blocks of stone fell from the face of the black tower and exploded when they hit the ground. The wind carried a fine snow of gray ash.

"Quite impressive," Brockton commented again.

Quellen shook his head. "Not my doing."

"What?"

"Let's get out of here," the elf said, panting. "The Molten Heath's coming alive under us."

As a second shudder shook the tower, they retraced their steps down the staircase.

Vaerix cast their blade aside and picked up the protesting Grisban.

By their side, Cyra twirled her blades, keeping Maesix at a distance.

Drys was there, too, pulling Maesix by an arm. "Enough of this," he said. Even though Vaerix noticed his eyes still burned with betrayal, it seemed he was taking Vaerix's teachings to heart for once. He would spare Maesix.

Vaerix threw Grisban over rheir shoulder.

"I'm not an invalid!" the dwarf groaned.

But Vaerix ignored his words. Blood was pouring from the cut in Grisban's shoulder, soaking his dirty tunic. His arm hung limply by his side.

Vaerix's eyes met Drys'.

"We'll fight another day," Vaerix said. Then they turned and ran, ignoring the outraged cry from Maesix.

Coward, he called them. He challenged them to stay and fight.

But Vaerix no longer had time for that.

There had been a time, Vaerix considered with a certain amount of amusement, when the shame of fleeing the battlefield would have been worse than facing defeat. And yet, they said to themselves as their legs moved in long strides, leaving the bank of the lava river and the battlefield behind, there were things that mattered more than shame.

"Put me down, I said!" Grisban barked.

Things like the life of one cantankerous dwarf.

Vaerix threw their head back and let out a long laugh.

A hybrid came at them, flapping their wings and gliding a few feet off the ground. He was intercepted by One Fist, who came running and slashed through their wing. The hybrid crashed to the ground, and the orc leapt over him and kept running, joining Vaerix.

"To the tower," Cyra gasped as she, too, drew level with them.

The earth shook again.

They veered toward the black wall of the tower. Two hybrids stood in their way, but they went through them like the wind. The two warriors barely put up a fight. They were intent on watching the sky to the north, where huge clouds of ash billowed, painted red by the raging fire fountains of the volcanoes.

Past the wall, Vaerix finally put Grisban down.

"Is he dead?" One Fist asked, his chest expanding in deep breaths. The orc was bleeding through a dozen small cuts but did not seem to mind.

"I am not dead, you blockhead!" Grisban tried to stand, but he swayed drunkenly.

Cyra pushed him down and sat him against the wall. She checked his shoulder and cursed under her breath.

"I'll need stitches," Grisban said.

The cut looked ugly to Vaerix. "Where's Tarha?" they asked.

Tarha ignored the hollow sound of the earth moving beneath her, and the shuddering. She added another handful of scraps to the small fire and breathed on the flames.

For a moment, pale yellow flames crackled and consumed the splinters of wood the orc had collected. The light from the fire cast Tarha's shadow on the dilapidated wall of the chamber. Then the fire died down, and the blackened remains coughed up a small cloud of smoke.

Tarha sniffed at the acrid smell and grasped her bone pendant.

Like many other times in the past, she focused her thoughts.

At the edge of her senses, she could feel the ghosts crowding around her. After centuries of waiting, they could feel something was about to happen. Something that centered on her, sitting lonely on the dirty floor of a buried chamber, under a smashed tower, along the forgotten border of a dwarven kingdom long gone.

Like the spirits she had used a while back, these were mere rags of ancient souls, remains eroded by time and ennui, dried-up remains of once proud fighters and colonists. A few still preserved a distant spark of who or what they had been – a conscripted man-at-arms, the one daughter of a gemstones merchant, an officer from the governor's guard. But most of them were just hungry will-o'-the-wisps, bundles of spiritual energy floating on the currents of the next realm. Devoid of thought or identity, only fueled by anger and hunger. And now, because of her, agitated in what a more naive observer could have called excitement.

But it was not just her.

Nor was it the earth moving, the mountains erupting into fire.

Something else was coming, making the spirits restless and furious.

She would use that fury.

The smoke rose in a faint spiral. Tarha ignored the increasing tremors and the sound of battle from outside. The broken tower above her acted like a beacon, calling out to the ghosts haunting this borderland. She was exactly where she needed to be.

She opened her eyes as the spirit approached.

He stepped over the dead fire and looked at her.

"I will need your help, spirit," she said. "One last time."

It was exactly like Vaerix had described, outside of the gates of the ancient dwarven city, almost like the past replaying.

The dragon appeared in the sky to the north. It flew over the mountaintops, pushing on the wind with wings that seemed to stretch forever. It drew closer and banked to the east in a great curve and at the same time dropped down, making straight for the hybrid camp and the dilapidated tower beyond it.

Cyra knew what was coming, but still she found it impossible to move.

It was a dragon. A true dragon from the Molten Heath. Just like in the old stories of the Third Darkness.

Powerful muscles moved wings through which the sunlight played as if through the glass windows of the imperial palace. A creature so large, it was hard to believe it should be able to fly and be so elegant as it crossed the sky.

As the dragon drew closer, Cyra realized how fast it was moving.

One of the wonders of Terrinoth she had dreamed about seeing in her travels.

The volcanoes thundered in the distance and the monster answered their call with a mighty roar.

She should have been more careful with her dreams, Cyra thought.

One Fist grabbed her by an arm and dragged her away. "Into the tower!" he shouted.

Vaerix picked up Grisban, who was no longer protesting, and they ran.

The dragon let out a screeching roar and it opened its maw, expanding its chest while its wings twisted, further reducing its speed.

Cyra leapt into the tower first, Vaerix by her side, Grisban in their arms. One Fist was trying to push the brass doors closed.

"Into the basement!" One Fist shouted.

"No!" Cyra snapped, thinking of the dwarves of long ago who had suffocated deep underground. "Upstairs!"

She remembered the underground chamber filled with bones in the buried city. Fire sucking the air out of their lungs.

Vaerix frowned. "Why?"

"Upstairs," she repeated, and without waiting for them she leapt up the steps.

"The sword poet is leading us to our death. Why would we go up?" she heard Grisban say. But he followed her.

She almost slammed into Brockton and Quellen coming down the staircase.

"A dragon's coming!" the younger dwarf said. Then he saw Grisban. "What happened?"

"We need to go up," Cyra replied and pushed him up the steps. "It's going to breathe fire," she said.

The elf looked at her, and comprehension dawned in his eyes.

"She's right," he said as he turned, limping as fast as he could up the stairs. "Upstairs, run!"

One Fist and Vaerix were pushing behind them.

Her breath catching in her throat, Cyra ran up the spiral staircase and finally emerged at the top of the tower. A blast of hot air caught her. She coughed and stumbled. Through tear-filled eyes she looked over the parapet. The tower was like an island in a sea of flames.

The hybrid camp was on fire, and so was the stretch of dry grass in front of the tower. The dragon was doing a slow circle above them, its wings almost perpendicular to the ground.

As the dragon's shadow crossed the river of molten rock, plumes of fire erupted. Again, the creature opened its jaws and belched liquid fire at the hybrid camp.

Vaerix watched her rise again for a second passage. "Levirax," they said, awe and fear in their voice.

They wanted revenge, and revenge was what Tarha would give them.

With the spirit of Ughat the Mace acting like a gateway to the shadow realms, Tarha called the spirits to her. The dead defenders of the Karok Doum, the warriors and the men-at-arms, the lost spirit strand of a once mighty kingdom, now languishing on the edge of the great darkness beyond.

The lone shard of bone on her neck burned like a hot iron in the palm of her hand, and it was like a fist was squeezing her heart with every breath. It was like her own life was being burned to fuel her call, to make her summons shine brighter in the dark.

And they came.

At first sluggishly, drifting closer in small steps. Cautious, or simply apathetic.

Distracted and slow to respond. But her message got through.

Come defend the tower. Come fight the dragons.

Tarha's knowledge of the War of Fire was limited at best. She did not know the facts, but she could see the consequences. She had seen them ever since she had come down the mountains with Brockton and the others. She had seen the clusters of spirits among the ruins, hanging by broken memories and distorted loyalties to the remains of their domain.

The black tower by the river of molten rock was one such places, a wreck from an ancient time, surrounded by a pool of unresolved lives.

A pool that normally was still like a swampland, but now was churning under Tarha's powers.

Come do your duty. Come for revenge.

Once aroused, the attention of the spirits did not take long to flare. They burned brighter in the dark. They drew closer. Most were little more than blue sparks of consciousness, centuries old, almost free of any intelligence. Others were dancing flames of hatred, all that was left of dead warriors still focused on their long-forgotten mission. A precious few retained most of their old self and came walking on ghostly legs, holding translucent shields and smoke-thin swords.

Come claim what's yours. Come to battle.

In normal circumstances, one like Tarha would never be able to cast so wide a net, to call on such a large army of the dead. But the circumstances in the Karok Doum were not normal.

The whole land was like a vast, endless battlefield, soaked in the blood and resentment of the fallen, and warped by strange, forgotten magic.

She called on that resentment. She used it to fuel and amplify her call. She made it her voice, echoing in the vast emptiness of the beyond.

Come fulfill your destiny.

Come and fight the dragons.

And in that vast dark emptiness, voices rose in response.

CHAPTER TWENTY-EIGHT
Dragon Rex

The hybrids were endowed with a modicum of fire resistance. Many of them, when the flood of flames swept the foot of the hill, simply stopped fighting and took flight. A few kept trading blows as they flew, and only the seriously distracted, the wounded and the dying remained on the battlefield, succumbing to the rain of fire Levirax was visiting upon them.

"What's she doing?" Brockton asked.

"She's culling the weak," Vaerix said.

They watched as Levirax once again rose in the sky, her wings causing small hurricanes in the black billows that rose from the burning grassland. A hot wind was rising from below, caressing with its warmth the skin of the companions atop the black tower.

A ragtag band of hybrids formed behind the dragon, loyal warriors following their leader. But they seemed to be keeping their distance, and Brockton thought they were as scared of their dragonlord as he and his companions were. They seemed small and insignificant compared to the colossal shape of Levirax, who paid them no heed.

Grisban cursed as One Fist pressed a rag over his wound.

"Now she will come for us," Vaerix said. "Where's Tarha?"

The dragon dove toward the tower. She did a first close pass, her large emerald eyes sweeping over Brockton and the others. Vaerix saluted her with their naked sword in a silent gesture of defiance.

Riding the wind, Levirax did a very tight turn and spread her wings to break her fall. Then her talons closed on the black stones of the tower and the building shuddered under the sudden impact of her massive body. She hung to the side of the tower, her wings outstretched and her long neck bent to bring her head level with Vaerix.

"What a way to go," Grisban muttered, trying to stand.

One Fist helped him up.

Levirax drew her head back, opening her mouth, a warm blast of foul breath washing over them. Ancient fire rumbled in her gut.

The floor shuddered, and Brockton could not tell if it was the energy coming from the dragon, or yet another earthquake. He had been told that in the final moments of one's life, memories of places and people would flash before one's mind's eye, like tapestries in a long gallery, but all he was able to think right then was how sharp and white Levirax's teeth were.

One of the obsidian tiles was torn from the floor and flew toward Levirax's snout. It exploded on impact, soon followed by another and another. The dragon pulled back, stung by that unexpected onslaught. Just like Brockton, she turned her eyes toward Quellen, who was leaning on Cyra's shoulder, his hands outstretched and bathed in a faint violet light.

Time seemed to slow down for Brockton.

The exploding tiles were not really hurting the dragon, but had distracted her, or at least given her a new target for her anger. Again, she reared, arching her neck and filling her lungs before she belched fire.

Vaerix leapt forward and stabbed her in the throat. The sword they had taken from Drys pierced the soft pale skin under Levirax's chin and sank a good two spans into the dragon's jaw. At the same time, One Fist lunged and sank his blade into the dragon's forepaw clinging on the parapet.

Levirax screeched in pain and jumped away from her perch, shaking her head and dislodging the weapon. She fell toward the blackened ground, then caught the wind in her wings and rose again, flying a tight circle around the tower.

"Now she's really mad," Cyra said.

Quellen sat down on the pitted floor and shook his head, too weak to speak.

"You all must go," Grisban croaked.

He had a pike he had found somewhere and he was using it as a crutch to stand. The wound in his shoulder was bleeding again, his tunic soaked in crimson.

"No," Brockton said.

"Go," Grisban repeated. He was following Levirax's orbit as she neared the tower.

"Listen," Cyra said.

Brockton frowned. He turned his head slightly, but he could hear nothing. Not the cries of the wounded or the crackling of the fires on the plain. Not the groans of the damaged tower under his feet. Not even the beating of the dragon's wings as Levirax drew closer.

Everything was perfectly silent, until it was not.

A distant hollow sound rose from beneath, like hundreds of voices humming an ancient song wordlessly, its strains at the same time familiar and strange to Brockton's ears.

"Sounds like Valnir's Call," Grisban said.

"What is that?" One Fist asked.

"Old dwarven battle song," Brockton replied. "Very old."

Levirax, who had been approaching the tower on a tightening spiral, flapped her wings and pulled back, as the red of the flames surrounding the tower faded, replaced by a cold, pulsating blue glow.

Tarha walked out of the buried chamber and into the open, and the ghosts of the Karok Doum followed her. They smothered the flames and lit the courtyard and the cracked walls of the building with their blue glow. She walked to the shattered bronze doors of the wall and then lifted her arms, a low chant pouring through her parched lips.

It was like the pulling of a bow, she thought, a reminiscence of her days as a young girl, when she and her brothers would run the fields looking for game. One would pull the string of the bow as far back as possible, the wood bending with a gentle creaking sound, and hold it there. She remembered the tension in her arm and her back, the string biting into her fingers, the power of the weapon wishing for release.

So felt the storm of spirits twisting around her.

A world-shaking power, crying, screeching, craving for release.

There was a black silhouette against the blue of the sky, surfing among the billows of black acrid smoke. It drew closer, great wings beating.

Tarha's gaze found the eyes of the dragon as it landed on the tower.

A good hunter, her brother Taran had taught her, was one that did not force their shot. They'd just align the arrowhead with the target and then the string would naturally slip through their fingers, as if by its own volition.

No tension, no stress. Just the bow and the arrow doing their work.

Tarha let go of her bone amulet, her palm marked by a black burn, the pain running through her arm, up into her heart.

But all that was of no consequence now. All that mattered was that she had her sights on the dragon, her arrowhead perfectly aligned.

And the angry spirits of the Karok Doum were free.

They surged through the air like a fountain of blue light, like a pillar of preternatural cold, the increasing snowstorm of ash flecks refracting and amplifying the ghostly glow. Most of the spirits shot straight up, while others strayed and circled around the tower. They followed different paths, but they all went for the same target and they all joined in a slow, ominous chorus as they did so.

The cold blue flame engulfed Levirax where she hung onto the tower, cutting short her fire-breath. A cloud of steamy air escaped her mouth instead, and then she let out a painful roar that turned into a strangled mewl as she let go of her grip and tried to fly away. The swarm of blue fires clung to her, inescapable. Levirax worked her wings to gain height and distance, but still the glow-worm swarm of spirits encircled her. Tiny sparks of blue light shot through the dragon's body, while larger strands of ghostly matter, like rags in the wind, clung to her limbs. Half-formed shapes of dwarven warriors, clad in ancient armor, crawled along her body in open contempt of the laws of gravity. They stabbed at Levirax with their spectral blades, tore at her with their fingers. Levirax coughed and her flight became erratic. Still a thousand voices sang a dirge-like dwarven chant, off-key and terrible. Levirax twisted and contorted in the sky, pain shooting through her body, and she flailed. Her wings flapped lifelessly and she fell to the ground.

Tarha watched the swarm of enraged spirits dissolve, each of them screeching its way back to their resting place.

She took a deep breath and crumpled to the ground.

Levirax pushed herself back to her feet.

She was dizzy and in pain, the cold burn of the ghostly attack making her muscles stiff, her scaly skin crawl. The pain was spreading where the blue ghosts had touched her. But worse than the physical distress was the anguish and pain in her mind. She had never felt like this, like her very soul had been crushed by the hatred and resentment of hundreds of voices screaming in her face their grievances, their pain, their emptiness.

She stretched her wings, tentatively, and pain ran like an ice blade between her shoulders. Dark patches marked her flying membranes, the veins broken, the bruises spreading. The pain reminded her of her unfinished business, and she looked up at the top of the black tower.

The sky was filling with specks of ash and volcanic glass, and pale violet lightning was tearing through the low clouds, a promise of the coming storm.

Did something still move on top of the tower?

Levirax did not know.

The landscape was a ruin of scorched earth and burning structures, all that was left of her army's encampment a jumble of blackened remains and isolated fires. She hated being so disappointed.

Anger flared in her spirit, chasing away the last lingering remains of the ghostly confrontation. The ache in her body was further reason to seek out her enemies and make them pay.

With a roar, she jumped into the sky.

She flew over the crumbling wall of the dwarven tower and rose in a tight path along the face of the building. Her talons found the arrow slits and grabbed the stones for support. She looked down on the tower's terrace. The traitor Vaerix and their cohorts were gone, seeking refuge and escape in the bowels of the tower.

Levirax grinned, the last strands of her recent distress dissipating.

She leaned forward, savoring what was to come.

She would put her lips to the opening there, now, and breathe her fire down the stairwell, filling the whole building with her flames.

Heat grew in her chest as she filled her lungs in preparation.

She paused for a brief moment as her senses perceived, with sudden horror, the presence of another.

Close, so close.

Levirax's head snapped back as Shaarina's talons sank into her, drawing a long painful line of fire along her side.

It had been five centuries since Shaarina had left the coziness of her lair to go out into the world. Longer still since she had to defend her title as Dragon Rex.

She was discovering anew the simple pleasure of soaring through the air, flexing her mighty wings. The activity was dissolving the kinks in her muscles, and her dead scales were falling off together with the volcanic glass incrustation and the grime that had made her skin brittle.

A new bright coat of color was revealed as she rose into the sky. A supple, healthy skin, her scales refracting the sunlight. Her wings stretched with ease as she climbed higher, above the volcanic ash and the sulfurous smoke.

Beneath her, volcanoes erupted with their thunderous voices as she passed.

The last time she had flown over the Molten Heath to do battle had been with Gehennor, who the humans had named the Unkind. A masterful understatement, that title.

Gehennor had fought fiercely, and their clash had shaken the earth, and caused the mountains to send fire up into the sky as the sun chased the moon. Shaarina remembered the excitement of those days.

Gehennor had been larger than her, but she had been smarter. That in the end was what counted.

Ruthlessness, and intelligence.

Like most males, Gehennor was never one for subtlety. But none of the others were particularly intelligent, save maybe Zir the Black, and even that had not saved her from Shaarina's fury. Even Zir had been blinded by the craving for power, dazed by the light of the Runebound Shards, forgetful of her responsibility toward the whole of Yrth.

A pity, truly. Shaarina had been quite fond of Zir. She still clung to the black dragon's captured hoard as a token of affection.

But now something was on the move again, the little upstart Levirax getting ideas of her own. She had found allies she believed Shaarina did not know about and was making plans. She had gathered the stray hybrids from the plains and believed she could be Dragon Rex.

As she slowly banked south, Shaarina reflected that Levirax was proof of how one single ill-advised act of mercy could be a hard debt to pay down the line. She should not have spared Levirax back in the day.

And yet, unintelligent but crafty, Levirax had been a useful tool for a while, and she had kept the dragon hybrids busy and mostly under control. But she had grown bold in her ambition and called others against Shaarina. The Dragon Rex worried about the deals her rival was sealing with other forces, far from the Molten Heath. It would displease her, should the upstart Levirax manage to involve others more powerful and smarter.

Levirax had not realized yet how vast the chessboard was, and how long Shaarina's reach was. She had been patient, a single move sometimes taking a century. When the Dunwarr dwarves had entered the game, she had welcomed the diversion, the sudden injection of urgency.

Levirax was about to tip the chessboard. The time had come to put the pretentious female back in her place.

Shaarina's ancient heart sang as she flew south toward the place where Levirax had gathered her army. And when she got there, she saw that much of her work had already been done for her by others.

She saw the burning plain under the snowfall of ashes, and columns of black smoke rising around the black tower. She felt, with senses for which the humans of Terrinoth had no name, the dissipating halo of raging ghosts.

She was surprised and delighted at the destruction. But there was still much to do.

She spied Levirax as she crawled up the black ruin and swept down to meet her, and to remind her who was Dragon Rex.

The black tower had shuddered when Levirax had perched on it, but now it rocked and tottered under the impact of the bodies of the two dragons. The structure creaked and cracked, ancient buttresses snapping under the onslaught. Blocks of stone fell and dust rained down on Brockton and his companions. A whole section of the staircase collapsed in a cloud of rubble just after they had descended it. A billowing pile of dust rose up the rest of the stairwell, choking them.

The remaining flecks of Tarha's spectral army flew around them like crazy fireflies, icy cold specks of blue light zigzagging through the air.

Vaerix carried Grisban, and One Fist supported a limping Quellen. Cyra was last in the line and cast worried glances at what little could be seen of the outside through the arrow-slits in the walls.

Brockton hurtled down the steps, covering his head with his right arm.

The twin roars of the two dragons fighting outside shook the tower.

Or maybe the earth was shaking, or the whole building coming down on their heads.

This was no longer their battle. All they had to do now was survive.

They ran out of the tower and there were hybrids there, surrounding the prone shape of Tarha. Brockton recognized Maesix, who had brought them here. The hybrid was prodding the orc with his foot.

There were seven of them, the hybrids that had regrouped and followed Levirax after her first fly-by.

As more detritus fell from the tower, the hybrids dispersed. Two of them flew out of the way, while the others scattered. Only Maesix showed purpose as he moved to intercept the fugitives.

With a ferocious screech, Levirax flew over them, her shadow obscuring the sky for an instant. Shaarina followed her and as she flew over the courtyard, she snatched one of the two fleeing hybrids in her teeth, crushed him and spat him away.

Brockton barely slowed his run, but Cyra let out a howl and ran past him, swords whirling. She slammed into the closest of the hybrids, shouldering him out of the way, before she did a half-turn and rolled on the ground in a crouch, coming back up on her feet by Tarha. Her blade clipped the wing membrane of Maesix as she moved into position and before the hybrid could respond, a huge block of black stone crashed between them.

More stones fell as Brockton moved to help Cyra pick up Tarha.

Beside them, Maesix blocked Vaerix's way. "You owe me one death," he said.

Brockton froze and turned to watch the scene. What folly was this, to fight while the whole world seemed to be coming down in flames around them?

Vaerix was cradling Grisban in their arms. They stopped, tail lashing nervously.

The ground reverberated with the shock of the two dragons crashing to the ground just outside the tower's wall. A cloud of fire rose in the sky. More chunks of glassy rock fell from the tower and exploded on the ground around them.

"There is no time," Vaerix said.

Maesix stepped closer, so close he was breathing each word in Vaerix's face. Ignoring the din and the chaos, he chuckled. "There is always time to die."

"Die, then," Grisban grunted and stabbed him.

It was a swift movement, his left arm extending, a blade slipping between Maesix's ribs. He let go of the hilt, his hand falling back, and the weapon stuck there, Maesix's eyes growing wide in surprise, just as wide and surprised as Vaerix's.

Vaerix froze and watched life seep out of their old friend's body. They felt a tightness in their chest. Then a square block of black stone struck Maesix in the head and he fell, soon buried by more rubble. But Vaerix had already gone, running for safety.

Brockton and Cyra staggered to the gate, Tarha barely standing between them. Brockton turned to look at the tower and saw Quellen push One Fist away and then lean on the wall of the building.

They spoke for the time of two heartbeats, and then the orc started running.

"Let's go," he said as he passed Brockton and the others. "He's holding the wall up until we're clear."

Brockton cast a final glance at the tall elf, who was slowly sliding into a sitting position along the shuddering black wall. The elf grinned and raised a hand. He looked tired, yet as self-assured as ever.

"Quellen," Brockton said.

Then Cyra was dragging him toward the gates as the snowfall of gray ashes intensified.

Madness.

There was no other word to describe what raged in Levirax's

heart as she flew over the collapsing tower, Shaarina drawing closer behind her.

Madness, brewing out of outrage for the sudden appearance of her enemy, out of pain for the wounds the Dragon Rex had clawed through her armored skin, cutting muscles and scraping bones. Madness fueled by anger and yes, by fear.

The unthinkable had happened. Shaarina had awakened.

Levirax did a tight turn that pulled on her wings and caused her lacerated side to flare up in pain, and she hurled herself head-on against Shaarina. The Dragon Rex filled her wings with wind, braking, and for a brief moment, while she brought her hind legs up to claw at Levirax, her soft pale underbelly was fully exposed. Levirax stretched her clawed hands, seeking the heart of her enemy.

The two dragons grabbed each other in a deadly embrace, and as gravity reasserted its authority on them, plummeted to the ground. A thick cloud of black cinders enveloped them.

The impact forced them to let go of each other and they moved apart, staring at each other, and roared their defiance. Levirax's side was bleeding and her narrow head swung from side to side. Shaarina's chest was covered in scratches and smoke escaped her nostrils. Both were dirty and bleeding, breathing heavily and trying to burn through each other's skull with the intensity of their glare.

Again, they raged at each other, their voices louder than the thunder of the volcanoes, their breath hotter than molten rock. They stood their ground, stretched their necks and shouted at each other, the sound causing the few remaining hybrids to flee in disarray, afraid of what was to come.

Rage was boiling in Levirax's mind.

She wanted a kill. To put an end to this ancient creature who for too long had held back dragonkind. The creature who had mocked her and caused her pain.

As Shaarina exploded in another resounding roar, Levirax moved, as fast as a snake, her maw seeking the other dragon's neck. Her long teeth closed just below Shaarina's head and Levirax twisted, putting the whole weight of her colossal body in it to try and snap her enemy's neck.

Shaarina rolled to the side. As Levirax fell on her, her hind legs snapped like a crossbow's spring and her talons dug deep into Levirax's abdomen, tearing a large wound open.

The new pain brought a piercing shard of reason back into Levirax's frenzied mind. She let go of Shaarina's neck and flapped her wings, getting as far as possible from the Dragon Rex's razor-sharp talons.

She circled slowly, a few feet from the ground, and Shaarina followed her with her silent stare.

This was going nowhere, Levirax thought.

She saw her hybrids as distant specks in the sky, fleeing.

There would be time to punish them later.

And the dwarves and their allies, and the Wingless One, running.

No time for those.

The tower was collapsing.

Levirax twisted in mid-air and accelerated in that direction, a crazy plan flashing in her mind.

With a roar that sounded like a mocking laugh to her ears, Shaarina took off in pursuit.

Quellen was tired.

His back was in pain, his feet had been walked raw, he was

weak from fatigue and lack of food. His legs were shaking as he slid down the wall of the tower and sat on the ground.

Just a brief rest.

Let the others go on.

Each individual stone in the tower above him was trying to escape his grip and come down on him to kill him. The ultimate failure of dwarven engineering.

He watched the others run out the bronze doors. He could not keep up with them. And he was not the kind that would go for self-sacrifice or such grand gestures. But he had more chances of getting out of this place alone and then rejoining his companions, rather than risking everybody's life by being dragged along with them on bleeding feet.

Let the dwarves and the orcs run. Quellen would go his own way.

The two dragons were fighting beyond the wall, their screeches rending the air. Like a cat-fight.

Quellen took one long rattling breath and waited.

The hybrids were gone, scared by the two behemoths they had served.

Now Quellen would rest for a spell. He would only need a few moments. Find his legs again, and then follow the others.

It stood to reason they'd go toward Black Ember Gorge. The fastest way back into Terrinoth, away from the Molten Heath and its warring monsters.

Just a few moments and he'd follow them. Follow them in his own time, at his own pace. Maybe do a little exploring on the side. Retrieve a few items from the ruins.

He just needed a little time to refocus.

Let the tower collapse, let the dragons kill each other, for all he cared. Let the hybrids go back to their primitive games of power.

The dragons chose that moment to fly over the wall. The smaller one first, wings beating with obvious difficulty, making a beeline for the tower. And the other behind, getting closer, its maw stretched and fire boiling in her throat.

A tired chuckle escaped Quellen's lips as he watched the two monsters come hurtling toward him. So much for all his plans and projects, he thought.

He took a deep breath, his eyes on the two colossal beasts filling the sky. He waited until he saw a ball of boiling fire in the mouth of the second dragon.

Archmage Quellen, he thought with a bitter laugh, who could kill two dragons with a single stroke. Then he just breathed out and let go of the black stone blocks of the tower.

The structure lingered for half a heartbeat and then collapsed with a sound that canceled any other sound, a black cascade of rocks that swept over the two dragons, crushing them.

A pity no one would be here to see it and tell the story, Quellen thought, and darkness once again closed on him.

Shaarina arched her back and shook off the rubble. She stretched her forelimbs and clawed at a large cube of obsidian, finally dragging herself free of the collapsed tower.

She rested on top of the black glass block like it was a pedestal and surveyed the devastation around her.

The sun was waning and the fires from the volcanoes painted the landscape red. A thin layer of ash covered every surface, and only the freshly piled ruins of the dwarven tower stood clean, like a pile of black rocks emerging from a gray sea.

Movement caught her eye, and she saw the crawling shape of another dragon, slowly walking away from the remains of the tower.

Levirax, one broken wing limp by her side, her body battered and wounded.

Defeated.

Shaarina's mood improved instantly.

She breathed in, filling her lungs, and then threw her head back and breathed a mighty pillar of fire straight up into the sky, while she bellowed a roar of unabashed triumph.

In the distance, Levirax stopped and turned to look at her. She bowed her head in a sign of submission and started away again.

Shaarina let her go unchallenged. It would be a long walk to her hideaway, and her faraway allies would not be pleased with her.

The Dragon Rex stretched like a cat, arching her back again and batting her wings, her tail swinging from side to side. There were aches and wounds, and her body was beginning to feel again the creeping tiredness that had become her daily companion.

She turned her gaze around. All that she could see was still hers.

Somewhere in the distance, to the west, she knew the renegade Vaerix and their dwarven allies were on their way back to the realm of Terrinoth.

Let them go, she thought.

Let them tell the world the dragons of the Molten Heath are not asleep and ready to defend their own.

There would be other chessboards and other games.

CHAPTER TWENTY-NINE
On the Border

Black Ember Gorge ran from east to west through the mountains, a narrow corridor of black volcanic rock, with a few solitary fir trees holding on for dear life to the steep slopes with roots like gnarled fingers. A constant wind howled through the high passes. In spring and in autumn it pushed stormy clouds through, and ice-cold rain.

Border duty at the tail end of the Gorge was not a sign of favor from the Guild Masters, and everybody in the patrol knew Hilmar Stone Heart had rubbed some old owl-faced pen-pusher the wrong way. As a consequence, now both he and his twenty men and women at arms would have to endure the weather and the territory, manning the Raven's Fort for one full month.

The barracks were reasonably clean, vermin-free, and the roof was mostly solid. Everything else, the soldiers had carried with themselves – food and provisions, firewood and fodder for their horses. They had been stationed a week in the box-like fort, sleeping rough and eating worse, the spring storms making their lives miserable and their armor rusty. Stone

Heart or not, some of the men said, the captain should learn diplomacy, for their sake if not for his own.

The fort had been built in the time of the War of Fire, halfway up the northern slope of the Gorge. A thick wall, a sturdy door, and two catapults to welcome any unwanted guest.

But no one really believed anything would come out of the east.

Not tonight.

Not in this weather.

And yet, just as the men and women under the southern porch were passing the bowls around and commenting on the food, a call came from the wall.

"No one in their right mind would cross the Gorge now," said Besso. He was quartermaster of the troop, an old dwarf with a dozen campaigns under his belt and little time for nonsense.

There was a hint of worry in his voice as he put down his food and hastened to the captain's quarters. As he approached, the door to the small room opened and Hilmar stood there, buckling his sword belt. He was a black-haired dwarf of middle age, with two white streaks in his beard.

"What is it?" he asked.

Besso shook his head. "Dunno."

They both ran up the rampart, rain splashing on their faces.

"Over there." The sentinel pointed.

The long shadows of the night were stretched across the floor of the gorge, but still Hilmar was able to pinpoint a small group of shapes crawling toward Raven's Fort under the rain.

"Adventurers," Besso said.

The Gorge led to the Molten Heath, whose ancient

mysteries sometimes attracted people with more courage than sense. The troop in Raven's Fort was supposed to prevent them from going in, as it was highly unlikely they would ever come out again.

And yet, here a handful of men came, from the direction of the Heath.

"Five men, crossbows and half armor," Hilmar commanded. "Let's go meet these travelers."

"Crossbows won't work well in the rain," Besso said. "Wet strings."

"Pikes then," Hilmar replied.

Besso had Hilmar's cloak at hand. The captain wrapped himself up, pulled the hood over his head and went to the gate of the fort, five men at arms falling in line behind him.

They walked to the bottom of the valley, just in time to meet the travelers.

"King of serpents," one of the men whispered as the newcomers drew closer.

There were five of them. A dwarf, two orcs and a human. And then a lizard-like creature, like a small dragon-kin. The human, a woman, was leading a pale horse. There was a rough bundle tied to the saddle.

Hilmar looked at the gaunt, dirty faces, the cuts and the bruises. Torn clothes, dented armor. They looked like they had been through a war..

"State your name and business," Hilmar called, standing in the middle of the road. He had his sword out, but kept it down as a sign of goodwill.

The dwarf came forward, limping. There were rags of a once fancy jacket over his shoulders.

"My name is Brockton, map maker to the Explorers' Guild,"

he said. His voice was raspy and broken. He was wearing dirty clothes and leaned on a staff as he walked.

Hilmar frowned. "Can I see your guild ring?"

"Why not get out of the rain first?" a gruff voice said, and it seemed to come from the horse. "Then we'll show you anything you want."

Hilmar took a step forward. "Grisban?" he called, recognizing the voice. "Grisban the Thirsty? Is that you?"

"I am thirsty, yes," Grisban replied, sitting up in the saddle and pulling back the blanket he was wrapped in. "And wouldn't mind a spot of stew and some fried bread, too."

The men watched them walk into the fort like they were ghosts out of some battlefield, and Brockton and the others did not feel much better than that. A barrack was cleaned up for them and a fire lit in the fireplace.

Grisban managed to dismount from Cloud, but did not make it to the barracks on his own. Vaerix and One Fist carried him inside, and the sawbones in Hilmar's troop came and gave him a good look. He was moderately impressed by the stitches Cyra had applied to the old dwarf's wound and much more impressed by Grisban's resilience.

"It's a wonder the old crow didn't croak," he said, pulling his beard.

"Can you help in any way?" Brockton asked.

The medic shrugged. "I can clean the cut and give you something to lower the fever. After that, we can only wait."

Brockton thanked him. Then he left the others to settle in and went to talk with Hilmar.

He asked for a message to be dispatched to Thelgrim as soon as possible and then requested writing implements and paper. While they waited for the Guilds to send word, he'd try and put down in writing everything he remembered. A poor substitute for his lost maps and notes, but better than meeting his masters empty-handed.

They sat in the stone room that had been given to them. A few men and women from Hilmar's force brought spare clothes, toiletries and other necessities. While Brockton sat in a corner writing, the others tried to clean up and acquire a semblance of normality. Cyra even managed to find a mirror, and she turned this way and that in front of it, commenting on how the short dwarven pants and tunic looked upon her.

They took turns by Grisban's bedside and on the second night in the fort, they took a moment to remember Quellen.

"He was so eager to dig under the ruins," One Fist said, shaking his head.

They all drank a toast to the elf.

"He'd be disappointed," Brockton said, "by how we're drinking beer."

The others laughed.

Emptying their cup in a single gulp, Vaerix turned it upside down and placed it on the fireplace. Then they nodded to the others and walked out of the room.

Cyra made to follow them, but One Fist stopped her. "They want to be alone."

There was a flap of wings in the dark, and then a black silhouette landed without a sound to perch by the spur of rock where Vaerix was sitting. Sparse woodland stretched below, dark conifers clinging to the sides of the gorge, and fireflies blinked through the underbrush. The night was silent and the world felt impossibly distant.

"I came to say goodbye," Drys said.

Vaerix masked their surprise behind a quiet grin. "You want your sword back?"

Drys smiled. "It would be nice to have it back."

"I am afraid it stayed with Levirax," Vaerix said.

Drys folded his wings. "Then it will just be goodbyes between us."

Vaerix sighed. "Our kind is too long-lived for goodbye to have a meaning," they said. "The Dunwarr dwarves have a saying – it is not the mountains that meet again, but people."

Again, Drys tilted his head to the side. "It's a strange saying."

"They are a strange people," Vaerix conceded. "But not unpleasant."

They sat side by side, looking down on the fort below. Trembling specks of light pinpointed where the men at arms were sitting around fires, consuming their supper.

"You saw much of the world and its strange peoples," Drys said. "It changed you."

"Maybe you were right," Vaerix replied. "Maybe I should not have come back. I did not do much good."

"Do you really believe it?"

"Maesix would still be alive," Vaerix said.

"Maybe he deserved to die for what he did."

Vaerix frowned. "The dead cannot change. They can't make things better. It's a pity."

Drys shrugged, his jaw tightening, his eyes suddenly hard. "What's done is done."

"So it is. But very little else is changed. Shaarina is still Dragon Rex, and Levirax still lives and plots. Of all my dreams about our kind's future, none has come to fruition."

"Yet," Drys replied.

Vaerix turned to look at him. "What do you mean?"

"You are a memory," Drys said. "One that neither Levirax nor Xenith were able to erase. A legend. The stories will be impossible to erase now, of how you faced Xenith and defeated him, and the way you did it. Stories will become examples. Each day we will rise and know you live, and by living you show us that another way exists, for those that have the courage to take it. To change their ways. And some will do."

Vaerix looked in his eyes for a long moment. "Some?"

They had seen signs in him of how things had changed. How he had changed, and how he fought such change. About how even dragon hybrids had gained new ways of living and thinking and remembering despite some of the dragonlords' oversight. And now they knew he was aware of his different outlook. The sadness of the loss melted as Vaerix realized everything *had* been worth it.

Drys shrugged. "More will change, sooner or later. When they find in themselves what it takes."

Vaerix sighed. "Will it take long, do you believe?"

"Who knows?" Drys looked down on the fires of the fort. "As you said, we are a long-lived people."

"Tarha."

The orc was sitting cross legged in front of the remains of a small fire. Black and gray ashes were in a small depression in the ground, no trace of fire or heat in them anymore.

Cyra could smell the smoke in the air. "I didn't know where you were."

Tarha turned.

"What have you done?" Cyra asked sadly. But she knew the answer, of course. She knew.

"What needed to be done," Tarha replied, closing her fist on the pendant on her neck and yanking it off. The leather strap snapped. She looked down in the palm of her hand and then twisted her wrist.

The bone shard fell on the ground and Tarha stood and stepped on it, pressing with the heel of her boot. There was a loud crack.

"He is free now," Tarha said in a low voice.

Cyra felt breath catch in her throat. "Oh..."

"Free of me," the orc went on. "Free of everyone."

She rubbed her foot in the dirt, spreading the fragments of the bone. The pendant shattered further, the tie severed.

The women embraced.

"I am sorry," Cyra said in a low voice. She pulled Tarha closer, clasping hands with her, as they had held hands in the buried chambers. "I am really sorry."

The orc shook her head and pulled back a little.

"They always called me the Widow," she said. "Now I have earned that name. Now I am twice a widow."

It took fifteen days for the emissaries from the Guilds to reach Fort Raven. They came with the men that would replace Hilmar's troop, a long train of mules and sour-faced warriors escorting five dwarves in velvet and shining steel breastplates, riding long-haired ponies with fancy saddles.

Grisban was sitting under the porch when they arrived. His shoulder was healing, and he was exercising it by tossing corks into a bucket, playing against One Fist and Cyra, while Vaerix watched. The old dwarf was losing badly, and cursed and swore the orc was impossible to beat at that game. Tarha sat alone off to the side.

They watched the Guildsfolk dismount and talk briefly with Hilmar and then with Brockton.

Looking good in his borrowed clothes, Brockton invited them into the barracks they had been occupying these last two weeks, and Tarha left as they entered.

"There go our bonuses," One Fist mumbled, collecting the bucket to count the corks.

"They can't deny us our due," Grisban replied.

One Fist mumbled something to the effect that he did not trust the Guild Masters.

"Much rides on what Brockton's going to give them," Grisban said. "And if they will be satisfied."

For two hours, the dwarves were holed up in the barracks. Twice Cyra tiptoed there to try and glean some information and twice she came back empty-handed.

The courtyard was busy with Hilmar's men at arms packing their gear and the newcomers getting ready to settle down. The two orcs, the woman, the older dwarf and the wingless hybrid attracted a lot of side glances and caused a lot of low-voiced talk.

Then the door opened and the five Guild members walked out briskly, Brockton behind them.

They had their ponies brought over and in a few moments were gone.

Brockton headed over to his companions.

"Your money's inside," he said. He looked at Tarha. "Yours too."

Then he glanced at Cyra. "And yours."

Cyra was surprised. "Mine?"

"Isn't she being paid by the Empress of Lorimor?" Grisban asked. When Cyra turned to look at him, he guffawed. "Come on, woman. I was not born yesterday."

Cyra snorted and shook her head. "Perhaps you aren't as dim as I'd thought."

"Everyone in my expedition gets paid," Brockton said, serious.

Grisban's eyes narrowed. "What about your maps?"

Brockton looked down and rubbed together his ink-stained fingers. "They were not overly impressed," he replied slowly. "Disappointed, I believe, is a word they used. But not more than thrice."

"Morons," One Fist spat.

"They were hoping for different news," Vaerix said.

Brockton smiled. "I believe so."

Quartermaster Besso came to them.

"Gentlemen and ladies," he said, "Captain Hilmar wishes you to know that we are moving in one hour. He'd be pleased for your company should you decide to join us."

Brockton looked at the others.

Grisban shook his head. So did Vaerix.

"Thank Captain Hilmar," Brockton said. "But we will be following you at our leisure."

Besso looked at them and then nodded. "Understood, sir."

"And tell your captain we'll find him in Thelgrim," Grisban added, "and the drinks will be on him."

EPILOGUE
Market Day in Vynelvale

The silver bell of the shop's door jangled.

"Welcome," the man behind the counter said. "How can I serve you?"

The newcomer pulled back his hood, revealing long brown hair and pointy ears. The shopkeeper's eyes widened. It was not often that an elf was seen in his shop.

"I am looking for…" The elf hesitated, looking around.

"For?" the man said expectantly. It had been a slow day for sales.

"You have spell books?" the elf said, moving to the bookshelf that occupied the whole right-hand wall.

"All of the classics," the shopkeeper said genially. "And maps too. And writing materials, because sometimes we want to write our own, right?"

The elf did not seem to pay him too much heed.

"Anything on dwarven runes?" he asked, as his long fingers caressed the backs of the exposed tomes.

The man behind the counter rubbed his chin. "Dwarven

runes – now that's a pretty niche subject. I don't believe I have anything right here in the shop, but–" his eyes were two calculating slits, "–I might be able to procure you something. Do you have any specific title in mind?"

The elf opened the satchel he carried slung over one shoulder.

"Something like this?"

He placed a very ancient book on top of the counter.

The short man looked down at the book, then up at the elf. He sniffed, and his fingers almost touched the ancient leather cover, but stopped just shy of it.

"This is old," he mumbled in a low voice. He leaned forward and studied the creases and lines on the dried-up cover. "Very old."

He looked up again, staring the elf in the eye. "Where did you get this?"

The elf arched an eyebrow. "The Karok Doum."

The shopkeeper scoffed. "The Karok Doum? Beyond the northern mountains?"

The elf did not speak.

"That's halfway across the world," the shopkeeper said. But his eyes kept going back to the old book.

"Are you interested?" the elf said.

The man crossed his arms and ran the tip of his thumb across his lips. "You are selling this?"

"I could, for the right figure. I no longer have use for it."

Again, the shopkeeper observed his unusual customer. His fine clothes a little worse for wear, his long hair a tad unkempt, his manner just the right degree of shady.

"I don't think I have that kind of money," he said finally. Not exactly a "no", still leaving an opening. He did not trust the elf, but the book was quite interesting. He could find a buyer, he believed.

The elf looked at him for a long moment. Then he stretched out a hand, delicately picked up the book and put it back in his bag.

The shopkeeper clicked his tongue. "Sorry."

Maybe it was better like this, he thought.

The elf shrugged, pulled up his cowl and was out of the shop without another word.

The shopkeeper went to the door and watched him go, his blue mantle easy to spot as he pushed through the crowd of Vynelvale's market.

Regret and greed played at the back of his mind for a few moments.

A book like that could be sold for a nice bundle. But on the other hand, the elf had given off some unpleasant vibes and the book was certainly stolen. What was an elf doing with a dwarf's spell book?

Not that he had anything specifically against stolen goods, of course, but there was a limit to the types of risks he was ready to run. The people in town called him Honest Grim, and he was happy to keep that name and that reputation, for the time being.

He followed the elf with his eyes until he disappeared in the distance, then went back behind the counter, waiting for the next customer.

ACKNOWLEDGMENTS

Writing a novel is supposed to be a lonely business, but there is a long list of people I wish to thank for the help and support they gave me along the way. That's what I am going to do now, and I am sorry if I forget anyone. It's very late in the night as I write this.

So, thank you to the authors and artists in the Descent franchise and Fantasy Flight Games, for creating a complex, fascinating world, and allowing me to play in it, and also for setting me straight where I misstepped along the way.

Thank you to the people at Aconyte Books, and to Charlotte Llewelyn-Wells, and Gwendolyn Nix in particular for her great support, kindness, and patience.

Meanwhile, in what passes for the real world, I wish to thank my Picnic Partners – Paola, Marina, Emanuele, Marco and Roberto – who helped me hold onto my sanity with our weekly games and by hanging out for lunches on market days.

Once again, I would have never made it without the help and support of my brother Alessandro, who kept things going in our lives while I typed away at this story.

And finally, a big heartfelt thank you to all the readers that came along for the ride. I hope you had as much fun reading this book as I had writing it.

Cheers.

ABOUT THE AUTHOR

Davide Mana was born and raised in Turin, Italy, with brief stints in London, Bonn and Urbino, where he studied paleontology (with a specialization in marine plankton) and geology. He currently lives in the wine hills of southern Piedmont, where he is a writer, translator and game designer. In his spare time, he cooks and listens to music, photographs the local feral cats, and collects old books. He co-hosts a podcast about horror movies, called Paura & Delirio.

karavansara.live
twitter.com/davide_mana

DESCENT
LEGENDS OF THE DARK™

EXPLORE THE DARK PASTS OF TERRINOTH'S MOST NOTORIOUS VILLAINS.

Waiqar, Lord of the Mistlands, is a necromancer of supreme power, arrogance, and skill. Driven by his hunger for absolute dominion, he has the whole of Terrinoth in his sights...

Zachareth, Baron of Carthridge, is a driven, ruthless and obsessive man. He must choose his true path – the path of virtue and heroism, or that of darkness and villany.